THE ROLE

RICHARD TAYLOR PEARSON

LETHE PRESS
MAPLE SHADE, NEW JERSEY

Published by Lethe Press
118 Heritage Ave, Maple Shade, NJ 08052
lethepressbooks.com

Copyright © 2016 Richard Taylor Pearson

ISBN-10: 978-1-59021-518-0
ISBN-13: 1-59021-518-4

Library of Congress Cataloging-in-Publication Data

TK

Cover art by Ben Baldwin
Cover design by Alex Jeffers
Interior design by Inkspiral Design

★

For my husband Brian.

Being cast as your partner in life is truly
the greatest role of a lifetime.

★

ONE

WHEN I WAS TWENTY, I thought all I had to do was get to New York City. Fate would surely smile on the brave boy who left Houston with nothing but a dream, right? Isn't that how it always happens? I'd find a little spot in Central Park to rehearse a monologue, and everyone who passed by would become entranced. A big-time agent would stumble upon the crowd, offer to represent me, and then I'd rush home to my shoebox apartment to tell my roommate. He'd be a writer, though I wasn't sure whether he'd be a journalist, a novelist, or a playwright. All I knew was that he'd have black hair, glasses, and be just a little too skinny to be considered hot; though, of course, I'd see his inner beauty. He'd offer me a glass of cheap Chianti and ask me to read his newest work. I would be so overcome by the beauty of his words that we'd push our beds and bodies together that night. We would make love, and I would finally know the kind of passion that I'd seen on stage so many times. The next morning, my agent would call and demand I rush to an audition. I'd kiss my new love goodbye, burst through the casting agency doors, and land the lead role. Then, when opening night arrived, the *Times* would herald me as Broadway's newest star. The city just needed me to get there.

Or not.

After five years in the city, the only part of that dream that's come close to true is that I did eventually fall in love with my roommate. My boyfriend Eric, and I have lived together for three years, but are still a few weeks away from our one year anniversary as an official couple. Eric is almost as I imagined him: skinny, glasses, black hair, and a writer. Though I suppose saying he's a writer is a bit of a stretch. He writes code for videogames, so it's not exactly a thrilling read. Still, I can't really complain. The city owed me nothing, but led me to the love of my life. The rest is up to me, so I keep auditioning.

"Hello, I'm here to audition for *Masque*," I announce to the front desk assistant of the casting agency.

"You and everyone else." He doesn't even bother looking up from his computer screen.

"Is there a big turn out?"

"Um, of course there is. It's a James Merchant production." He stops browsing the web to give me a withering glance.

"Oh." James Merchant is basically Broadway royalty. An absolute genius director. I spent almost twenty-four hours waiting outside the Delacorte Theatre in Central Park last summer to get free tickets to his reimagining of *Much Ado About Nothing*.

"You do know who that is, right?"

"Of course! I love his work!" The words come out so eager they sound false.

"I'm sure you do," he says, with a condescending smile. "Anyway, auditions are being held in Studio 6B. So you go down the hall, take the first left, and it's the second door on the right."

"Thanks so much. Have a nice day," I reply instinctively. Five years in the city has yet to wipe out the southern charm my mother instilled in me.

To get to the studio I have to make my way through the gauntlet of actors who are warming up, practicing lines, and coming and going from other auditions in various states of anticipation, exultation, and disappointment. Although these places were designed to house multiple auditions at a time, the cheapskates who built them cut every corner imaginable so the walls have about as much sound insulation as a paper bag. While each of them is trying their best, the combination of a woman belting out the hits of *Wicked*, a man wailing unintelligibly through a monologue, and the blaring hip-hop a group of dancers is using to rehearse their choreography disorients me for a moment. I lean against the wall, hoping the dizziness will pass, when suddenly the door next to me swings open and pins me against the wall.

"Ah!" I yelp, as the door handle barely misses punching me in the gut.

"Oh, man! Hey, are you okay back there? Sorry!" I instantly recognize the voice coming from the other side. Kevin Caldwell. Most people probably know of him from his minor roles on television. Kevin played a charismatic cult leader in a Lifetime movie, and had a short recurring role as a sexy undercover cop on *Law & Order SVU*, but I met him long before his brush with television fame. After I finally made it to New York, I enrolled in an acting class that was supposed to help me break into the business. Kevin and I were scene partners, so we spent countless hours together that summer. Unfortunately, I spent most of that time trying desperately to get him to fall in love with me instead of getting casting directors to notice me.

"Kevin?" I ask, as the door pulls away.

"Mason? Oh man! Is it really you?"

"Have I changed that much?" My heart races as he looks me over, and I feel my face flush as I take him in. I thought that over the past few years my mind had exaggerated how gorgeous he was, but Kevin looks even better than I remember. Six feet tall, with the lean and toned musculature of an Olympic swimmer, Kevin is one hundred percent leading man material. He actually seems to glow, partly because of the way his wavy blond hair always manages to catch the light, but it's more than just superficial, he radiates confidence like a true star. He's like the sun god Apollo, only in designer jeans. I have a hard time looking directly at him for more than a few seconds.

"Of course not! You look just the same as I remember."

"I hope not! I'm hideously out of shape now." To most of the world this isn't true, but in terms of gay New York theatre boys, I'm practically a lost cause. Since I'm only five foot eight inches tall, my thirty-two-inch waist typecasts me as the "less attractive best friend" whenever I audition.

"Don't be ridiculous. You've still got the cute 'boy next door' thing going on," he says. It's the nice way of saying "less attractive best friend."

"Thanks. Hopefully that's what they're looking for."

"So, you're here to audition?" Kevin asks, eyeing me suspiciously.

"Yeah, for *Masque*," I say, and Kevin breaks out a huge smile. I try to smile back, but realize I've been smiling since I saw him. Everyone always smiles when they look at Kevin. It's like an instinct, the same as raising the pitch of your voice when you talk to a baby. I often wonder if Kevin even knows that people can frown, outside of times in which a script specifically calls for it.

"I bet you'll do great!"

"If I even get seen. You know how it goes when you don't have an Equity card."

"You're not Equity yet?" he asks, making me feel like even more of a failure. Membership in the Actor's Equity Association requires the equivalent of fifty weeks' worth of work in theatres that adhere to union standards. Of course most union theatres hire actors who are already members of the union. This makes sense because one of the perks is that every union member is seen before the casting directors will even consider seeing non-Equity. It's a big advantage.

"Nope. I've only got thirty-six weeks of work on my resume."

"Oh, that totally sucks," he says, his smile fading quickly.

"Yeah, but you've got to keep trying, right?"

"Well…right," he says, and then drops his voice to a whisper. "Look, I probably shouldn't be telling you this, but I'm working the audition for *Masque*. I'm the reader." Meaning he is the person who reads with whoever is auditioning when a scene has more than one character.

"That's a great gig."

"Right, so…what part were you thinking about trying out for?"

"Part? Oh, I was just hoping to be in the ensemble."

"Mason, come on, you can talk to me," he says, throwing one of his long, lanky arms over my shoulder. The second his skin touches mine, a shiver runs from the top of my head all the way down to my toes, and Kevin pulls me in a little closer. He knows exactly what he's doing. The arm-over-the-shoulder move was just one of many tools Kevin liked to use to get me to partake in whatever mischief he had planned. It was never enough for him to just go out and do outlandish stuff in the city. He needed an audience, and he knew how to get me to follow him anywhere.

"Honestly, I'll take anything."

"I didn't ask what you'd take." He brings his lips close to my ear and in a rich baritone, speaking slowly, so as to draw out every word, says "I'm asking what you want."

"Well…" I start, but my brain feels like it is short-circuiting. I turn my head as far away from him as I can, and eventually I can finish the thought. "I thought I might be a good fit for Lord Dyne, the advisor. That's why I planned to use a Polonius monologue. Last time I did it, I was cast as Cinna the Poet in *Julius Caesar*. So I'm pretty confid—"

"Dyne? No way, I bet they want someone older," he says, before returning my face to meet his. "You should try for Caleb."

"Isn't that a lead?"

"Yeah. Why?"

"I'm not really a lead actor kind of guy," I say, causing Kevin to look at me as if I'm some sort of alien. I guess if I were Kevin, I'd also find it odd that anyone would pursue a supporting role. They're not glamorous, but as some Greek philosopher once famously chiseled on a wall: KNOW THYSELF.

"What kind of guy are you then?"

"Oh you know, the leading man's best friend, his lackey."

"Then Caleb is perfect for you. His whole thing is that he's a manipulated innocent, and who wouldn't see that when they look at your little face?" he says, pinching my cheek a little too hard.

"Ah! Not so rough." I rear back.

"Sorry, but…I mean, look at you. You're adorable! Even that vest looks a little period."

What I wear to auditions is more of a uniform than anything else – white button down shirt layered under a slate gray vest, black tie, dark jeans, and knock-off designer boots. The vest is my favorite, and not just because Kevin complimented it, but because it was made specifically for me. It was part of my costume in a show. Ever since then, it has served as my own personal corset, helping me hide the ten extra pounds I seem incapable of losing.

"I'm just not sure I'm what they are looking for. I think that—"

"Mason," Kevin interrupts. "Stop making excuses! Do you know how lucky you are to run into me?" He seems to have already forgotten that he's the one who hit me with a door only a few minutes ago. "How many times are you going to have someone on the inside?"

"You're right."

"I know I'm right, so just listen to me and do exactly what I tell you. Go sign up on the non-Equity list, and then use your phone to look up the first scene in *Edward II* by Marlowe. The end of the scene has a monologue by Gaveston that would make the perfect audition piece for this show."

"Okay, but even if I manage to memorize it in time, what's the point? There's a ton of people here. They probably won't even see any non-Equity people, let alone one who's so late to sign up."

"Have a little faith, Mason," Kevin protests. "You focus on learning that monologue, and let me worry about trying to get you inside. If they like you, you'll get to read with me. It'll be like old times."

I blush at the mention of old times. I would've thought a couple of years away from Kevin's glow would have made him easier to be around, but it hasn't at all. In fact, I've seemingly lost my tolerance completely. He's more intoxicating than ever, but unlike before, I have Eric now. Thinking of him helps me remember I'm stronger than I was back then.

"Okay. But if this works, don't show me up like you did in class! We all know you're brilliant," I say, rolling my eyes.

"I'll see what I can do. Remember, stay in the waiting room no matter what. If I don't get you in, drinks are on me."

"I think you're more excited than I am," I say, finding it hard to keep pretending I'm not thrilled at the chance to get seen.

"It's just…well…it's just really good to see you again!" He flashes me one last smile before returning to the room.

I always wonder whether it's just me, or if everyone else feels slightly depressed when Kevin turns his gaze away from them. I shake my head to clear it. I don't have time to lament. I need to get my name on that list and start memorizing. Something tells me the other part of my Broadway dream is about to come true.

TWO

I HAVE TO STEADY MY hand as I write my name on the sign-up sheet. Being in the twenty-fourth spot would usually fill me with despair, but Kevin's optimism and confidence has given me a sense of hope that I haven't felt in ages. After so many years of failure, I thought I'd trained myself to become numb to the excitement of auditions. It was the only way to cope with the years of having the door slammed in my face, but today I can't seem to stop myself. It's thrilling to have hope, to believe I might actually be cast, but it's also scary. The thread that has allowed me to hold on to my dream of being on Broadway is so frayed that I fear I could snap it completely if my aspirations are revived only to once again feel the sting of rejection.

I need to stop thinking.

To distract myself, I stare at my phone. After looking over the lines of my new monologue a few hundred times, waiting around to see if my name gets called goes from boring to agonizing. The itch to text Eric is strong, but I resist it. When we stopped being just roommates and began dating I would constantly update him about my auditions, but after a few weeks I stopped. He took each rejection much harder than I did.

"Why won't they ever give you a shot?" he asked over dinner one night, although he already knew the answer.

"It's not their fault I'm not in the union."

"But they could at least see a few people. I mean, you get up so early."

At that point, I had yet to learn how to contort my body out from under him without waking him. Nowadays I'm like some sort of ninja, able to do my entire morning routine completely undetected.

"I'm sorry I woke you up."

"It's fine, I just wish they saw what I saw," he said, looking at me with his big amber eyes.

"So long as you see me that way, why does it matter?"

"Because you're so talented. It doesn't seem fair that they won't see you just because you haven't worked on enough professional stages."

"It's not supposed to be fair, it's show business," I said, giving him a kiss. After that night, I stopped texting him about auditions. Talking about bad news is always harder for Eric, predominately because he's not had a lot of it in his life. Eric was a gifted only child, and that meant he spent a lot of time alone. By the time he was six he knew all sorts of things: how to say the alphabet backwards, the capitals of all fifty states, and that he was undeniably gay, although he didn't tell anyone until many years later. Instead, he spent most of his high school career overcompensating for this assumed "flaw." His perfect academic record and numerous extra-curricular achievements earned him admittance to Columbia. He told his parents about his admission and being gay in a single sentence. "I got into Columbia. Oh, and also, I'm gay." In the end, he'd worried for nothing. His parents weren't even surprised; they just hugged him tight and told him they loved him. Then they joined PFLAG and have probably been to more LGBT Pride events than Eric and I combined. I love them very much. My parents, on the other hand, still insist Eric and I are only roommates. They even rationalize that we sleep in the same bed as us trying to save money on rent.

The idea that today I could finally tell Eric some good news about an audition is enough to give me the strength to calm down and redouble my efforts to learn my lines. I lose track of time, but somewhere between five minutes and an hour later, a rather large man trundles into the center of the room and makes an announcement.

"Hello boys," he says, in a high-pitched voice that seems especially odd considering his mammoth proportions. "Welcome to the audition for *Masque*. My name is Jerry, and I'll be your monitor for today. Before we begin, I want to let you know that it looks like we'll only have time for

Equity today. We thank everyone else for coming out, but request that any non-Equity actors leave so we can continue on with the audition. Of course, if there is extra time, we will call those actors in the order in which they signed up on this sheet, so it helps to keep your phones on and stay in the surrounding area. If you're interested, please sign up if you haven't already done so. Thanks."

As the other non-union actors begin to pack up their things and leave, I pretend to be ignorant of the announcement by putting in my headphones and nodding along to imaginary music. In reality, the only thing I keep hearing is Kevin's voice telling me to stay in the room. The monitor begins checking everyone's Equity card, and eventually he comes to me.

"Hey sweetie, can I see your Equity card?"

"Sorry, I'm not Equity."

"Oh, didn't you hear me? We aren't seeing non-Equity today," he repeats.

Stay in the room.

"Oh, I heard you, but one of my Equity friends is already in there. Can I just wait here? It's kind of cold outside, and we haven't seen each other in years," I say in technical honesty.

"Well...we really aren't supposed to, but, whatever, so long as you know it won't get you an audition, I guess it's fine."

"Thanks so much! I promise you won't even know I'm here." I scroll through the menu on my iPhone to look busy, mouthing the words to my monologue instead of lyrics.

"What're you listening to?" he asks, once all the other actors have either left or gone inside.

"Lines," I reply. "I decided to learn a new monologue for this audition."

"I told you..."

"I know, don't worry. It's for next time. I haven't done a show with period dialogue in a while. Better to be prepared, you know?" I'm never getting in that room. A pain in my chest wells up as a sense of defeat quickly wraps itself around my heart. Kevin's going to have to buy some strong drinks tonight. I'm not sure how many Cosmos it takes to anesthetize someone whose lifelong dream has just been shattered.

"What's it from?"

"*Edward II*. My friend recommended it for auditions like these."

"Marlowe? That's a smart move. I'm pretty sure they've heard every monologue Shakespeare ever wrote at this point. They're so over the bard!"

"Thanks, but I'm sure they'll see plenty of talent," I say, deflecting the compliment.

"I wouldn't be too sure. No offense to your friend in there, but they haven't been too happy with the turnout today. Of course, they didn't even want to audition the other lead, but their celebrity fell through."

"Who was it?"

"Well you know they'd never tell me, but I'm pretty sure it was Jake Gyllenhaal. I think his people were afraid of what the role might make people suspect, you know, given his history."

"What do you mean?"

"Check out the breakdown for Caleb," he says handing me a piece of paper.

```
Caleb: Under 6', innocent, a man manipulated
by Ezio. Must be able to handle Elizabethan
speech without a British accent. Must be
comfortable kissing and touching another
man. Possible nudity.
```

"Oh, I see your point."

"Too bad though. I'd love to see him and the other leading man. They'd make a delicious sandwich!" he says, though I'm not sure whether he means he would enjoy watching them kiss or eating them. Or both.

"So…is there a lot of sex in the show?"

"Not sure, but one of the sides has a really hot scene. Take a look." He hands me a copy of the short scenes that directors use to see how actors work together. I take them and quickly scan to get the point of each scene. The theatre gods have smiled upon me again. If I'm lucky enough to audition, and they like what they see, Kevin and I will be reading these scenes. Although I know the chances are remote, I can't stop the fresh wave of excitement and anticipation that crashes over me.

The first scene reveals Count Ezio meeting an injured Caleb who has returned from the battlefield. The count takes an immediate liking to him, despite his lowly station. This seems to cause some concern with the nobles of the court. The other two scenes are two different attempts by Ezio to seduce Caleb, one of which works out much better for Ezio than the other. The writing feels familiar, but I can't quite place who it reminds me of. However, one thing is certain—compared to most new works, this script is surprisingly good.

A quick glance at my watch tells me it has taken me longer to read over the scenes than I thought, and I can't help but be happy that the day is almost over. In an hour I will either have been seen, or I'll be starting a long night of drinking. I devote what is left of my time to thinking about Kevin's acting style. It's been years since I saw him perform, but when we were in class together I memorized everything about him. I want to be prepared for anything he might throw at me, and am relieved that, in the scene, Caleb lets Ezio take control. Having played lackeys for years, I'm certain I can handle that. Still, I remind myself, memorization is key. Looking Kevin in the face can make even a seasoned actor lose their place.

"Mason?" Kevin whispers as he sticks his head out of the door.

"Kevin!"

"This is your friend?" The monitor looks suspicious.

"That's right, Jerry. I told him to come. Think we can sneak him in?" Kevin pleads, making puppy dog eyes.

"Well, he's pretty far down on the list. It wouldn't exactly be fair." The monitor crosses his arms.

"Who cares about fair? He's here, and everyone else went home."

"They went home because I sent them home. You know the drill. I have to call the names on the list in order to see if they can get back here in time." He reaches for his cell phone, but before he can even unlock the screen Kevin grabs it out of his hand. "Hey! Give that back!"

"Come on, Jerry, you don't wanna go through all that hassle. Wouldn't it be so much easier to just do his paperwork and call it a day?" Kevin asks, stretching his arms up to reveal tight, tanned stomach.

"Nice try, but you'll have to give me more than a peek if you want me to bend the rules."

"I'm off limits, but…" Kevin pauses for a moment, transfixing the full power of his gaze onto Jerry. "Do you remember that hipster you saw me with last week?"

"The one with the sleeve tattoo?" His eyebrows perk up.

"I'll give you his resume and phone number. He told me he would do *anything* for an audition. With your connections I'm sure that could be arranged."

"I don't know…"

"Jerry, take it from me. You're getting the better bargain. That guy's got a mouth like a Hoover!" Kevin tilts his head back and closes his eyes, seemingly lost for a moment in the memory of a rather intense orgasm.

"I'd rather him call me," Jerry haggles.

"Deal!" Kevin says, handing Jerry's phone back to him. "Now can Mason come in or what?"

"Yes, but first I need you to go back to the room. I'll introduce him." Jerry says, escorting Kevin back beyond the door.

For a brief moment I am alone. Posters of famous shows line the walls; I wonder if the actors depicted on them once had a moment like this. Did they know then that their audition would get them on Broadway? I gather my audition pack, turn my cell phone to silent, and toss my hair to give it a ruffled look. I say a little prayer to the theatre gods, letting them know I understand how they've blessed me. No one gets an opportunity like this without divine intervention, so I resolve that this is my final attempt. If I don't make it this time, I will never audition again.

"Here, kid. Give them this with your resume, and blow them away," Jerry says, overemphasizing the word "blow" as he hands me a form.

I walk down a short hallway, and each second seems magnified, like the way time seems to slow down when something truly important is happening. Everything I see seems clearer, in shaper focus. Every sense is heightened.

I enter the room to find three exhausted-looking men seated behind a table. After handing them a copy of my resume and form, I spot Kevin standing in the corner. He gives me a quick smile as I walk to the center of the room, and I feel somewhat lighter and more confident than ever before. I tell myself not to worry about the men in the room; I can't control how they will react to me. No, all I can do is present myself to them, and do my best, so I stare straight ahead and smile.

"Mr. Burroughs, I applaud your tenacity in staying so long, however we do not have much time. Please begin whenever you are ready," says the man in the middle as he strokes his scruffy goatee.

In the moment before I begin, I am aware of my own body more than I have ever been. I take one last inhalation of air and hold it for just a brief second. This is the final breath I will take as a struggling actor. Either I will land a role today, or I will give up on this silly dream forever. The thought sends adrenaline coursing through my veins, and for a quick second it feels like I could do absolutely anything.

And so I begin.

When I exhale, I feel everything start to dull, almost as if I am not even in my own body. I say the first line, and notice my voice is pitched a little lower than usual. The voice isn't mine, but some character that my actor's instincts have decided to create. I forget where I am, and although I'm aware I'm talking and walking around, none of it feels like it's in my control. Time is speeding past, as if compensating for having felt so slow just seconds before. I only have a few more lines left before my monologue is over, before everything could be over for good. I close my eyes, trying to savor these last few precious seconds, but time keeps pressing on.

When I open my eyes again, all I can hear are the last auditory traces of my final line hanging in the air. It's over. I've no idea whether I said any of the lines correctly, or if what I've done could even be considered acting. I swallow hard and steady myself before returning my gaze to the men seated at the table. For the first time in my career, I see something new: each pair of eyes is not only looking at me, they're smiling too.

"Very good, Mr. Burroughs. Now if you don't mind, I'd like you to go back outside and ask the monitor to give you the sides for Caleb. We will send someone to fetch you when we're ready," says the goateed man, pointing generally toward the door as he returns his attention to the array of papers before him. I exit the room and close the door behind me.

Leaning back, I close my eyes and the goofiest grin crosses my face. They want to see more; my last audition isn't over yet.

"Excuse me?" I hear a voice say, and when I open my eyes my smile quickly fades.

At first I think I'm looking into some sort of bizarre mirror that is showing me a younger version of myself. The figure before me is my height, with full black hair that is cut short like I wore it in college. He's even wearing a vest similar to my own.

"Excuse me?" the doppelganger repeats, more loudly. "I need to get in."

"Oh…I…Yes! I'm sorry. I thought I was the last one."

"So did I," he says, glaring as he hurries past.

I make my way down the hall to the waiting room and find Jerry thumbing through headshots of gorgeous men.

"They told me to ask you for the sides."

"Yes, Mama!" Jerry says, affecting his best drag queen voice. The fact that it's deeper than his usual speaking voice is odd, but given his hulking frame, it fits him better.

"Thanks," I reply, taking the pages I'd seen earlier. "Any clue who that other guy was in the hall?"

"You mean Alex?"

"Umm…maybe. Does he look like me?"

"I mean…sort of. In a younger, thinner kind of way."

"Gee, thanks."

"You asked. Anyway, I wouldn't worry about it. He might be better looking but…." Jerry trails off.

"But what?" I ask.

"But, let's just say he and Kevin aren't on good terms,"

"Have they worked together before?"

"Not professionally."

"Oh." As lovable as Kevin is, he is not without enemies. A lot of people hate him out of jealousy. However, Jerry's tone and choice of words makes me think that Kevin and Alex must have dated, and when Kevin dumps a guy, it's not a pretty picture.

I'll never forget the first time I encountered one of Kevin's ex-lovers. It was the summer solstice of my first year in the city, and the heat was unbearable. Kevin and I had been rehearsing a scene for class in a poorly ventilated studio space all day, and I was about to head home when Kevin asked me if I wanted to go out clubbing. A lot of the guys from our class were meeting at a new bar in Hell's Kitchen, and had, of course, begged Kevin to make an appearance. I've never really enjoyed dancing at clubs, but Kevin was looking especially sexy that night. While I considered his proposal, he used the bottom of his tank top to wipe his face, revealing beautifully sculpted abs glistening with sweat. It was an invitation I couldn't pass up.

The club was packed, and the scent of steamy bodies was so acrid I felt like I could taste it. In all directions shirtless guys writhed to the beat of a heavy dance remix of a Rihanna song. I was already regretting my decision to come along, but, before I could make up an excuse to leave, Kevin threw an arm over my shoulder and guided me through the crowd. The sea of flesh parted for him as if he was Moses, and I followed him to the bar.

"Gimme two Manhattans," he ordered, projecting his voice over the thudding music.

"Two?" I asked, eyeing him with suspicion as the bartender set about preparing our order.

"Yeah, I hope you like whiskey," he said, winking as he handed me one of the two cocktails.

Wanting desperately to fit in, I took a huge gulp. The booze burned so badly, I could barely choke out, "Oh, I love it."

"Drink up. I wanna dance."

"Okay." I took another burning swig. I wasn't sure whether he meant dancing with me specifically, but I wasn't about to ask.

Kevin finished his entire drink in less than a minute, but it took me a little bit longer. The second I set down my half-full glass, he pulled me onto the dance floor. I did my best to keep time with the steady bass beat, but he danced with the confidence of a true performer. His footwork had serious flair; before long everyone around us was staring. Aware that my two-stepping was just embarrassing compared to Kevin, I started to back up but he grabbed my hand.

"What are you—"

"Just follow my lead," he said, placing his hands on my hips and guiding me to keep up with him.

I'd like to say I'm a good partner to dance with, but I'm pretty sure Kevin was just an amazing lead. Our bodies moved in tandem and quickly went from dancing to something more like aerobic grinding. Feeling our bodies on one another was electric, and the whole room seemed to melt away.

"God, it's hot," Kevin said, stripping off his tank top and cramming it in his back pocket.

"I think you're making it hotter!" I replied, emboldened enough by the rush of alcohol and excitement to run my hands down his smooth, taut shoulders.

I felt the entire room burn with jealousy as I reveled in the exquisite sensation of Kevin's body under my fingers. As the music played on we became more and more entwined, until our bodies were moving together in perfect sync I couldn't help but wonder if Kevin wasn't just enjoying moving to the music, but also dancing with me. Seeing us move together, everyone else seemed to give up on the idea that they might go home with Kevin that night, and they all went back to dancing around us.

The only exception seemed to be one guy who was watching us very intently from just a few feet away. While Kevin was clearly the hottest one in the club, this guy was a close second. Dressed in tight jeans and an even tighter t-shirt, there was little left to the imagination; yet his tear-filled eyes and pained expression presented a stark contrast to his firmly gelled hair and muscled build.

"Your turn!" Kevin smiled as he gripped the bottom of my shirt and started to yank up. I quickly clamped my hands down with as much force as I could to stop him. Even though I was certainly skinnier back then, I've never been confident enough to take off my shirt in public.

"No."

"Don't be so shy." Kevin tried tugging again, but this time I pushed his hand aside. Seconds later I felt a big push, which sent me stumbling into two guys who were making out.

"Sorry," I apologized, turning around to see what had sent me flying.

"What the hell are you doing?" Kevin yelled at the sad muscle boy who had been watching us.

"Do you know him?" I yelled over the music. Kevin's face had physically changed into something utterly unrecognizable on him. A scowl.

"Yeah, we used to…um…date."

"Oh."

"Let's get out of here." Kevin took my hand and led me out of the bar, but the muscle boy was right on our heels.

"Wait," he called after us, but Kevin kept going.

"Why not just talk to him?" I asked. It wasn't hard to see that getting dumped by Kevin could make someone do crazy stuff. I mean, my one-sided love affair with him was hard enough. I could only imagine how much more painful it would be to have him reject me after knowing him as more than just a friend.

It turned out that Kevin was as gifted at hurting someone as he was at charming them.

"Wait here," he said, spinning around to face our stalker. "God, can't you get a clue? Get lost!"

"Please don't say that," the muscle boy mumbled. "I don't want to give up on you. I can't."

"So you're just going to…what? Stalk me till I come back? That's your plan?"

"I didn't know what else to do. I thought if you'd just give me a chance…"

"You thought? You thought!" Kevin said in an increasingly mocking tone, before letting out a cold-blooded cackle. "Thinking isn't your strong suit. I've told you that. Whatever you thought, you were wrong. We had fun, but it's over, so just get out of my life."

"But why? What did I do wrong?"

"Nothing! Nothing wrong, nothing right, you did nothing. Everything we did was my choice, my decision. Dating you was like dating a puppet."

"But I…I was just…"

"But nothing. Look, Pinocchio, you're fine, but I'd like a real boy," Kevin said, phrasing the final insult in a way that made me wonder if he'd rehearsed it beforehand. The guy started to sob, but Kevin showed no remorse; he turned away and, with just a few strides of his long legs, was beside me once more.

"You're really just gonna leave him like that?" I asked, unable to believe anyone could leave someone crying in the street.

"It's fine. Just start walking. Don't look at him. Guys like him always turn on the waterworks as a last resort. Ignoring them is the only way to make sure they don't come back." Draping his arm around me, he flashed a smile as he steered us toward another bar. No trace of the villainous mask he'd been wearing remained; instead his expression was, again, that of a local hero.

That was the only time I ever saw first-hand that Kevin was capable of being so vicious, but it was unforgettable. I knew then that I had to find a way to stop loving him. If he ever let me in, only to shut me out after a few weeks, I wasn't sure I'd survive the heartache.

"Gurl! Wake up!" Jerry's loud drag queen voice knocks me out of my daydream. "They're ready for you, go!"

As I grab my pack, I realize I must have missed seeing Alex leave. I wish I'd been able to see his face to gauge how well he thought he'd done, but as I enter the room the answer is clear. The blatant traces of annoyance on the faces of all three men, coupled with Kevin's smug smile, make it clear that Kevin has given me the encore I had hoped for. Now I just need to give the best reading of my life.

THREE

"Mr. Burroughs, thank you for staying with us. Have you familiarized yourself with the material?" asks the goateed man who spoke earlier, while gesturing for me to stand in the center of the room.

"Yes, I have. It's practically memorized," I say, hoping my confident tone doesn't sound too boastful.

"Excellent, before we begin I'd like to talk to you for a few moments. For starters, my name is David Stein. I'm in charge of casting, and I'm a co-producer with our author, Colin Shapiro," he says gesturing to the man on his right, who is so thin and frail that he almost looks like a skeleton wearing an Andy Warhol wig.

"As in Colin Shapiro who wrote *Twisted in the Night?*"

"See that Colin? You've not been forgotten," says a stout, red-bearded man to the left of Stein.

"Forgotten! Of course not, you made history with that show. I wished I'd lived here to see it," I say, finally recognizing why the script felt so familiar. Colin Shapiro was a Broadway legend in the eighties. He wrote three Tony Award-winning plays in a row, and when he accepted the Pulitzer for *Twisted in the Night* he shocked everyone by announcing his retirement.

"How very kind. I do hope to make a splash with this one too," he says, and I can't help but be thankful I didn't know who he was before now. I doubt I could've kept my cool during my monologue if I'd known I was in the room with him.

"Leave that to me," says the man with the red beard. "I am James Merchant, the director." As if being in the same room with renowned playwright Colin Shapiro wasn't enough, the idea that James Merchant is also here makes me forget how to breathe. He isn't at all as I imagined him to be. Given his genius, I expected him to be some tall and lithe Steve Jobs-looking guy. Instead, he looks more like that dwarf from *Lord of the Rings*. Gumtree? Gimlet? Eric would be so disappointed in me for not remembering his name.

"It's an honor, sir. I saw your production of *Much Ado about Nothing* three times last year. It was incredible." I sound more like a fan boy than I mean to. As my words hang in the air, I take a shaky breath and try to recall everything I've said in this room before I knew who was in it. I can't recall anything, though. It's like my memory has been erased. Afraid this means I won't remember my lines, I clutch the paper copy Jerry gave me.

"Did you now? That's good to hear. However, *Masque* is a different animal despite the similarity in period."

"Of course. So, is there anything I should know before we begin?" I ask, hoping for a little direction.

"I'm sure there are a great number of things you *should* know, but right now I'm only interested in one thing. Chemistry. We've seen a lot of people for this role, seasoned professionals, even some celebrities, but they lacked the ability to connect to our leading man. I need an actor who can do more than just keep up with him. I need someone to push him further, to make him work, and for some reason this been difficult to find. So chemistry, Mr. Burroughs, is what I'm looking for."

"He must be quite an actor."

"Well, you would know, wouldn't you? After all, he's the one saying you're the miracle we've been looking for. I thought you two were friends," says Merchant, extending his right hand toward Kevin.

"Kevin's the lead?"

"Yes. Didn't you know?" asks Shapiro.

"He said he was the reader."

"Well, I am," Kevin explains. "It was the only way I could be part of the casting process without raising suspicion."

"How charmingly deceitful, I see someone's already getting into character," Shapiro says with a nod of approval.

Merchant's eyes focus on Kevin and then move to me. "Indeed, so it would seem. Well, that should make this somewhat interesting, so while the moment is still fresh, let us begin."

After having done nothing but wait all day, I wish I had more time. My brain feels foggy, unable to cope with the fact that I am auditioning before theatre royalty with Kevin Caldwell, of all people. I look at Kevin, and, as he smiles, I remember how to breathe. Chemistry is something I think we have, and I hope it'll be enough, because I have to begin.

"Your Lordship has been most kind in inviting me to dine here, but surely it is a waste to bestow such finery on someone of my station." The line feels good to say, because I mean it. Kevin hasn't even spoken a word, and yet he seems completely different. His posture, his face, everything about him is somehow changed. How did I ever think that acting with him was a good idea? I'm out of my league.

"Do you think of yourself as having such little value?"

"As my own man, I know my worth. But to a count? I cannot imagine you've need of a discarded soldier."

"'Tis true, as a count I have no need of you, but I am more than my title. I too am my own man, and, like all men, I have desires and wants." Kevin moves toward me and hooks his index finger on the top of my vest.

"I thought you would want for nothing. Is not everything within these lands yours?"

"Everything?" he asks, and then pulls me to him. "No, there is plenty within my borders that I cannot have."

Looking into Kevin's eyes, I have to fight the urge to shrink, but decide to challenge him as Merchant requested. I entwine my hand with his, and drop my voice into a deeper baritone to ask, "Is there anything I can provide?"

"Oh, of that I am not yet certain, but I hope to discover all that you can offer in due time. That is, of course, provided you are not otherwise occupied?" Kevin begins undoing the buttons of my vest, and while I want to stop him, I let him continue.

"I have a modest farm to tend to, but it has little need of me while the ground lies frozen." As Kevin finishes the last button I quickly turn away, and catch sight of Merchant. He's not even watching anymore, seemingly more concerned with the papers before him than what we are doing in front of him. Flustered, I quickly look down at my script to compose myself before continuing. "I am happy to provide whatever service your lordship asks of me." At the word "service" I feel Kevin's breath upon my neck, as he wraps both arms around me.

"It pleases me greatly to hear those words from your lips," Kevin says, running his fingers down my chest. However, he doesn't stop there, and when he attempts to slide them into the waistband of my jeans, I bolt up and cross as far away as I can.

"Do you mock me, sir?" The text mirrors a question of my own. Kevin is moving things way beyond what is customary for an audition. I'm starting to understand why they've had difficulty casting someone to play Caleb.

"Not at all. I have meant no offense." Kevin's eyes plead with me to return to him, but I stand my ground.

"Forgive me, sir, but my words have never garnered praise." I stress "words" in the line to make it clear that I am referring also to his actions.

"I fear you have spent your life surrounded by fools, for anyone with true vision can see what an amusing treasure you are."

When I first read the script, I thought the next line was Caleb's way of stating again how unworthy he is, but now I deliver the line as someone who is insulted.

"An amusing treasure?" I ask, my tone causing Kevin to look up, and for a moment I see a look of fear in his eyes. "Surely your lordship could summon up any number of people better suited to entertaining your desires. I am a—"

"My little Caleb," Kevin interrupts, cutting off my line. "Think not of me as your lord tonight. Call me Ezio. I would like us to be friends. Would you embrace me as you do your fellow soldiers?" Kevin oozes charm from every pore as he approaches me, backing me into a corner, leaving me nowhere to run.

"Ezio, I will gladly embrace you, but do not ask it as a comrade. For if we are to be friends, I hope you never know the life of a soldier. The horrors on the battlefield are not for a man as refined and fragile as you." Standing as tall as I can, I place a hand on Kevin's chest to keep some distance between us. However, Kevin uses this against me by grabbing my wrist and pulling me toward him, clutching my head to rest on his chest. I look up at him to deliver the next line, but as I open my mouth Kevin cups his hand to my jaw, and brings my lips to meet his for a kiss.

For a moment I forget myself, lingering on Kevin's soft full lips, unable to stop myself from comparing them to Eric's. But soon all traces of Eric vanish, as my memory calls forth the many nights I spent dreaming of this exact fantasy. I remember believing with every part of me that if Kevin could know what it was like to kiss me, he would feel every ounce of love I had for him, and he would know nothing in the world could ever rival such passion. I feel Kevin's tongue on mine, and everything seems to go hazy. It's as if Kevin's some sort of predator whose saliva has the ability to knock out his prey. The sound of pages dropping to the floor brings me back to the present, to the audition, and I regain enough sense to push him away, but I can't seem to think of what the next line is. I look to Kevin for help, but, to my surprise, he seems as lost as me.

"Let's stop there, shall we?" Merchant says as I bend over to collect the script.

"Sorry, I lost my place for a moment."

"Oh, don't apologize, Mr. Burroughs. I rather appreciated your interesting interpretation with those few lines."

"Plus you were at a disadvantage. It would be hard keep your place when Mr. Caldwell decides to veer so far from the script," says Colin, shaking his head in disapproval.

"Sorry, I was just caught up. It felt different, but also…right." Kevin says, giving Merchant a look I can't quite figure out.

"Yes, different is certainly a word for it, though I'm uncertain if Ezio would be so brash. This play is all about seduction; it needs to build slowly to really rev up the tension." Merchant says, jotting down a note.

"Mr. Burroughs, thank you so much. I believe we've seen enough to make our decision," says Stein.

"Oh, are you sure? I know the other scene."

"Yes, I'm sure you do, but we've run out of time," Stein explains.

"Well, thank you, thank you so much. It's been an honor," I say, quickly grabbing my pack and heading for the door.

"Hold up! I'll walk with you."

"We are not through with you, Mr. Caldwell. We still have some matters to discuss," Stein says, causing Kevin to pout like a kid being forced to miss recess.

"Oh...right. Well, I'll see you later then," Kevin says, giving a short wave. The gesture feels inconsequential compared to the intimacy we had during the audition. Even though I know it was just for the scene, I'm amazed by how quickly Kevin can just turn it off. Unsure of what to do, I simply nod to him as I close the door, but I can't help feeling like I've been kicked out of bed.

I walk down the hall in an absolute haze. Before I know it I realize I've boarded the subway home, even though I barely remember leaving the agency. Did I even say goodbye to Jerry? I feel guilty for not remembering to thank him, but am not entirely certain I didn't.

The train is crowded with people getting off of work, which is unfortunate because I should definitely sit down. My limbs are like overcooked noodles, and, as the car takes a hard left, I accidentally knock into someone's shoulder. Before I can apologize, they are exiting the car, and only then do I realize I should be, too. Utterly depleted, I shuffle like a zombie the rest of the way home. After a few attempts of getting my key into the door, I enter the apartment and flop down onto the couch. My vision grows hazy, like a scene from a Lifetime movie when a girl has been roofied, and seconds later I am asleep.

FOUR

"**M**ASON! MASON! WAKE UP! HELLO? ARE you in there?" Eric yells, violently tugging me back and forth to wake me up.

"Hmm? Oh, what time is it?" I ask, certain I fell asleep only a few minutes ago.

"It's 8:30, would you wake up already? Everyone's been trying to get ahold of you. Where's your phone?" he asks, his pale complexion marred by the red blotches he gets when he's really annoyed.

"Calm down. It's in my coat. What's the big deal?"

"Someone from some agency has been calling me over and over since you weren't picking up your cell! I didn't even know my number was on your resume!"

"You're the…," I let out a big yawn, "alternate number."

"Well, they said you needed to come back. I've been trying to reach you for hours, but you wouldn't pick up, and I couldn't get out of work. What happened at your audition today?" he asks as he retrieves my phone from my coat.

"I auditioned, and Kevin was there, it was…Oh my god! Shit!" Seeing that I have twenty-two missed calls and sixteen new voice mails throws me into such a panic I forget how to retrieve the voicemails. After watching me fumble for a few seconds, Eric takes the phone from me, presses one button, and hands it back.

"Hello? Is this Mason? It's Jerry from B&R casting. Where are you? You walked out, and they need to see you again. Call me back, and get here fast," he says followed by a beep.

"Mason, where are you? I just got a call from some guy at an agency. He says you need to come back. What's going on? Why don't you ever answer your phone?" I hear Eric's voice yell in my ear while, beside me, he silently glares at me.

"Mason! It's Kevin. Dude, where the fuck are you? Call me back. I'll try and keep Merchant busy, but I don't know how long I can...oh, shit! He's coming!" The message abruptly stops.

The next few messages are just the sound of someone hanging up after a long sigh. Clearly, Eric has been trying every ten minutes. I listen to them one by one, until I make it to the final message.

"Mr. Burroughs, this is James Merchant. I would like to discuss your audition. Please call the office. I do not enjoy being kept waiting."

Did I get it? He didn't say that.

I save the message, and replay it a few more times. After the third time, I realize I won't be able to divine anything concrete from it and hearing Merchant's harsh edge on each word becomes too much for me.

"Mason! Talk to me! What's going on?" Eric asks, looking at me with deep concern.

"I'm not sure. They said they needed to see me again. But...but... they told me they were done! I've got to call them back!" I say, scrolling through the list of unrecognized numbers on my caller ID.

Matching the numbers to the voice mails, I call the agency back first. It rings once, and then I hear Jerry's voice. My heart jumps, but right before I begin talking, I realize it's the agency voicemail. He yammers on about various options, and then finally I hear the beep.

"Hello? This is Mason Burroughs, I auditioned today for *Masque*. Mr. Merchant said I should call. Please call me back. I promise I'll answer." I hang up and move onto the next unrecognized number. No answer again, and when the voicemail picks up it just repeats the number I dialed before asking me to leave a message.

"Hello? Kevin? I'm trying to leave a message for Kevin Caldwell. It's Mason. Sorry. My phone was on silent, so I didn't get the calls till just now. I left a message. Mr. Merchant called—I have a number, should I call him back personally? Oh I'm getting a call on..." I say as I hear the call waiting beep in my ear and switch to the incoming call. "Hello?"

"Mason? Finally! What the hell happened to you?" I can barely hear Kevin over all the noise in the background.

"I was just leaving you a message. My phone was on silent, and I fell asleep."

"Merchant is so pissed." His words make my chest tighten.

"What do I do? He left me a message, so I have a number. Should I call it?" I ask, unsure if I even have anything to lose by attempting it.

"Don't call him. I've got Jerry's number. I'll call him, and call you back. You better answer your phone this time." Kevin hangs up before I can reply.

"Who was that?" Eric's blurts out, annoyed at being kept in the dark.

"Kevin. He's going to call the monitor on his cell."

"Kevin, as in..." I can see a flicker of panic flash across Eric's face. I was still hung up on Kevin when we first started living together. Eric saw first-hand what a mess my fascination with him made of me.

"Yeah, Kevin, the guy from my acting class. I ran into him today, and he got me an audition. He was the reader."

"I thought all actors read," Eric says, misunderstanding the term.

"The reader is the person who reads lines with you when you do a scene for an audition, but Kevin's also playing the lead, so it was...is... confusing."

"You're not kidding."

"I'm trying." It's hard to concentrate on anything, my mind's so busy thinking of a hundred things at once.

"It's okay, Mason. Just breathe."

"I am," I say, but no matter how much air I suck in I can't seem to expel it except in short staccato bursts like a woman in labor.

"You said something about someone calling a monitor? Like a computer screen?" he asks, rubbing my back while I attempt to breathe.

"Jerry is the monitor. The guy who makes the audition go smoothly."

"Sounds like he did a great job," Eric sarcastically replies, but when I try to laugh it sounds more like a cough.

"I don't think it's his fault. Anyway, Kevin's calling him to find out if Mr. Merchant will still see me."

"Okay, and who is he?" Eric sighs, obviously tired of constantly having to prompt me for information.

"The director. He's famous. He did that *Much Ado* I always talk about."

"Oh god, please don't start talking about that again," Eric jokes, pretending to cover his ears.

"This is serious! He's directing the show I auditioned for today. I think he liked me."

"Really? That's great!" Eric's whole face lights up at the potential for good news. He has the best smile. I think it's because of his dimples, or maybe just that it's unmistakably honest. In either case I can't stop myself from kissing him. The second our lips touch, I think of what Kevin did in the audition, and immediately I feel guilty. Even though it was just for the audition, I'm uncertain whether I should mention the kiss to Eric. Lackeys are pretty asexual, so there's never been occasion for it to come up before now. Under normal circumstances I doubt Eric would care, but because it was with Kevin, it's different.

Before I can decide, my phone rings, and I break the kiss to answer it.

"Man, you are going to owe me big time if this works out," Kevin says, his voice clear in the absence of the background noise from before. "Jerry says to come by the agency tomorrow at 3:00 p.m. Call me the second you know anything. They loved us! I told you Caleb was perfect for you. Just don't pull a stunt like this again."

"I didn't do it intentionally; I was unconscious. They said they were done."

"Yeah, well, Jerry was supposed to stop you. He says when you walked by without a word he thought you hadn't done well. Colin and I fought for you, but Merchant isn't convinced."

"Fabulous," I deadpan. "Any advice on how to score some points with him?"

"Merchant thinks you won't be able to handle the pressure, and this disappearing act didn't exactly help. But if you could butch it up a bit, that'd probably help a lot."

"Excuse me? Since when did you turn into Mr. Garr?" The guy who taught our class essentially gave me the same note every day for three months: "Butch it up, Mary!" Given that my name already started with the letter M, it only took about three days for it to become my official nickname.

"Hey, don't shoot the messenger."

"You're right, sorry. What exactly did he say?"

"He just worries you're a bit...umm...soft," Kevin says, clearly rephrasing whatever horrible term Merchant actually used.

"I see, well, I did just start with a trainer at the gym."

"That's perfect! Try to find a way to mention that. Merchant's trying to get more sex into the show, and he likes the whole Abercrombie look."

"Great. So I just need to become butch and sexy in eighteen hours," I say, certain I'm completely screwed. Transformations like that only happen in fairytales or on reality TV shows.

"You can do it. It's basically down to you and Alex, and we've got something between us," Kevin offers, though I'm not sure if the "us" he's referring to is me or Alex.

"History?"

"Chemistry," he corrects, and hangs up without even saying goodbye.

"I think I caught the gist of that one. Anything I can do?" Eric asks, helping me up and then giving me a long hug. Eric understands how much I loathe the idea of working out and that asking me to reign in my natural flair feels like sticking me back in the closet.

"Yeah, help me pick out something from Abercrombie that will make me look butch," I say, making finger quotes around the term.

"I'm a game designer, not a miracle worker," he says, modifying one of the few *Star Trek* lines I know.

"It's hopeless. This is why I never audition for big roles."

"How big is it?" he asks in surprise, making me realize I hadn't mentioned that I was in the running for a lead role yet.

"Let's just say if it were a video game, I'd be on the cover. It was all Kevin's idea. What am I going to do?"

"We'll find some clothes for you tomorrow. Have you eaten?" he asks, kissing me again.

"No. I'm not hungry."

"But this could be your last chance before the diet and work-outs."

"Don't start," I say, not wanting to get his hopes up, or mine.

"Fine, you're right, but what would you do if I got us pizza from Amelia's and a bottle of wine?"

"Do you really have to ask?" At the mention of Amelia's stone oven pizza, my mouth begins to water.

"Nope," Eric whispers, going in for a long kiss. Unfortunately, I'm still having trouble breathing, so when he starts using tongue I push him away.

"I'm not sure what was the bigger tease; that, or the offer of pizza."

"I never tease!" he says, and then rushes out the door. Alone in our apartment, I look around, knowing that if tomorrow goes as I expect, I'll be seeing a lot less of it.

★

I ARRIVE AT THE CASTING agency a few minutes early, decked out in my new look: baseball shirt and cargo pants. According to Eric, it makes me look more athletic, but I'm pretty sure I just look stupid.

"Mmmm, gurl, look at you! Why weren't you rocking this yesterday?" Jerry says, once again using his drag queen voice.

"It was a gift from my fairy godmother." I smile, imagining Eric in tiny fairy wings.

"Well then, Cinderella, you best get to the ball! Mr. Merchant is in the conference room down the hall. Third door on the right."

"Got it."

"If he decides to cast you, don't leave. I've got a ton of forms for you," Jerry says, and as I pass him he slaps me hard on the ass like he's sending me out onto the field. I half-expect him to say "Go get 'em, slugger!" As my left butt cheek burns, I'm utterly convinced jocks must reserve that kind of homoerotic play for when they're wearing pads. That, or maybe they don't slap that hard and Jerry was just trying to cop a cheap feel. I am so distracted by that thought, and the pain, that I enter the room without even knocking.

"Mr. Burroughs, how kind of you to reappear," says Merchant, barely looking up from the papers on the table in front of him.

The sound of his voice makes me go completely numb, obliterating the sting from Jerry's swat. As I stand there, I seem to forget the most basic things, like how to stand like a person who isn't a nervous wreck. I shift my posture to try and look more natural, but instead realize it looks like I am posing for him in the door frame. Quickly, I attempt to adjust back to before, but it also feels wrong. I have no idea how long it has been since he spoke, but it feels like ages. Finally I manage to untie my tongue enough to reply.

"I'm so sorry, Mr. Merchant. I had silenced my phone before I auditioned, and I fell asleep the second I got..."

"I'm not interested in your excuses, now please sit down. We have plenty to discuss, and I barely found time to be here at all."

I flop into the chair, spreading my legs in a wide stance, and slouch forward. Eric had me rehearse this sitting position for over an hour last night. Apparently perfect posture isn't masculine. It took some work, as slouching hurts my back, but it does the job. Merchant looks up.

"All right. What do you want to know?" I ask, hoping to seem more dominant.

"I want to know why someone with a resume like yours even auditioned for a role so clearly out of his league." Merchant asks pointedly, and although I want to lean away, I don't move.

"Out of my league? I admit it's not the kind of work I've been doing lately, but that doesn't mean I'm incapable of doing it," I say, confident in my answer because I anticipated the question.

"Capable, perhaps, but I need someone who will do more than tread water, Mr. Burroughs."

"So what is it you want me to say here? That I'm hungry for the role? That I'm ready to fight for it?"

"You can save those platitudes for your *Wicked* audition, thank you. You brought out the best in Kevin with only a few lines, so you have my attention, but my concern now is how you managed to do it."

"Well...we've worked together before."

"Yes, I'm aware, but that was years ago, correct?"

"Yeah, we were scene partners in a class."

"Is that all?" Merchant asks, studying me very carefully as I consider the question.

"Well, we were friends."

"Were?"

"Yes. You see, Kevin's career took off pretty big after the class. So… we lost touch." I say, causing Merchant eyes to widen.

"Really? The way Kevin vouched for you…I'd assumed you remained friends."

"Oh…well…I mean it was great to see him again. It felt like old times." I backpedal, wondering what on earth Kevin told them.

"Yes, that's exactly what I suspected." Merchant says, folding his arms. "You've reminded Kevin of a time where he was forced to work on his craft."

"What?"

"Kevin isn't like you, Mason. He's a born actor, an artist. He doesn't spend years working on audition pieces, he just walks in and lands the role. However, natural talent is as dangerous as it is helpful. If Kevin can get away with doing a half-ass job, he will, but when he read with you, well, he could see how hard you were working, so he couldn't get away with phoning it in."

"Because?"

"Because, although your audition was far from perfect, you succeeded in challenging him, which meant that Kevin had to actually do something to keep up. Of course, once he started trying, it didn't take long for him to put you back in your place."

"What do you mean? You wanted chemistry, didn't that kiss show we have it?" I ask, unsure how I could be faulted for causing Kevin do to exactly what Merchant wanted.

"The kiss proved that you are like all the rest; unable to avoid succumbing to Kevin's charms."

"I can resist Kevin. Believe me, I've had plenty of practice. But yesterday he wasn't auditioning, he could afford to take big risks."

"And if you had the role, you think you're prepared to take risks like that?"

"Of course! This show is the kind of thing I've been dreaming of doing my entire life. The real question is, are you willing to take the risk by casting me?" The question feels more like a challenge, and I worry I may have gone too far.

"I believe in calculated risk," Merchant says, touching his temple with his index finger, "and there are things you can do to improve your odds. As of now, you are too rough to be able to act alongside Kevin, especially on a Broadway stage. However, with my help, you could be more than ready by opening night."

"I'll do whatever it takes."

"So you would not object to working with me, off the clock, in additional rehearsals?"

"I'd consider it a perk," I say, the hair on the back of my neck beginning to prickle. I've never had a part this big so close within reach.

"I doubt that will be true for very long, but I believe you. Of course, we'll also need to do something about your physique. No one will believe you were a soldier as you are now."

"I've got a personal trainer."

"Not anymore. Honestly, they deserve to be fired if this is the best they can do with you. No, I will select a trainer for you, and you'll do exactly what they prescribe."

"Anything else?" I ask, afraid to even breathe.

"At this moment, I think that is enough. I suggest you rest up while you can. Rehearsals begin in three days, and I don't want to hear you slept through it. Please arrive for our first private session an hour before rehearsal. Provided you do that, then...I suppose the role is yours." Merchant extends his hand to me and smiles.

"Really? Oh...Mr. Merchant! Thank you. Thank you so much! You won't be disappointed," I say, leaping out of my chair. After quickly shaking his hand, I grab him in a big hug.

"Yes, yes, Mr. Burroughs, that's fine," he says, tensing his shoulders and taking a step back to extricate himself. "Now, please go fill out your forms."

"Oh, yes, right away." I say, too happy to be ashamed of clearly overstepping my bounds with him. I close the door and bolt down the hall, never more excited to fill out paperwork in my life.

FIVE

FROM THE CIRCUS OF SOUNDS emanating from behind our front door, I can tell the party is already underway. Still dressed in the clothes of a stranger, I flex my hands, cramped from hours of paperwork. Why did they need my address seven different times? Of course, I would have been done sooner if my cell phone hadn't exploded with constant phone calls and texts of congratulations. It feels silly to even think about complaining about that, though. I just can't believe how fast word got around after I told Eric.

"Mason! I don't even know what to say. This is so...oh...I don't know...just get home quick, okay? We have to celebrate!" Excited, he'd hung up before I could tell him it would probably be awhile.

This is a moment I've been dreaming of for as long as we've been a couple. I'm going to walk through our door, greet him with a kiss, and finally tell him I'm going to be a working actor on Broadway. The prestige is really the important part, but I'm also looking forward to the paycheck that goes with it. Eric saved me from waiting tables, landing me a slightly more stable paying job doing data-entry from home. It's a pretty easy gig, but I only make enough to cover my half of the rent and utilities. Whenever we go out, Eric pays for me. Or, as he puts it, us. I can't wait to beat him to the check when we go out next time.

"Congratulations!" my friends collectively roar, descending upon me as soon as I open the door.

"Eric?" I call, searching for his short black hair amongst the human rubble.

"Here!"

"Give them some room," someone says, and as everyone parts, I finally see Eric's sweet, dimpled smile a few feet away.

"I'm going to be on Broadway!" I rush up to him and throw my arms around his neck.

"Then I guess I've only got a few weeks before I've got to share my shining star with the rest of the world," he replies, pulling me in for a kiss. Considering we are surrounded by our friends, I'm surprised when he slips me the tongue, but I'm not embarrassed at all. It's like the end of a fairy tale for me, even though my dreams of being on Broadway are really just beginning. When Eric finally lets me go, I notice something peculiar about the apartment.

"Why's everything covered up?" I ask, holding up what appears to be a wine bottle in a brown paper bag.

"Why don't you open it and find out? We've got a pool going on how long it takes you to guess."

"All right, but you know I hate surprises." Eric's track record for surprises is abysmal. I normally have to return them. But I like just about everything in a wine bottle, so I relax and pull the tiny string cinching the bag closed. The second it reveals a bottle of Amarone wine, I get the clue and start laughing.

"Time is ticking," Eric reminds me.

"Brown paper packages tied up with string, these are a few of my favorite things!" I sing, and everyone applauds.

"Six minutes since he walked in the door. Steph is the winner!" Eric says, handing our friend a fan of dollar bills.

"What was your bid?" I ask him.

He grins. "Three minutes, fourteen seconds." Only Eric would think Pi would help him in this area.

"You're such a nerd." I tap the bridge on his glasses and kiss him again.

"You love it."

"I love everything about you. But I'm a little curious how you managed to get all of this done in two hours."

"Well everyone helped, plus I decided to take some time off."

"I thought you were in crunch mode right now."

"We are, but the minute I told my boss why I wanted the rest of the day off, he pulled this out of his desk. He says congratulations by the way," Eric says, tugging a magnum of champagne out of a chilling bucket.

"Oh, my! It looks expensive."

"It is."

"He really shouldn't have. It's too much."

"We'll put it to better use than he would. But before we pop the cork, are you ready for your surprise?" Eric asks, flashing a Puck-like grin.

"This isn't it?" I'm not sure if I can handle much more.

"Follow me," Eric says, handing me a glass of wine as he leads me to our bedroom door, which suspiciously is closed.

Instead of coats all over the bed, there is nothing but roses. Cellophane wrapped bouquets of every color are piled on top of another, surrounded by overflowing vases that cover every spare inch of space on the floor. Their floral aroma is as overpowering to my nose as their sheer number and variety are to my eyes, and I feel tears begin to well up in my eyes.

"Oh Eric! This is too much! Did you rob a flower truck?"

"No. Everyone brought you a bouquet. I assume you know which one's mine."

"Of course. You're the only one who didn't get roses," I say, pointing out the bouquet of moonlight lilies.

"Your favorite."

"Yes," I say, kissing him once again. "This really is too much."

"It's what you deserve! To Mason!" Eric says, raising his glass in a toast.

"To Mason!" everyone shouts from the doorway as they begin to flood into the room.

After clinking about twenty glasses, I drain half of my wine in one big gulp. Feeling light-headed, I grab onto Eric's arm.

"Let me fix you a plate." Eric knows that I will most likely pass out before the party is over if I continue to drink on an empty stomach. I've always been the lightweight in the relationship.

While I wolf down a plate of my favorite snacks Eric does a great job of keeping people entertained. Once I've sobered up a bit, I insist that Eric let me help out, and I start seeing who needs a refill. I laugh when I spy the last of our Halloween candy has been set out for the guests. Eric got to choose our costumes this year, so we went as the most iconic video game duo ever, Mario and Luigi.

"Mason!" I hear someone yell from behind the front door, followed by three hard knocks. Assuming it's a rather late guest, I open the door without checking the peep hole.

"Kevin?" I ask, unsure if I'm more surprised that he is standing at my door, or that he appears to be drunk out of his mind.

"There's my man!" he slurs, pointing at me with a mainly empty bottle of Jack Daniels.

"Are you all right?"

"Of course I am. Happy birthday!" he says, lunging at me in an attempted embrace, knocking me to the floor.

"Is everything okay?" calls Eric. I can hear him approaching from the other room and try to disentangle myself from Kevin.

"Everything is amaaaaazing," Kevin singsongs.

"Do you know this guy?"

"This is Kevin. Kevin, this is my boyfriend, Eric," I say, pushing Kevin off of me so I can stand up.

"Your boyfriend?"

"Yes," I say, annoyed at the surprise in his voice.

"I didn't know you had a man. He's looks….smart."

"And you look drunk," says Eric, taking off his glasses and cleaning the lenses with his shirt. I notice Eric's bicep is flexing a little harder than it should.

"You're right…but you know what…I'm a sexy drunk," Kevin slurs, flashing a smile at him.

"This is Kevin?" Eric asks, unable to conceal the judgment in his face or voice.

"I'm the star," Kevin says in a loud stage whisper.

"And don't all stars need their beauty sleep? Maybe you should lie down," Eric says, using his calmest and most placating voice. Eric's boss has been known to get hammered on the job, which is not a fireable offense if you happen to be the son of the owner. Eric's always the one who manages to get him to sleep it off. He's like a horse-whisperer for drunks.

"See? You're already trying to get me into bed. I am a sexy drunk. Right, Mason?"

"Right. Just let me make sure the room is ready," I say, dragging Kevin toward our bedroom.

"Want me to get him some water?" Eric asks, helping me lift Kevin up.

"No, I'll get it."

"You sure?"

"It's fine, but I'd appreciate it if you got everyone to stop staring."

"Done," Eric says, helping me get a better hold of Kevin before turning around. "Okay everyone, grab a refill. The Wii Tennis Tournament is about to begin!"

After getting Kevin into the bedroom, I clear a swath in the pile of bouquets as he leans against the door. Within seconds he begins to slip down, and so I do my best to stand him back up, but the second I try to move, Kevin starts to slip again. For the first time in my life I'm happy our bedroom is so tiny, because with just a little adjusting I manage to get Kevin to fall face first onto our bed simply by tipping him forward. Thankfully, his face manages to miss the thorns of a bouquet by a few inches.

"Whoa, is your man a florist?" he asks, throwing them aside and knocking a vase over.

"No, it's because I got cast."

"No one ever brings me flowers."

"Really?" I ask, curious as to how this could possibly be true.

"Yeah, leading men never get flowers. You girls get everything," Kevin says, flipping onto his back and closing his eyes.

As obnoxious and irritating as Kevin's being, it's hard for me to get mad at him. When our places were reversed, Kevin was my knight in shining armor. We were at a cast party on the last day of class, and I was so sad about never seeing Kevin again I decided to get absolutely wrecked on boxed wine and equally cheap vodka. My memory of that night isn't clear and after a certain point it just goes completely blank. The next thing

I remember is waking up in a cab with Kevin, and then him walking me up four flights of stairs to my apartment. God knows what would have happened to me if he hadn't been there.

As thankful as I am about it, I do wish he'd quit snickering in his sleep.

"What the fuck is so funny?" I ask, stupidly trying to find sense in the mind of a drunk.

"You….You're…Oh man…You're….," he replies, before sitting up and starting to laugh.

"I'm what?"

He makes a show of trying to pull it together. "It's a secret….I have… to…to…whisper it to you." He erupts into even higher peals of laughter.

"Fine," I say, leaning in.

Kevin grabs me, pulling me close, and begins to ferociously invade my mouth with his tongue. I try to pull away, banging my fists on his compact chest, but he has no problem overpowering me. I panic and begin to scream, which is strange since my sound goes into Kevin's mouth. I look at him with wide eyes, horrified by the knowing look he is giving me. He's clearly aware of what he is doing. Even with the strength brought on by panic, I can't seem to push him away. Just as I am about to try biting down, Kevin releases me and tosses me on the side of the bed.

"What was that?" I shout, rubbing my aching jaw.

"A congratulatory gift. I got you the job, now you can give me one. You know, quid pro quo and all that," he says, grabbing his crotch.

"Wait…what?"

"Normally I'd expect more than a blowjob, but since we're old friends…"

"What? Wait, are you serious?" I ask, unsure which is more unbelievable, that Kevin thinks I would do this, or that he would want me to.

"Oh my god, Mason, chill the fuck out. I'm just kidding."

"Well, it's not funny! Wait…are you even drunk?"

"Fooled you," he says with a wink. "Look, I didn't know you were having a real party, or that you had a boyfriend. I'm sorry, man. Just let me make my exit. Walk me to the door, and help me get a cab, whaddya say?"

"Anything to get you out of here."

"Ouch. Jeez, don't get all pissy. I was just following orders," he says, but before I can question him further he stands up and walks out the door, once again feigning intoxication. Without a word, I adopt my role to keep up this charade, and escort him downstairs.

The November night has turned bitterly cold, so there are only a few people still out and about on our block. Unsure what to even think at this moment, I sit on the steps next to Kevin. All my emotions seem to have blended together, leaving me numb and somewhat dazed. I let out an exasperated sigh, which materializes in the frigid air.

"I know you need to get back up to the party, but there's something I really need to know," Kevin says, his eyes focused on the sidewalk.

"What is it?"

"What were you thinking about when we kissed in the audition?"

"Well...at first I was thinking how different you kiss, you know, compared to Eric. But also I was thinking about how I'd imagined kissing you, and about Merchant wanting chemistry. It was a lot of things. Why?"

"You gave me the biggest hard-on ever, that's why. I haven't been able to stop thinking about it," Kevin says, adjusting himself.

"Is that why you tried to practically devour my face just now?" I say, still very aware of the throbbing pain in my jaw.

"Yeah, I'm really sorry about that. Especially since you're with that guy."

"Eric."

"Yeah, please apologize to him for me. I promise I'll be good from here on out. Except on stage, where, you know, we're supposed to be in love."

"I'm not sure it's love."

"Seems like love to me."

"I'm sure it does. See you in a few days."

I walk back up to the apartment, making sure to put on my best "everything is fine" face, before generously filling my glass with wine.

"You all right?" Eric asks, eyeing my glass.

"Yes, Kevin sends his apologies."

"He's a hot mess. I mean...I can see why you were into him, but..."

is he always like that?"

"No, I think it was some kind of actor hazing thing," I offer as a weak explanation.

"Don't worry about it then."

"You're right."

"Of course I am." He grins. "Now, let's break out my boss's gift. We need champagne!" With a pop of the cork, the party resumes.

SIX

THE REHEARSAL SPACE IS NOT at all how I imagined. Instead of walking though Times Square into a gilded lobby with carvings of cherubs and lush red carpets, I am outside a drab warehouse a few blocks north of the Port Authority. I check my phone to be sure I'm in the right place before pressing a chipped, painted button on an ancient intercom.

"Name?" the voice crackles.

"Mason Burroughs," I yell into the box, unsure if I needed to press the button to be heard.

"Downstairs, second door on the right," the voice snaps before buzzing me through.

I grab the freezing door handle and yank hard, not wanting to ask them to buzz me again. After descending the cold cement stairs into a crypt-like hall that's lit with garish fluorescent lighting, I make my way toward the door, but a woman blocks my path.

I don't need to be told who she is; she has all of the obvious signs of the job. Oily hair pulled back and clipped, dark circles under the eyes, and of course the unofficial uniform: comfortable, though hardly flattering, black slacks, a white collared shirt with a black cotton sweater vest layered over it. Complete with the almost action-figure like set of accessories of a huge binder in hand and various pens and pencils tucked into every pocket, she can only be one thing.

"Mr. Burroughs, I presume?" she asks, barely looking up from her binder.

"Yes. Nice to meet you."

"I'm Jenna, your stage manager," she says, shaking my hand and confirming my assumption. "Mr. Merchant has already informed me of your arrangement."

"Arrangement?"

"Yes, any work you do before rehearsal will be off the clock for union purposes. Please only sign in once you two are finished," she says curtly, and then quickly walks away.

I'd spent the better part of the past two days reading countless interviews of actors who'd worked with Merchant, hoping to find some hint about what I could expect in these sessions, but I wasn't able to even find anyone acknowledging they existed. Though I was somewhat curious to find that when I typed "James Merchant Private" into Google it suggested "James Merchant Private Sessions," and further down the list, "James Merchant Private Torture." However, when I searched those things nothing came up.

Not wanting to be late again, I enter the room and see Merchant seated at a large rectangular table. Unlike our other meetings, I notice that he does not look the least bit exhausted. As I approach the table, his gaze is so palpable that I begin feeling I've done something wrong before we've even begun.

"Ah, Mr. Burroughs, so nice to see you can arrive on time," he says, not-so-subtly reminding me that my mistake has been neither forgiven nor forgotten.

"Of course. Would you like to begin?" I ask, trying to sound unafraid.

"Eager are we? That's good. However, before we begin, I need to explain some things. You may be seated."

"Okay," I say, taking a seat and pulling out a notebook.

"You won't need that." Merchant says, snatching the book out of my hands.

"But I—"

"I know, you just want to do a good job. Believe me, I understand. I've worked with actors like you many times. Every single one of them hated my approach at first, and I have no doubt you will, too. But I've found that every actor was able to work through this, so long as they understood that everything we do in these sessions is necessary."

"All right."

"There are a few rules – three to be exact – that you must agree to abide by during these sessions. The first, and most important, is that everything we do in this room is secret. And I mean absolutely secret. Should you divulge my methods to even a priest, I'll know and I will fire you immediately. This is not limited to the present either. If you reveal anything after opening night, I will make sure the only acting jobs you can get are in community theatres in Tuscaloosa. Will you honor this first rule?" he asks, leaning back in his chair, which seems absurdly nonchalant.

"So I can't tell anyone? Not even my boyfriend?" I ask, stalling for time. This must be why I couldn't find anything on the internet.

"Yes, Mason. Not even him. This role could change your future, but time is not on our side, so our work will be intense. I cannot have you discussing it and analyzing it with strangers who don't see the bigger picture. Now, do you agree or not?"

My mind races through various problems with this. What if this is a casting couch situation? The idea repulses me, but I try to remember who I'm dealing with. This is James Merchant. The man is a genius – a respected, famous genius. He wouldn't do anything to me that would get him in trouble. But then why the secrecy? Is this a test?

"Yes. I will keep it secret."

"All right. The second rule is that we shall always be honest. Given the first rule, there is no need to lie, is there?"

"Agreed," I say, not wanting try his patience.

"Excellent! All that is left, then, is my third and final rule. You will do whatever I ask, to the best of your ability, so long as it is legal," he says, stroking his beard and smiling at his own caveat.

"I will try to the best of my ability."

"No! You will *do* what I say to the best of your ability," he corrects.

"I will *do* what you say to the best of my ability," I affirm, keeping my tone neutral.

"Excellent. Now please stand up and remove your clothes." The words leave his mouth in such a calm and flippant manner that it takes me a minute to even understand the request.

My brain goes blank for a moment, then rewinds the past few minutes back. I cannot have heard him correctly, but I know I did. I start to wonder if my instincts about the casting couch were correct, and I think I'm going to be sick.

Every part of me wants to protest, but I force myself to stop and think before I say anything. I feel trapped, horrified with myself for agreeing to this, and knowing that if I refuse to do as he asks, I'll be fired before I even make it to the first official hour of rehearsal. Determined to thwart his expectations, I start to strip.

In an effort to express my anger, I undress down to my boxer briefs, throwing each article of clothing down to the ground with as much force as I can muster. The cold floor leaches the heat from my body through the soles of my bare feet, making my nipples stand at attention. My knees begin to buckle due to the cold, or possibly the embarrassment, and I lock them to prevent Merchant from noticing my discomfort.

"Is there an issue?" Merchant asks, eyeing my underwear.

"No...I...didn't know if you meant these as well," I explain, taking them off and throwing them on top of the pile of clothes in front of me. The cold has done nothing to help me in the size department, and I wish the heat that seems trapped in my flushed face would disperse itself lower.

"How do you feel?" Merchant asks, as he gets up and begins to circle around me.

"Horrible," I reply, honoring the second rule of honesty.

"Why?" he asks, again in the same calm and measured manner.

"Because I agreed to do this, and there is no way to avoid it."

"How does that make you feel?"

"Stupid, embarrassed, angry..." I list, my voice barely audible.

"Why?" he repeats.

"What do you mean 'Why?' Because it does!" I shout, over-articulating each word as I glare in his direction. My eyes having welled up with hot tears, so I can no longer see him clearly. I have to fight to keep them from spilling down my cheeks.

Merchant sighs and circles me, watching me quiver like a frightened animal for what feels like days. My breathing becomes labored, and although I try, I cannot help but let out louder and louder whimpers with each inhalation.

"Mason," Merchant says, his tone softening. "I know this isn't easy... but I need you to go deeper. If you do...it will get better. Now tell me *why*. Why is being naked causing you to feel this way?"

"Because you're watching. I'm...cold. I feel unprotected. I hate that you're seeing me this way. I feel judged by you. It isn't fair. It isn't fair at all!" My throat grows tighter with every word, and I can feel myself becoming unhinged.

"Mason, focus!" Merchant barks, quieting my hysteria. "Keep talking. Keep going!"

"Going with what? I know I'm not what you wanted. I'm a disappointment, a fluke. It's not exactly new to me. My parents spent years wishing I was different, and you're even worse. You don't wish you had a straight actor, just a better looking one!" With that, the last of my strength drains from my legs; I slump to the floor in a heap of tears and broken cries. In between sobs the only thing I can think is: No, nothing is worth this.

Merchant puts his hand on my shoulder. The contact burns like acid, and I yelp as I shrug it away.

"You may put one thing back on," he says, and I immediately grab my shirt, hoping to cover as much as possible. "While I understand no one would enjoy this situation, do you always feel like that when you are naked in front of someone?"

"No."

"When do you feel differently?"

"Well...when I'm with Eric," I say, ashamed of the idea of him seeing me like this.

"Why?"

"Because he loves me. When he looks at me, he sees the best possible version of me." To Eric I'll always look as good as I did on the day we met. It took him hours to notice I'd dyed my hair red last summer. It wasn't a great look for me, but to Eric I was as cute as ever.

"You'd do well to try and see yourself like that, too. Now remove your shirt and put these on," Merchant commands, tossing me my underwear. The second time I remove my shirt feels even worse. No longer fueled by anger, it feels like I'm ripping off the first layer of my own skin. I don't have the strength to simply stand at attention, so I allow my neck to bow. My eyes focus on the gray cement floor, and I hug my arms around my stomach to shield it from view.

"Why did you choose this?" Merchant asks, holding up my shirt.

"It covers the most."

"Still…you understand most men would have covered the bottom half first."

"I have less of a problem with that part," I admit.

"Why?"

"Because I don't have a lot of control with what I've been given, and I've never received any complaints," I say, letting out a short static bark of a laugh as I recall the goofy faces my lovers have made during sex. For a moment I almost forget that I am being tortured.

"Good! Laugh! It's okay."

"No, it's not. This isn't funny."

"No, it's not. But I wonder why you think you're a disappointment."

"Because I know you didn't want an actor who looked like this."

"And what is so wrong with this?" he asks, seizing a handful of flesh from around my stomach in one quick movement. I gasp for air, shocked at the force of his grip. Barely able to breathe, I am unable to cry out as his fingers dig beyond the soft tissue and bury themselves deep into my abdominal muscles.

"Because I'm fat, okay? I know I'm fat."

"Fat? Mason, this is fat," he says, finally letting go of my stomach, so he can lift up his own shirt and smack his swollen belly. "You're not fat, you're weak."

"I'm not weak."

"Not as weak as I thought."

"Is that what the point of all this is?"

"I needed to know exactly what I'm dealing with," he says, returning to his seat at the table. "Like most people, you see the worst version of yourself. You must learn to see yourself as others do, and not just in terms of your body but every aspect of yourself. You must know what you are showing the audience."

"And you think this is how to teach me?"

"I do, and believe me, none of these sessions will be any easier. However, I can assure you that they will make you stronger, and, by opening night, no one will see you as anything less than perfect. Now get dressed, the read-through will begin shortly."

Not having to be told twice, I quickly grab my clothes and hear Merchant begin to shuffle through his paperwork. Despite the fact I'm in a hurry, it takes me a while to get re-dressed. My thoughts are focused more on reviewing the moments that have just passed. Knowing why he did it makes it seem less awful in retrospect, and I'm shocked that I no longer feel embarrassed. Rather, I feel a sense of accomplishment. Merchant has seen the worst, and yet he said I would be there on opening night. I will prove him right. I won't be weak forever.

"One more moment of your time Mr. Burroughs," Merchant says, just before I open the door.

"Yes?"

"It has come to my attention that Mr. Caldwell paid you a visit over the weekend."

"Yes. He...stopped by while we were having a party," I confirm, unsure how much Merchant knows, or why this is even being discussed.

"I know what happened, but I would like to ask that you blame me instead of him."

"You?"

"Yes. You see, Kevin was sent there by me, but he took some liberties with the direction I gave him. I apologize for that, and please know I have told him to keep your relationship strictly professional." I'm unsure what to even make of that. Does this mean Merchant is also working with Kevin, and if so, what instruction had he given him?

"Sure, but...what did you tell him to do?" I ask, hoping Merchant has some answer which will help me make sense of Kevin's behavior.

"I'm afraid that telling you would hinder the work we need to do. Just try to forget it ever happened. You'll learn the truth eventually," Merchant says, once again tapping his index finger on his temple.

WHEN I RETURN FROM SIGNING in, I'm amazed how quickly Jenna has managed to transform the room. Long rectangular tables have been arranged in a square, and a script binder bearing each actor's real name, as well as his or her character's name, has been placed in front of each seat. After I find mine, fatigue from my morning session with Merchant begins to set in. It isn't until someone waves their hand in my face that I realize I've spent the past five minutes staring off into space.

"Hello? Are you there?" a woman asks.

"Oh, I'm sorry. I guess I zoned out."

"Happens to me all the time. I'm Julia," she says, simultaneously offering me her hand and dropping her Prada purse in the seat next to mine.

"I'm Mason."

"Oh, so you're Mason." she says, removing her coat. From her angular face I had assumed she was a rather petite girl, but her draped blouse and skintight jeans reveal that she has the hourglass figure of a 1950's starlet. It then dawns on me who I'm talking to.

"Julia Pierce? Wait…are you…her?"

"Guilty as charged."

Julia was nominated for a Tony Award for playing the Marquise de Merteuil in Merchant's sexually scandalous production of Les Liaisons Dangereuses. Consequently, she was in all of his productions, until just a few years ago. I remember fantasizing about how she must have been his muse, and seeing her now, I can see I was probably right. She projects a divine combination of grace and power.

"I can't believe it! I'm such a fan of yours."

"And I'm quickly becoming a fan of you! Tell me, have you worked with James before?"

"Oh…no. Any advice for a newbie?"

"My usual advice for ingénues is don't sleep with him," she says, with a wry smile.

"Heh, I don't think I'll have that problem."

"Not unless his taste has drastically changed." She winks. "Anyway, I wouldn't worry too much. James was always rather gentle with the men."

"I'll try not to," I say, finding that comment hard to believe after my morning session.

"The maestro enters," she whispers. As Merchant walks in, the room falls silent.

"Good morning, cast. I hope you had a pleasant weekend, because, after this morning, we will be working through this script as fast as possible. But before we dive into the text, I'd like to hear a bit from our playwright. Colin, why don't you tell the cast what it is that has brought you out of retirement?"

"Well, I've been working on this for years, but I'll spare you the boring details. Let's just say that when you get to be my age, you think back on the moments of your life, and spend countless hours doing nothing but mulling over questions that haunt you. For me, one in particular." Colin's voice is warm yet fragile.

"And what question is that?" Merchant asks.

"Were the shortcuts I took in life, worth it?"

"What do you mean by shortcuts?" Merchant prompts, though I suspect he's already very aware.

"I mean the moments where we make a bargain to get ahead. When I was working on *Twisted in the Night* I bought Ritalin off of some kids, so I could focus and write. The pills certainly helped me, but I was irresponsible with them. Taking them to stay awake for days, I was consumed by the project. When my lover tried to take them away, I lunged at him, and we had a huge fight, which ended with my kicking him out into the street. It wasn't until days later, after I finished the play, that I learned he had been killed. Those pills were a shortcut to finishing on time, but...at what cost?"

"Is that why you retired?" asks a man with strikingly pale skin and snow-white hair.

"The short answer is yes. That play made my career, but to this day, I cannot sit and watch a performance of it without being distracted by the memories of the fight we had that night. The last words I ever said to him were the worst sentences I've ever constructed."

"Thank you, Colin, for sharing that with us," Merchant says, before turning his attention to the pale man who spoke up a moment earlier. "Marshall, since you spoke first, perhaps you could introduce yourself?

Tell us your name, your character, and what shortcuts in life you have taken."

"Oh...er...well..." he sputters.

"Name?"

"Right, sorry, my name. I'm Marshall Kiff, I play Dyne, and....well...I guess the time I bought a term paper?"

"So...your degree is a lie? I'm shocked! Clearly you shouldn't be playing the advisor!" Merchant says with overdramatic indignation, causing everyone, even Marshall, to laugh.

"It's true! I'm such a fraud! Though, in my defense, the paper I bought was on quarks, which I don't think have anything to do with theatre."

"What's a quark?" Julia asks.

"I've no idea; I never even read the paper."

"Did you at least get a good grade?"

"The paper landed me a B, allowing me to pass the class with a respectable D+."

"High honors indeed! Now, let's see, Julia, why don't you go next?" asks Merchant.

"If that's what you want, certainly. I'm Julia Pierce, I play Mina, and well...I'd say these babies have helped me out of plenty of situations," she says, cupping her rather full breasts and pushing them together to maximize her cleavage.

"I'd wager they have also managed to put you in a few bad ones, too," Merchant jokes, making me wonder if he's referring to their intimate past.

"True, but for the most part, showing off my set has opened a lot of doors. It's like shortcut city!" Julia shimmies and we all applaud.

"All right, all right, we get it. However, you bring us to a classic idea found throughout many stories. The use of beauty, of sex, to get ahead is perhaps the most common, I'm certain it's something Kevin could tell us about?" Merchants points to Kevin who's pretending to manicure his nails to demonstrate his vanity.

"Oh sure...pick on the pretty boy! I'd say Julia's gotten a better deal than I ever have. I've never gotten anything based on looks alone. Everyone who's opened a door for me has insisted on full contact," Kevin says, trailing his fingers down to his crotch and then grabbing himself like he did the other night.

"Don't think I haven't let a guy get healthy handful!" Julia grabs Marshall's hands and tries to get him to squeeze her breasts despite his shrill screams of protest.

"Yeah, I guess it matters how big the favor is. I mean, I avoided being charged with breaking and entering by blowing a security guard once," Kevin says with a shrug, as if it is hardly worth mentioning.

"Doesn't that only happen in porn?" I ask, trying hard not to let my imagination run away with itself.

"Well…actually it does sound like it, but then the guard would have been hot. Not this one. You see, me and this other guy—"

"Other guy!" I break in, and most of the room starts to hoot and holler.

"Settle down everyone. Mr. Caldwell please continue," Merchant says, and I note the eyes of a handful of pretty ensemble members are focused very intently on Kevin.

"Yeah, you see, we had snuck into this fancy gym in the Flatiron Building because the guy was into pool sex. We got caught, and instead of calling the cops, the guard said he'd let us go if we let him watch and finished him off."

"I'd hate to see what happens when you order a pizza," Julia says, causing the room to titter with laughter.

"I'll tell you about that sometime, but if anyone needs some after-hours time at the gym, I've got a lifelong pass. It's a great place to get steam, or blow some off." Kevin winks, causing me to look away and blush.

The very thought of Kevin flirting with me sends my mind back to the total mouth invasion at the party, and I try even harder to make sense of it. Merchant's cryptic excuse makes me even more curious to know what Kevin was trying to accomplish. It isn't until I hear my name that I notice I've gone off into my own little world, and I ask Merchant to repeat his question.

"Care to introduce yourself?" asks Merchant, clearly not for the first time.

"Oh, yes, of course, sorry. I'm Mason Burroughs, I play Caleb, and I guess the biggest shortcut I ever took was cashing in the inheritance I got from my grandparents."

"What did you get in return?"

"Two years in the city, and the benefit of never having to speak to my parents again."

"Would you say it was worth it?" Colin asks, intrigued.

"It led me here, which is a dream come true." As if on cue, the doors to the studio fling open, and in walks someone I'd definitely never dreamt of seeing again.

"Ah, Alex," Merchant says, bolting up and leading my doppelganger to an empty seat next to me. "I'm glad you got my call."

"So am I." He smirks.

"Cast, this is Alex Twyford, the final member of our cast. Alex will be understudying for both Mason and Kevin."

"Sorry for barging in, I just didn't want to miss anything. Have we begun the read-through?"

"Not yet, we were just about to. If everyone wouldn't mind turning to the first page? Mason, you've the heavy burden of the first line," Merchant says, adding yet another pile of pressure onto me.

"Stop!" Jenna calls. "We need to take a break. It is 10:00 a.m. now. Actors, return at 10:20 for the beginning of the read-through. Water is on the table outside. Restrooms are down the hall on the left."

As the other actors disperse I stand up to stretch. Turning my head from side to side, I try my best to stop staring at Merchant and Alex, who are having a rather intense looking chat in the corner of the room.

"Hey," I hear Kevin say from behind me.

"Oh…hello." I turn to face him, surprised that when we make eye contact he immediately shifts his focus to the floor. Seeing him drained of his usual confidence is so jarring that I don't know what to say, and so we stand in an awkward silence.

"About the party…," Kevin begins.

"Don't worry about it."

"I hope I didn't ruin the night."

"No, not really," I lie, remembering I told Merchant I wouldn't hold Kevin's behavior against him.

"Oh…good."

"So, that Alex guy?" I ask, annoyed that I can't seem to stop fixating on him.

"Yeah?"

"Do you know him?"

"Well…."

"Bitch! Yes, you know me!" Alex interrupts, in an affected voice similar to Jerry's drag queen persona. "Now get your skinny ass over here."

"Hey Alex," Kevin says, giving him a stilted hug.

"Nice to officially meet you, I'm Mason," I say, extending my hand.

"Have we met before?"

"I was at the audition."

"Oh right, sorry, I forgot. It's been such an intense morning. I mean, I crawl out of some guy's bed and am about to do my walk of shame when – bam! – my phone rings, and Merchant and my agent are telling me how they need me to come to rehearsal. I was pretty sure I was dreaming, but here I am! I mean I've haven't even had a chance to change!" I wonder when Merchant made this call. Was it after our session? Does he really think this guy is better than me?

"Yeah, I was saying something similar right before you arrived."

"Oh, did I interrupt? Sorry, to steal your spotlight," Alex smiles, making me completely sure he isn't sorry at all.

"Mason will have plenty of time in the light." Merchant says, joining the conversation.

"I know!" Kevin smiles and throws his arm around me again. "Was I right or what? He's perfect!"

"He could be. We'll just have to see," Merchant replies, quickly patting his own belly and shooting me a glance.

"I'm looking forward to getting to read the entire play. I don't even know what happens in the end," I say.

"None of us do," Merchant says.

"What?" I panic at the concept.

"Colin has two endings. I convinced him to watch some of the work we do before we settle on which one to use."

"But without an ending…I mean…is that normal?" I ask, unsure of how I will be able to develop a character without knowing how the ending works out.

"Normal? Oh, sweetie, is this your first Broadway show?" Alex asks, a wicked grin spreading across his face.

"Yes."

"I guess I'll learn your lines first then." The confidence in his nasal voice sets my teeth on edge. I try to think of a good comeback, but the moment passes. Fortunately Merchant comes to my rescue.

"Mason, it's not uncommon with new works. We'll let you know when the script is finalized," he says.

"So we don't need to worry about memorization then," Kevin says with a big smile.

"Don't memorize if you can't adapt, but I would like scripts out of hands as soon as possible," Merchant says sternly, causing Kevin to drop his smile as fast as it appeared. "After all, I suspect your hands will be busy."

"I like the sound of that!" Kevin says, dropping his hand to pat my ass.

"Ah!"

"Mr. Caldwell, I told you…"

"Sorry, sorry. Professional. Got it," Kevin affirms half-heartedly.

"I think we need to get back to the table," I say, wanting desperately to get away.

"Yes, I'm so interested to hear you read," says Alex, as I walk back to my seat.

Once everyone has returned, I say the first line, and the read-through begins. The first few scenes aren't bad, but it doesn't take long to get overwhelmed. Being a lead, I no longer have the downtime between scenes I'm used to, and, as I sip from my water bottle during my brief pauses, I notice my voice is getting exhausted faster than ever before. Still, I'm relieved by how smart and complex the script is, although I barely have time to appreciate it.

The themes of the show are simple to understand: love, betrayal, passion, and revenge. However, the plot itself is a complex web of secrets and scandal. Kevin's character, Ezio, starts off as a reviled count, who becomes infatuated with my character, Caleb, a solider wounded in battle.

Hoping to charm and ultimately seduce Caleb, Ezio uses his wealth to build schools and libraries, and in the process learns to see the value in the common man. While Ezio's early attempts to get Caleb into bed have been unsuccessful, after Ezio's change of heart, he begins to woo Caleb with love instead of lust, which ultimately results in Caleb returning his affection.

The nobles of the court despise Caleb and fear the lower classes will be influenced to rise up. They enlist Mina, a lady of the court, to seduce and lure him away from Ezio, but her attempts to use sex and bribes on Caleb fail as miserably as Ezio's. Caleb is only drawn to those who love him with a pure heart. It isn't until Mina loses herself in the game of seduction and begins to actually fall for Caleb that she captures his attention. While she is keeping him distracted, the nobles manage to bribe the guards to refuse Caleb re-entry to the castle. When he finds his way blocked, Caleb threatens Ezio's wrath, but, as a commoner, he is powerless without the count by his side. Caleb writes Ezio a letter explaining he has been barred from the palace, and begs Mina to deliver it to him. Mina takes the letter, but upon reading Caleb's sweet and loving words, she is filled with jealousy and gives it over to the conspirators. Seizing on a new plan to depose Ezio and banish him and Caleb forever, the nobles lift Caleb's ban. Ezio is so overjoyed to have Caleb back at his side that he throws a lavish masked ball in celebration. Mina decides not to attend, planning to mend her broken heart by traveling abroad, instead. But while waiting to board her ship, she overhears the conspirators' true plan: they don't mean to simply depose Ezio at the ball, they plan to kill him, and Caleb, too. Mina rushes back to the castle to warn Caleb, but her efforts are complicated by Ezio's last-minute decision to switch costumes with Caleb, in order to spend an evening as a commoner.

"But Ezio, I cannot pretend to be the count!" I say, turning the page to find the next line, only to find myself staring at a blank page.

"To be continued," Merchant says, smiling as the entire cast groans. "All will be revealed in due time. I know it is frustrating, but Colin and I have a difference of opinion about who the audience will be rooting for."

"What did you have happen originally?"

"Don't answer that," Merchant snaps before Colin can even begin.

"I'm afraid I'm sworn to secrecy."

"Don't focus on the ending. There is plenty of work to be done. Now, if there are no other questions, I'd like to thank you all for your time. Jenna has some announcements to share before you leave."

When I am handed my rehearsal schedule, I am concerned how little rehearsal time is on it. From morning to night I am scheduled to do a variety of things, but while most people seem to be rehearsing, my schedule is labeled with something called "Lycan." I have no idea what that means, but I notice Kevin is scheduled to be rehearsing with Alex while I'm doing it, which makes me question, who is the real understudy?

SEVEN

As I walk home, I consider what I'm going to say when I walk through the front door. I know I promised Merchant our sessions would remain a secret, but what happened this morning feels too big to keep from Eric. Ever since Merchant grabbed me I feel like my body is different, as if it has changed in some way. I know Eric will go ballistic if I tell him, but I also know he'd never hide something like this from me. What does it mean that I am actually considering not telling him?

I wonder if Merchant would even know whether I spoke to Eric. After all, he's not going to go blabbing about it. But I worry that keeping it secret has some point; Merchant said everything he asked me to do has a purpose, so if I tell anyone, it might change how I think about it. Still, whenever I have done shows, I've always needed time to decompress. Talking about rehearsal is what helps me return to the real world. Instead, Merchant is asking me to turn life into another stage, and I am not sure I'm that good an actor. I have to tell him.

As soon as I've reached this decision, a feeling of relief comes over me, Then my phone rings.

"Hello?" I ask.

"Mr. Burroughs, this is Jenna. Mr. Merchant has requested you meet him at the space at 8:00 a.m. tomorrow to continue your work," she says, once again using a rather curt tone.

"All right."

"Good. Oh…and he asked you to wear something fitted," she adds before hanging up.

Merchant will know if I tell anyone, even Eric.

I spend the remainder of my walk figuring out what I will say. Recalling what I've been like with Eric after other first rehearsals, I hope I can get away with passing off recycled memories from my past as the present. Wanting to avoid too many questions, I allow myself to look as exhausted as I actually am before trudging through our door.

"Hello?" I call into the apartment, mentally blocking myself from thinking about my earlier strip tease as I shed my winter layers.

"In here."

"Your star has arrived." I collapse onto the sofa where Eric is furiously pressing buttons on the PlayStation controller.

"Hold on, let me save. I just slayed a power demon."

"My little hero," I say, imagining Eric would look pretty hot wielding a sword in some tight armor.

"Right, but enough about my quest. I want to hear everything!"

"No rush."

"You look like you've got a lot to talk about," Eric says, making me wish he'd just keep playing his game.

"I'm not sure I even have the strength to go into it."

"Maybe this will give you some," he says, giving me a quick kiss as he lays the controller down on the coffee table.

"Okay…well…for starters the guy who looks like me is in the show. He's my understudy, and he's a mess."

"How so?"

"He's loud, conceited, demanding, prone to calling people 'bitch' as a term of endearment."

"So he's an actor," Eric jokes, as he usually finds other actors annoying. I'm not sure why I'm the exception to that rule.

"It's not just that. He is so condescending."

"Again, you're just describing an actor."

"Forget it." I retreat to the kitchen and begin assembling dinner, relieved that I can pretend to be annoyed and avoid discussing the show further.

"No, no, I'm sorry. I'm actually interested in hearing about the show.

What's the director like?"

"Oh, him. He's a real pro. We didn't really get to do much beforehand, but he was amazing in rehearsal. I think I'll really like working with him," I say, looking Eric in the eye, hoping it will lend some authority to my blatant lie.

"Really? That's unusual."

"What?" I panic, opening the fridge to block Eric's view of my face.

"It's just that you normally complain about your directors. What kinds of stuff did he have you do?"

I feel the heat flush to my face and attempt to counter it by sticking my whole head inside the whirring refrigerator. I take a deep breath and deliver the lie I came up with on my way home.

"Nothing really. Just a bit of movement, breathing exercises. Honestly, I think he just gets off on making me come to rehearsal early. Hey, did you get the salmon I asked for?" I say, even though I can clearly see it on the shelf in front of me.

"It's right in front of you. Maybe you should sit down."

"I'm fine. Besides, it'll take you an hour to do what I can do in twenty minutes," I say, knowing Eric's never been a great understudy for my long standing role as family chef.

"Okay, but don't complain about the way it's cut up. Chelsea Market was completely mobbed after work."

"Oh…right. I guess I never went during the rush." It's clear Eric and I really need to sit down and revise our old routines for stuff like this.

"How was working with Ella Fitzgerald?"

"Who?" I ask, confused by who he could even possibly be referring to.

"The crazy drunk blonde?"

"Oh…I think you mean Zelda Fitzgerald. Ella's the jazz singer."

"Whatever. How is he?"

"He's fine. He told some crazy story today about getting caught having sex in a gym."

"Charming," Eric says, his tone dripping with sarcasm.

"Give him a chance. He did apologize about crashing the party. He seemed genuinely embarrassed about it."

"He's an actor. Of course he did," Eric is quick to say, making me feel even worse that he doesn't see the actor I am, doesn't know I'm lying to his face.

"Is that what you think whenever I apologize?"

"You're different," he says, unintentionally twisting the knife in my heart.

"I think he was sincere, and I'm good at spotting a fake." I take his hand to really sell it, and feel a tiny twinge of guilt that I'm using my actor skills on him.

"Fine, fine. Tell me about your part. Is it really big?"

"It's definitely called a lead role for a reason. I'm barely ever off stage," I say, feeling exhausted just talking about it.

"Lots to memorize?"

"Well...yes. But there's more to it than that. This isn't going to be like the other shows I've done. There's so much to do."

"I know that. But that's a good thing right? This is what we've been waiting for. You, making it as a working actor."

"You're right, it's just that...well...it's a lot more intense than I imagined. It's only day one, and I feel like I'm already behind," I say, still processing the lack of the ending, Alex's bitchy remarks, and being stripped naked within the first hour of rehearsal.

"You can do it, though. Remember, they chose you for a reason." Eric slides his arms around me and kisses the back of my neck.

"Why don't you set the table for dinner? It'll be ready soon," I say, afraid that if he is any nicer I won't be able to stop myself from confessing.

"In a minute," he whispers, slowly walking his fingers up my abdomen.

He touches the spot where Merchant grabbed me. "Ah," I gasp, wincing in pain.

"What's wrong?"

"Nothing. I just hurt myself when I was doing some stretches this morning."

Eric squints. "But I thought you said it was easy."

"It was. I just overextended. I'll be fine by tomorrow."

"You need to be careful. I know you want to do a good job, but you've got to recognize your limitations. You can't just start running a marathon if you don't work up to it." Eric ran cross country in high school, so he's overly fond of using running metaphors to make a point.

"I know."

"I know you do, but I need to say it anyway."

"Why?"

"Because we both know what you're like when you get cast in a show. Even when you have small parts, you let it consume you, you get obsessed."

"And I suppose you never do that? How many times have I had to pry a Red Bull out of your hand? How many nights have I found you passed out at the keyboard?" I reply, projecting my voice louder. I usually don't use my theatre training whenever Eric and I have an argument, because it freaks him out, but I'm tired and this kind of thing really irks me. Eric likes to pretend that I'm the only one who ever has issues like this.

"That's just it, we depend on each other, but this time, we're both going to be so busy. I'm trying to be there for you."

"And I appreciate it, but you're overreacting."

"I'm just trying to stop something small from being a bigger problem down the road," he says, his voice trembling. "I know you hate it when I talk about this stuff, but I'm worried you'll try to do something drastic again."

Early on in our relationship, I was playing a junkie in some show that was a sad knock-off of *RENT*. I was concerned that all the other guys were much skinner than I was, and so one night I tried to lose weight by taking a bunch of laxatives. Eric found me around two o'clock the next morning, curled up against the toilet screaming in agony from stomach cramps. It took hours for it to work its way through my system, but he sat outside the bathroom door most of night and talked me through it. After that I worked with a therapist a bit, but Eric and I have never really talked about it.

"It's so unfair for you to bring that up now," I say, wishing I could tell him the truth, just so we could leave that memory where it was.

"I know, I'm sorry, but…I don't want to miss seeing the signs again. I should have noticed something was wrong, but I missed it," Eric says, his whole body shaking.

"Eric, come here," I say, hugging him as tight as I can. "You didn't miss anything, I just did something stupid. But I'm going to be pushed harder than ever before, and what I need when I come home is someone who is going to support me. Not suspect me."

"I'll try." His amber eyes are glassy, and I know he's trying so hard to be strong right now.

"That's all I ask. Now, go set the table, so I can get dinner done."

"I love you," he replies, giving me a quick kiss.

"I love you, too."

I TRY TO SLEEP, BUT I can't seem to stop thinking. My thoughts ricochet, from my session with Merchant, to my fight with Eric, or my rehearsal schedule which doesn't seem to involve very much rehearsal. I toss and turn so much that eventually Eric flicks on the light.

"Mason, I can't sleep with you flopping around like that."

"I know. I'm sorry." I grab my pillow and head for the couch, hoping that if I manage to watch a little television my brain will stop. I find a *Law and Order SVU* marathon, and just as I'm about to fall asleep Kevin walks on screen. It's strange to be able to look at him without him being aware of me. I fall asleep sometime after his second episode, but it doesn't last long. A full hour before my already early alarm, I turn onto my stomach and am up like a shot, after the spot on my abdomen grazes one of the couch springs. The spot is barely covered by the upholstery, thanks to Eric's ass making a deep groove there from hours of gaming. It takes every ounce of restraint I have not to wake him by yelling out in pain.

Certain I won't be able to get back to sleep, I get dressed, grab my pack, and make my way to the rehearsal studio. With so much time to spare, I figure I can consume and burn a few extra calories. I grab a bagel from the place on the corner, still hot and smelling of yeast, and begin my fifty-block walk to the studio. The city feels sleepy, though of course never asleep, and when I reach Times Square, I can't believe how deserted it is.

I take a seat on the ruby red TKTS stairs. I've never seen them so vacant. I moved here shortly before they were constructed, and yet, they've become a piece of the city far faster than I have. Even after five years in this city, I'm still an outsider. I continue to dodge people as I walk through crowds, get lost in the areas of the Village where there are no numbers, and at least apologize to the homeless when they ask for a handout. I guess the staircase was born here, and that seems to make things easier. I'd always thought I was a displaced New Yorker, especially since I never fit in back home. In Texas I stuck out, like a puzzle piece that had been put into the wrong box. I figured once I came here I'd snap right into place, but it's hard to find your place in this city. However, with this role, I'm beginning to feel like I finally belong.

I arrive at the rehearsal space early, but it takes me a lot longer to get into my fitted clothes than I anticipate. Any movement that stretches my core abdominal muscles pains me, thanks to Merchant's prodding. The spot bothers me beyond just the pain though; every time it hurts it reminds me that I'm keeping a secret. One that is even harder now that the spot has turned into a black and blue bruise about the size of a door knob. My lie about overextending won't work if I'm not careful about hiding it from Eric. Until yesterday I never realized how often I'm naked in front of him. Between showering, sleeping, and sex, assuring he doesn't see my bruise won't be easy.

The guilt of keeping things from Eric weighs on me like a phantom chain which seems to get heavier the more I think about it. After being buzzed in, I look at the door to the rehearsal space, and take a deep breath. Based on Merchant's own words, it's likely that whatever awaits me behind that door will be even worse than what happened yesterday, and so I try to prepare myself for that as best I can. Usually, in moments like this, I would think of Eric to give me strength, but, thanks to Merchant, thoughts of him are more draining than invigorating. Recognizing this saddens me, but I know that, to survive, I have to try something else, and so I focus on the fact that while Merchant's forced me to wear a mask at home, inside the studio I can still be myself. This realization gives me strength, but as I open the door I question if it will be enough.

Merchant, seated just as before, motions for me to come forward, but I barely notice him at all, as Kevin is standing next to him. Shirtless. Out of pure instinct, the nice way of describing lust, I stare at his lithe torso and sculpted abs. Lit by the stage lights high above, he looks like an angel, and I feel a sudden spark of excitement jolt through me. I start to feel bad about it, but remind myself that guilt and Eric are out of my mind for today, and so I permit myself to enjoy this new found energy.

"You're early," Merchant says, his voice knocking me out of my head and into the room.

"I had a rough night."

"Is that right? I will keep that in mind then. Today is going to be physical, so if it gets to be too much—"

"I'll be fine," I interrupt, unable to bear another lecture about my health.

"Just let me know," Merchant finishes, dropping his smile and donning a scowl.

"Yes. I will. Sorry. I just…I'm anxious to begin."

"That's good to hear, but your health is important. If you get hurt, I'll be forced to use Alex."

"Then let's be careful," Kevin says, eyeing me up and down in a way that makes me wish Merchant hadn't insisted I wear such tight fitting clothes.

"That's up to both of you. Now Kevin, I would like you to stand here," Merchant says, positioning him just a few inches in front of me.

"Anytime," he says, taking an exaggerated breath so his bare chest brushes against the tight t-shirt I'm wearing.

"Mr. Burroughs, please look at Kevin instead of the floor."

"Yes sir," I obey, trying to keep myself from drooling as I stare into his eyes.

"I have called you both here today, because I want you to develop a personal warm-up together. You will do this every day. It needs to remind you both that while your characters are strangers, you should almost be able to read each other's minds. I am aware the two of you have a history, which should help, but throughout this process you will undoubtedly become even closer."

"Sounds good to me," Kevin says, with a wink.

"This isn't a joke, Mr. Caldwell. It's essential. There should be some awkwardness during these sessions. The exercise I have crafted is an adaptation of the Meisner approach to acting. His sentiment, 'The foundation of acting is the reality of doing' is the primary focus, and you should keep it at the front of your mind throughout the rest of these sessions. Do what comes naturally, act and react. Leave Kevin and Mason at the door, and when I officially begin this exercise, I expect you two to be in character. Is that understood?"

"Sure," Kevin says, stretching and yawning as if he couldn't be more bored.

"Yes," I respond, wishing both of us were taking this seriously.

"Very good. Now, how do Ezio and Caleb meet?"

"I…er…Caleb comes to provide a status report on the war and explain why he has been sent home," I say, shocked to hear me refer to myself as Caleb so fast.

"Correct. Keeping this in mind, I would like both of you to leave this room and re-enter as your characters. Take a few moments to experiment before returning to the room. When you come back, I would like you to walk toward one another, and with each step, really explore how these two men see one another for the first time. Try to mirror one another's pace as best you can, and explore how you can communicate a change in speed or direction without speaking. Eventually, end up standing exactly where you are now. Once you've done that, stop, and I'll give you further instructions. Any questions?"

"Which door do I exit from?" Kevin asks, his former lackadaisical demeanor vanishing in an instant.

"I would prefer you enter from the side. Mason, you should use the front."

Even though I know which door he means, I turn my head to look at it anyway, and when I turn back, Kevin is already gone.

"Did you have a question?"

"Well…not about the exercise," I say, trying to think of something to ask, to explain why I'm still in the room.

"Something else then?"

"Why is he shirtless?" I blurt out, amazed at how stupid the question is.

"Then your question is about the exercise. I told you everything in these sessions has a purpose."

"But what is it?"

"Don't think about it now, but be sure to remember it. I need you to focus on the task ahead. Please do not enter until you are ready to introduce me to Caleb," Merchant says, confusing me even more.

Outside I recall the most basic building blocks of creating a character. Posture. Movement. Voice. Remembering Caleb was a soldier, I draw myself up to perfect posture, lock my legs, and turn my head sharply from side to side. The rigidity and precision of this type of movement is fun, but when I decide to try pivoting my torso, I barely turn a few degrees before I feel my injury flare up. Just like Caleb, I too am injured.

Realizing this similarity, I continue to play with Caleb's posture and movement. At first, it seems there is no way to move without engaging my abdomen, but I keep experimenting to try and find some way around the limitation. Eventually I find that, by pushing my chest forward and walking with wider stance, I am able to reduce the amount of strain, but walking that way is nearly impossible. My first few steps are more like a mummy, but as I fine tune it, I notice I am propelling myself forward by rocking my hips back and forth. It takes some getting used to, but eventually I'm gliding up and down the hallway with ease.

All that is left is the voice, but I worry I've spent too much time outside the door. When I said my lines in the audition, I'd used my lower register, so I decide to repeat that. I know Merchant told me to wait until I was ready, but I don't know if that will ever be true. It's time to fall or fly.

I might have opened the door, but it is Caleb who walks through. Through his eyes the bare studio is a medieval throne room. I hear the flicker of candles in the chandelier above. I smell the cold stone, dusty tapestries, and the faint hint of cinnamon that permeates the air. My heartbeat accelerates upon seeing Ezio for the first time. As Caleb, I let myself drink in Ezio's image. Only a god would know how to construct a face so perfectly, for even if I were allowed to choose every aspect of my own visage, I would never have come close to this. If I could wear a mask, it would have his features. Full red lips, long dark eyelashes, but it is really his eyes that make everything work, two apatite gems sparkling behind the most flawless of faces.

As we move closer together I can feel him watching me with the same intensity. Our steps grow bolder, wider, faster, and then we both slow down again. Turning directions, we circle the room. With a smile, I can see his excitement, telling me to move faster. We bound about the room, perfectly mirroring one another, but each time we close the distance between us our pace drops as we get lost looking at one another again and again. We feed off one another's cues, until finally we meet at the center, breathless and eager to see what Merchant has planned for us to do next.

"Very nice. Now, I would like us to move on to the second part of this exercise. Caleb, close your eyes. Ezio, I want you to walk around the room, as quietly as possible, and stop when you hear this sound." He strikes the floor with something metal.

The sound draws my full attention. It is cold and frightening, almost like a gunshot, and I get goosebumps. The darkness I'm plunged into by closing my eyes feels unbearable, having just spent so much time basking in the radiant glow of Ezio. Not wanting to be without it, I try summoning it from memory. In my mind, I retrace the lines where I once beheld him only moments before, and for a brief second it almost works. But then I notice that the room has gone completely silent. Fearing I've gone deaf, I listen hard and am relieved when I briefly make out the sounds of my own breath, as well as the faint hum of the air conditioner high above me. I listen for any sound of movement, but nothing comes, until Merchant strikes the floor again. I am practically deafened by the abrupt blast of sound.

"Where is Ezio?" Merchant asks, his voice coming from behind me at a distance.

"I'm not sure."

"Then guess."

"To my left?" It seems as good a guess as any.

"Wrong. Try again," Merchant says, and strikes the floor again.

I will my ears to ignore the echoes of sound Merchant has created, and try to find any sound of movement. I slowly turn in a circle, hoping it will help, but no matter what I do, I can't seem to pick anything up until Merchant strikes the floor again.

"Where is Ezio?" he repeats from the same location.

"To my left," I guess again.

"Wrong. Last chance."

Unsure of what to do, I try putting my ear to the floor, but all this accomplishes is practically deafening me when Merchant strikes the floor again.

"Where is Ezio?"

"Left?"

"Open your eyes," Merchant says letting out a huge sigh.

The second I do, I want to die of embarrassment, as he is standing one foot in front of me. I cannot tell if he has even moved at all.

"Ezio, it's your turn."

The pain of having not been able to find him, even though he was so close, burns within me, and I quickly dart away when Merchant strikes the floor. With my eyes open, I finally see he is holding some sort of metallic staff. Yhe top of it is curved like an ornate shepherd's staff, but the hook closes, so I've no idea what it would be used for. When I see that he is about to strike the floor, I hold my hand for him to stop. I then creep to about eight feet behind Kevin, who has decided to lay down on his back, with his hands crossed over him like a vampire. He is so still he looks like he's asleep, he doesn't react at all when Merchant finally strikes the floor.

"Where is Caleb?"

"There," Kevin responds, cool and confident as ever, as he points above his head directly at me.

"Correct. Try again."

Merchant strikes the floor again, and I redouble my efforts to be absolutely silent. It must have been luck, or maybe my footsteps weren't as soft as I thought, but this time I was sure he would fail just as I had. To throw him off I make my way across the floor behind Merchant, hoping that by putting him between us, it will confuse Kevin.

"Where is Caleb?"

"There," Kevin repeats, pointing toward Merchant and myself.

"Excellent. Try once more."

This time I don't move. I stand exactly where I did before. Whatever Kevin is doing to find me, he won't be able to do it if I stay still. As the moments tick by, I watch him, trying to figure out his system, but his face is perfectly placid.

"Where is Caleb?"

"There."

"Perfect. Open your eyes. The exercise is over."

"What do I win?" Kevin asks, smiling as he leaps to his feet in one fluid motion.

"I'll think of something. Now, Mason, you are going to spend the rest of the day with Mr. Lycan. Jenna will give you directions, he expects you within the hour. Kevin, you will be working with Alex today. Oh, and you might want to put this back on," Merchant says. He tosses Kevin's balled up shirt directly at my head, which Kevin catches just a few inches from my face.

"Thanks," I say, feeling like a saved princess in a castle.

"No problem." The fabric cascades down his frame like a curtain, telling me the performance is over. It makes me blush to realize that with Eric banished from my mind, Caleb wasn't the only one who enjoyed the show.

EIGHT

"Who is Mr. Lycan?" I ask Jenna, as I officially sign in for the day. The name is the only thing on my rehearsal schedule for the entire day.

"I honestly have no idea. I know he lives at this address, and he was hired by Merchant. He's apparently very expensive, so I'd be on your way. He had a messenger deliver this a few minutes ago," she says, handing me a thick envelope which has been addressed to me by hand.

Inside are instructions on heavy parchment, but the lettering is so ornate that I can't make it out.

"Hey, Julia," I call, seeing her pass by.

"Mason!" she sings, air kissing my cheeks.

"I got this package. Can you read what this says?"

"Oh my, this is beautiful!"

"And illegible."

"Don't be silly. It's plain as day. It says to walk from here to 74 Commerce Street, located next to the Cherry Lane Theatre, and…um… once there, call three times with the mouth of the lion."

"What does that mean?" I asked, finding the instructions as puzzling as the handwriting.

"I don't know, but knowing Merchant, I'm sure it will make sense once you get there. It says you should leave the moment you receive this."

"Okay, thanks for your help."

"Anytime. Let's talk later!" She says, dashing off with more grace than I would have imagined her heels would allow.

After my second fifty block walk of the day, I arrive at a beautifully preserved brownstone nestled on a quiet street in the West Village. The street is a true rarity because it bends in the middle, in a city that was built on a grid. Lycan's apartment is situated in the corner. As I approach the front door, Julia's words prove true, when I find a silver door knocker shaped like a lion. Heeding the last of the directions, I knock three times, but nothing happens. So I sit down on the steps and wait.

As time slowly passes, I think about my morning session with Kevin, fixated on the memory of his perfect body. For years I'd always wanted to stare at him like that, but had never allowed myself to. Whenever he stripped down in dressing rooms, or out at a club, I always averted my eyes after a few seconds. I knew how intense my crush on him was; I didn't need any more fuel on that fire. If only he had managed to become less attractive in the past few years, it would have been wonderful. But he hadn't. I know that if I'm going to put walls up about Eric in rehearsal, I also need to shut down thinking of Kevin outside of it. But, unlike with Eric, I can't seem to get the image of Kevin out of my head. The more I want to forget, the more vivid the memory of him becomes. I can feel myself getting hard, and know I've got to stop.

To distract myself I decide to try to sneak a peek through the mail slot, and kneel down as casually as possible. Just as I put my face up to the slot, the door swings inward and I fall forward into the foyer. My chin comes into contact with the hardwood floor, and I bang my left hip on the threshold, causing me to call out in pain.

"Mr. Burroughs?" I hear a lyric tenor voice ask, as I quickly push myself off the ground.

"Yes. Oh my god, I'm so sorry. I'm here to meet Mr. Lycan," I say, finally getting a good look at the man. Dressed in a tank-top and cargo shorts, it's clear he's in amazing shape, maybe even better than Kevin, but his body isn't beautiful. His arms and legs have dozens of scars, some are just small slivers, but others are massive. The most noticeable is a huge crescent-shaped one on the right side of his shaved head.

"I'm Alistair Lycan, are you all right?"

"I'm fine. Mr. Merchant sent me."

"Yes, we have lots of work to do. Come in," he says, leading me into his living room, which looks like some sort of museum. Every surface is covered with art or artifacts from around the world. I only recognize a few things—a Buddha statue and a tapestry with that elephant god from India—but most of it I've never seen before.

"Wow, your place is incredible."

"Thank you, it's been in the family for generations, but I've spent the past ten years updating it. I wanted to create a space that allowed me to work from home."

"Right. And what exactly do you do?"

"No one told you?" he asks, seemingly offended.

"No, sorry."

"I've been enlisted as your personal trainer and dietician."

"Oh..."

"I'm sorry he didn't warn you."

"It's fine, I should have guessed," I say, my ears growing warm as I blush in shame. I look away, pretending to be distracted by one of the many artifacts in the room.

Jenna said this guy cost a fortune, so Merchant must think I need more help than I thought.

"Would you like some tea? I just brewed some, and I'd like us to chat a bit before we begin."

"That'd be great."

"Excellent," he says, walking over to a silver tea set on an antique credenza.

"So you're a professional trainer?"

He tilts his head to the side and studies me. "I'm more of a metropolitan medicine man."

"What does that mean?" I ask, taking the cup from him.

"Well, I'm more than just a physical trainer. I've spent years learning about all types of medicine. But I did get my start in physical fitness. I mainly worked with dancers back then, but one day a client who was a Hollywood director asked me if I could design a training regimen for some actors he was directing in a film. It made a big splash at the box office, and once word got out, well...it became my life for most of the nineties."

"And after that?"

"I've been on a hiatus of sorts," Lycan says, fingering the huge scar on his head. "I couldn't do much after my partner and I were caught in a rock slide while climbing Pico da Neblina in Brazil."

"Oh…"

"I managed to stay harnessed in, but most of my anchors were knocked away. They estimate that I fell about 100 feet and hit my head, as well as just about everything else, on the cliff face. It was days before Jake and the rescue team found me, and when they did…well, they were pretty sure I would never be able to walk again."

"Really? You'd never know. I mean…you walk just fine."

"I run fine too," he says with a smile, "but it took years, and I saw everyone from specialists to witch doctors."

"So what was the cure?"

"I've no idea, it was probably a combination of several things, but I like to think that maybe what really healed me was that it gave me a new passion in life. I used to be solely focused on turning people into machines of muscle and paid very little attention to the fact I was tearing them down to do it. Having been torn down myself, I learned that what I truly love is giving people a new life, and so I've studied with healers from all over the world to make that a reality."

"That's really amazing," I say, finally taking my first sip of tea. It tastes like fresh cut grass and a pine scented air freshener.

"Are you all right?"

"What is this?" I ask, setting the tea cup down and pulling my water bottle out of my pack.

"I'm sorry, it's wheatgrass tea. I should have warned you. I forget it can seem very intense if you've never had it before. I've been drinking it for years."

"Why?" I say, guzzling as much water as possible to wash out the taste.

"It's great for internal wellness."

"I'll have to trust you on that."

"That's the idea. I'll modify your diet plan to make taking your daily dose a little easier. Many people find it easier to shoot it like a shot."

"I'm terrible at that."

"Well, I'm here to train you to be better," he says, with a smile.

"Right, so what did Merchant ask you to do with me?"

"He sent me the script, and asked me to help you find Caleb's body."

"Is it around here?" I joke, looking around the room.

Lycan let's my joke hang and die in the air before replying. "Come with me." He leads me through two French doors, to a small enclosed garden out back.

"It's warm," I say, impressed, considering it was fifty degrees when I was waiting outside his front door only moments ago.

"It's enclosed at the moment. I retract the glass ceiling whenever I can, though."

"That's incredible."

"I'm glad you like it, we'll be doing most of our work here. But first, I'd like to draw your attention to the sculpture on the far wall," he says, pointing to a life-sized stone torso in the corner.

"Not a lot left of it," I say. The head, arms, and most of the legs are gone.

"Yes, alas, but this sculpture is important. Have you ever seen it before?"

"I don't think so."

"Well, you might not have seen this one, but I am certain you will recognize what it inspired. This is a copy of the Belvedere torso, which inspired artists for many years, including Michelangelo's 'David'."

"I know that one, but he doesn't look like this." I always thought David was kind of hot. Especially that slight "V" shape around the hips. Lycan's statue isn't like that at all, the muscles aren't lithe, they're giant and bulky.

"Is something wrong with this body?"

"It's just so…big," I say, repulsed by the idea of being any bigger than I already am.

"Don't worry, I don't plan on turning you into The Hulk. However, I'm sorry to tell you, your body won't ever look like Michelangelo's 'David'. Your bone structure and body shape simply won't allow it.

Though…Bernini's vision might work."

"Who?"

"One minute," he says, picking up a huge book from a stone table. "What do you think of this?"

I take the book from Lycan, and stare at the picture. A statue of a man, David, I assume, with a sling in his hand. At first all I focus on is his face, which is kind of funny, because he is biting his lip, but after getting a better look at his body, I can see what Lycan meant about the statue in front of me. While the bulk is gone, the shapes are the same. It's just that now, everything is in proportion. It isn't exactly an Abercrombie body, but it's one I'd be pleased with.

"Can you really make me look like that?"

"When Bernini started, it was a chunk of marble, but over the course of seven months he chipped away until it became what you see there. I am certain that, with my help, you can mold your own flesh to have the same form in seven weeks." If that's true, then Lycan's worth whatever fortune Merchant is paying him.

"If we start today, we'll be done just a few days into our preview performances. Our first real audience."

"So what do you say?"

"Let's get started!" I say, feeling completely reenergized. Maybe that wheatgrass stuff does work.

"That's the spirit, now drink your tea," Lycan says, wryly, refilling my cup.

NINE

I AM SO MENTALLY AND PHYSICALLY exhausted that I have to stab my key at the lock a few times before I actually manage to get it open. Letting my pack crash to the floor, I stumble in and drop onto our couch.

"Ouch!" Eric yelps in pain. I realize the lumps I've landed on are his shins.

"Sorry." I shift my weight to allow Eric to move his legs.

"Long day?" he asks, too engrossed in the game he's playing to look over.

"Definitely, you?"

"Pretty much, but I'd say it's worth it. Pretty cool right?"

"Huh?" I ask, fatigued just by the effort it takes to project my voice.

"The game. It's going to come out in just a few weeks. This is our demo, it goes live tomorrow." Eric points to the screen where a fantastical world is displayed. A knight in black armor tromps around running through fields and slashing at monsters, taking them down with a single blow.

"It's....colorful." My limited video game knowledge makes me about as perceptive a critic as Eric is when I drag him to obscure Shakespeare. "I'm assuming you're the knight?"

"Yeah, watch this," Eric says, as his fingers seem to press every button on the controller in rapid succession. The knight on the screen glows blue, and then slices straight through some sort of troll monster. The camera lingers on the guts that spew forth, and the scream of the monster echoes throughout the room from our surround sound.

"Ugh, that's disgusting!"

"I know," Eric brags, as he executes another series of button presses to cause his knight to spin around and slash a zombie's legs off.

"Poor guy."

"What?"

"That one you just killed. That's how I feel."

"What?" Eric repeats, before finally pausing the game in order to look over at me. His expression changes from confusion to horror. "Good god! You look like death!"

"I feel like it too."

"What the hell happened?" Before I can reply, he bolts up and runs to the kitchen.

"They hired a trainer for me, apparently some sort of miracle worker," I say. Just the effort of projecting my voice loudly enough for Eric to hear me in the other room is enough to exhaust me.

He re-appears. "But you look even worse than yesterday!"

"I'm fine."

"Fine?" Eric asks, pressing a cold glass of water into my hand.

"You've looked worse than this after a run," I remind him.

"Wait…did you run here?"

"Yep."

"From where?"

Tilting the glass almost completely upright, I gulp down as much as I can, and let the rest flood over the sides of my moth, down my neck, and onto my chest. Within seconds the glass is empty, and starting to fog up in my hot hands. Eric refills it, but makes sure I look him in the face before he hands it over. After I drain it too, I'm able to find the strength to sit up, hoping it'll make the answer easier to hear.

"Liberty State Park."

"As in…you ran here from New Jersey?" Eric asks, pulling out his iPhone.

"Yeah."

"But…that's like four miles!" he says, showing me an estimated route on the screen.

"More, actually. I had to do laps while on the ferry."

"Mason, I thought you said you were going to be careful." Eric flops back onto the couch in a huff.

"I thought you promised you'd be supportive."

"I know, but—"

"No 'buts.' I told you, I'm going to be pushed hard. So I wasn't prepared today. Tomorrow I'll be sure I wear better shoes, bring more water. I'm not dead; I'm not maimed; I'm just tired. Quit overreacting."

Eric exhales deeply, but then nods. "You're right," he says. "I'm sorry. It's just hard for me to see you like this."

"Well, look on the bright side, me being this tired means we'll sleep in the same bed tonight."

Eric smiles. He always sleeps better with his arms around me. "No tossing and turning tonight?" he asks.

"I don't think I have the strength to move."

"Are you sure?" He kisses me, and pulls me onto his lap.

"Maybe later," I say, remembering that I still have a rather visible bruise to hide.

"It's just that it's been so long."

"It's only been two days."

"Exactly," he says, artfully unbuttoning my jeans with one hand.

"You're making this very hard to resist."

"Focus on the hard part, and less on the resisting," he says, stripping off his shirt.

"You're not playing fair."

"No game designer ever does."

Even after spending my morning drinking in Kevin's ideal form, there's something especially magnetic about Eric's body. For a man of his height, his tiny waist and milky complexion make him look like an elf from one of his games. I trace my hands over his shoulders, and down his back. Just the feel of him is enough to make my fatigue melt away. My body is far more interested in getting off than complaining about the abuse it's been put through.

Shifting me from his lap onto the couch, he slides both hands

underneath my waistband and yanks my jeans and boxers off. Before
he can grab my shirt, though, I pull him on top of me. I run my fingers
through his hair, guiding his lips toward mine. Our kisses are short at
first, but grow a little longer each time. Recalling Kevin's total mouth
invasion makes me realize how lucky I am that Eric prefers to work up to
using a lot of tongue. To reward him, I pull out an old favorite, breaking
off our kiss so I can slide my teeth along his neck. He whimpers with joy
and shifts his body down, to give me better access to his neck.

Each pass I make causes his entire body to undulate in excitement.
His flannel pajama pants tickle my thigh, and I let out a tiny giggle, before
managing to reclaim my focus. I realize I've been somewhat cruel in
keeping his erection locked behind fabric. I kiss my way down his body,
and then finish undressing him.

Thoroughly absorbed by the image of his naked body on our couch, I
stare at Eric's dick which, for the first time in weeks, is positively wet with
pre-cum. Proud that I can still turn him on this much after two years, I
shift to the floor so I can really drive him wild. However, before I can even
begin, Eric stops me.

"Wait," he says, tugging at my shirt.

"Don't," I reply, trying to hide the panic in my voice.

"What's wrong?"

"Nothing, it's just…I love you, but my knees aren't exactly thrilled
with our hardwood floors. Do you mind if we move this to the bedroom?"
I say, hoping the truth of that statement will cover up the fact I'm mainly
interested in preventing Eric from seeing my bruise.

"I like that plan," Eric smiles, dashing into our thankfully dark
bedroom.

TEN

FOR THE PAST THREE WEEKS, every day has been the same: I wake up, run, and then head off to my private session, where I'm humiliated for my continued failure to find Kevin. After that I rehearse for the rest of the morning or until Merchant gets so fed up with me that he has Alex take over. Next, I run forty blocks to meet with Lycan, who is waiting to have me work out even more by doing everything from Yoga, to climbing ropes, to fencing. Once he's done with me, he hands me my dinner, a snot yellow corn gruel I can barely stomach, which I carry back to my apartment, where a copy of the newest iteration of the script is waiting for me. I fall asleep reviewing all of the notes about the blocking Kevin and Alex worked through, only to wake up and do the same thing the next morning.

It sounds worse than it is, though I did have to send Eric to his parents' for Thanksgiving alone this year. I couldn't bear the idea of looking at all that food, and then digging into my gruel. But, aside from that, in many ways it's been a blessing. I'm so exhausted by the time I get home that I don't have the strength to care about lying to Eric. The lie feels smaller these days, much like my bruise and waistline. The progress Lycan has made with me in such a short time is incredible; I've already lost more than fifteen pounds, and can see the faint outline of muscles underneath what's left of my thinning later of fat. I'm consistently aware of how much progress I'm making thanks to a practically mute young woman named Robin, who is an assistant to the costumer. For the first week she barely said two words, but as my numbers have gone down more she's been slightly more friendly, by which I mean she finally told me her name.

I would worry about becoming vain if I had time, but my brain is usually too tired to do anything other than review the ever-changing script each night. Colin, it seems, has become completely unglued. My character changes so much from day to day that I get confused about my motivation to do anything. However, instead of complaining I have to be thankful, because the difficulties with the script are probably the only reason I haven't been fired yet.

"Mason, I like what you're doing with that cross away from Julia," Merchant said yesterday, stopping rehearsal. "However, since Colin moved the scene where you and Ezio first touch to later in the act, I'm not sure Caleb would be so distant. So let's run it again, and Alex? Would you mind relieving Mr. Burroughs? His time is up for the day."

The words are like knives. Alex has had more rehearsal time in one week than I have in two, a fact he adores repeating to the cast whenever I'm within earshot. At this point, I've begun to fear that when I sign in, the word understudy will be next to my name, instead of his.

"I've got to do something," I repeat to myself over and over, my breath steaming in the cold air outside Kevin's Chelsea apartment. I never thought I'd resort to stalking hum; even when I was practically his shadow I never went this far, but I'm desperate. Hopefully he'll give me what I need even without a bribe of hot coffee, because it's practically iced by now. I assumed he'd have left twenty minutes ago. Now I'm not sure either of will have enough time to make it to our session. It's unlike Kevin to be late, what could be keeping him?

Just then, he steps out into the morning light. The sun's rays, breaking through the yellow foliage of the nearest tree, hit him so perfectly I have to wonder if he was delayed because he was waiting for his light cue.

"Hey!" I shout, flashing my best "this is not completely crazy" smile.

"Mason? Jesus, what're you doing here?" he asks, his eyes wide as he stares at me. Then he quickly turns back to the door.

"I figured we could walk together, I wanted to—" I stop mid-sentence when I see someone else emerge from Kevin's door. Alex. He breaks into the most sickening grin when he sees me, and I drop both cups of coffee, their chilled contents spilling out onto my shoes and the sidewalk.

"Oh dear, it looks like we've been discovered." Alex tries to drape his arms around Kevin, but is shrugged off.

"Mason! Oh, I completely forgot, we were supposed to meet early right?" Kevin's eyes urge "follow me." It's familiar to me, because I've seen it every day during our mirror exercise.

"Yes, and you're late!" I say, channeling all my embarrassment into rage. "Honestly! Do you just think I have nothing better to do?"

"Well, do you have time now? I mean before rehearsal?" Kevin asks.

"Not really, I like to get to rehearsal early so I can practice," I say, bumping his shoulder as I storm off towards the subway.

"Don't bother," Alex quips.

"Alex." I hear Kevin chide.

"Oh, sorry. Did I say that out loud?" Alex feigns, his grating voice fortunately less audible with every step I take.

"Mason wait!" Kevin calls, I hear his footsteps as he races to catch up with me. I push myself to go faster. Unfortunately, despite all my training, Kevin's both taller and in better shape, so he has no trouble keeping up. After two blocks he's managed to get so far in front of me, he starts walking backwards so he can face me. "So are you really mad? Or...."

"What?"

"Well I mean, we didn't really have a meeting. You can stop pretending to be pissed off."

"I am pissed off!" I say, upping my pace so that I'm basically running.

"But why? I mean what were you doing there anyway?"

"I was hoping to talk to you."

"So talk."

"There's not enough time. We're supposed to meet Merchant in ten minutes. I can't afford to be late."

"Right," Kevin says, his voice heavy with sarcasm. "Because being on time has worked out so well for you?"

"God, you sound just like Alex."

"Just because he's bitchy, doesn't make him less right."

"Take that back!" I yell, charging at him.

"Make me take it back!" he yells, planting his feet, but before I can crash into him he grabs me by the shoulders. "Stop focusing on the wrong stuff! The only thing you're in charge of is finding Caleb."

"I'm trying."

"No, you're not. You're too busy worrying about the script, or how you look, or Alex!"

"Of course I am! I'm working myself to the bone, and I'm barely in rehearsal." My knees threaten to buckle, and my entire body is vibrating, but I continue to stand my ground.

"That's just it! You aren't in rehearsal even when you're in the room. Your job is to find Caleb and show him to us. I saw him when you auditioned, and again when we did our first session with Merchant, couldn't you feel it?"

"Yes," I mumble, unable to look into Kevin's venomous eyes.

"Don't you fucking look away from me," he says, shaking me.

"I'm sorry. It's just...the script keeps changing, and you and Alex are doing so much work that I'm having to catch up on."

"Quit making excuses. None of it matters if Caleb isn't even in the room. So either bring him back, or quit wasting my time," he says, releasing me and breaking into a full-on run.

I want to run after him, but I can't seem to move. His words echo in my head. Is he right? I've spent a lot of time focusing on how things will look. How can I not, though? It's all related. How can I find Caleb if my character changes from to day to day? How can I be someone, if I don't know who they are?

Yet I know it must be possible. Kevin has become Ezio every morning, and with each day he becomes more real. I think back to what he said, about when he saw Caleb in me, when I felt him, but it was all so hazy. In a fit of desperation I conflated my old desire for Kevin to bring out Caleb's passion for Ezio. To know the life of a wounded soldier, I melded my character's pain with my own injury and feelings of being flawed. How does any of that help me find Kevin in a room?

As much as I hate to admit it, Alex and Kevin are right about one thing. Nothing else I've tried has worked at all. There's no possible way I could suck more. If I want to keep this role, I've got to bring Caleb to life. I have to trust that the rest will come, if I can do that.

My newfound determination enables me to move again. With each step I take, I feel stores of energy burst open, sending my entire system into overdrive. I can almost sense the synapses in my brain firing faster, making my vision clearer, and my nose more sensitive. Everything, every sense, begins to tingle at once, like a superhero. It's a bit overpowering at first, making me wonder if I'm about to have a psychotic breakdown, but after a few moments I just enjoy whatever natural high I've tapped into. I know I should take the subway, but I'm already late, and I can't stand the idea of waiting for a train. So I run.

"It's Mason Burroughs. Let me in," I command, as I slam my hand onto the buzzer.

I swing the studio door wide open, and begin kicking off my shoes and stripping off my socks without even acknowledging Merchant or Kevin. The floor is like ice, but I feel more connected to the room this way.

"You're late, Mr. Burroughs," Merchant says, and while I can read his disapproval clear as day on his face, I'm beyond caring. I'm tired of being a disappointment.

"I'm ready to begin."

"Very well, Mr. Burroughs. I'll leave you to it."

I take my place across from Kevin, determined not to take a single step until I can feel Caleb. I can see Kevin change, his demeanor, his posture, everything. I study his bare chest, remembering how allowing myself to drink in the sight of him brought forth Caleb before, but nothing comes. Time passes, and eventually Kevin takes a step toward me, but I stand my ground. I will make him stand there forever, before I give into him. I will make Kevin take back what he said, and I will never allow some sycophant to play this role. My role. I am Caleb. I can feel it now, again, only bigger and bolder than before. The rest of me, not just a wounded soldier, or lust filled man, but all of me. All of him. We become one. My vision flutters, the room becomes a palace, and for the first time in three weeks I can see Ezio through Caleb's eyes once more. I take my first step toward him, and we begin.

As Caleb, I give myself time to appreciate how beautiful Ezio is, but refuse to let that be all he discovers. When he wants to rush, I focus on the feel of the cold floor beneath me, and it helps me assert myself. My mind whispers to Caleb that there's no need to rush. Ezio isn't going anywhere, so we have all the time we need to observe and learn what we can as we draw ever closer to him. Finally, Ezio and Caleb's faces are only inches apart, and I can feel my blood grow hot.

"Close your eyes," Merchant whispers, as if he has sensed the difference too, and is afraid of disrupting us.

Before complying, I lay down on the cold floor. As my body's temperature balances out, I close my eyes, and the exercise begins. This time, however, I am not alone in my search.

"Where is Ezio?" I hear Merchant ask, after stabbing the floor with the staff. The sound is so close, that I realize he must be inches away from me, and I can feel his anticipation. I think about Kevin and Ezio. Where would he be today? Kevin is probably curious about what is going on, happy that I've managed to find Caleb again, and annoyed that it has taken this long. Ezio is certainly intrigued, but also cautious about who I am. Together, they both want me to find them, but neither wants to make it so easy I could guess by chance. So where would that be? I scan my mental map of the room, and instead of stabbing blindly, I use my knowledge to rule out what I can, little by little the room becomes smaller, until finally there is nothing but the answer.

"He's right above me," I say, imagining him watching over me like the Colossus of Rhodes.

"Correct!" I hear Merchant cheer.

Happiness and pride swell up within me, but, as it does, I can sense the world around me starting to shift; my connection to Caleb and Ezio falters. I'm not done, I tell myself. I have to do it again. It's painful to avoid happiness, especially given the misery of the past few weeks, but I cannot lose focus. I redouble my efforts in tracking Kevin and Ezio, their thoughts, emotions, everything. They both know they will know have to do something unexpected now, they need to make Merchant see that it wasn't a fluke. Still, they know that my chances of finding them again are not guaranteed. If I were them, I'd try to do something kind of funny, and then I remember the time I made Kevin laugh the hardest. We were playing a drinking game, and I was supposed to do a handstand while on top of a table in the green room. If I could do it for sixty seconds, Kevin would have to drink, and kiss whoever was to his left. That would have been me, so I tried my best, but the table wasn't very steady and it actually collapsed. I wasn't seriously injured in the fall, but the only thing that kept me from crying was that I made Kevin laugh so hard that he could barely breathe. That, and the Long Island Iced Tea they gave me afterwards.

"Where is Ezio?"

"On top of the table!"

"Correct! By Jove, I think he's got it!" Merchant exclaims. I chuckle at the idea of Merchant as Henry Higgins and me as his Eliza Doolittle. Still, having done it twice, I'm confident I've finally figured this out. So for my final guess, Kevin and Ezio are going to give me a real challenge. In their determination to make it difficult though, it will also be predictable. A throwback to our first session, he'll be less than a foot away.

"Where is Ezio?" Merchant asks, his voice brimming with such excitement that I can hear the smile on his face.

"Right here!" I say, putting my hand out in front of me and striking Kevin in the chest.

"Correct! Open your eyes!" Merchant crows.

"You did it!" they yell in unison.

"I did it!" I yell back. My entire body is tingling with excitement. I can't stop smiling.

"Now the real work can begin! I need to make a few calls, so I'll see you when rehearsal starts," Merchant says, stuffing his pile of papers under his arm and exiting the room.

"That was incredible," Kevin says, hugging me so hard he lifts me off the ground. "I mean, I knew you had it in you, but not like that."

"I can't believe it worked! It's like I could feel everything you were feeling."

"Exactly! My god, that was so intense," he says, finally putting me down.

"I owe you big time."

"Nah, you did all the work. Besides, what's really important is that the show is the best it can be."

"So you think I'm a better Caleb than Alex?" I ask, lacing my hands around his neck.

"Oh Mason," he says, dipping me back. "Alex is nothing compared to you."

ELEVEN

For the first time ever, I rehearse the entire day. It's disorienting to go in and out of character as we stop and start. Fortunately, Kevin is there to help me through it. There is such a subtle change that overcomes him when he is Ezio; a thousand things are different, but it's so microscopic that most people would never be able to tell. However, through Caleb's eyes, I'm never fooled.

Alex paces along the side of the stage as I go through the scenes. Whenever I forget a line, he yells it out. I notice Kevin's eyes roll each time it happens, and after the third time Jenna puts him in his place.

"No one asked you. He'll call line if he needs it. I'm on book, so just sit down!" she yells. When she's finished, the entire cast breaks into whispers and snickers.

I can't help but beam as Alex sulks in his chair. After that, I don't drop any lines, and everything just comes naturally. We do most of the scenes in the first act a few times, as Merchant fine tunes small beats within each one. It's strange how different the moments feel each time we do them. Merchant has a knack for making things more intense with each run-through, which makes the displacement of going in and out of character even harder each time. Finally, it's the end of the day, and I am thrilled to have made it through the entire first act I notice the nods of approval from the cast as I gather my things.

"Great job!" Julia says, looping her arm through mine. "Any plans for tonight?"

"Does the gym count?"

"Don't they ever give you a break? I mean you've practically transformed in the past three weeks," she says, squeezing my bicep. The fact I have one for her to squeeze makes me smile.

"Thanks, but I think I've got plenty of room to go."

"Whatever you say, but I hope you'll come out with us soon. I've barely gotten to know you!" Julia says, air kissing my cheeks before heading out.

"Hey Mason, you've got a delivery!" Jenna thrusts an envelope into my hands, as I sign out. From the handwriting I can tell it's from Lycan.

"You get mail in rehearsal?" Kevin asks, once again draping one of his long arms over me.

"Only from Lycan."

"What's it say?"

"He says congratulations on my morning session, and that tonight I'm allowed a reprieve from my diet." I say, and then smile. The words are music to my ears. My stomach grumbles in excitement.

"Was that you?"

"Sorry, it's been a long time since I had real food."

"Then let's go out. We really should celebrate!" Kevin says, so excited it's almost alarming.

"I thought you were going out with me," Alex interrupts, eyeing Kevin.

"I don't remember us having plans."

"Well, I plan to get wrecked tonight, so I figured you'd want to come along." Alex nods his head to not-so-subtly indicate I'm the reason.

"No, thanks. Mason and I are going out tonight. I'd invite you, but we're just going to be talking about lead actor stuff," Kevin replies, pulling me closer.

"That could be me too."

"It could, but I don't think it will be," Kevin replies, once again reminding me how good he is at hitting people's weak spots.

As Kevin escorts me out, Alex remains fixed, glaring at me with a level of disdain I'm not sure I've ever experienced. I'm used to being the cast member everyone likes, but I guess being a lead makes that impossible.

"There's a great vegetarian place a few blocks from here," Kevin offers, hugging his coat to himself.

"I told you I wanted real food."

"So?" Kevin asks, clearly not understanding how exciting this is for me.

"So I was thinking Burgers? Pizza? Chinese?"

"Chinese!" Kevin shouts, grabbing my hand. "I know just the place."

I'm not used to holding hands with someone else; Eric's hands are always so hot that it's uncomfortable, and PDA wasn't exactly accepted in Texas. I remember, as a kid, dreaming of another guy taking my hand, and how important I thought that was. Figuring there's no harm in indulging my childhood dream, I lace my fingers with Kevin's.

"Not going to invite Eric?" Kevin asks, squeezing my hand a bit.

"He's working late tonight, besides I thought you said it was just us tonight." I squeeze back.

"That was just to get rid of Alex, I don't want to come home and find him on my doorstep."

"Oh, yeah, sorry about doing that this morning."

"What?" Kevin asks, seeming to have forgotten about my little stalking session. "Oh no, I didn't mean you."

"It's cool, I just had no idea you two were together."

"We're not. We were just having a bit of fun."

"You must be kinky then."

"What?"

"The only way I can think of having fun with Alex would involve a ball gag," I joke, imagining how delightful it would be to shut Alex up with one.

"Sounds like you're the kinky one."

"Not really, but desperate times call for desperate measures."

"I'll keep that in mind."

After a few more blocks we arrive at the restaurant. The place looks like every other Chinese place I've been to, so I'm not exactly sure why Kevin's so keen on it. It takes longer to be seated than it does for our dishes to arrive, and although this fact would normally give me pause, it's just another exception to today. I immediately begin scarfing down sauce-drenched chicken and rice, before my body can remind me that I don't need to eat everything on my plate.

"Umm, Mason?" Kevin asks, looking at me like I'm some sort of alien.

"Sorry, I know I'm eating like a pig."

"No, it's not that, but you're using your chopsticks the wrong way."

"What?" I ask, now returning the "are you an Alien?" glance.

"You pick stuff up with the square part, not the pointy end."

"No. I'm pretty sure you pick them up with the pointy end."

"No. You use this part," Kevin insists, pointing the square end of a chopstick at me. His lips tightly pursed making his face comically serious.

"Kevin, you look like a warrior holding the blade of a sword and trying to stab people with the handle." I smile, thinking how much Eric would enjoy that metaphor.

"No. That's what you're doing."

"You're kidding me right? Google it."

"Fine, I will."

I am pretty sure smart phones were designed for moments like this. I don't even care about the food anymore. It'll be far more delicious to see the look on Kevin's face as Wikipedia gives him his answer. His eyes dart back and forth like, and within a few seconds he hits it. For a split second his jaw hangs open, but he is quick to recover.

"Well…that is just stupid. My way is easier."

"A fork is easier, but you use the pointy end with that too," I laugh, still amazed that Kevin Caldwell, the golden boy, has been using chopsticks incorrectly his entire life.

"But…why didn't anyone tell me?"

"I suppose there are a few possibilities. Either they didn't notice, didn't know, or didn't want it to ruin their chances of getting into your pants."

"But I've corrected other people."

"Were you on a date?" I ask, picturing Kevin turning the chopsticks around for some moon-eyed boy, who is petrified to say anything that might hurt his chances of getting him in the sack.

"I don't know. Probably."

"Mystery solved then. Do you need me to teach you the right way?"

"No. I'll manage."

"Suit yourself."

Kevin is a quick study, and by watching me for a few minutes he is able to adjust his technique. However, the amount of energy and focus it takes him use chopsticks correctly is highly amusing. It's so strange to have our positions reversed. For once I am better at something. I revel in the level of mastery I can demonstrate with my chopsticks, and show off by swooping the tender morsels of chicken around before planting them in my mouth. It's a petty thing to gloat about, but with Kevin, there are so few chances.

"I can't believe this. I'm not even half done, but I don't think I can eat any more." I remember hating my skinny friends for statements like these, but now I can understand why they said it. I'm about to burst.

"Lycan really has done wonders with you. I mean it's only been three weeks, and you look amazing."

"Yeah well, it's not all peaches and cream. In fact, it's neither of those things."

"He has you on pinole, right?" Kevin asks, referring to the gruel-like sludge I've been consuming for the past few days.

"How did you know?"

"I see him once a month for supplies and a tune-up. Before it became popular, he was the only person I knew who could get it."

"Why would you want it?"

"I don't look like this by magic. I have to work at it just like you. But I don't get to use rehearsal time to do it," he says, making me wonder if he is jealous that I do.

"Well, you're doing maintenance. They're trying to perform alchemy on me!"

"And they are doing a fine job at it from what I can tell."

"What?"

"I mean I can only see so much, especially now that your clothes basically just hang off you, but I'm sure Eric's been more than pleased to have you in bed every night."

"Well...our schedules haven't exactly given us a lot of time to see one another. At least not consciously."

"Meaning?"

"I'm normally asleep by the time he comes home," I say, trying to remember the last time I spoke to Eric. We've been texting back and forth, but it's been a while since I actually heard his voice.

"Well, I'm sorry, but if I came home to you in my bed, I'm pretty sure I wouldn't be able to just let you sleep." It takes me a minute to realize what Kevin means, predominately because it is one of those moments I used to fantasize so much about. It's not quite like déjà vu, but it's close. I decide to play it off, assuming he is just being nice. People like Kevin never really think that about people like me.

"Given who I saw you with this morning, I'm not exactly sure that's a compliment."

"As you said, desperate times call for desperate measures," Kevin says, mimicking my chopstick loop pattern as he places a piece on his outstretched tongue.

"I'm pretty sure you could get anyone you wanted, regardless of the circumstances," I say, noticing multiple men around the restaurant who are watching him.

"Really? So does that mean I can call you tonight when I can't sleep?"

"Funny, but still, you could easily find someone better than Alex!"

"You really don't like him do you?"

"What's there to like?"

"I can think of a few things," he says, eyeing me up and down. "However, it's not important. I thought we were supposed to be celebrating! Let's grab a drink, I know the perfect place."

"Okay, but only one, we've still got an early morning tomorrow." I'm pretty sure I'd never be able to succeed in our sessions while hung-over.

"Then I'll make sure it's a good one," he says, motioning for the check.

Kevin pays and we head for the exit, but as we pass the kitchen he grabs hold of me and pushes me through the swinging door. Suddenly we're surrounded by waiters bearing trays of food and busboys with tubs of dirty dishes, all of them yelling at us in other languages. Kevin keeps pushing me until we reach another door, and emerge in the alley behind the restaurant. We pass by giant dumpsters that reek of rotting food, making me wonder about what I just shoveled into my mouth at dinner.

Kevin keeps pulling me until he stops in front of a rusted red door that practically blends into the brickwork.

"What are you doing?" I struggle to break free.

"Grabbing a drink." Kevin knocks loudly on the large metal door.

After a few moments a thin-faced man opens the door slightly. "May I help you?"

"Table for two," Kevin says, pulling me closer to him.

"Name?"

"Tower," Kevin says.

The man smiles and opens the door wide. "Follow me," he says, leading us through an elegant parlor lit by candelabra light. The place is quiet, except for the faint murmur of hushed conversations, emanating from behind thick black curtains. Finally, tucked deep into one of the back rooms he motions for us to ascend a small circular staircase where a table and antique loveseat are waiting. Once we are up there, the man bows to Kevin and then leaves without another word.

"Tower?"

"It's a password; this room is reserved for people who know it."

"Should I ask how you learned it?"

"Similar to how you did," he smiles, handing me the menu. "I came with the right person."

The menu describes drinks that make no sense. Aperol, Amaro Nonino, Chartreuse, I've no idea what any of it is. Fortunately they seem to have organized things by taste, so I focus on the page marked "sweet and sinful."

"Have you ever had this one? The Royale?"

"No, but I'm sure it's good. Everything here is."

"What are you getting?" I ask, noticing Kevin's not even looked at the menu.

"It's not on the menu."

"Maybe I should get it too then," I say, but Kevin shakes his head.

"I don't think you'd like it."

"Why not?"

"It's really strong. How about I let you taste it, and if I'm wrong, we'll switch."

"Deal."

Kevin writes our order on a piece of paper, and places it in a black envelope that he retrieves from the last page of the menu. He then drops it into a small slot in the center of the table.

"Where does it go?"

"This table is directly above the kitchen. Most people just press a button that turns on a light, but this table is special. I've heard there is an even more elaborate one set up in the basement, but I've never met anyone who knows how to get to it."

"Even more elaborate than this?"

"Yeah, it actually used to be a secret gay bar in the twenties. They had all these special signals to warn patrons if there were police. When we're done we'll leave by the hidden exit behind you." Kevin shows me a large iron door hidden behind a tapestry, before sitting back down. I feel his leg press against mine. Although it's not erotic, it feels strangely intimate.

"Wow, I had no idea this kind of place still existed."

"It's probably the last good secret in the city."

"Thanks for sharing it with me."

"My pleasure."

A tiny bell rings, and the man who sat us enters with two drinks on a silver platter. In total silence, he sets a ruby-colored martini in front of me, and a honey colored concoction in a brandy glass in front of Kevin. He exits without a word.

"To your incredible breakthrough," Kevin raises his glass.

"To making it through rehearsal." I clink his glass with mine, and then take a sip. The sweet taste of oranges and peaches flood my mouth, followed by the ghosts of raspberry and jasmine.

"Are you okay?"

"God yes, this is amazing. Want to try?"

"Sure, try mine too."

Kevin's drink is the polar opposite of mine. Spice and smoke assault my tongue, followed by a sharp bitter aftertaste of clove. I choke a bit as it burns down my throat. Kevin smiles, but his face shudders as he sips mine. We quickly trade back glasses.

"I thought you liked whiskey." Kevin drains half his glass in one gulp.

"I liked it when you ordered for me, what it was didn't really matter."

"Does Eric order for you?"

"He knows what I like," I say, wondering if I should text him. It's getting late.

"Would he have ordered that?"

"Probably not, he prefers wine, so he'd be even more clueless about the menu than I was."

"So I guess he doesn't know everything you like," Kevin says, leaning in for a kiss.

"Kevin, stop." I turn my head so he ends up kissing my cheek instead.

"What? Why?"

"Because, I'm not like that. I've got a boyfriend."

"I know, but we're friends right? It doesn't have to mean anything. Besides it's clear you want to." Kevin slides his hand up my thigh.

"I love Eric." I stand and start for the door.

"No one is saying you don't. It's just that we have to be lovers on stage, more than that really; the audience needs to feel passion between us. We need to be really comfortable with one another," Kevin says, standing and walking toward me.

"And you think surprising me with an ambush make-out session is going to make me comfortable?"

"Sorry, I didn't think you'd mind. I mean, the entire cast of *Cabaret* would make out before a show."

"That was in the theatre."

"So you'd be fine if we were there instead of here?" Kevin presses his body against mine, pinning me to the door.

"It's not that, it's that I don't want to confuse things. I need boundaries to keep everything straight in my head."

"How about this? I'll quit pushing outside rehearsal if you'll really give it your all while we're working."

"I'll give you everything I've got on stage," I say, determined to make the deal stick.

"All right then," he says, backing off and returning to the table.

"Kevin?"

"What?"

"I just want to say that I really am thankful for everything. It all... well...it means a lot," I say, hoping this will help keep us on friendly terms.

"It's no problem, man," he says, leaving some cash on the table.

TWELVE

Standing in the spray of the shower is the best moment of my mornings these days. I've never worked harder in my life than I have this past week. To compensate for the fact I'm now in rehearsal all day, Lycan has upped the intensity of my workouts by making me do all my runs with weights strapped around my arms and legs. As I adjust to it, he makes them heavier. I'm now running around with weights that make me twenty pounds heavier than I was when he met me. As if that wasn't exhausting enough, Merchant has begun to push us even harder in the morning sessions. Kevin and I must now literally move, think, and breathe as one person. Any flaw in precision results in his berating us while we do push-ups—in sync of course. Rehearsal isn't a total nightmare, though, now that Alex seems to understand that I'm not going anywhere. Still, I constantly feel his eyes on me, just waiting for me to mess up, so I spend what little free time I have each evening making sure I'm up on my lines and blocking. Everything I do seems to be in service to the show. If it weren't for Eric, I'm not sure I'd remember there was anything else in the world.

Despite living with one another, we have almost exclusively communicated with each other through text messages since my breakthrough. So when I hear him come in, I'm more than a little excited.

"Is that a pre-bed shower or a morning shower?" Eric asks, in a voice that makes me wonder if he's drunk or sleep deprived. Or both.

"I'm on my way out."

"Really? What time is it?"

"It's a little after five, have you been coding all night?" After wiping a window to see through the steamed up glass the question seems stupid. The rainbow of stains on his t-shirt and bloodshot eyes are answer enough.

"Well, I don't know. Larry sent me home after I fell asleep at the keys. My forehead almost deleted half the night's work."

It's hard to hear that Eric's working himself to death. Like me, when he gets fixated he's not the best at personal maintenance. It hurts me to know that unlike the times before, I'm not able to be there to support him. Usually, when he is in crunch mode like this, I try to do lots of things to make the few hours he gets to have at home as nice as I can, but this time I don't have the time. I turn off the water and grab a towel, but I'm too concerned for Eric to really commit to drying off before walking back into the bedroom. "How much longer till launch?"

"Five hundred and forty-eight hours."

"Meaning?"

"Three weeks, one day, and change," he says, seemingly exhausted by the effort of brushing his teeth and simultaneously doing the calculation.

"Wait," I say, grabbing my phone off the nightstand and pulling up the calendar. "Does that mean your game launches the day after previews start?"

"Yep, but don't worry. I told them I needed the night off."

"I bet they loved that," I say, my voice dripping with sarcasm. The company Eric works for seems to be annoyed that he has to actually eat and sleep when they get down to the wire. I swear, if they could chain him to the desk, they would. I can't believe they would really give him that night off.

"They were uncharacteristically cool with it. They said I can have it, provided I really buckle down between now and then."

"Wow, that's great. I'm so relieved. I want you to be there on the first night, so I guess you'd better get as much rest as you can. Gotta have a clear head to make your deadline!"

"That's the plan," he says, before letting out a big yawn. "I love you."

"Love you too," I say, watching him strip off his clothes and put them in the hamper. I'm a little ashamed by how quickly my dick rises to attention at the sight, but most of me is more concerned with drying off to be sure he doesn't fall asleep before I can get to him.

The hours I've spent making out with Kevin have been maddening. His tongue on mine, our hips grinding against one another, the passion between Caleb and Ezio is so intense for me that I've almost come in my pants on two different occasions. But Kevin is never satisfied, and despite my attempts to deal with my frustrations with my own hands, neither am I. Even as a teenager, I've never wanted it this bad. I mean, Eric and I used to barely be able to go two days, and now it's been almost a month. I've been dying to see how he will respond to my new body. Unfortunately, by the time I've toweled off, he's already asleep and drooling.

"Eric?" I whisper, pretending I don't know he's asleep. He doesn't even move, so I pack up my things and head out for my morning session with Merchant.

After being buzzed in, I am surprised to find Jenna blocking the door to the rehearsal space. Until now she's pretended to be completely blind to our sessions, ignoring me as best she could.

"I'm sorry, Mason, but Merchant has decided to cancel your session this morning."

"What? Why?"

"He'll explain it later, so just sit in the green room or come back in an hour. I don't have time," she says, before closing the door on me.

I make my way to the green room, and make a pot of coffee. I wish I'd known this earlier. Even if Eric and I hadn't managed to have sex, it would have been nice to wake up to him, and remember at least that much of my old life. Merchant is usually so many steps ahead that doing things last minute just doesn't seem right. Before I can get too anxious, I open my script binder and study it. I have a suspicion that I need to be prepared more than ever today.

"You made coffee?" Kevin shuffles in looking like he braved a hurricane to get here. His hair is wild, his eyes are puffy, and notice he's wearing the same thing he wore yesterday.

"Uh yeah, want me to grab you a cup?"

"You're an angel."

"Here." I set down a large mug in front of him. "Do you need anything else?"

"Advil?"

"I think I have some in my bag."

"Like I said, an angel."

"Long night?"

"Yeah, sorry. Is Merchant pissed?" he asks, washing the pills down with coffee.

"Oh, I don't know. He canceled our session when I got here."

"Really? Guess I dodged a bullet then."

"Unless he canceled because you're hung over."

"How would he know?"

"He seems to know everything." Since rehearsal started, nothing has seemed to surprise Merchant, except maybe that I passed his test. Even then, he seemed to already have a plan in place for when it happened.

"Good point, but if he knew I was going to be hungover, he'd have sent a car."

"You think?"

"I know."

"So why do you think it was canceled? Now I'm nervous."

"No idea. I'm going to grab a shower."

"Really?" In all my years working in the theatre I've always wondered why dressing rooms had showers. The only person I could think of who would actually need it would be whoever plays Elphaba in Wicked, and maybe the Phantom, because they have such elaborate makeup.

"Yeah, wanna join me?" he asks, taking off his shirt.

"No thanks, I just had one," I say, trying to will the blood back to my head. The combination of Lycan's diet, constant exercising, and making out with Kevin for hours a day, has apparently made my dick think it's a teenager again.

"Well, the invitation's open anytime."

I return to my script, but the sound of the shower is distracting. As I read about Ezio and Caleb's love affair, I can't seem to stop imagining Kevin soaping himself up. I picture the water pounding off his muscles, his curly hair weighted down, and the twitch of his biceps as he lathers himself.

"Darling, are you all right?" Julia asks, plopping yet another designer handbag down on the table. She seems to carry a different one every day.

"What?"

"Your face is all flushed." She lays her cool hand against my cheek.

"Oh, is it? Must be the coffee. It's still too hot for me to drink."

"I'm not sure the heat is the reason to avoid drinking it. God knows how old that stuff is."

"I just made it."

"I was talking about the grounds."

"Oh."

"Anyway, I've been trying to get a moment alone with you all week," she says, grabbing my hand.

"Oh, sorry. I've barely had a moment alone with myself."

"Don't apologize. I've worked with Merchant before. I understand. I'm just glad I'm not too late. You see, my husband and I are planning to throw a little Christmas soiree. He's schmoozing investors and I'm entertaining the cast. Do you think you might be able to put in an appearance?"

"You're married?" I ask, finding it hard to imagine any man being okay with how flirtatious she is.

"Sort of."

"What's a 'sort of' marriage?"

"I guess you'll have to come to the party to find out. You will come, right?" Julia says, making the invitation impossible to resist.

"Doesn't sound like I've got much of a choice."

"Not really, but I like to give the illusion."

"All right, do you mind if I bring my boyfriend?"

"Kevin? He's already coming."

"Kevin and I aren't together," I correct her. I wonder how many other people in the cast have also made this mistake.

"Oh? I'm sorry. I just assumed—stupid me—I thought you had this whole showmance thing going on."

"Nope. I'm already spoken for."

"Then he's welcome, too!"

"Thanks. His name is Eric."

"Mason! A word please?" Merchant beckons, as he approaches me.

"Go on. I'll give you the details later," Julia says.

"Have you seen Kevin?" Merchant asks, as he drags me into the rehearsal studio.

"Yeah, he's taking a shower."

"Good, this afternoon is going to be very different. And I need you to do something for me."

"Okay," I say, worried I won't be able to remember any changes after having worked so hard to cement the lines and blocking in my brain.

"The lines are all the same, but at the end of the scene where Mina is brought to the mirror to spy on you, I want you to see her and stop Ezio momentarily. Keep him at bay for a bit, and then instead of him subduing you, I want you to claim your desire for him. Caleb should become wild, like an explosion, I want to see what it looks like if we see Caleb release all this pent-up desire at once. Can you do that?"

"I'm pretty sure I can." If there's one thing Caleb and I have in common these days, it's pent-up desire. "Does Kevin know about this new plan?"

"No one else knows. I'm counting on you. I'm adding a lot of elements today: sets, costume pieces, lighting, even some music, so we're going to walk it a couple of times, but when you rehearse it, do it like you always have. Only change when our guests have arrived. If I'm right, I think this might get us exactly what we need."

"Actors, please make your way to the stage," Jenna calls, and Merchant hurries off before I can ask what he means by "guests." Within minutes the entire cast is in the room.

"Ladies and gentleman," Merchant says, projecting his voice. "This afternoon we are going to have some guests. Producers, investors, as well as our playwright, all of whom are anxious to see what we've been doing down here. I can't emphasize enough how important this afternoon is, but please know that if we succeed, as I expect we will, it will mean big things for the future of this show. So please, I know it's going to be hard to be quiet, but, if you need to talk, do it in the hall. I don't want any distractions."

Jenna picks up from there, with more specific instructions. "We will be doing a slow walkthrough to set up some preliminary lighting cues and get used to the pieces of the set we will be using. Everyone should check the racks outside to see if you've got a costume to try on. Principals, your costumes are located across the hall. It took a lot of persuading to get Ms. Taylan to let us use them, since they aren't complete, so please be as careful as you can. We will begin the walkthrough in ten minutes."

Seeing the rest of the cast members flit about all at once makes me finally recognize how big the ensemble is. The sheer number of bodies makes it clear just how isolated I've been. Leads always seemed busy to me, but I never thought about how hard they must work to insert themselves into the cast dynamic later on. In all my past shows, I had plenty of time to establish a rapport with everyone. We would spend hours sitting around in the green room, trading war stories or waiting to see if the actors on stage would mess up. The knowledge that there are at least five guys, not to mention Alex, sitting around hoping I'll fail does nothing to help my nerves. I try to distract myself with finding my costume.

Assembled on the rack, it is breathtaking. There's a thin, cream shirt with long, billowed sleeves tapering to cinched cuffs, dark red riding pants, knee-high leather boots, a scarlet vest, and the most exquisite frock coat I've ever seen. The coat looks like it's made of moonlight, and I notice that an outline of gold embroidery in a rococo-inspired pattern has been threaded into it so that it shimmers almost as if it's enchanted. I can only imagine what it'll look like in a few more weeks.

The pants are tiny, but, to my surprise, it doesn't take much effort to fasten them about my waist. I guess they've been making alterations based on the periodic measurements Robin's been taking. The shirt is loose, but the vest contours to my frame much better than the one I wore to my audition. I have to remember to thank Lycan, next time I see him. He really has guided me through a transformation. As I approach my reflection in the mirror, I can feel myself almost start crying from absolute happiness. I actually look…handsome.

Wanting to see the full look, I grab the coat, which turns out to be far tighter than the rest of my clothes. Although it is designed to be worn open, I know that it would never be able to close around me at this point. I try not to let this get to me, and distract myself by spinning around in it;

unable to stop marveling at how the fullness of the hem allows it to whip about like a tail as I dash and twirl about.

"You look incredible!" Julia says. She's draped in a cobalt blue ball gown with butterfly sleeves, and a corseted top that amplifies her already generous cleavage. A silver pendant nestled there has the effect of drawing the eye to the spot even more. Considering even I have trouble looking at her face, I doubt most men will be able to look anywhere else.

"So do you! Here, let's see what we look like as a couple."

"Stars in the night sky," Julia says, as we look at ourselves in a full-length mirror leaning against the wall.

"And blinding ones at that. Julia, I swear, you're the only person who could make a corset appear effortless," Kevin says, sidling up to her on the other side. Standing next to her, the champagne and crimson colors of his costume really pop. His burgundy silk shirt is tightly tailored to his body, and he's left several buttons undone to display his smooth, sculpted chest. His vest has a brushed metal look, like copper that has lost its luster from being touched by too many hands. Instead of a coat, he wears a blood red cloak with faux garnets around the hood and gold embroidery along the base.

"A woman never reveals her secrets, though you do make it hard to resist." Julia says, adjusting the angle of her face slightly to be even more flattering in the mirror.

"She's right," I confirm. "Your costume is amazing, and it's so complete. How many times have they fit you?"

"Oh, only one so far," Kevin replies. The costume designer must have memorized him. It fits him perfectly. "But look at you, Mason! Wow. For a poor soldier, you sure manage to clean up nice."

"Thanks, I think the royal treasury was hit hard to make this," I say, twirling around to show off the whole ensemble.

"It's no wonder I make you switch part of your costume. That coat is incredible."

"Oh…right." I had forgotten about that. At least it explains why it barely fits me.

"Let's see what it looks like when we switch."

It pains me to surrender my beautiful coat, but like a good servant I oblige my ruler, and drape his cloak over me. It's a shade brighter than my crimson vest, but the russet fur trim helps bridge the gap between them. I flip the hood over my head, and turn back to see myself in the mirror. With my face hidden, it's even harder to believe that the body I'm looking at is my own, and I can't help smiling.

Pleased with how the cloak enhances the rest of my costume, I turn back to face Kevin. It is clear that the coat was meant for him. While it certainly made me look noble, it fully transforms him into a count. That it seemed to be a part of my costume even for a moment is hard to believe. Neither Caleb nor I could deny Kevin or Ezio once we saw them in it. Like so many things, it was destined for the truly blessed.

"You look like a king," Julia says, taking his arm and looking at herself in the mirror by his side.

"Or a god," I say, but when I see Kevin's wicked grin, I instantly regret it. "We better switch back. I don't want them to wait on us."

We begin the rehearsal by walking around the parts of the set that have been brought in for today. After we stumble through the first act once, Merchant demands we stop holding our scripts, and my memorization is truly tested. Thankfully my recall is good, but I know with Colin in the room, my paraphrasing will not go unnoticed, so I call for the line if I'm unsure of the exact wording. Of course Kevin has no issues, and this helps me relax a little. Once the investors see Kevin, he'll have them writing checks so fast it won't matter what I do.

Merchant is really quiet for the most part, which makes me nervous, so I find it hard to keep from pouring my all into it. But every time I start projecting or really emoting Merchant demands that I "save it for the run through."

"Chaise entering," Jenna barks, as I approach the center platform where the final seduction scene is supposed to take place. Two stagehands enter, struggling a bit with the awkwardly proportioned lounge chair. The upholstery is virginal white and the wood frame has been painted gold. The quality of it makes me wonder how much was spent on it, but it all makes sense once Kevin lowers himself onto it and strikes a pose. His costume compliments the upholstery perfectly, as if it was some sort of accessory that came with him in a package. When he closes his eyes, he looks like an angel stretched out on a cloud.

"Lunch time!" Jenna calls out, not bothering to check with Merchant.

"Thirty more minutes!" Merchant insists, throwing his hands up in annoyance at being asked to stop before he is satisfied.

"It's been five hours. Equity rules state..."

"Fine," he yells, and sits down to review his papers again.

"Cast, you've got one hour, return here at 1:12 p.m. Please don't eat in costume. Lunch has been provided today, since we don't want anyone leaving the space. Please pick up your meal in the green room. If there are any issues see me," she says, and quickly I start toward the hall to hang up my costume.

"Mason, wait up," Kevin calls after me.

"Hey."

"Hey, I was wondering if you and I could work on the kiss."

"Now?" I ask, unsure how to honor my deal with Kevin and hold back as Merchant requested at the same time.

"I thought we had a deal."

"We do. We do. I'm just starving, and I wanted to get something before the investors showed up."

"Can we at least run it once? If we don't have an ending, we really need to wow them."

"Fine. Give me my cue," I say walking over to the chaise to prepare.

"Why?"

"Because it's part of the scene. Look if you'd rather just wait till we are in the moment..."

"No! It's cool. You ready?"

"Yes."

"Then stay with me tonight. Do not run to Mina, but rather see if she runs to you. Her engagement is bound to be long, and you have my word that, if she comes to you, I will retreat. Love me tonight as I love you, and when the morning light shines in, if you still love another, I will resign that you are a war I cannot win."

Kevin's speech is so spellbinding, as he inhabits the character of Ezio, that I move toward him without even thinking that's exactly what Merchant blocked us to do. I lower myself onto him, straddling him on the chaise, and slowly kiss his lips. I try to hold back, but I get lost in the pleasure of the sensation. While Caleb's instincts are somewhat clumsy, I'm able to help him use our body to its full potential. Having spent so much time in Kevin's head, it's almost too easy to rile him up. Just as things start heating up, though, his arms go limp and he breaks away.

"What's the matter?"

"It's just not right. When Caleb kisses Ezio there is so much going on. It should be big, like light shooting through darkness."

"Well, unless you've got something in your pocket, you seem pretty much ready to explode."

"That's not the problem. It's just so…mechanical. There is something missing." He says, shifting so I'll get off of him.

"Well, maybe it'll be different once we have all the other things in place: lights, costumes, furniture, plus the whole of the play. All of that will help build to this."

"Okay, but if not, can you stay late tonight?"

"Like I said, we'll work on it till we get it right."

"Thanks, I'm sorry to be such a perfectionist."

"Don't be sorry. We both want this show to be the best it can be. Now let's get some lunch."

The green room has a very different vibe when the entire cast is relaxing in it. I'm used to being quiet and still, since I'm usually in there alone, but today it's loud and full of energy. I take a seat next to Julia, hoping she will help me transition into making friends with the rest of the cast. Most of the guys are too busy talking about Kevin to notice me, and when Julia refers to them as "Kevin's Club" I smirk, remembering that a few years ago I could have been considered a founding member.

I tried everything to keep Kevin in my life after our classes were over, arranging elaborate reasons for us to meet-up. Eventually though, I saw that it was never going to happen. Kevin wasn't going to just wake up one day and see I was the guy for him. So I let nature take its course, and when I stopped desperately trying to keep us together, we quickly drifted apart.

"What are you so lost in thought over?" Julia asks.

"Kevin."

"Oh my! But I thought you said you were taken."

"It's not that. Kevin and I used to be friends."

"Friends or lovers?" she asks, clearly expecting the latter instead of the former.

"Friends, but I dreamed of being his lover. That's what makes this all so strange."

"Makes what so strange?"

"Kevin seems to think our passion is lacking."

"That is strange," she confirms, dropping her voice even lower and scooting closer.

"I know. I mean, I fantasized about this kind of thing."

"Maybe that's your problem."

"Huh?"

"I've been the object of affection a lot, and I'll tell you, it's not as great as it sounds. It's nearly impossible to live up to the expectation," she says, her usual smile fading.

"But I'm not in love with Kevin anymore."

"I wasn't talking about you. I mean, have you ever considered that maybe you're the one on the pedestal?"

"Is that a joke? Look around. Those are his fans, not mine, " I say, subtly nodding my head at Kevin's Club. All he's doing is sitting down with his script, but the way they're looking at him, you'd think he was turning water into wine.

"I don't think they matter much to him, but even if they did, Kevin's character certainly has you on a pedestal."

"So what do you do when you're up there?"

"Find someone like me, who can teach you how to wield an actors' finest weapon," Julia says, grabbing my hand and pulling me into the hall.

"Where are we going?"

"The stairwell," she answers, pushing me through another door and then shouldering it closed behind us.

"Why here?"

"Shut-up and sit on that step," she demands, and as I take a seat she begins pacing back and forth. "Mason, you're very smart, at least for an actor, so I'm going to try and explain this as best I can."

"Explain what?"

"Do you see what I'm doing right now, this pacing, pay attention to it. Notice the speed, my expression, and the sharp turns I make just moments before I hit the wall." It's true; her body narrowly avoids scraping the cement, which seems particularly impressive given her Marilyn Monroe figure.

"Yes, could you stop? It's making me nervous."

"Exactly, it's making you nervous, yet you are in no danger. Correct?"

"Well, Merchant would probably be pretty mad if you—"

"Stop thinking about Merchant!" Her voice echoes up the stairwell. "We only have a few minutes. I need you to focus on me."

"Okay, but stop pacing."

"Never." She begins moving faster with each pass. "Have you ever heard of Antonin Artaud?"

"No."

"He was famous in France in the late eighteen hundreds. He created this thing called Theatre of Cruelty."

"Is that what this is?"

"Somewhat," Julia smirks. "It played with the idea of using theatre as a way to make audiences feel things like fear or pain. In the most famous performance, audiences were shown what it was like to be in the mind of the truly insane."

"You're making me crazy. Please stop," I beg, but she persists. Her eyes seem to be getting wider with panic as she keeps increasing her pace.

"Focus. There is nothing else but you, me, and these walls."

"Fine, but slow down."

"I'm not going to slow down Mason." She starts going even faster.

"Stop," I blurt out, realizing that I've been holding my breath as I watch her.

"Never."

"I can't stand this! Stop." I bolt up from the step and grab her into a tight hug.

"Feel this? Feel our breath? I've been pacing yet you're the one out of breath."

"Yes."

"Now close your eyes for a moment." I comply, and I feel Julia's hands slowly run down my shoulders, then to my arms, the tips of my fingers, and back up to my chest. She drags her index finger down the center of my body until she lands at the button of my jeans. With a swift movement she undoes the button and unzips my fly. I start to panic and open my eyes.

"Julia!" I say, knocking her hand away and quickly trying to button my jeans back up. Unfortunately, my semi-erection makes it more difficult.

"Don't worry, the lesson is over. The best thing about teaching this to a guy is I don't have to even ask if I got it right."

"Oh my god! I'm so sorry!"

"Sorry? Don't be! Whenever this works on a gay guy, I feel a little extra pleased."

"I've never…I mean with a girl." This being my third hard-on today makes me wonder if I've developed some sort of problem.

"Mason, all I did was get your blood pumping fast. That's the part that matters. Everything else is just biology. You'd have been stiff if a dog just rubbed against your leg. It doesn't mean you're not gay. Believe me, I know women who have tried this trick to get a gay guy in bed, the effects don't last that long."

"So then what's the point?"

"The point is, it's theatre. Your job isn't just to get Kevin's blood pumping, that's easy; you and Kevin have to raise the heat in the entire theatre. The entire audience should be able to feel exactly what you feel you in that moment, so much so that they find it hard to stay seated. Find a way to show them how intense you feel. You can't keep all inside, you have to share it. Make them want to take it home."

"I see. Thanks Julia, I think I understand."

"Good. I'll look forward to seeing you tonight. I promise I won't tell your boyfriend I know how lucky he is," she says, grabbing my ass on her way out of the stairwell.

"Hey!"

"Come on babe, we've only got a few minutes to get back into our costumes."

AFTER CHANGING CLOTHES, I MANAGE to make it into the rehearsal space just as Merchant begins his post-lunch announcements.

"Welcome back, everyone. I was just told by Mr. Stein that the investors will be here shortly. Therefore, we will be resetting for the top of the show. We'll begin as soon as they arrive," Merchant says, motioning for Jenna to put this plan into action.

"But what about rehearsing the last scene?" Kevin asks in an alarmed voice.

"Run your lines somewhere until it's time. You've got your blocking."

"But...."

"Is there a problem, Mr. Caldwell?" Merchant asks.

"No, no problem," Kevin says, with an audible swallow.

"Good."

By "shortly" Mr. Stein must have meant "momentarily," as he and a group of about twenty sharply dressed men and women show up before Kevin and I have finished running our lines. Their presence causes everyone to move even faster as they reset the stage, and five minutes later I find myself primed at center stage.

I remind myself that no one can start this thing until I say my line. Unfortunately, it, along with the rest of my dialogue, has seemingly vanished into thin air. The more I try to remember it, the more the exact phrasing seems to retreat, becoming lost inside my head. Everyone's eyes are on me, so I close my own, hoping that I'll forget about them like an ostrich with his head buried in the sand. I take another slow inhalation, purse my lips as if I was going to whistle, and allow my breath to slowly release. I feel it wash over the space, breathing life into the world of the play. When I open my eyes, the lines return to me, but they don't feel like lines. They are thoughts, and with Caleb's voice I speak them with pride.

"My liege, I have been sent from the fronts of battle, to deliver unto you, this message."

The show goes smoothly from there, and I find some relief in having an audience watching us. Kevin is dazzling, feeding off the energy of the crowd, making him easy to fall in love with. I'm starting to worry that perhaps I'm not resisting him enough, but the second Julia enters as Mina, I am saved by her radiance. Before I know it, I'm off stage, with two members of Kevin's Club helping me do a quick change into my final

costume. The next scene is the big seduction scene with Kevin, and I think
of Merchant's instructions, hoping that I can find a way use Julia's advice
to give him what he wants.

Even though the set isn't really fully constructed, looking through
Caleb's eyes, I am truly there. Four sturdy, pearl white walls, each of them
with crown molding painted gold, in the French Rococo style, create
a little love nest. Heavy tapestries hang on the walls, and the scent of
orange blossoms permeates the air. The room is not entirely comfortable,
made overly warm from a lack of ventilation and the heat from numerous
dripping candles that are lit all around.

"Where have you brought me?"

"To my inner sanctum. Come, Caleb, share in my delight, and suck
the milk of Venus with me," Ezio says from the chaise lounge, his chest
glistening as the flames illuminate the sweat on his smooth chest.

"I dare not your lordship, for that is the Cup of Counts." I start to
pace a little, just as Julia did earlier. I look around the room, as if I know
something is not quite right.

"Caleb, my pet, do not fear. Are you not swathed in the makings of
a count? Surely, donning such apparel is far more offensive than sipping
with me behind closed doors."

I begin to panic, and quickly cross over to the table with the chalice.
I grasp the silver cup, the cool metal so sharp in contrast to the heat of
the room. I set it down with a hard thunk, and cross the stage again, this
time moving to the mirror. Using its reflective surface to see what Ezio is
doing behind me, I watch him as he slowly undoes the buttons of his vest
and throws his clothes to the floor. In repose on the chaise, he looks even
more like a sculpted figure, and I feel my own temperature rise. I slide my
sleeve along my brow, trying to wipe away the sheen of sweat, unable to
keep my eyes fixed on him for more than a few seconds.

A whimper of fear escapes my lips, and Ezio sits up, extending his
hand out to me. His very essence appears to pull me in, almost as if he
was supernatural, and yet something in me finds the strength to resist. I
walk away, but before I know it I am pacing back toward him, as if we are
magnets and I keep flipping from one pole to the other. The distance and
speed increases with each pass, as Caleb and I attempt to make a decision.

Can we give in? Should we?

"Caleb?" Ezio whispers. His silky voice teases my ear and the last of my defenses crumble. Finally, I resume Merchant's blocking, and make my way over to Ezio.

Seated next to him on the chaise, I am keenly aware that the only thing preventing our knees from touching is the light fabric of our stockings.

"The gala has brought many people within your walls tonight. Are you certain we are alone?" I ask, noticing Kevin's chest is rising and falling with the same ragged breath I had when I watched Julia. Even though nothing has happened yet, I feel I have already begun to sin.

"I assure you, this chamber is the most private in the realm."

"Then if it please you, I shall share your cup," I say, as I tip the chalice to my lips.

Although I'm drinking grape juice, I am so wrapped up in the moment that I could swear it is real wine. On Caleb's tongue the juice is transformed, and I detect the sweet tastes of pear and apple, along with the acid of the grapes. No sooner has the liquid passed my lips, than I become all too aware of how swelteringly hot the room is. I throw caution to the wind, along with my shirt and vest, and creep ever closer to Ezio's side.

When our bare shoulders brush against one another, a flash of desire courses through me. I spring to my feet again, pacing even faster. Then it hits me: This is what was missing. I was so worried about helping Caleb please Ezio, I was letting my experience guide him. However, in knowing how to please him, the sensation of discovery was dulled. The question of how someone like Ezio could spark such a hunger in me is something I've been ignoring, because while the answer is obvious to me, it's not to Caleb. I can sense in him the fear that comes from seeing the parts of yourself you never wished to know. I take another swig of wine, hoping to calm my nerves.

"Drink again, my little angel. But as you do, tell me, what do you know of love?" says Ezio, refilling the chalice for me, and taking my hand.

"I know that it causes men to do mad things."

"Could you ever be mad for me?"

"Of course."

"How?" he asks, tracing the line of my cheekbones with his index finger.

"If anyone were to harm you, I would be overcome. Mad with grief, I have no doubt that I would rush to avenge you."

"You care for me so much?" Looking at me with such innocent eyes, I let him gradually pull me down so that I'm resting my head on his chest. Listening to his rapidly beating heart makes aware that I have accomplished my goal. I feel what little control I have starting to wane, but I fight to maintain it, promising Caleb that I will unleash him when the time is right.

"Ezio, you know I do. I fought for you before ever seeing your face, and hated you for it. But now, I would gladly go to battle for you."

"Yet with you, I no longer thirst for blood."

"And the people love you for it."

"Then they should all love you. Yet tonight, shrouded in your clothes, the entire court treated me as one treats a dog. They are fools. Do they not realize that all the blessings of this past year were inspired by you?"

Hearing the slight rancor in his tone opens a wound I never knew existed. As Caleb, it never occurred to me that life could be anything other than the way it was. Through Ezio's eyes, though, I finally question the injustices inflicted upon me.

"Why should they pay me any attention? Mina has abandoned me, and to them I am nothing but a wounded soldier."

"Mina! That viper. At the first test of her love, she fled from you," Ezio says, rising up from his reclined position, causing me to sit up as well. Taking a huge swig of wine directly from the flagon, he turns to me. "How can you continue to harbor such affection for her? How can I get you to love me as you love her?"

"I love you as best I can, but you are never satisfied. Mina grew with what affection I showed her. She wanted me as I was, and never asked for more."

"Yet she found you lacking."

"She did not wish to battle for my love. To her, love is not a war."

"Then she does not love you. I could never give you up without knowing I gave everything to keep you. True love is not polite, it does not lie down like a dog. No. It fights, and while I may never have fought on the fields of battle, I will fight for you for as long as I draw breath." Somewhere in the distance, I hear stringed instruments begin to play, long and extended phrases that grow shorter, increasing the tension with each repetition.

"But Mina is gone, you have no one to battle with."

"She may have fled the land, but her ghost still haunts you."

"And how do you plan to do war with a specter?"

"By bringing you here and asking you, not as your ruler, but as your lover, to stay with me for one night. Try to love me as I love you, and when the morning comes, if Mina is still in your heart, I will resign that you are a war I cannot win." The honeyed words drip from his ruby lips, and I believe him. I believe that he loves me, and that if I am willing to give him everything I have, it can be enough.

I grab the silver cup and tip it to my lips, taking another full and hearty guzzle, before embracing him at last. Wrapping my arms around his muscled frame, pulling our hips together, and then, with no other motion, kissing him. Unlike the other times when I relied on my own experience to guide him, Caleb experiences the full glory of his first kiss, making it almost impossible to keep his desire in check.

"My god," the whispered words fill the entire room, and I know the voice is neither mine nor Ezio's. I bolt up, knocking Ezio aside, and step toward the mirror on the wall. It takes me a few minutes to even recognize myself, to remember my own face, but as I stare straight ahead, I can feel her. Mina. Mina is on the other side. This is the moment that Merchant was talking about, but although I know how to do what he is asking, it makes no sense to me in the moment. How can I betray Mina, and fall into the arms of Ezio, when I know she will see? The idea is hard to justify in my head, but Caleb isn't exactly interested in thinking anymore. With each step closer to Ezio, I can sense the depth of the awakening the kiss between us has created. No, there is not stopping him now, nothing I can do will douse the fire that Ezio has lit tonight. If I am to burn in hell, I shall at least burn bright.

Holding his face between my hands, I kiss him with renewed vigor, managing to not only match his intensity but eclipse it, pushing him to keep up. No longer concerned with just his pleasure, I guide his hands to my ass, showing him how much I want him. The music that was barely audible before, now seems to swell as the light drains from the room, but even as we are consumed by the shadows, I know this moment has forever altered us.

"Hold," a voice cries out, followed by a great murmur of voices and a soft sound of applause. Light returns, illuminating the stage and reminding me that I am in a play, that none of this is real. The intensity of being Caleb is hard to let go of, and it takes me a few minutes to remember who I was before rehearsal began. I look up at Kevin, his face frozen in shock and confusion, as if he is looking at a stranger. When I try to move, his arms grip me tighter and I feel an urgent need to get away. I press harder to escape, and he drops his arms to his side. I scramble to get my shirt back on, and toss Kevin's next to him, but he makes no move to get dressed. I can't believe how well Julia's trick worked, but now I wonder if she had another lesson to teach, one that would allow me not to be spellbound by experiencing that each night, and remember that in the real world, Eric is the only man I could love like that.

THIRTEEN

I TEXT ERIC ABOUT THE PARTY, and am surprised when he agrees to put in an appearance. I hope that by seeing him, I'll be able to stop thinking about either Kevin or Ezio. Honestly, I'm not even sure which one is still haunting me. Maybe it's both. I feel like I've lost my virginity again. I keep smiling, singing to myself, remembering how incredible that moment felt on stage. It's what I remember thinking love was: swelling music, wild passion, the idea that nothing else matters. But that's just the superficial stuff. True love is much deeper than that. It's about being a couple, two people who are both better because they live for each other as well as themselves. Seeing Eric as he exits his office building finally helps me remember that.

"Wow!" he says, looking me up and down. "What happened to you?"

"What?" I ask, fearing he can detect what happened.

"Mason! You look incredible! Are those my jeans?"

"Yeah, you don't mind do you? None of mine fit anymore." I couldn't believe that Eric's clothes fit me at all. Of course, since he's a lot taller than me, I've had to roll them up at the cuff.

"Not at all! I'm just shocked. I mean, I knew you'd been working hard, but, you look completely different." He circles me, patting my arms and legs.

"Are you frisking me?"

"Sorry, but even my clothes are kind of baggy on you."

"You'd have gotten a much better view if you'd managed to stay awake this morning."

"What?"

"I was hoping to show off my new body this morning, but by the time I got out of the shower you were drooling," I say, grabbing his mouth and kissing him.

"Hey!" Eric says, stopping me. "I'm happy to skip the party if you'd rather..."

"No, we have to go. But maybe you can come home for an hour before heading back?"

"Only if we don't stay too long."

"Then let's go!" I say, kissing him again.

★

"How do you know this lady again?" Eric asks, noticing the high-fashion design scheme of the lobby. From the outside, Julia's building looks like an abandoned warehouse, but in typical Chelsea fashion, the interior has been extensively modernized. Lacking a six-figure salary, I feel like an intruder.

"She plays the woman I'm supposed to be in love with."

"And she lives here?"

"I don't understand it either. I mean, I thought she'd be in something nice, but not like this." I make a mental note to ask Julia what her "sort-of" husband does, after she explains what one is.

"Can I help you?" a man in a perfectly tailored three-piece suit asks from behind the front desk.

"We're here to see Julia Pierce."

"You must be with the actors. Take this and use the elevator on the right to go to the roof," he says, handing us something that resembles a gold credit card.

When the chime sounds and the elevator doors slide open to reveal the rooftop, I almost press the button to immediately go back down. All of the guests are in cocktails dresses or suits. Foolishly, I assumed Julia was throwing a party for the actors, and so I chose to wear Eric's skinny jeans with a hoodie in an effort to be more casual with the rest of the cast.

Thankfully, I've got my stylish pea coat, but I don't think I can stand the heat of wearing it all night. Even though it's the middle of December, Julia has made sure no one will be cold on the roof tonight. Heating lamps are tucked into small alcoves with couches, while iron firepits glow in the center of the larger seating areas.

"This is your cast?" Eric asks, sounding as intimidated as I feel.

"No, I've never seen these people before."

"Mason, over here!" Julia calls, projecting her voice through dozens of bodies. She's waving, but I don't need any help finding her, since she's practically spilling out of a low cut dress. The gown is really stunning, but it looks more like something reserved for the red carpet than a cocktail party.

"Julia, I wish I'd known the party was going to be like this. I look a mess."

"You're fine! The ones in suits are Charles' friends. We thespians have taken over the bar area," she says, before turning her attention to Eric. "Now who is this?"

"Oh, I'm sorry. Julia, this is my boyfriend Eric. Eric, this is Julia. She's my leading lady."

"Eric! It's delightful to meet you, though you might want to be careful when I introduce you to the rest of the cast."

"Why?" he asks, giving me a nervous glance.

"I think most of the boys were hoping you were a figment of Mason's imagination. You should hear how he talks about you. He is clearly smitten. Though now that I see you, well, I'm not sure he did you justice."

"Oh, I like you." Eric says, smiling bigger than I've seen in ages. "Maybe you'll be willing to trade some information with me. I'll tell all of Mason's secrets if you'll tell me about the show. He's been very tight-lipped about everything." He takes her arm in his. It's clear Julia's gift for flattery works on everyone.

"Eric seems to think that there is more to rehearsal than I tell him, because this time I'm not complaining," I say. " Maybe you can demystify it for him, while I get you both something to drink?"

"Bring me whatever you're having," Eric says.

"I'll stick with white wine, dear. Tell them it's for me. They'll know what that means."

Normally, I'd worry about leaving Eric to survive among the actors, but his smile tells me he'll be fine. Thankfully, the bar is only a few feet away, but the "bartender" seems to have been chosen more for his looks than his skills as a mixologist. I settle in for a long wait, and watch him as he slowly makes drinks. His pompadour haircut and scruffy beard make him look like one of a hundred hipsters, but his flannel shirt has quite a few undone buttons to show off his shaved chest. His muscled pecs twitch along with his biceps as he rattles the cocktail shaker. While I'm sure most New Yorkers would think he's attractive, I've never been into the Brooklyn bohemian look. Maybe it's because I grew up in Texas.

"Two glasses of Cabernet and a white wine for the hostess," I say, when it's finally my turn.

"Oh, sure thing. Hold on though, I'm gonna go raid her secret stash," he says before disappearing, leaving me with dirty looks from a crowd of thirsty guests.

"I think there's another bar on the other side." I turn just in time to see Kevin flash his trademark smile, while the guests who were lined up behind me stampede across the roof in search of their libation of choice.

After what happened this afternoon, I was worried what seeing Kevin was going to do to me, but being with Eric revealed all of that for what it was: merely the illusion of passion. While it was strong in the moment, now it has completely faded away.

"Is that true? There's another bar?"

"No idea, but, I didn't want witnesses if I was going to pour my own." He steps behind the bar.

"You can't do that!"

"Why not? What are you drinking?"

"Cabernet. Two glasses."

"Wow. You might want to slow down there."

"One is for Eric. Julia is working her usual charm on him right over there."

"Oh! Then let me at least pour you two glasses of the good stuff. Let's try this bottle of 'Gueule de Loup,'" Kevin says, flipping his own personal whine key out of his pocket and then expertly sinking the screw into the cork of a dusty, dark green bottle.

"Of what?"

"It's French. It means 'Mouth of the Wolf.' It's one of my favorites really, but it's hard to come by."

"How have you had it, then?"

"I've dated a sommelier or two. It's a perfect choice for you though, given what you pulled in rehearsal." He delicately pours the garnet liquid into two tulip-shaped wine glasses.

"How do you figure that?"

"You kiss like a beast! I couldn't believe the difference between what we rehearsed and that. You're an animal."

"I take it you don't think we need more rehearsal on it, then," I say, rubbing my finger along the rim of the glass and smiling.

"I don't know. I wouldn't mind running it a few more times."

"That wasn't the deal. You said you wanted passion, you got it. Why don't we try working on the rest of the play?"

"But that's not as much fun."

"Work rarely is, Kevin."

"Shit! Here he comes. I'll take this to Eric. You take Julia's," Kevin says, dashing from behind the bar with the rest of the bottle clutched to his chest. Not sure whether Julia will be able to appropriately referee Eric and Kevin together, I grab the wine out of the bartender's hand and quickly make my way back. Julia and Eric are sitting on two of the couches that are surrounding a table with a built-in fire pit in the center.

"Here you go, Julia. Thanks for the help, Kevin."

"Any time."

"Now, does everyone know one another?" Julia says, looking from Eric to Kevin.

"We've met," Eric responds, his smile fading.

"We have?"

"Yes, but I can understand why you don't remember me, you were drunk."

"Oh right. The day Mason got cast." Kevin says, putting his arm around me.

"Right. Speaking of drinks, Julia, what's in the glass?" I take the opportunity to shrug off Kevin's arm by leaning over to examine the drink.

"A chardonnay from Chassagne-Montrachet. Charles bought a whole case. It starts off like any white wine, crisp and clear, but then bam, you're smacked with this luxurious hint of peaches and apricot. It's divine."

"It should be. I bet it cost him a bundle," Kevin says, once again flexing his wine knowledge.

"What exactly does he do?"

"Charles? Finance. I'd explain it to you, but I've never been able to understand it when he tries to tell me about it."

"I don't get investing either, but thankfully Eric does," I say, giving him a peck on the cheek.

"Only a little bit," Eric blushes.

"So, I want the scoop. You said you'd explain your arrangement."

"Oh, it isn't that mysterious," she says, pausing for dramatic effect. "I'm a mistress."

"Really?"

"Yes, really. But it isn't like it matters. James' wife knows me. We're friends."

"Then why are you…" I start, but falter, unable to think of a nice way to ask about her situation.

"A mistress?"

"Yes."

"Charles and Delia are rich, but most of their money is held in trust. Delia loses everything if she becomes divorced. It's completely silly, but her father had some snake of a lawyer make it that way. Apparently she did something to piss him off, and so he's trying to make her pay for it even from the grave. Anyway, they can't divorce, but Delia's got a lovely man she lives with at their summer home."

"How did you meet?"

"Funnily enough, Delia was the one who introduced us. She saw me in *The Children's Hour* at the Gloria Maddox Theatre. The whole night I could feel her eyes on me, and when I walked out of the place, she was waiting."

"What did she want?"

"I thought she was interested in me – you know, in that way – and

I was all set to break her heart, but then she rushed up to me and said: 'You must meet my husband!' Well, needless to say, my 'This bitch is crazy' whistle was blowing, but before I could get away from her she started telling me about their arrangement."

"I can't believe you didn't run."

"I tried! But I was wearing very high heels in those days. So anyway, Delia had met a man, and while Charles claimed to be fine with it, she knew he wasn't. She was trying to find someone for him, and she thought we would be great together. She offered me a ride in her town car, and when I declined, she gave me her card. She begged me to call her in the morning."

"And you did?" Eric asks, leaning forward like an excited kid at story time.

"Are you crazy? No! I threw it away after she was gone. But the very next night, I saw her and Charles in the audience. Just like her, he couldn't take his eyes off of me, and he actually yelled out when I died at the end. It was so sweet. They invited me out for drinks afterward, and I figured it couldn't hurt if they were buying."

"Girl after my own heart," Kevin says, taking a huge drink from the square tumbler he's been nursing.

"Of course, darling. Anyway, I won't lie; it was a little awkward at first. Charles was clearly still in love with Delia, but he seemed to like me all right. Delia practically pushed us together. She took him to see the show every night, and after each show she sent us out onto the town. She made the reservations, we showed up. The last night she arranged a private dinner at Tavern on the Green. It was the best meal I'd ever eaten in my life."

"I miss that place," I say, having only dined there once. Eric had insisted we go when he read it was closing. The food wasn't great, but the evening was still special. The Taven was steeped in New York history.

"Then I won't taint the memory of it by telling you what happened after dessert," Julia laughs. "By the time the production ended, Charles looked at me the same way he looked at Delia the night we met. He said he was star-struck, and he couldn't stand that he no longer had an excuse to see me every night, so he asked me to move in here. It sure beat the roach-infested closet I was living in. He sent flowers with a moving van, and after that, I knew he could handle me. I've been here ever since."

"He sent movers?"

"Yep, they were gorgeous, too. So hard to turn down."

"So you two are monogamous then?" Kevin asks.

"More or less. I mean we've had a few nights, one with Delia and her lover, Tim, and we've both had a few trysts. We have safety guidelines about any play on the side, but we don't really discuss extra lovers."

"Then how do you know he's had others?"

"Oh, there's something about being with someone else that makes you rediscover what you already have."

"I see," Eric says, shifting in his seat in a way that means he's uncomfortable.

"Don't worry darling. I'm happy with what I've got," I say, giving him another quick peck on the cheek.

Julia beams at us. "You two are adorable."

"You two are lucky," Kevin says, taking another deep drink.

"What exactly is that you're drinking?" Julia asks.

"A Caldwell Clan. My dad came up with the recipe after my mom forgot to re-stock the bar before going to visit her sister. He was too drunk to get to the liquor store, so he mixed the remnants of various rums with splashes of whiskey and gin. I like to throw in orange juice, but he drank it straight up."

"It looks pretty clear tonight," I say, eyeing his glass.

"Certainly clearer than when you tried it."

"You drank that?" Eric asks, seemingly shocked I hadn't told him.

"I tasted it after rehearsal one night. It's way too intense."

"Yeah, well, I needed something to come down from rehearsal," Kevin says.

"Why? What happened?" Eric asks.

"Oh, nothing, we performed for some investors, and it just got very intense." I shoot Julia and Kevin a glance trying to indicate not to talk about rehearsal.

"Mason and I have a little secret, Eric, and we can't tell you in mixed company. It'd ruin it for Kevin," Julia says, coming to my rescue.

"What?" Eric and Kevin say at the same time.

"Leading lady secrets," I say, covering my mouth and pretending to whisper into Julia's ear.

"No fair!" Kevin and Eric continue in unison.

"I believe a change in subject and a refill for Mason is in order," Julia says, grabbing the bottle off the table.

"I'm barely done with this glass."

"Nonsense, it is my duty to see you are wined, dined, and entertained! Kevin, I've already told my best story, I want one from you."

Eric takes a big swig and then turns to Kevin. "Mason says most of your stories are like bad porno films."

"I prefer to think of them as excellent porno films." Kevin winks.

"So, that's all your life is?"

"Eric!" I shoot him a look.

"No," Kevin says, laughing it off. "but I like to give an audience what they want. So, if you want something else, I'm happy to oblige. You choose the topic, I'll tell the story."

"Okay, well...did you become an actor because everyone thought you were hot?"

"Nope."

"Good. Tell us about that then."

"That I can do, and I'm happy to report, it's a sex-free zone!" he says, draining his glass, and emptying the rest of the wine bottle into his tumbler. "I was a jock in school. I wasn't captain of the football team, but I played just about everything. When football ended, I would shift to basketball, until baseball started, which I sometimes would quit early so I could help out the soccer team. It just depended on where Coach needed me. I wasn't great at any of them, but I was reliable. This of course meant I spent a lot of time in the locker room and showers."

"I thought this was supposed to be sex-free," I say, seeing Eric roll his eyes.

"It is. Stop imagining me naked, and listen, Kevin retorts. "Now where was I? Oh, right, I spent a lot of time with my teammates, but I didn't particularly like them. They were morons, and while I never made stellar grades, I had more to talk about than banging chicks, which I never did, and sports, which I played but never really cared about."

"Then why did you play?" asks Eric.

"If you'd ever met my dad you'd understand. It wasn't really a choice. My dad thought he was a superstar in high school, and as his only son, I was supposed to be just like him, whether I liked it or not."

"How? I mean did he…" I start.

"Beat me? Yes, but I'm getting ahead of myself. You see, the coach saw that report where the Dallas Cowboys got better if they did ballet, so he decided we were all going to do that, too. If we wanted to be first string, we had to enroll at Mrs. Moore's School for Dance. I didn't dare tell my father, but I got my dance shoes and tights, and showed up for class. To my surprise, most of my teammates were also there."

"Did they look as good as you did in tights?" I ask, unable to get the image of a seventeen year-old Kevin in a leotard out of my head.

"No, but few people do, and I not only looked good in them, I was awesome in them. Mrs. Moore took a liking to me almost instantly, which was great because she was kind of a monster to everyone else. She sounded like a Hungarian Harvey Fierstein. I think she had cigarettes for breakfast and lunch and a nice big cigar for dinner."

"How glamorous," Julia deadpans.

"In her own way, she kind of was. She'd been a Follies girl in the 1930's, but she left New York when she met her millionaire husband. They moved to Minneapolis, where she opened up her school."

"That *is* glamorous," Julia replies.

"Old world glamour, that was her. Anyway, after the off season was over, and football was going to start up again, the coach said we didn't have to take dance anymore. I was sad because I liked it, but I knew my dad would kill me if he found out. I couldn't handle sneaking around, since I was already very busy hiding being gay and hating sports, so I told Mrs. Moore I was done."

"Then what happened?" Eric asks. I'm a bit shocked that he's so interested.

"She slapped me in the face, and said I was a fool."

"No!" we all yell.

"Yes! She said it was my decision to throw my life away, but, she wanted me to go with her to see some real ballet before I gave it up for good. She told me to meet her downtown at the Orpheum that weekend. I told her I had a game that night, and she said if I was smart I'd quit playing with boys, and be a man."

"If they make a movie of your life story, I know who I want to play," says Julia.

"I'm pretty sure she'd insist on playing herself."

"She's still alive?"

"Oh yes, I hear she is still kicking kids around, though apparently she now whaps them with a cane."

"I definitely want to play her now," Julia says.

"So what did you do?" asks Eric, still interested.

"I went to the game."

"No way!" we all scream.

"I couldn't get away with skipping out. My dad went to every game. When I tried to see her again, she refused to see me. I went to her school every day, for months, but she wouldn't even acknowledge me. Finally I stopped trying, but I couldn't get over how much I missed performing."

"You mean you missed boys in tights," I say, assuming Kevin is probably leaving out a few stories where he seduced some of the ballet boys.

"A little of column A, a little of column B. Anyway, that spring, instead of baseball, I auditioned for the school musical. They posted the cast list the same day my dad found my ballet gear in my room."

"What happened then?" asks Eric.

"I got the lead role and three broken ribs within about an hour of each other. I told him I hated sports, and that I loved ballet. When he called me a faggot, I told him that was exactly what I was. He beat the shit out of me."

Julia clasps her hands together. "Where was your mother?"

"Gone. She was seeing some guy on the side, who she, thankfully, married after divorcing my dad. She actually already had the papers drawn up. When she came to see me in the hospital she handed them to him right there. She remarried that summer. By fall, we'd moved away and I'd transferred to a performing arts magnet school."

"What happened to your dad?" I ask, shocked that Kevin had ever had anything so terrible happen to him.

"Nothing, really. He was the same asshole he ever was, drank himself half to death, and had a heart attack."

"I'm so sorry," I say, having to fight the urge to take his hand.

"Don't be. My mom and Paul, that's my step-dad, are great. He was the one who put me through college and sent me to New York." Kevin turns and looks at Eric. "So, that's how I became an actor. It's my least sexy story."

"I think it might be your best."

"You should reserve judgment till you've heard some of my others."

"I'll consider it."

"So did Mrs. Moore ever speak to you again?" Julia asks, the idea of playing her clearly still in her head.

"Speak? No, but she does respond to my letters. Of course, they have to be written by hand."

"How Dickensian of her. I hope I'll be like that in my old age, eccentric but in a sort of noble, frozen in time kind of way," Julia says, looking off in the distance. I chuckle at the idea. Julia would be a fabulous modern day Mrs. Havisham.

"What's so funny?" Alex asks, sitting down next to Kevin.

"Oh, hi Alex."

"Hey," he replies, his nasal voice hanging too long on the "e" vowel.

"You're Alex?" Eric asks.

"Pretty sure that's been established. What, are you slow?"

"He's as charming as you said," Eric says, giving me a kiss.

"Alex this is Eric, my boyfriend."

"You have a boyfriend?"

"Don't pretend like this is news!" Julia says, slapping Alex on the wrist. "He talks about Eric constantly!"

"Well, you know, understudies rarely get to spend quality time with the leads," Alex backpedals, rubbing the spot Julia smacked.

"So true, but I'm happy to answer any questions you've got. I know it might be hard to see everything from the wings." I say, reveling in the chance to rub Alex's face in my success.

"I see more than you might think," Alex replies, shooting a glance at Kevin.

"Okay, well, I'd love to chat more, but unfortunately I think we need to get going. I've got a delightful training session in the morning, and it is going to take us forever to get home."

"So soon? Bummer!" Alex says, snuggling up to Kevin.

"Do you need us to get you a car?" Julia asks, making me question the last time she took the subway.

"No, we'll be fine. Thank you so much. I'm so glad to have a face to put to the name," Eric says, squeezing her hand.

"Likewise. I'll make sure Mason behaves in rehearsal, so don't worry."

"You promise?"

"Leading lady's honor," Julia replies, clutching her fist to the center of her cleavage.

"Oh brother," Alex quips.

"You guys headed back to the East Village?" Kevin asks.

"Yes."

"Mind if I come with you? I promised some friends I'd meet them there. Their show should be ending now, so I might actually be on time for once."

"You're leaving me all alone?" Julia pouts.

"Excuse me!" Alex balks.

"Sorry darling,"

"Oh Julia, we need you to entertain the ensemble. Clearly, nothing is more dangerous than an understudy with too much time," I say, nodding toward Alex.

"Fine. Just remember me when you win a Tony. I expect a special thanks and at least half of the swag from the gift bags."

"I'll make sure all my Chanel goes to you," Kevin says, giving her a kiss on each cheek.

"Without Julia, I'm lost, thanks for everything," I say, pretending to clutch my Tony.

"That will do, boys. Now go have fun. A diva's work is never done."

"I'll meet you guys at the elevator, I need to grab my pack," Kevin says, before practically sprinting toward the bar.

"So that Alex guy is the understudy?" Eric asks, looking over his shoulder.

"Ugh, yes. He's the worst."

"But you do realize he looks like you, right?" Eric asks, still looking at him.

"Yes, though at least now I'm the thinner one."

"True, but…he kind of looks like the you I'm used to."

"Please don't tell me you have a crush on him."

"What?" Eric asks, finally turning to look at me. "Of course not, but if you could mute him…well…no, not even then."

"Good, besides, I thought you hated actors. Except for me, though I gather Julia is a new exception?"

"I can't believe you never talk about her." I've never seen him so enamored with another cast member. He generally finds actors, especially loud boozy ones like Julia, really annoying. Though I guess, standing next to Alex she seems more refined.

"I don't really see her off stage that much."

"It's true. Whenever he's not with her, he's with me," Kevin confirms, re-appearing with his pack in hand.

"Do you even know the names of the rest of cast?" I ask Kevin, as we get on the elevator.

"Not really, Merchant confuses me by calling people their real name half the time, and their character name the rest. So I have no clue. I guess I'll just wait till I see the program, and match their names to their headshots."

"I've always wondered if leads did that to me. Once a show was up, they always knew my name."

"Well, that won't work this time," Eric says, chiming in just like the elevator, when the doors open.

"What?" I ask, as we head into the street. Having been so remarkably warm on Julia's roof I forgot how cold it was. I quickly button all the buttons on my coat.

"Mason, your headshot basically looks like a 'before' of a 'before and after' shoot now."

"He's right." Kevin confirms, throwing a long arm over each of us as we make our way our way to the subway. "Seriously, you should do something about that before the show starts."

"Oh, I never really thought about it, but I guess so."

"How about tonight? One of the guys I'm meeting has his own studio, he's an absolute genius, and he takes booze as payment."

"I don't know…"

"Come on, you're barely going to get any sleep as it is. Come out with me, let's party like fucking rock stars."

"No, not tonight. Besides, all the liquor stores are closed," I say. Eric exhales deeply as if he's been holding his breath.

"That's why I grabbed these from the party!" Kevin says, reaching into his pack and then presenting an expensive-looking bottle of scotch and another bottle of the wine we'd been drinking.

"Kevin! Take those back right now!"

"Why? Those investors didn't respect what they were drinking tonight. To them, this stuff is standard, but in our world, it's exceptional. It's currency. Let's use these gifts to make some serious art tonight."

"Well…," I can hear my resolve breaking. The idea of a free photoshoot, especially since I dressed to show off how much progress I've made, is hard to turn down. Plus, it just sounds fun. Crazy, but fun. I've been working so hard, I feel like I deserve a little adventure.

"You can't seriously be considering this," Eric says. I can't believe the judgment in his voice.

"Why not?" I ask, as I swipe my Metrocard and walk through the turnstile.

"Where do I even begin? You really think it's a good idea to show up to your trainer's house, who the director is paying for, after a night of partying? Plus, I thought we had plans."

"You're right. Sorry. Of course, it's just…I thought it might be fun. Maybe we could just go for a little while."

"Mason, I barely have enough time as it is. I should be at the office with everyone else, but I rearranged my schedule to be with you."

"I know. You're right. Sorry Kevin, but I just can't."

"It's cool. I'll text you where we end up. Just in case you want to join us later. Are you taking the M train?"

"No, we need the F," replies Eric, though honestly either would work.

"Ah, well I guess this is it then." Kevin says, as an F train pulls into the station.

"See you tomorrow," I say, waving goodbye.

"Yeah, tomorrow." Kevin grabs me and pulls me into a hug. He kisses me briefly before letting go. I barely make it into the car before the doors close.

"You two seem…close," Eric says, once the strain starts to move. He continues to stand after I've taken a seat, which seems odd, as there are only a few people on the train.

"We're old friends."

"Old friends who kiss?"

"Well, we kiss on stage a lot. Why, are you jealous?" I tease, finding the notion both flattering and hilarious. Eric doesn't seem to think it's a laughing matter, though.

"Should I be?"

"What? Wait, you're not serious are you? That's about as likely as you having a crush on Alex."

"No, it's different. I mean, every time I see him he's got his hands all over you. And the way he looks at you, it's just…wrong."

"Eric, it's just the play. Kevin barely even hugged me until the day I auditioned. It's something we've had to work on."

"I bet you must hate that," Eric replies, shuddering in disgust.

"Actually, I kind of do. It's been so long since I kissed anyone but you, I'd forgotten how good you were at it." I stand up and try to kiss him, but he doesn't kiss back. "Eric?"

"I'm sorry, but knowing he's been slobbering all over you isn't exactly enticing. I know it's stupid to be jealous, but Kevin has this…this…" Eric stalls, searching for the right word. "This effect on you. He always has. I mean, when we met, you were so in love with him. You didn't even see how much I wanted you until he was off in L.A., and even then it took months."

Eric and I started living together when I decided to purge my obsession with Kevin from my system. I remember when he texted to tell me he was moving California. Eric came home to find me drunk, singing

"We Do Not Belong Together" from *Sunday in the Park with George* on a loop. He stayed up with me till dawn that night, holding me as I cried, making me play video games to forget, even for just a few minutes. For weeks he helped me remember that there was more to this world than Kevin Caldwell, and finally, one day, I just woke up and realized how lucky I was to have Eric in my life. He loved me at my absolute worst, in a way no one else in my life, even my parents, ever had. That morning, when I first said "I love you, too" was a big one for us. We instantly went from friends to lovers.

The train takes a sharp curve, and I clutch Eric tight to me. "I wasn't in love with him, it was a crush. I love you."

"I love you too, but—"

"But?" I repeat, unable to believe that he is qualifying this.

"But this production is changing you. Kevin is changing you. You barely look like yourself anymore. You look like him, and now you're starting to act like him, too."

"Why? Because I want to have some fun?"

"Because you'd rather have fun with him than be with me! I've killed myself for the past week to spend this night with you, and you were willing to throw it away. How do you think that makes me feel?"

"You're blowing this out of proportion. I considered it for a second, but you just assumed I would say yes. How do you think that feels? Do you really think I'd be so selfish? That my love for you is somehow less than your love for me? If Kevin had friends who worked at Sony, and had a prototype of a new game system, would you have still wanted to go home with me? Can you honestly tell me you wouldn't have spent a few seconds pondering that offer?"

"That's not the same thing. Kevin and I don't have a history together."

"Why does that matter? The fact that you'd be tempted, without the history, proves my point."

"You know what? Fine," Eric says, as the train comes to a stop once more. "You're right, Mason. So why don't you just go and play with Kevin? It's clearly what you'd rather be doing. I need to get back to the office anyway." He turns and exits the train. Before I can think to follow him, the doors close and we speed away.

Trapped, I pace back and forth, ignoring the stares of the few other passengers in the car. I can only imagine what they must have been thinking, watching us fight that way. I exit the train at the next stop and run up to the surface. I start to backtrack to the previous stop, but about halfway there, I stop in my tracks. Vicious words swirl about my head, so vehemently, that I worry they might actually appear on my face like a tattoo. That I'd considered saying them for even a second makes me worry that Eric might be right; maybe I am starting to be more like Kevin. I take a sharp turn, heading north toward the stop where Eric bolted, but after a few blocks I turn and walk back the other direction. I feel lost. Tonight wasn't supposed to turn out like this. I've never seen Eric like this before, he's never been the jealous type, and the worst part of me why that is. Was it because he never thought anyone else would want me? That's not true, I know that, but much like the voices that told me I was too fat or too stupid to succeed as an actor, it's hard to silence the thought once I've had it.

I wander aimlessly, further and further away from our apartment, afraid that Eric will be waiting for me there, and that I'll say something I'll regret. I consider texting Kevin, but I don't. If Eric is right about anything, it's that I've got to be clearer about our boundaries. After an hour or so I realize I'm en route to Lycan's home. It makes sense, considering how many times I've run there over the past few weeks. My only hope now is that Lycan will be as wise about my heart as he is about the rest of my body.

FOURTEEN

I ARRIVE AT LYCAN'S HOME WELL before dawn. There don't appear to be any signs of life, and I tell myself I need to wait until the hour is decent before knocking. With my pack still at home, I have nothing but my slowly dying cellphone to keep me occupied. I set it to silent mode before the party, so I expect to once again have missed calls and text messages from Eric, but this time there's nothing. I scan through the texts from the past few weeks until I find the memory of how excited we were the last time this occurred, which makes me realize just how much has changed in such a short time. Back then, the biggest fight we'd ever had was about who had to get up from the couch to get the we'd ordered. I consider hopping into a cab to make my way home, but I know that there isn't enough time to have a real conversation and I don't even know if he'll be home. Still, I know I should say something, so I text him.

"I love you. I'm at Lycan's. Be home later."

He doesn't respond, so I decide to sit on the steps and rest my head against the door. The biting cold of night has crept into my bones. I long for Eric's unnaturally hot hands to hold me, but that just makes me sad all over again. I focus on my breathing and try to clear my mind. Eventually, I go into a trance, and my brain seems to shut off completely. At some point I hear a sound, coming from behind, but before I can react, I experience the all too familiar feeling of falling across Lycan's threshold.

"Mr. Burroughs? What are you doing here at this hour?" Lycan asks, extending a hand to help me up.

"Umm...well..."

"I appreciate you wanting to be early, but, considering you even beat the paper boy, this borders on being more problematic than productive."

"I just didn't have anywhere else to go," I admit, and something about saying it out loud causes me to burst into tears.

Without a word, Lycan ushers me into his parlor, sits me down, and vanishes disappears into the next room. I try to pull myself together, to tell myself that this is not how a professional actor should behave, but just as soon as I am about to stop crying, it starts all over again, only louder and wetter than before.

"Drink this, it'll make you feel better," Lycan says, returning with a hot mug of something.

"What is it?"

"Trust me, you'd rather not know. Just drink." Knowing Lycan, he's probably right, but I still sniff to try and prepare my taste buds for what is to come. I get nothing, but I'm not sure if the reason is lack of scent or the fact that my nose has clogged up from all the crying. Lycan looks at me expectantly, so I drink. The taste is an unpleasant pairing of vinegar and honey, which takes effort to swallow, but as the warm liquid trickles down my throat, I begin to feel pleasantly buzzed. Suddenly I want more, and before I know it I'm barely stopping to breathe, as I drain the cup down to the dregs.

"Is there more?"

"I think you've had enough. Drink some water. It'll help with the thirst."

My mouth feels funny, and I'm suddenly aware that I can't stop smiling. It reminds me of the time I had laughing gas before I got my wisdom teeth out.

"What's happening?" I ask, more curious than afraid.

"Don't worry, the effect only lasts a few minutes. Just enjoy it. You're fine. I'm right here and I'm not going anywhere."

"Okay."

"So by the looks of you, can I assume you haven't slept?"

"No, but I'm not tired."

"Good to hear, but you will be by the time your appointment should actually begin. So I guess we'll move it up to now. Through that door you'll find some clothes in a chest. I'm sure something in there will fit. Once you've changed, please meet me in the garden and you can begin going through the Sthira Bhagah," he says, referring to the series of yoga poses I've been doing with him. The idea of contorting my body should be unpleasant, but for some reason it sounds really good to me.

Once I step inside the room, I notice something is strange about it. Unlike the rest of the house, where every surface is covered with ancient relics or mementos of his many adventures, this place is almost completely bare. The only items in the room are a bed and an old cedar chest. It feels almost too empty, as if, by opening the door, I've ruined something that was being held in mint condition. Taking as few steps inside as possible, I quickly strip off clothes, tossing them to the floor. However, I then think better of it, and decide they should be folded neatly in a pile, because I worry that any chaotic mess might interrupt the strange energy of the room. Opening the chest, I find there are plenty of perfectly folded shirts and shorts. I think back to when I met Lycan, about how he got his scar, and wonder if these clothes might belong to his partner. I feel uncomfortable about removing them from their place, like wearing the clothes of a dead person. I keep imagining that scene from Indiana Jones where he takes the idol and unwittingly unleashes a giant bolder. Whatever was in that drink seems to have made me slightly silly. To steady myself, I close my eyes and take a big breath. However, it doesn't seem to work. The euphoric effects of the drink seem to kick into overdrive, because I decide that shorts and shirts are for losers. I walk into the garden clad only in my boxer briefs.

"That should certainly allow you to move freely," Lycan says. His eyes take in my body, and he seems proud of what he has helped me accomplish so far. "Please, begin."

The garden area is surrounded by bricks on all sides, but the glass roof makes it feel like we're outside. Usually, the space feels a little claustrophobic. Particularly because Lycan is always hovering over me so he can make tiny adjustments as I shift from pose to pose. However, today everything feels easy and bright. I feel a real sense of calm and control that I've never had before. I'm no longer forcing my body to do something, instead I am working with it to achieve the goals that Lycan has set for us.

"So, why were you early?" Lycan asks, tilting my chin ever-so-slightly to fix my posture.

"Eric and I got in a huge fight about Kevin and headshots on the subway. It got so bad that he ducked out, leaving me on the train," I say, sharing a little more than I would have normally.

"What was the issue?"

"Kevin wanted to get his friend to take headshots of me tonight, but Eric said I needed to sleep. You know, because I had to be here in the morning. He said I was choosing Kevin over him."

"Did you want to go with Kevin?"

"I didn't even say that! I just considered it, and Eric got all mad."

"Well, did you?"

Talking while holding these poses is exhausting, and I breathe heavy to consider his question. Why was I so interested in going with Kevin? "I did."

"Why?"

"Because he was right, I don't look like I used to, but for some reason I couldn't see it until he pointed it out. Honestly, this is all really new to me. I'm not used to liking how I look, so I wanted to document while that feeling was in me. Because, I don't know how long it will last." The answer falls so easily from my mouth, it's like I was given the question ahead of time.

"I think it's time we moved outside," is Lycan's only response.

"We are outside."

"No, we're in my garden."

"Oh…Right." I follow him back into the house. Just before I reach the front door, Lycan grabs my shoulder and pulls me back.

"Mr. Burroughs, while I've no issue with your attire within the confines of my home, I have neighbors who might find it slightly scandalous. In addition, I am responsible for making sure your body is in peak condition, and it's the middle of December, so I'm going to have to insist you put on some more clothes."

"I don't have any."

"I told you, they're in the chest."

I take a step, but stop again. I don't want to go back into that strange room. "It's just that…the clothes in there…whose are they?"

"Mine. Why?"

"I just thought they might be his." I worry that, since I've never seen Lycan's partner around, this might be a sore subject.

"Whose?"

"Your lover. The guy you went climbing with? You know, when you had your accident."

"Jake? He and I weren't lovers."

"Oh. Sorry. It's just…I call Eric my partner, and the room just looked so…preserved," I attempt to explain.

"It's not preserved, it's new. I just finished having it remodeled."

"I'm such an idiot."

"No, an idiot is one who insists on being blind to his own mistakes instead of learning from them. You, are not that. Or, at least, you won't be if you go get dressed."

"Oh! Right, sorry," I say, quickly walking back toward the room. I hope Lycan will chalk my behavior up to a combination of exhaustion and the effects of the drink he served me.

The second I put on clothes, the spell I've been under breaks, and I feel myself crashing from the high I've been riding. The lightweight thermal shirt I'm wearing feels like a suit of armor, weighing me down. I'm acutely aware that I haven't slept in hours, and I feel a wine-induced hangover coming on. There is no more chatter, as Lycan has me run circles around his block, changing my stride and posture to vary which muscles are being taxed the most. All I can think of now is how to keep going without vomiting in the process. Lycan is clearly aware of just how difficult this is, but while he continues to be encouraging, he never lets up.

"Good, now I want a lap on your toes, run like you've got stiletto heels on," he commands, but before I can even get around the corner, I know I've lost the battle. Without deciding to, I stop moving. For a second my legs cease shaking, but then they give completely. I fall onto my knees, then forward, putting my hands out in front of me to catch myself and scraping them across the rough asphalt in the process. I end up on all fours, like a dog. Then the drinks from last night make their return appearance, up and all over the sidewalk. The taste of Lycan's potion mixed with wine causes me to gag and choke, until everything in my entire digestive track is evacuated. My abs cry out in agony after each wave, since they were already exhausted by the Sthira Bhagah; and I worry I might pass out from the pain.

"I know it's hard, but just try to breathe. Honestly, I'm impressed you made it this long," Lycan says, applying something cool and damp to the back of my neck.

"I think I'm okay now."

"Let's get you inside and clean you up," Lycan says. Throwing my arm across his shoulders, he helps me to my feet.

Lycan deposits me in the bathroom. Like the rest of his home, it's immaculate, and spacious in a way that makes you question whether or not it could actually exist within the confines of the house. Vatican-quality mosaic tile is cover the walls, depicting mountains and streams all around. The images are so vivid that it gives the illusion that the marble bathtub in the middle of the room is actually in some mythic wonderland. The antique bronze handles turn at the lightest touch, making the experience even more luxurious, and water flows into the deep marble basin from the mouth of a spigot shaped like a lion's head. It's been years since I took a bath. After a little tinkering to get the water just right, I lower myself in. As the water rises around me, the sensation of weightlessness does wonder for relieving my pain. Part of me want to stay here forever, and never leave, like a hero after a quest. At the same time, though, I know I'm far from done, and we've only got three weeks remaining to our first preview performance.

Thinking about the future reminds me that I'm due at the rehearsal space this afternoon. With my workout completed, the main thing I need now is sleep, though I worry whether or not I'll be able to fall asleep, considering how I left things with Eric. I borrow Lycan's robe to make my way to the guestroom where I left my clothes. I get lost in the twists and turns, and end up having to up one flight of stairs in order to reach another that descends near the parlor. Unsure where Lycan is, especially since I seem to have walked through most of the house, I jump when the front door opens and he walks in.

"Sorry, didn't mean to scare you." Lycan is the only person to have ever taken my disdain for surprises to heart.

"No, I'm sorry, for everything. Thank you for...for...everything." I say, feeling embarrassed by my inability to express myself better than this.

"My pleasure. Now, I'm afraid the heat from the subway might cause you to collapse again, so I've arranged a car for you. It will take you wherever you want to go."

"Oh, I don't have any cash on me."

"It will be billed to Mr. Merchant, so don't worry. Do you have everything?"

"I think so. I'll return the clothes I borrowed once I do laundry."

"Don't worry about that for now. They're just clothes. If they are meant to be mine you'll return them eventually. Focus on your training, and I'll see you at our next appointment."

"Yes. Thanks," I say, but after I've stepped outside, I turn around. "Lycan, can I ask you something?"

"Of course."

"What am I going to say when I get home?"

"Even the sturdiest of ships can bend and break in a storm. In that moment, repairs are quick and crudely made, but they ensure the journey can continue. When the seas are calmer, the crew works together to reinforce her hull, to see that she will not break again. They devote their time to refine and restore what they once had, but the new wood can take years to blend in with the rest," Lycan replies, and while I ponder what he means, he shuts the door.

I think about his words the entire ride home, and wonder what quick and crude repair I can make, but nothing comes to mind. Aware I have so little time, I walk into our apartment without a plan, armed only with a prayer that the words will come to me.

The apartment is spotless, which tells me I'm in real trouble. Eric only cleans when he's upset. From the gleam on the hardwood floors, I'm not sure any apology is going to work.

"You're home," Eric says, walking in from the bathroom. He's wearing yellow rubber gloves and holding a bottle of bleach.

"The apartment looks really nice," I offer, hoping his reaction to the compliment will give me a clue how to approach him.

"Yeah well, despite being up for the past thirty-six hours, I couldn't sleep for some reason," he says, walking in an arc just to avoid me, to replace the cleaning products under the sink. After slamming the cabinet door, he looks at me for second, opens his mouth, but then stops before speaking. Instead, he looks down and dabs a sponge at some tiny fleck on the gleaming counter top.

"I'm sorry."

"I bet."

"No, I'm really sorry. I know that sounds lame, but just look at me," I say, and to my surprise Eric does actually look up, but it's not in a good way. I imagine that if this were one of the games he designs, he'd be able to actually kill me with the stare he's giving me. "You're mad, and you deserve to be. It was really insensitive of me to even consider going with Kevin after everything you'd done. I don't want to make excuses."

"Because you know there isn't a good one?"

"Because I've been trying to think of something to say that's better than that, something that lets you know how sorry I am."

"Mason, I believe you're sorry. Being sorry is good, it lets me know you haven't changed completely, but the Mason I know wouldn't have even considered going off with him like that. Whenever you're around him, you're like this different person. Not the person I love."

"I know. It's just difficult. I mean, he makes me a better actor."

"You've got to stop attributing all your success to other people."

"I'm not! Eric, I know you don't like him, but Kevin is helping me. I've learned so much from him. Without him, Merchant would have fired me." I wonder if saying even this much breaks Merchant's rule, but then I think of what Lycan said, and hope that this is a quick and crude path to repairing things. Maybe if I can let him know something of the pressure I'm under, he will understand.

"Why would he have done that?"

"I just wasn't doing well in rehearsal, and when he put Kevin next to me, it was obvious how outclassed I was. I couldn't even tell who was more frustrated, me or Merchant, but Kevin talked me through it, and…I don't know. Something just clicked. I wouldn't even be in the show anymore if it wasn't for him."

Eric runs his hands through his hair, and lets out a long sigh of frustration, but when he looks at me, the anger in his eyes is gone. "Why didn't you tell me things had gotten so bad? Is that the reason you wouldn't talk about rehearsal?"

"Honestly, I didn't want to face it, but Kevin made me, and he helped talk me through it. I owe him a lot for that."

"Look, I'll agree things are definitely different," Eric says, leaning back against the stove.

"But nothing is different between us," I say, hoping I'll be able to patch this hole with the answer my brain has finally constructed.

"Yes it is. Mason, I—"

"Just let me finish. Look, I have changed in a lot of ways, but I can't change how much I love you. Nothing can. You remind me which parts of me are worth preserving. Things that, even if I could change, I never should. You're my beacon, Eric. It's probably unfair for me to call you that, but it's what you are. You give me so much, and I'll never be able to repay you in kind, but that's why this show is so important. I want to become a person who can give you, what you give me."

Eric smiles, small at first, but then he breaks out into a big goofy grin and pulls me into a tight hug. "I guess you finally found something to say."

"Clearly, I needed to be closer to my inspiration," I reply, and we both let out a tension- relieving laugh, not because it's funny, but because laughing together lets us know we can continue on with our journey.

FIFTEEN

"WE HAVE AN ENDING!" MERCHANT trumpets, striding into the rehearsal with pages in hand. A large black man follows him, pushing a cart with new scripts which he begins passing out. Given that this job is usually Jenna's, I scan the room for her, only to realize she's not here. In fact, I haven't seen her all morning. Merchant crosses to a whiteboard and begins writing out character names, drawing a complex web of lines as he continues to speak. "Colin and I discussed it, and we've decided that neither of his original endings were right."

"Why not?" Marshall asks, prompting Merchant like a good lackey.

"It was the performance of our two leads. The passion between you two changed his mind. I hoped it would, but I didn't expect Colin to be so inspired that he'd rewrite the ending in a single night."

"So who do I end up with? I'm dying to know!" I say, looking at both Kevin and Julia.

"Dying is exactly what you do."

"I die?" I exclaim, not having meant it literally.

"Yes, at the hand of Marshall!" Merchant draws a line connecting our names.

"Me?" Marshall says, looking similarly shocked.

"Yes, it would appear that there is more to our Lord Dyne than we ever knew. Your entire motivation for getting Caleb and Ezio has been changed. You are now the hidden leader of the conspirators. Colin has added a series of tiny moments showing you tug at strings from the shadows as a brilliant puppet master."

"And what about me?" Kevin asks, looking uncharacteristically ill at ease.

"Ah, our Ezio. Colin and I argued the most over you. In the current draft, the audience didn't really know whether or not they wanted you to succeed in seducing Caleb. Your blinding obsession over Caleb was coming across as more creepy than romantic, and this created a problem, because when you two got together, they didn't know how to feel about how much they liked it. So we've changed some things around, with Dyne creating roadblocks, forcing you to flex your power to keep Caleb at your side. With the blame more on Dyne, you will be seen as loving instead of devious."

"And what becomes of poor Mina?" Julia asks, as she quickly flips through the script looking for her scenes.

"Mina! Well, you are sadly manipulated more than anyone. Colin hasn't finished all of your scenes. I had to practically rip these pages out of his hands, but I assure you, the audience will pity you almost as much as Caleb."

"Yeah, about that. I die now?" I ask, still looking for clarification.

"Yes. In a noble sacrifice, you stop Dyne from killing Ezio, and both of your lovers surround you while you deliver this glorious monologue. He seemed almost possessed as he wrote it, talking to himself, ranting. He couldn't seem to get the words on the page fast enough."

"Is he all right?" I ask, knowing all too well how exhausting bursts of creativity like that can be. Colin is so frail and old, I worry that the kind of exertion Merchant is describing might be too much for him to handle.

"Yes, I gave him a brandy to calm him down and he promptly passed out. Don't worry though, I've left Jenna to look after him," Merchant explains, finally making her absence make sense.

"So, where do we begin?" Marshall asks, looking utterly delighted by the changes in the script. I feel the tiniest twinge of jealousy for Marshall. To have the lackey role elevated in such a way is something I always dreamed of. I would have been thrilled by the chance to push myself, while still keeping my toes in familiar waters. Dyne is still a lackey, but now he has razor sharp teeth.

"I can only work on what we have so far, and that mainly involves Kevin and Marshall, but the opening scene now includes all of you, so I'd like us to start with working through that," Merchant says, pacing around the room with a type of nervous energy I never knew he had. It's strange to see how frantically he works when he isn't ten moves ahead. The lightning-quick pace really demonstrates just how much of a genius he really is.

"Can we get a moment to review the changes?" Kevin asks, in an uncharacteristically strained voice.

"Of course, Mr. Caldwell, of course, but today is just about adjusting the blocking. None of you should worry about acting. Don't even commit this to memory; Colin will probably change it all around by tomorrow. Today, I just want us to explore what we've been given. Once you've read through the scene, please walk on stage."

Reviewing the script is pretty easy for me. I have the same opening line, and the changes are minor. I'm the first to walk onto the stage, and Julia is only a few seconds behind me. Marshall and Kevin, however, have been given several pages of new dialogue. After Marshall joins us I look up to see what's taking Kevin so long. He keeps flipping the page over to scratch notes on the back, the lines in his furrowed brow getting deeper by the minute. In class, Kevin gave cold readings with such ease that seeing him process these revisions with this kind of intensity is unsettling. When he looks up at me, I smile encouragingly, but it seems to make things worse. Instead of smiling back, he stands up, whispers something in Merchant's ear, and leaves the room. Merchant doesn't move at first, but after a few seconds he nods to the large black man who is standing in for Jenna.

"Fifteen minute break. Be back at 1:12," the man announces. Although I've been doing nothing for the past thirty minutes, the anticipation of the moment has drained me. I quickly make my way to the break room for coffee.

I'm alone for a few minutes before Kevin comes in and pours most of the pot into a travel thermos. Given the change in supply, I decide to forgo the second cup I was considering. He seems to need it more than I do.

"Quite a change," I say, stating the obvious as he sits down across the table from me.

"It's a fucking disaster," he says, pulling a flask from his bag and pouring a capful of clear liquid into his thermos.

"Are you okay?"

"Of course not! I've been working with Colin on this script for a year, and Merchant comes in and fucking neuters my part."

"Because they gave Dyne something to do?"

"Because they gave him my power! Without that, Ezio's just some spoiled brat."

"He was always spoiled."

"Yeah, but now that's all he is. Ezio was a conqueror. He knew how to get what he wanted. It's why he's so good at seducing you."

"But you weren't likable."

"Well, maybe I don't care about being likable. I'd rather be ruthless than stupid!" he slams his thermos onto the table.

I look at Kevin, never having seen him lose his cool like this. His breath is ragged, and I'm not really sure how to handle this. "Maybe you should talk to Merchant?"

"Oh, I will," he says. "This is not what I signed up for." He stands so quickly the chair falls over. When he glares at it, his expression shocks me. It's the same horrifying mask from all those years ago.

"I'll get it," I say, but don't, because he suddenly turns and leaves the room. I hurry after him. He doesn't make following him easy. All the hallways in the rehearsal space look the same, but having had a lot of practice in finding him, I manage to keep up without him noticing. I panic when he reaches a dead end, but instead of turning around he starts pounding on one of the doors with his fist. His fury seems to almost visibly swirl around him. When no one opens it, he starts to turn back toward me, so I slip into an empty practice studio and hide behind the door.

I peek into the hall through the small gap between the hinge and door. A set of sharp knocks tap out on a door nearby, followed by some murmuring and then silence. Assuming Kevin must have gone into the other room, I'm about to step from my hiding place when he and

Merchant storm past the door and into the room. I panic, unsure if I should make my presence known, but when I hear the anger in Kevin's voice, I don't dare.

"What in the hell do you think you're doing?" he demands. I'm shocked to hear him speak to Merchant this way.

"Mr. Caldwell, you were hired to do a job."

"I was hired to play the role Colin wrote for me, not this trash you put him up to. I told you, I'm not interested in playing another stupid, pretty boy."

"Then stop acting like one."

"I will when you give me something else to work with. You promised me a part that was going to make me. You owe me." At that, I can't stop myself from taking a peek around the edge of the door. I try to keep myself hidden, but their eyes are locked onto one another so intensely, I doubt they would notice if I was standing next to them.

Merchant is not fazed by this at all, and his expression remains stoic. "I don't owe you anything. However, I will consider speaking to Colin about your complaints if you stop this pathetic whining. Otherwise, I'll have to start finding a replacement, and I don't think either of us wants that."

Having been terrified of being replaced, I can't believe that Kevin isn't remotely fazed by Merchant. Instead of shrinking back, he cackles with laughter. "I'd love to see you try," he says, the look on his face as sinister as his tone. "If I'm going down, I'll take you and the show with me."

"What do you mean by that?"

"You've got to be kidding! What do you think will happen if I told everyone about your little private sessions?"

"You chose to attend those. I offered you my services as a tutor free of charge."

"Tutors don't normally strip their students. Think what the press will say about that."

"Mr. Caldwell, I knew the risk I was taking. I'm fully prepared for you to walk out and tell the world. So by all means do it, tell everyone how I humiliated you, objectified you, say whatever you like. Everything I've done is to make this show a masterpiece. So when it succeeds without you, the only thing people will think about you is that you are difficult to work with. Divas don't work on Broadway. Actors do."

"If the script isn't fixed by tomorrow, I'm walking," Kevin says, heading for the door, forcing me to duck back behind it.

"The story depends on people wanting you to succeed. No one will do that if you're a tyrant," Merchant says.

"They will if love is his weakness."

"Then you'd better show me it can be yours," Merchant says, followed by squeak of Kevin's shoes on the cement floor, as he abruptly halts.

"What?"

"Mason gave you everything to crumble, and yet you still wanted more. You will break him if you keep that up. If you want Ezio to keep his power, you have to be willing to give it up. You have to be willing to lose this fight."

"Fine, but don't call me back until you've got the scenes revised," Kevin says. I fight to hold in a gasp as he goes past, exiting the room.

For a few minutes, I don't hear Merchant at all. It's so quiet, I'm sure he will hear me breathing, and discover me, hiding behind the door. That thought, plus the reality of Kevin's threat, is enough cause me to panic, and again I start to feel like I'm not getting enough oxygen. I try my best to take deep silent breaths. I feel utterly powerless. Doomed. The room begins to feel like it's closing in on itself, but then I hear a knock on the other side of the door. I shrink back and bump into the wall behind me. I put my hands over my mouth to stop from crying out in pain.

A long shadow extends onto the floor. "Mr. Merchant, Colin is demanding to speak with you." It's Jenna, seemingly back from babysitting Colin.

"Good, I need to speak with him anyway. Let the actors have an hour's break, and tell Alex he'll be standing in for Kevin this afternoon," Merchant instructs. They exit, but I wait several minutes before moving at all. It isn't until I hear the clatter of the punchbar being hit on the door at the end of the hall, that I finally wedge myself out from behind the door. My legs shake so badly, that I collapse onto the floor. I take deep breaths, trying to calm myself down and make sense of what on earth I just witnessed.

SIXTEEN

ERCHANT CANCELED OUR MORNING SESSION, but I expected that. Yesterday's rehearsal with Alex was a complete and total disaster. Without Kevin, I couldn't manage to bring Caleb to life, but no one even noticed; we were all too busy watching Alex, whose version of Ezio was so bad it was comical. Unlike Kevin, who portrayed him as dark and brooding, Alex's version of the Ezio was vapid and effeminate. It so closely matched what Kevin warned Merchant about, that I wondered if Kevin told him to do it that way. When we got to the scenes where I had to kiss him, it got even worse. Unlike Kevin or Eric, Alex seemed to believe passionate kissing involved licking his partner like a dog. Whenever we'd stop, I'd get the towel from my pack to dry my face off. Disgusted, Merchant dismissed us early, canceling rehearsal for this morning as well.

After my morning session with Lycan I have a few hours to kill before I'm due at the theatre. It's the first moment in ages where I've had a chance to catch my breath, but it's hard to enjoy. The show has been my entire life for the past few weeks, but now it feels broken. I fear what another day of acting with Alex will be like, not just because he's terrible, but because I couldn't seem to find Caleb with him as Ezio. I doubt Kevin ever let having Alex as a scene partner distract him from his work, and neither should I, but I'm not sure how to do it. Kevin and I have history, and my old feelings for him are part of what gives Caleb life. Without him, I'm not even sure how to begin, but I resolve to find out. If anything,

I've learned that a true actor can't rely on anyone but himself on stage.

When I press the buzzer to be let in, no one buzzes back. Considering I'm over an hour early, I'm not surprised, however I'm craving caffeine, so I head to the nearest Starbucks. Though I'm completely certain Lycan's dietary restrictions don't include it, I treat myself to a large latte with an extra shot of espresso, and find a window seat. I expect to be able to admire the fall colors on the trees lining the street, but am shocked to realize the season has already moved beyond it. I've been so preoccupied with thoughts about the show that I missed the crimson reds and vibrant yellows I adore. I can't help but feel a little like one of those leaves myself these days, my body transformed into something bright and bold, yet still made up of what I once was. I sit and watch the rest of the world go by. It's funny; even though there are tons of people coming and going on the street, it all seems rather placid compared to the drama of rehearsal. I worry that I'm beginning to sound like a diva, until a real one walks in.

"Julia!" I say, causing most of the patrons to turn and look at me. I guess I've yelled louder than I intended. I'm not entirely sure why I'm so excited to see her.

"Mason?" She walks over and gives me a side hug.

"How's it going?"

"Would you hold my purse?" she asks, depositing yet another designer bag in my lap before I can even reply. Clearly, coffee is the only thing on her mind.

I am so used to giving her my undivided attention on stage that I feel compelled to watch her wait in line. It's strange to see her do something by herself. In the show she has servants, and she had an entire staff at the party. As usual, her makeup is artfully applied, but her bubbly personality seems to be missing. I wonder if this is what Julia is really like in the backstage of her life, or the result of caffeine withdrawal.

"Sorry about that," she says, returning to the table. "I'm just not myself until I've had at least one cup of coffee, and Charles broke the coffee grinder this morning. He dropped one of his cufflinks in the thing."

"Did you try it? I mean, you never know, maybe you could sell coffee with specks of platinum in it. Coffee snobs will drink anything," I say.

"That's true. You know, before him I used to drink anything, even that stuff in gas stations," she says, taking a sip and then screwing up her face in disgust. "But I'm afraid he's ruined me. I can barely stomach commercially sold beans now. He imports his own from a small artisan roaster in Arezzo, Italy, and really, nothing else can compare."

"I'll have to take your word on it. I don't foresee myself having that kind of problem any time soon."

"You never know."

"Right. Anyway, so I went by rehearsal this morning, and no one was there."

"Not even Tiny?" she asks, but I've got no idea to whom she could possibly be referring.

"Who?"

"Tiny. Jenna's assistant. He's the one who works the buzzer."

"Wait, are you talking about the big black guy?" I ask, wondering if she means that guy who was filling in for Jenna. I was so busy with Lycan when the rehearsals began that I was never formally introduced to him. He was simply there one day, filling in, and no one else seemed to think it was noteworthy.

"That's the one. He's a total sweetheart and he's probably the most amazing assistant stage manager I've ever seen. When he is supposed to be on book, he doesn't even have to keep it open. He just knows everyone's lines. He even prompted De Niro once."

"Wow, I don't think it ever occurred to me Jenna even had an assistant."

"Mason, what do you mean? Do you think she also sets the lights and sews the costumes? You need to pay more attention. I know it is cheesy, but the little people really do matter."

"I know, I've just been so busy."

"Well, you're not busy now. Let's go, I'll introduce you around." In the time it takes me to grab my pack, Julia consumes her entire cup of coffee in two unladylike swigs. Once she's drained it she grabs my hands and pulls me out into the street back toward the theatre while giving me a full rundown on the entire cast and crew. Considering her heels, I'm impressed how fast she can walk, especially since she is pulling me along with her, but in typical Julia fashion she makes it look effortless. I try hard to listen and commit some of the information to memory, but she is talking so rapidly that it all falls in one and out the other. In a matter of minutes we arrive back and the door, and this time we are buzzed in. Julia's face lights up when she sees Tiny behind the glass.

"Tiny, have you been formally introduced to Mason?"

"Why no, I haven't," he says. He has a southern accent and a voice so deep it practically makes me vibrate. "He always seems to come in just when I've stepped away. Jenna covers for me on bathroom breaks." He can barely look my in the eyes and when he finally does he quickly shifts his gaze to his shoes. Everything about Tiny seems contradictory. For a guy who is almost twice my size, it's disarming how bashful he is.

"Must be the morning coffee. It's nice to officially meet you," I say, starting to extend my hand, but I stop when I remember he's behind glass.

"You too. I'm looking forward to the show." The buzzer goes off again, giving us all a cue to get back to work.

For the first time, I'm not the first to arrive, so it's strange to walk into the space and find the entire cast and crew milling about.

"Actors, please settle down," Jenna calls. Her hair is pulled back in an exceptionally tight bun today. "I just heard from Merchant, and he'll be here in ten minutes with the new script. It'll take some time to make enough copies for everyone, so he's asked that we run the dance sequence in the meantime. Leads, please go down the hall to meet with Ms. Taylan, for a fitting."

Julia, Marshall, Alex and I head that way. Kevin is nowhere in sight.

"Mr. Burroughs, I presume?" says a pencil-thin woman short, platinum blonde hair, cat-eye glasses, and a thick French accent.

"That's me."

"I am Ms. Taylan. I believe you already know Robin," she says gesturing toward the woman who has been taking my measurements for the past few weeks while hardly ever uttering a word. Robin nods her head precisely one degree in acknowledgment before returning her attention to organizing the clothes on the costume racks.

"Yes, she's been taking my measurements."

"And now we will finally see if she got them right."

"Well, I think I've lost a few pounds since last week," I say. Behind me, Alex mutters something nasty underneath a series of feigned coughs.

Taylan bristles at the sound and then whirls around, pointing toward the door. "If you are sick, get out!"

"But—" Alex protests.

"'But' nothing! Out! I don't have time to be sick," she shrieks, before pushing him out the door. "Mr. Burroughs, please put on your costume, and we'll see what we can do."

Not wanting to get on her bad side, I begin to strip off my clothes. Julia and Marshall giggle, which causes me to immediately panic that I'm still some sort of fat, hideous blob. However, when I look up, they point toward a changing curtain, set up only a few yards away, which I quickly duck behind.

"What do you think?" I ask, drawing back the curtain and straightening my posture to model for Taylan.

"That is the wrong coat. Get the cloak from Mr. Caldwell's rack," she replies, and Robin leaps to her feet and begins thumbing through Kevin's rack to find it.

As Robin thumbs through Kevin's clothes to find my cloak, I can't stop thinking about him. If he was here, he'd be helping me, telling me how good I look, making funny comments, and showing me how to interact with Ms. Taylan. Yet, without him here as a crutch, I feel like I'm actually getting to know them.

"Robin! Bring me Mr. Burroughs' chart."

"Yes, ma'am," Robin says, quickly retrieving it and handing it to her. Taylan studies it, and me, for a few moments. She pokes and prods at me, pulling bits of fabric, raising my arms, and then pushing them back down. She makes tiny clicks with her tongue, each of which Robin appears to hang on, desperate for her approval, but when Taylan lifts the back of my cloak she gasps.

"Aiya, this will not do! What were you thinking with the waist of these pants? Mr. Burroughs' ass has more than enough work to do in this show, but you think they should be the only thing holding up his pants as well? No! no!" Taylan says, lightly tapping Robin on the arm. "The waist must be taken in to here!"

"Oh!" Robin exclaims, hanging her head in shame.

"Sorry, it's probably my fault, I've been doing everything I can to get my waist as small as possible," I say, trying to cover for Robin. Given how many times she's measured me, there is no way she would mess up something like that. It's got to be my fault.

"I'll fix it immediately!" Robin says, grabbing the cloth to my waist and furiously pinning it there. She moves so quickly, it's no surprise when she accidentally pricks me.

"Ouch!"

"Shush!" Robin says, bizarrely insisting that I be the quiet one for once.

"Sorry," I whisper, though I'm not really sure I should be the one apologizing.

"How can anyone lose weight so fast?" she asks, making me want to laugh. Only a costumer would find my weight loss annoying.

"My apologies for the inconvenience," Merchant's voice chimes in. I try to turn to see him, but Robin whacks my hip so hard that I immediately refocus my eyes forward while she continues to pin my clothes.

"Not at all," Taylan says. "You warned us this would happen, and you were true to your word. Honestly, I thought the progress on his measurement chart seemed impossible, but he is as transformed as you promised. Do you expect him to change much more?"

"Mason is about done, but it's possible he'll lose another inch off his waist and add some more muscle in the arms."

"Fine, but don't get carried away. People always think taking things in is easy, but it's not. I don't want anyone to think I'm losing my touch. Everything must be perfect."

"Give him another week, and I'll have Lycan start him on a maintenance plans. Honestly, Mason, I'm impressed. You got there a lot faster than I thought. Mrs. Taylan should be happy you're ahead of schedule."

"Simone isn't happy until opening night, and even then it's a toss-up." It's him. Despite Robin's threats, I can't resist turning around to look. Kevin is leaning against the door frame, posed like James Dean, wearing the requisite black leather jacket and white t-shirt. He's definitely reclaimed his cool.

"Mon cher! Why are you so late?"

"I didn't know I was supposed to be here until I was already late."

"My fault entirely, I assure you," Merchant says, his mannerisms and tone slightly camp for a straight man. I don't know what to make of that. Is he putting up a front for us, or does Ms. Taylan's French fashionista persona just rub off on people? "While you finish with Mr. Burroughs, I need to speak to Kevin. Don't worry, we won't be long,"

"Very well, but you don't have much time. Kevin's costumes are ready for their final fitting, and Jeannette and I will be done with this one in no time at all."

I want to find a way to eavesdrop again, but I can't move while I'm being fitted. When he returns, Kevin's Cheshire Cat grin tells me he's pleased. Once I get a script from Jenna, the reason is clear. As much as I am appalled at Kevin's tactics, the changes from Colin are even more brilliant than yesterday's. Marshall's role is somewhat diminished, and Kevin's power has been restored. I still die, but now there's a twist to explain why. Dyne still desires power, but instead of manipulating Ezio, he manipulates Mina. When Ezio confesses his love for Caleb, Dyne reveals the lovers to Mina and places a dagger in her hand. She barges in, driven mad with jealousy. She tries to kill Ezio, but Caleb takes the blow, and in his dying speech explains what Dyne has done. He speaks of his love for both of them and begs that they care for each other. They promise they will, and Caleb uses his last bit of life to join their hands.

The prose of Caleb's new speech gives me goosebumps. I'm excited to get to deliver it. Even after one read, it's hard to imagine the play could end any other way. Finally, the show feels complete.

For the next hour I'm on my own, as I am basically a wallflower during the beautifully choreographed dance scene being rehearsed, so I focus on learning my new lines. The language is so incredibly poetic it rolls off the tongue with ease, and after a few quick runs I've got it memorized. For the first time I find myself in rehearsal with nothing to do, so I try to really soak in the moment, and just enjoy watching the cast and crew at work.

I try to notice something unique about each of the actors, something I cam compliment them on after the show opens, things calm down, and I finally get the chance to know them. To help me keep track of it all,

I making notes in the margins of my script. I have to identify them by their character's name, but after a while I feel a sense of accomplishment. It's strange to have worked next to these people for weeks and still know nothing about them. Their smiles and laughs in the moments of rest let me see just how deeply they've bonded. I hope that when we start doing full run-throughs of the show they will adopt me into their family.

Merchant approaches. "Are you ready for the new scene?" he asks, taking a seat next to me. I'm surprised by how put together and relaxed he looks. Clearly, he didn't lose much sleep over Kevin's threats, and Alex's pathetic attempt at playing Ezio.

"Yes, it's a great monologue."

"I agree. Colin was inspired."

"Anything I should know?"

"No." His answer is sure and final.

"Did you need something then?" I ask, giving him another chance to tell me why he came over.

"I just needed to know you were prepared. Please get to your place for the start of the scene." He stands, and walks away.

I thought, after everything that happened yesterday, the pressure was going to be on Kevin. It appears, though, that like always, it's still all on me.

We start by quickly walking through the seduction scene. Merchant makes minor adjustments, but we quickly get to where we left off. I mime kissing Kevin, making annoyingly loud kissing sounds in an imitation of Alex, and laughter erupts around us. Julia's cackle practically rattles the mirror, but Kevin just glares at me. I stop, and Julia enters the scene. The dialogue of the confrontation is rapid fire, reflecting the true chaos of a climax, and before I know it Julia lunges toward Kevin with the dagger.

"Stop," Merchant calls out, and joins us on stage. "Let's slow this down, and work it out beat by beat. Now, the key to this is that we have to really put energy into the placement. Julia, I want you to run at him with the knife held out in your downstage hand. Kevin, I want you to look like you are ready for her, and Mason, I don't want it to be too obvious that you are going to get in the way, so when Julia says her last line, what was it again?"

"You would dare think of returning to my side? I will have none of you that his venomous lips have touched, which leaves you nothing to offer."

"Right. When she says that, I want you to turn your back to her and face the audience. Then, for a few seconds I don't want anyone to move. I want tension here. Julia, you need to look like you are about to give up, and then make a dash for Kevin. Mason, the second she does, you are going to turn around and block her."

"Does it matter which way I turn?"

"Turn all the way back around, so that'd be over your left shoulder. You're going to take it in the gut, facing Julia." I turn as he instructed, and manage to block Julia.

"Now Julia, we need to see you pull your arm back before you stab in. It will help it look fatal. Mason, when she stabs you, I want you to pull your arms around her in a tight embrace. When you feel the stage knife hit, make sure you give it a good vocal. Not only when it goes in, but when she pulls it out. Can we put all that together? Let's do it in slow motion for starters."

We start to slowly go through the motions, but I miss my cue, and Julia manages to reach Kevin before I've even turned around.

"That would be a rather different ending. Is there an issue Mr. Burroughs?"

"I can't see when she starts."

"Julia, can you give us a growl when you start?"

"Like this?" Julia says, giving a shallow, flirtatious growl.

"No, I want something more frustrated than foreplay," Merchant says with a smile, and we can't help but laugh. Except for Kevin.

"Okay, okay, let me try again. How about this?" she asks, letting loose something more like a high-pitched yelp of a wounded dog.

"Not quite. Maybe we should have Ezio try and stab Mina instead."

"Oh, come on," Julia protests.

"That! Take that emotion, and growl." It works. Julia gives an exasperated guttural growl of frustration, and we all break out into applause.

"Brava! Okay, from the top."

I manage to save Kevin this time. Julia strikes a direct hit on the point that Merchant bruised all those weeks before, but it doesn't hurt at all. When the point of the knife retracts, I'm astonished how impenetrable my abs feel. I fall to the floor in feigned pain, ready to deliver my final monologue.

"Let's stop there," Merchant says, before I can utter a single syllable. "We will work the ending tomorrow. Do you guys think we can do the whole scene from the top for real, or do you want to walk through the stabbing again?"

"Can we do it a few more times?" I ask, knowing I'll need to store it in my muscle memory. I don't want to be distracted when I become Caleb again.

"How are we on time, Jenna?"

"You've got twenty minutes before we break."

"All right, let's do this once more. Then we'll have everyone else get ready for the top of the scene."

We go through it again, and it works even better than last time. I manage to get there just seconds before Julia, and Merchant seems pleased.

"Places for the top of the ballroom scene!" Jenna barks, and before long, the scene is underway.

Even without the costumes and lights, getting into character is easy. Caleb's presence has been bubbling underneath my skin since I saw Kevin again. When the music of the dance begins, my consciousness recedes and Caleb claims my body as his own.

The scene is just like before, until we get to the final kiss.

"Try to love me as I love you, and when the morning comes, if Mina is still in your heart, I will resign that you are a war I cannot win." Although I have heard Ezio's declaration before, it brings me back to that same moment of ecstasy. It feels like a Pavlovian response, and I instantly hunger for Ezio's lips to kiss me once more. In a matter of moments he has me back on the chaise and is undressing me.

"My god." Mina's words come again, and although there is less of the set present to hide her, from Caleb's perspective she remains hidden. When I return to Ezio, I once again force him to share the reins, making the seduction into something more mutual. But things are different this time. Ezio seems to hand over control completely. I lower myself onto his lap, but he doesn't claw at me, rather he begins to shudder and shake. His trembling makes things awkward so I pivot myself off of him, and draw him to my chest. I take a deep breath and let it slowly pour out as a cool stream onto his neck.

Without a clear understanding of why things have stopped, I feel Caleb's presence fade slightly, forcing me to step in and keep things going. I keep expecting Merchant to stop us, but he doesn't, and I wonder if Kevin has been given secret instructions, like I was when we performed this scene for the investors. The primal urges between us seem to have settled now, and when I turn Kevin's face to meet mine, there are tears running down his cheeks. I cannot tell if they are happy or sad, but I kiss them away, and when he smiles, our lips meet once more.

"This cannot be!" Mina says, entering with a dagger in hand. Sensing the danger to Ezio, Caleb's spirit returns to full control of the situation, and I can feel my muscles twitch in anticipation.

"Mina! What are you doing here?" I spring over the clothes on the floor as I attempt to put some distance between Ezio and I, knowing there is no way to take back what she has seen.

"You dare to ask what I am doing after I find you like this?" Her eyes are wild and her delicate hand is solid white as it firmly grips the black hilt of the blade.

"It is not all it seems. I would return to you if I thought you would have me."

"You would dare think of returning to my side? I will have none of you that his venomous lips have touched, which leaves you nothing to offer." Shamed and stung, I cannot face her. I turn away to figure out whether I am a fool for trying to love two people at the same time, but my thoughts are interrupted by the sound of Mina's battle cry. With only seconds to spare, I manage to place myself between them. The knife slides into my flesh, and I call out in pain.

"Thank you!" a voice calls out, and the world around me cracks and crumbles, shattered by the voices of phantoms I do not know. I become aware that my body has begun to sweat, a reminder that I am human.

I am Mason.

Unlike last time, I feel almost nauseous returning to myself. The emotions from the passion and confrontation continue to flow through me, and my body is agitated by the stress of the illusion. I hold my stomach as I take a seat off stage, giving Merchant the floor.

"Are you all right? The knife didn't hurt you did it?" Merchant asks.

"No, sorry, just a bit nauseous from...everything," I offer, hoping he will understand.

"I see. If things don't improve in a few moments come to me immediately."

"I will."

"Excellent work everyone. Colin has assured me that there will be no more major changes to the script, so those of you who are not off book should start memorizing now. We have an audience in three weeks, and I want us to have as many good preview performances as we can, because the official premiere date has been moved up." The news breaks over us, but none of us dares make a sound. I exchange wide-eyed glances with Kevin and Julia, both of whom seem equally concerned. Merchant appears to notice, but keeps silent.

"Why?" Marshall asks, and I'm thankful that he is willing to be the whipping boy for all of us.

"It's related to a potential change to a larger venue. I'm told the lawyers are finalizing plans that will have us opening in style, but I won't say more until it's official. I expect you will all be discreet. Any leaks will be dealt with harshly." The entire room sits up straight. "Jenna will forward you an updated rehearsal schedule. We will spend the next two days revisiting old scenes and working in Colin's revisions. We will have our first stumble-through of Act One on Wednesday, Act Two will be Thursday, and Friday we will run the entire thing from start to finish. You will all have Saturday off while so we can install the set, but Sunday is going to be our first tech rehearsal. Everyone should be completely off book on Monday. Do you have anything to add, Jenna?"

"I need you to submit your bios and headshots for the playbill to me by Sunday. Brevity is encouraged. You are released."

The mention of headshots reminds me I need new ones, a fact I know is true, because it's the one thing Kevin and Eric could agree on. I decide to ask Merchant for a recommendation, hoping that by following his direction, I'll avoid any future disasters where that topic is concerned.

"Certainly, I'll talk to Lee. He's doing the promotional material," he says. "It'd be nice if Kevin got new ones too, just so we could control the way you're both presented in the program. You've seen your schedule for the photoshoot, right?"

"Yes, it's tomorrow night. I'm excited about it! I just hope the photographer doesn't mind the additional work. I wasn't really looking to spend a fortune so…"

"Lee will be delighted to do it for free, and if he's not, I'll remind him he owes me one." Clearly everyone Merchant deals with ends up owing him something. I wonder what favor I'll be asked to fulfill for him.

SEVENTEEN

As I get ready for the photoshoot, I take a moment to look at myself in the mirror. Merchant's friend "Lee" turned out to be Liloun Kwan. I didn't recognize the name, but Eric completely flipped out when I told him he was going to be shooting my headshots. Apparently, he's someone important in the graphic design world. Eric talked about him like I do Ian McKellen, which makes me incredibly nervous. As proud as I am about my new body, I worry what a famous photographer will think.

I try hard not to see the flaws. My stomach, while now flat, still lacks the deep dividing lines which outline each abdominal muscle. The strong definition in my calves and things is grossly out of proportion with my only slightly-enhanced arms and shoulders. Everyone keeps saying how good I look, but it's only in contrast to how I was before. In an effort to really see the progress, I decide to put on the vest and shirt I wore to my audition. When I bend down to take them from the lower rack of our closet, I catch a glimpse of myself in the mirror, and finally see it.

Bernini's *David*.

Using my phone, I pull up the sculpture that Lycan showed me almost six weeks ago, when we met. To truly compare, I strike the pose. My body is almost a perfect replica. In fact, as I look closer, I am amazed to find that I'm actually in slightly better shape than the figure Bernini sculpted. Moreover, the flaws I found in myself just moments ago, not only exist in the statute, they're more pronounced there. I can't believe I never noticed it before. I stare at myself for a long while, willing myself to truly see my own reflection, until the phone rings.

"Hello?"

"Mason, this is Jenna," she says, not really needing to introduce herself. "I wanted to let you know that the venue of the show has officially been changed to the Lyceum Theatre. It's going to take us all day to move everything we need into the space, so your shoot has now been pushed back to 10:00."

"That's kind of late for a photoshoot isn't it?"

"Do you need the address?" she asks, ignoring my question.

"No, I know where it is." How could I not? It's the oldest continuously running Broadway theater, and the place where most of Merchant's most famous productions have been performed.

"Good. Don't be early and don't be late," she says crankily, and then hangs up.

★

My ears celebrate the snap of my boot heels striking the marble floor in the lobby, each step bringing me closer to the stage. When my foot finally touches the old hardwood floor, a feeling of accomplishment washes over me. I truly feel I've made it.

Constructed on stage, draped in expensive fabrics and colored lights, is the room I envisioned through Caleb's eyes. Calling it the seduction chamber does not do it justice. It's a den of sin. The details of the set so accurately resemble my own fantasy that it feels as if the designer plucked the idea out of my brain. Only slight differences seem to have been made in order to make the room even more dramatic. High quality LED candles installed into antique bronze wall sconces provide flattering lighting. The old chaise has been replaced by a new, fleshier one, cover in a fabric so smooth and plush that it invites the world to recline in its tender embrace. Silver flagons of sanguine liquid are placed near platters teeming with flowers and ripe fruit, filling the space with an earthy aroma that seems to change and evolve with every breath.

"What do you think?" Kevin asks, dropping his bag and falling onto the chaise.

"I'm pretty sure it was designed so I wouldn't think."

"Yeah, it's pretty heavy-handed. We'll get used to it, though."

"I guess. Have you seen anyone else?"

"No, but they've got to be around here somewhere."

"We are," a voice says over the loudspeaker. I recognize it as Merchant. I realize he must be up in the light booth, using the speaker system known as the "god mic" to project his voice out into the house.

"Hello?" I say, looking out into the audience as the house lights slowly fade, hiding the empty seats in darkness.

"Hello," I hear someone reply from stage left. I turn and see a tall man of Asian descent. He is dressed in a tight, purple t-shirt and dark, skinny jeans that have been sliced open by a razor every four inches from the thigh to the shin.

"This is Mr. Kwan," Merchant's voice booms all around us.

"Lee is fine," Kwan offers.

"I'm Mason." I shake his hand.

"I'm Kevin."

"Nice to meet you both. Shall we get started?" Lee asks, removing the lens cap of the rather expensive-looking camera hanging around his neck.

"Shoot Kevin first. Mason come join us up here," Merchant commands.

"Yes, Great and Powerful Oz," Kevin says, projecting his voice loud and clear into the darkness. Lee grins at this; I roll my eyes.

"How do you get to the booth?" I ask.

"Exit, stage left even," Kevin says, doing a spot-on impersonation of Snagglepuss.

I head backstage and marvel at the way the place is set up. The theatre was built over a century ago, and as a result it doesn't have the big open space like the modern ones I worked with. Instead backstage there are tiny nooks and crannies, with stairs leading all around. It takes me several minutes to finally find the way up to the booth.

When I walk in, I find Merchant and Jenna standing before a long, slanted window that looks out over the house and onto the stage. Beside them, a curly-haired woman sits in front of a massive light board covered with buttons and dials.

"Mason, I'd like you to meet Laura Jilg, our lighting designer."

"Hi," she says, waving to me for a second before returning her fingers to the sliders on the lighting board.

Over the next few minutes she works on adjusting the lighting, occasionally speaking into her headset, giving orders to her assistants who are on the catwalks above the stage, until finally a cue is set and she saves it to the software. Below us, Kevin walks onto stage, directed by Merchant, and Lee shoots him from every angle. It looks pretty simple, so I begin to relax.

"Mason, we'll be using the final seduction scene for the promo shots," Merchant says.

"That's fine. Whatever you need." The minute the words are out of my mouth I realize: I'm half-naked at the end of that scene.

"That's the spirit. We'll just run it like normal, stopping and starting if necessary. Lee will be shooting it, but try to ignore him."

"Umm...."

"Is there a problem?" Merchant says, turning to glare at me.

"I'm a little worried about the nudity."

"What happened to 'whatever you need'?"

"I know, but photos last forever." Over the years I've given a lot of thought to being naked on stage. I always knew that, if it was necessary, I would do it. However, the idea of lasting evidence of it, beyond memory, is harder to handle.

"Mason, I have spent a fortune in time and money working on you and your body," Merchant says.

Clearly, I am now paying the price. "I...I know that."

"Believe me, I'm not going to do anything to jeopardize my investment. You have my word, none of the photos will compromise your modesty."

"Oh. Well, okay then."

"Good, now get down there. It's your turn for headshots."

While I'm not thrilled at being forced into this, I decide to look on the bright side. I won't be able to maintain this statuesque form forever, so it'll be nice to have a record to prove that, for a few moments in my life, I had a truly beautiful body. Since Merchant was clear I have no choice in this matter, I decide to let my vanity loose and strut onto the stage.

"Did you bring other clothes?" Lee asks, looking at me through the lens of his camera.

"Yeah, a button-down, and a vest and tie to dress it up," I say, grabbing some newly-purchased clothes from my bag.

"Anything more casual?" he asks, taking my picture even though I'm not really doing anything.

"More casual than what I'm wearing?"

"Yes. I thought the point of these was to show off your new bod."

"Who told you that?"

"I did," says Kevin, joining us both on stage.

"Shouldn't you be with Merchant?" I ask, hoping he'll leave me alone. My body might resemble a work of art, but having Kevin around would make that fact much harder to remember.

"Nope, I'm all set."

"I didn't interrupt your photoshoot."

"Well, I'm a pro. Besides I'm sure I can help. For starters, put this on," Kevin says, throwing me a shirt. When I unfold it, it looks like just a regular old, black and white striped polo shirt. However, I notice that instead of cotton, it appears to be made out of some sort of springy mesh, synthetic fabric. As I pull it back and let go, it becomes slightly translucent the farther it is stretched. It has an Armani label.

"Whose is this?"

"Mr. Burroughs, quit talking and do as you are told," Merchant's voice booms like an angry god.

"Fine." The second I lift my shirt over my head I hear the camera snap. Three more shots click by before I manage to get my shirt all the way off, and when I open my eyes and see the camera, I freeze. Lee has a field day, his camera clicking as fast as Gene Kelly tap danced in the movies, capturing my horror-stricken expression.

"Your shirt is in your hand," Kevin reminds me after a few seconds. His voice is warm, but even that doesn't help melt my frozen stance. Finally, he walks in front of Lee's shot, takes the shirt, and begins to put it on me himself. "Let me help."

"Thank you," I whisper, once my head is through the shirt. Just like the Tin Man after Dorothy applied the oil, I have the ability to move once more.

"Okay, so let's position you here for starters. Now look into the light," Lee says, moving me around the stage like a chess piece. I feel the warmth of the stage lights hit my face, so I know Merchant is watching and giving Jilg a ton of modifications. The lights dim, and my face feels cooler, but then new lights come up and start baking me again.

"Lift your chin a little, and think of hope," Kevin directs, and before I know it, he is leading me through a whole series of poses and emotions. Lee is completely quiet, but he takes shots of everything in the photo session, from me changing clothes to drinking water. Eventually the clicking falls into a rhythm. The stage lights flicker on and off like stars, and I glide from spot to spot, following Kevin's lead. It feels like we're dancing, even though we're far apart. Eventually the shutter clicks begin to slow, and I find myself center stage, bathed in light.

"Think of the curtain call on opening night," Kevin prompts, and I imagine the sound of applause that will fill this room. In the tradition of male actors, I clasp my hands in front of me and take a bow. The noise grows louder, and I think about how in just a few weeks, a real audience will see me in this show. I lose myself in the moment, and quickly toss my head back. When I face forward again my smile grows as I imagine Eric seated in one of those chairs on opening night.

"Perfect," Lee says, with one final click. "I think that's enough. Want to see?"

"I'd love to."

"So would I," Kevin says, draping his arm around me.

Even though the image is small on the electronic preview screen, I am dumbstruck. The shot is close up, but captures most of my torso. Having swung back up from my pretend curtain call bow, my shoulders are pushed back and my posture is slightly elongated. My arms have pulled the Armani shirt's fabric tight across my body, revealing the new, lean muscles underneath. However, my face is the most captivating part. My smile is pure, almost child-like, and the lights from the stage sparkle in my eyes. It's the proof I was looking for, the testament that, for a brief moment, at least, I was as divine as Kevin. Lee has managed to capture it forever.

"You look hot in this one," Kevin says, passing the camera back to me, showing me one of the shots from when I was frozen. The torso is certainly mine, but I have a hard time believing it, because my stare is so vacant. However, something tells me Kevin's used to admiring guys with that expression.

Suddenly the lights shift dramatically, and Jenna trudges onto the stage dragging a costume rack.

"Merchant has you dragging costumes?" Kevin asks. While Jenna is in charge of about a hundred things, costumes are something she actually doesn't have to deal with.

"No, Taylan," she confirms.

"Why?" I ask.

"Apparently someone—" she says, flopping her wrist out in what I assume is an imitation of Alex. "—had the bright idea to try on your pants from Act One. Clearly, they didn't take into account the size difference as they split down the middle. To make matters even more fun, the moron didn't tell anyone! So Taylan and Robin are trying to salvage them. Honestly, the way they are hovering over the thing, you'd swear she was doing fucking heart surgery."

"Knowing Simone, she'd probably say her work is harder than heart surgery," Kevin jokes.

"Days like today make me wish I'd become an accountant. Anyway, Merchant said to put your costumes on and get ready for the rest of the shoot. I'll see you in the morning,"

"You're leaving?" I ask, though I certainly can't blame her. She looks even more exhausted than I did after my first training session with Lycan.

"Amazingly enough, yes. Merchant's orders. Apparently he understands I need some sleep to function tomorrow. It's going to be hell. Don't break anything, and put those costumes back when you're done."

"Sure thing. Just promise me you'll take a cab home."

"I'm taking a town car," she replies, smiling for the first time. Seeing her display emotion is such a rarity that I consider hugging her.

"That's pretty swanky."

"Merchant treats me well, otherwise I'd quit. That reminds me, you two should take one of these." She holds out a card. "It's Merchant's private car service. You can use it on nights when you've got an audience. Just don't abuse it. It's one of the few special perks of being a lead."

"Thank you!" I say, grabbing the card and then hugging her. Jenna immediately stiffens like a board. I guess I misread the moment, because she quickly leaves once I let go. Feeling awkward, I stuff my hands and the card deep into my pockets.

It's clear that Ms. Taylan and her staff have been hard at work. Where I once had one costume, I now have six, and most of them look complete. I grab the pieces for tonight and change backstage. There have been some major alterations to my shirt; it's no longer billowy but has been tailored to fit me. The blood-red cloak is heavier now, and the gold embroidery along the bottom is finished. I also see a big wad of white cotton cloth draped over a new hanger. Unfolding it, I realize that I have been supplied with period underwear. They are short breaches, with a drawstring waist. I quickly finish dressing and make my way back. I know that if I don't hurry, my resolve to actually go through with this will probably crumble.

"My, Simone has really outdone herself," Merchant says from the booth. His voice seems louder than ever.

"Mr. Merchant would like you to have these," Lee says, presenting Kevin and I each with a black gift box tied with a crimson ribbon.

"I am going to make a big presentation about this tomorrow, so please act surprised, but I want some shots of you with these," Merchant says.

Feeling confused but curious, I look to Kevin for guidance. He simply smiles and holds up three fingers. He counts them down, and I know this means he wants us to open them at the same time. Our minds and bodies are in perfect sync, ripping off the ribbon and opening the top of the box at the exact same time to reveal a pair of Venetian Carnival masks. Kevin's is a full face mask, entirely coated in gold, adorned with white feathers and what I assume are fake diamonds. It's flawless, but his real face is still more beautiful. My mask, on the other hand, is certain to make me all the more attractive. Even though it's only a half mask, obscuring everything above my top lip, I can tell it will give my face a more angular and interesting shape. The sharp lines that run from the base of the nose out toward my ears give the illusion of prominent cheek bones, so my face will appear to have more depth than it actually does. Instead of feathers and jewels, the mask is adorned with gold stenciled notes on aged sheet music. I try to sight-read it, but the notes are either random, or I am too rusty to pick out the melody.

"Kevin, your mask is called a Bauta. It is the ultimate symbol of anonymity," Merchant says, his voice quieter than before, though he's still projecting his voice over the god mic. Calmed by the lower volume, I release a breath I hadn't realized I was holding. Kevin turns around and places the mask up to his face. Seeing the black satin straps, I volunteer to tie it in a bow for him to hold it in place.

"It's perfect. I can see why Mina is fooled," I say, once he has turned around.

"That's the idea. Mason, yours is a Columbina, named after a famous actress who didn't want to cover her entire face. Her reason was inspired by her vanity, but that is not the reason I chose this for Caleb. Can you guess why?" I ponder this, as Kevin returns the favor and helps me fasten it. Although he ties the bow tighter than I would have liked, once the mask is secure, something seems to click inside of me. The answer – Caleb's answer – springs forth.

"Because I'm divided?" I reply, and at the moment it feels not only correct, but true.

"That is the gist of it. I prefer to say he is split between two worlds and two loves."

"I'll be sure to say that, if someone interviews me."

"I would appreciate that, as would Simone. Now then, let's run the scene."

The lights change, and I follow Kevin off stage so we can make our entrance. By the time I reach the wings and look onto the set, Lee has disappeared. I don't have time to try and figure out where he's shooting from because Kevin grabs my hands and pulls me back onto the stage. His touch awakens Caleb within me, and when I walk back onto the stage, I know it is Ezio behind his mask.

The costumes, lights, and full set make Caleb's life force more potent than ever before. Whatever normally tethers me to the scene seems to have left me adrift, and I feel like I'm having an out-of-body experience.

I am a member of the audience, watching myself perform. I'm not even sure I have any control at all, which should be frightening, but the scene unfolding before me is too gripping for me to bother with fear. I wonder if Kevin feels like this, too, if his spirit is somewhere out in the audience as well, watching Ezio from afar.

The pace of the scene is faster than we have ever rehearsed it; the only pause comes when Ezio begins to remove my mask. I am called back into the pocket of my mind that I share with Caleb.

No longer a spectator of the scene, I am overcome by the intense sensations that Caleb is feeling. Once Ezio's mask is gone, I reach out to touch his face, like Adam's hand reaching toward God on the ceiling of the Sistine Chapel. However, when I make contact something strange happens: I feel Caleb's presence retreat, and the entire illusion of the world seems to fade almost beyond sight. I no longer see Ezio, I see Kevin.

I think about stopping, of breaking away, because I know this is wrong. It's not Caleb and Ezio enjoying this moment; it's us. I hesitate, but Kevin does not. He kisses me again and I sense this deep hunger for me within him. I remember believing that if I could kiss him like this, he would feel my passion for him and fall for me. The memory seems to seep into the present. It's like I'm twenty-two again, lying in bed, pretending Kevin is there beside me. I try to stop myself, but Caleb returns to me again. I am somehow myself and Caleb as well, uncertain whether the lips I am tasting belong to Kevin or Ezio.

The passion between us feels otherworldly, mythical and ancient, and I lose track of everything that is happening. We tear at our clothes, buttons popping, fabric ripping, trying desperately to feel the entirety of the other. His flat stomach rubs against mine, creating warm friction that grows hotter as he moves even faster.

"You're mine. God, you're finally mine," Kevin whispers in my ear.

"Stop!" Merchant's voice booms over the god mic, sharply bringing me back to reality.

"What's up?" Lee asks, walking on stage and staring up at the light booth. He shields his eyes with one hand and firmly plants the other on his hip, seemingly annoyed by the interruption.

"I'm coming down," Merchant replies.

As the house lights come up, I notice the door from the lobby opens, and everything seems to slide into slow motion as I see Eric walk in. The second we lock eyes his smile melts into an expression of absolute horror. I can only imagine how this looks to him, seeing Kevin and I wrapped in each other's arms.

"Eric? What are you doing here?" I ask, pushing Kevin off of me. Eric shakes his head and turns to walk out. I grab my clothes, clamber off the stage, and run after him.

"I came to see the shoot. I wanted to meet Mr. Kwan," he answers, turning back around to face me. Despite his usual pale complexion, he looks practically ghost white.

"How did you get in the building?"

"Some lady let me in. She said you were rehearsing."

"We were."

"Is that what you call it?" Eric asks, his eyes narrowing.

"What?"

"Mason, look at yourself! You're fucking naked!" It isn't until he points this out that I become truly aware of it. Now I know how Adam felt.

"Eric, it's just part of the show," I say, trying to close the distance between us and also pull my clothes on. Unfortunately, I manage to do neither.

"How stupid do you think I am?" he asks. His eyes are wet and glassy with tears, and as they start to trail down his cheeks he has to remove his glasses to wipe them away. "I want to see the part of the script where it says you two fuck on stage."

"We...we weren't," I stammer, uncertain how I can ever explain this. "Things just got out of hand. Normally someone stops us."

"Clearly, they'd have to. You two were like animals, like dogs!" he says, his feet twitching seemingly uncertain whether he wants to fight or flee.

"Eric, I'm sorry. Will you just stop so I can explain?" I ask, grabbing onto his waist.

"No!" he pushes my hands away. "You always have some explanation for why you and he are in situations like this. I'm tired of trying to believe them."

"Excuse me, but I can assure you that he is telling the truth," Lee says. We both look, and find him standing just in front of the stage. The light from his iPad throws a pale blue hue across his face. "In fact, I was the one who asked Merchant not to stop them."

"Oh, Mr. Kwan," Eric says, his attention distracted for a moment.

"Please call me Lee. Here, take a look. As you can see, here are the headshots, and these are the photos from the rehearsal." He holds the camera out, so that Eric can see it.

"I assume this is Eric?" Merchant asks me, having made it down to the stage at last.

"Yes." I say, relieved by a chance to think while I make introductions. "Eric, this is James Merchant, the director."

"Oh, hello," Eric says not even bothering to look up from the iPad. Given everything that's gone on, I can't believe he seems to have forgotten we are having a fight, but I use the time to actually get dressed while I try and figure out why Eric is behaving so oddly. His face is transfixed as he keeps sliding his finger across the screen to scroll through the images.

"This is why," Lee says, pointing to the screen.

Eric looks at it for a long time, then up at me, and finally down to the floor. Lee walks over to me to show me what he has captured. I am surprised to find the shot is taken at a far distance, which somewhat obscures the fact that the two bodies engaged in a kiss belong to Kevin and myself. Lee appears to have taken it a split second before I heard Merchant stop us. Considering how my headshot felt like it captured and even enhanced the emotion of the moment, I'm surprised that this one feels muted. There is no trace of the primal forces that were driving what was going on; instead everything looks delicate, almost fragile. Kevin's back is arched in a concave motion, while mine is convex due to the curve in the chaise, giving the image almost a yin and yang quality. Still, even under these circumstances, I'm pretty sure it's clear there was more than just acting going on. Looking at it, I expect Eric to practically explode with rage, but as he stares at it, something appears to have clicked inside his brain, almost as if someone has thrown cold water on him. As relieved as I am by this, it makes no sense, which ends up making it more unsettling than if he was still angry.

"I don't get it," I say to Lee, who smiles and holds up one finger, motioning for me to wait. He takes the iPad back and sets it on the floor. He places both hands on it, like a concert pianist, and begins to dance his fingers across it. Lee is clearly a master of his craft, but it is far from effortless. Unable to really follow what is happening, I look at Eric, but he is fixated on Lee's hands. Merchant grips my shoulder firmly, and gives me a look of reassurance, but I shrug it off. I am through with his meddling destroying my relationship with Eric.

"Look at it again," Lee says, handing the device back to me. In a matter of minutes, he has performed a miracle, converting the various images of Kevin and I entwined to be the eyes of a mask. To my relief, his editing has made it impossible to even tell which one of the figures is mine. Through his tinkering, our bodies have been drained of their color, and our faces have been blended into the smooth surface of the mask. At first glance, I doubt people would even notice, but the longer you stare, the better you see the piece's static erotic quality.

"Where are we?" Kevin asks, proving my point.

"Look at the eyes and lips," Eric answers, even though he hasn't even seen Kwan's modified version. Since Eric's psychic powers are generally only existent his video games, I'm guessing that this isn't the first time Kwan's used this concept.

"Lips!" Lee says, and quickly grabs the iPad. "How did I miss that?"

The room goes silent again.

"Sorry, I didn't mean to ruin the shoot," Eric says, unable to look up from the ground. The fact that now he thinks he did something wrong is too much.

"No, don't apologize! I should have stopped it before it got to that point." I glare at Merchant and Kevin. "It won't happen again."

"Mason…," Kevin says, probably guessing where my mind is going.

"Merchant, from now on Julia enters the second Kevin starts to strip my clothes off. I won't be losing these," I demand, pulling on the fabric of the underwear.

"We will discuss this later," Merchant says.

"No, we will not. I am not asking you. If I have to stop him, I will, and it won't be pretty."

"Mason, don't," Eric interjects. "It's just a play. I was wrong, it isn't worth—"

"Isn't worth what?" I cut him off. "You have no idea what he's put me through. I've given him everything I can. If I don't stop him now, he'll just ask for more, and more, until there's nothing left."

"Not another word, Mr. Burroughs," Merchant says through gritted teeth.

"Why not? You changed the script for Kevin." Both Merchant's and Kevin's eyes widen.

"I don't know what you are talking about."

"What was it you said that time? Something about only being able to have power if he was willing to give it up? You said I would break otherwise, and I guarantee, I'll do more than that if you don't listen to me and fix this."

"I'm curious how it is you heard that," Merchant says, his shocked expression letting me know I've finally taken him by surprise.

"Are you going to deny that you said it?"

"No." He smiles. "I was as right then as you are now. I will make sure that the change is made."

"I'm glad you agree." That I've won so quickly feels almost too easy. It makes me wonder what it will cost me later.

"Eric, I must apologize for everything. Mason is right. I have asked a lot of him. I asked him to keep many secrets. I assure you that I did so with good reasons, and I am confident that when you see the entire play, you'll agree it was worth it. That said, until now I hadn't stopped to consider it might cause so many...problems. Therefore, given your involvement in everything, I am more than happy to make an exception for you."

Eric looks over at me. "Um...okay?"

"Mason, I assume you and Eric have lots to discuss, and you don't have much time. You are expected to be back here in just a few hours, so is there anything else?" I rack my brain to think of anything else, but nothing comes. I can't help but feel I've left something out, that I've left a loophole for Merchant to slip through, but I can't see it.

"No."

"You're certain?" he says, making me even more paranoid that I'm missing something.

"Yes."

"Then once you've changed out of your costume, you are released."

I don't need to be told twice. I grab Eric's hand and practically run out the door to change. Merchant was right; we have a lot to discuss.

EIGHTEEN

WE HAVE TO NEGOTIATE A deal so Eric will quit interrupting me while I tell my story. I tell him to write down questions as I go, and in exchange for his patience, I promise to answer all of them once I'm done. I try to be as thorough as possible about everything that's happened over the past five weeks, and once Eric realizes he's going to be listening for a long time, he requests that we move to the kitchen. He starts making a midnight feast, while I explain Merchant's training sessions, Kevin's demands, and everything else. With no more secrets to burden my conscience, it's like I've tossed aside a heavy mantle. Every aspect of my life is just as I have always wanted; I am a lead who is going to be a star on Broadway, and I'm in love.

I would've thought that grilling burgers on the stove and making homemade fries would have distracted Eric from my story, but he is a master multi-tasker. I suppose this shouldn't be shocking, considering how many applications he juggles to do his graphic design work, but it is strange to see him demonstrating more than just some basic culinary skill. When I tell him I hid behind the door to eavesdrop on Merchant and Kevin, he simultaneously writes something down and flips a burger patty into the air, catching it seconds later directly in the center of the pan. As the resident chef of the apartment, this near vaudevillian flare in the kitchen makes me curious, so I stop my story to question him.

"Have you been moonlighting at a diner while I was rehearsing?"

"What?"

"Since when do you know how to flip burgers?"

"Oh, well...sorry. I know you're on a diet, but I couldn't take it anymore, so I started watching The Food Network."

"Do you think that's such a good idea?" I say with a look of suspicion. I went through a Food Network phase myself last year. Eric loved it for a while, until he got our credit card bill. We are still paying off the Kitchen-Aid stand mixer I bought.

"So far things are under control, but I get why you were tempted. After three days I felt drawn to that Williams-Sonoma in Columbus Circle. If the check-out lady hadn't said the price aloud as she rang it up, we would have difficulty paying our rent this month, even with your paycheck. Why is a cast-iron pan five hundred dollars?"

"Because they last forever," I say, almost wishing he had bought it. Clearly we both need a Food Network Anonymous group.

"Anyway, that's where I learned the secret to a good flip. It's all about confidence."

"How many landed on the floor?"

"None, I practiced with one of your rice cakes."

"I'm glad to know there is an actual use for those. They're practically inedible."

"Then I bet you'll love this!" Eric slides a juicy burger and fries in front of me.

"The second I bite into it, Eric bombards me with questions, making it impossible to enjoy. I can't even tell if Eric has simply failed to become a better chef, or if it's his questions that are leaving the bitter taste in my mouth. Either way, the burger tastes about as good as a stale rice cake. Still, at least it has cheese. As I doctor the burger with some salt and mustard, Eric starts going through his list. Since I'd been very meticulous in my explanation, he mainly just wants to confirm that some of the unbelievable things I said are actually true.

"He made you take your clothes off?"

"Yes, it was terrible."

"Kevin really used blackmail to change the script?"

"I told you what he said. Sounds like blackmail to me." We go on like this for quite some time.

"So can you explain what you meant, about playing Caleb? You make it sound like you're possessed." This question is a little harder to answer.

"Well, that's kind of what it feels like. As the scenes get more and more intense, I tend to forget I'm actually on stage. The first time it happened, it was kind of scary. We were in the studio, but I could have sworn I was really in a medieval castle."

"So are you, like, on auto-pilot?"

"No, not really. It's just that I don't feel like myself. When I see Kevin on stage in the beginning, it's really like we are meeting for the first time. Everything is like that, new and exciting; it's easy to get lost in the moment."

"Is that what happened tonight?" he asks, after having to work a little too hard to swallow a french fry.

"I think so. It's hard to tell. Being on that set really amplified everything. I forgot who I was."

"I've never seen you look like that."

"What do you mean?"

"Mason, you looked like you were in complete bliss. I could feel it from where I was sitting, your enjoyment of it, of him." Eric uncorks a bottle of wine, but when he tries to pour himself a glass his hand is shaking too badly.

"Let me," I say, taking over and pouring us both a glass.

"Thanks. I'm just a bit frazzled."

"But why?"

"It was just hard to watch you like that. It didn't feel like a play."

"Well it's not supposed to. It's more like a dream."

"But that's exactly why I'm worried. How can I compete with a fantasy? With Kevin."

"It's not Kevin. It's his character. Just like it's not really me, it's Caleb when I'm on stage. I don't even feel like me. The memories I created for Caleb are all I have to guide me, I actually forget that everything is scripted."

"But you remember your lines?"

"Yeah, they are kind of hard wired into my brain." I'm actually surprised that I never get notes for screwing up the lines. It always feels like I'm making them up as I go along.

"So, is that different from the other shows?"

"Yes. I've never had an experience like this. In the other shows I spent so much time off stage, it was easy to remember it was all pretend. But now, I barely have time to change clothes between scenes. So, I can't ever leave my character."

"Do you think Kevin is the same way?"

"What do you mean?"

"Do you think he gets lost like you do?" It had never occurred to me to ask.

"I assume he does. It's thanks to him I learned how to do it. Why?"

"It just felt like Kevin was up there, not a character. So when I saw you kissing him..."

"You didn't see me. It was Caleb and Ezio. They have good chemistry, just like you and me," I say, leaning over to give Eric a big kiss. It feels far more sweet and loving than whatever primal urge Kevin and I explored. That had been a dream of a moment, allowing me to fulfill some childish fantasy. Fully awake and in the real world, it is easy to see that what Eric and I have is real. With all the secrets gone, tonight is not about re-forging our bond, but, rather, celebrating the one that we have. We are just like that ship Lycan discussed, and having survived this, I know we will weather any storm.

★

I'M CERTAIN WHOEVER CAME UP with the concept of ennui was at a tech rehearsal. For the ensemble, it usually involves standing on stage for a few seconds, and then being quarantined in the green room for hours. Meanwhile, the principal actors are asked to go through each moment of their scenes in tiny bursts, so that all the technical aspects of the show can be finely tuned. Ten minutes of the show could take over an hour to properly light, requiring the actors to repeat the same few lines like a broken record. The only benefit of tech is that you don't really have to act, and today I'm happy to simply phone it in.

Exhausted from the day before, I can barely remember what I am supposed to do in a scene for more than thirty seconds at a time, so the sloth-like pace suits me fine. Unfortunately, I only remember the way scenes went before I started to let Caleb really take over, so we have to stop even more than usual.

"Mason, you haven't been making that cross upstage for the past week," Jenna says, referencing her notes.

"Sorry, what have I been doing instead?"

"You don't remember?" Kevin asks, raising his eyebrow in suspicion.

"I get kind of caught up in the moment." This is mortifying. I feel like I've been caught cheating on my homework.

"Stand there. Kevin eventually comes to you."

"I've had to," Kevin sourly replies.

"Don't get snippy, Mr. Caldwell. Mason's instincts have been correct. It works better this way," Merchant says, from his seat in the house. "Can we bring up the red on stage right a little?"

"How's this?" Laura replies using the god microphone. The stage lights radiate even brighter, warming my face.

"Much better," Merchant replies, walking up, down, and across the aisles in the theater to see it from every angle. "Set that. Julia are you ready for your…"

"Here!" Julia trills, as she runs on stage.

"Great. While Laura makes sure that is set, we need to discuss the timing of Mina's entrance." In a flash Jenna has joined Merchant, and as soon as she clicks her pencil for lead, Merchant explains that Julia's entrance will be earlier.

"So, when exactly would you like me to come in?"

"When Kevin starts stripping Mason. It is important that you come in before he actually takes everything off. I want to avoid any awkwardness of Mason scrambling around trying to cover himself before giving his final monologue. We want the audience to look at his face, not his cock." Merchant impresses me by making my demand seem like his idea.

"Got it. Such a waste though," she says, with a wink.

"I'm sure you'll see enough backstage."

"Oh, I know, but what about the audience?" Good old Julia, always thinking of the crowd.

"I think they see enough."

"I don't," Kevin chimes in, putting his hand on the small of my back. The gesture feels strangely more personal, even though it is less contact than his usual arm over the shoulder move. I move away, and then pivot to face him.

"I'm happy to show them anything of yours."

"I'll take that into consideration," Kevin says, biting his lip to try and stop a curious smile.

"As will I," Merchant says with a similar smile. "Please take your places."

The scene runs smoothly, but is incredibly complex for lighting. The audience needs to be able to see Julia, but they can't use bright lights because it would ruin the lighting on us just a few feet away. Kevin and I both have to lie there in our underwear, so that they can fine tune the lighting to tread the line between pornographic and tastefully erotic.

They tinker with the cue forever, so Kevin and I are forced to continually make-out, while they debate just how to light Julia. Unfortunately, Kevin seems to have forgotten that he doesn't need to act during this rehearsal, and insists on kissing me with so much enthusiasm that it almost hurts. As the rehearsal drags on, I can't believe I ever wished for this to happen. Unable to take it anymore, I clench my teeth to block Kevin's aggressive tongue.

"You were a lot better at this last night," he whispers in my ear.

"So were you."

"What?"

"Could you back off a little? This is only a tech rehearsal."

"They need to see what it looks like. Maybe if you weren't making me do all the work…" he justifies, and then brings his lips down to me once again.

"They can see what they need without you slipping me the tongue."

"Look, if you want to keep your clothes on, we need to make this look really good."

"Sorry, it's just…I can't stop thinking about Eric."

"Then you should be really interested in getting this right. If it doesn't look at least as intense as last night, Eric's going to think something is actually going on between us," he says, his expression serious and intense.

"I guess you're right."

"I've got plenty of experience with suspicious boyfriends."

"I can't blame anyone who dates you for being suspicious."

"I meant avoiding them. The only boyfriends I have are someone else's," he says, enunciating each word after a trail of kisses that slowly make their way from my lips to my hips.

"That's not what's going on here."

"If you say so."

"It just got out of control."

"Mason, don't try to lie, we were in total sync. I could feel it. You wanted me. I can only imagine the shots Lee would have got if your boyfriend hadn't interrupted us," he says, as he starts to work his way back up my body.

"Stop," I say, as I feel the situation getting out of control again.

"Do you really want me to stop?" he asks, kissing my lips as he resumes thrusting and grinding against me. A reasonable question, since his erection is sliding up against my own. Thankfully, I'm wearing my boxer briefs under my breeches. Otherwise the tented fabric would be much more obvious.

"Slow down!" Merchant cries out, and we both freeze. "We're not to that point in the scene yet. We'll let you know when we need you to get there. You guys can give it a rest for a few minutes, just hold your positions."

I fall back against the cushions and try to catch my breath. Kevin's entire torso glistens with sweat, and as he pants for breath, light reflects off his dewey abs. Once I get up and walk around a bit, I can feel the blood returning to my head.

"When I say stop, I mean it," I say, unsure if I will ever have the strength to resist more than that.

"We're supposed to at least pretend to be into one another."

"Exactly, we are supposed to be pretending. That means there is a line, and I'm tired of you redrawing it. I'll make Julia come in sooner, if you keep it up."

"Okay, you're right. So how about we come up with a signal or something, you know, so we don't go too crazy."

"That's actually a good idea," I say, with a smile.

"Don't sound so surprised."

"Sorry, how about if I press two fingers on your neck, you stop?"

"That could happen anyway, I was thinking we need a safe word. You know, like people have during really kinky sex." Try as I might, I can't imagine Kevin in bondage gear, so his familiarity with this concept is pretty intriguing.

"How about 'wait?'"

"You will be tempted to say that anyway. It needs to be something random."

"Like?"

"Tower. Just say tower, and I'll stop."

"The password for that bar?" I wonder if there is more to that word than I originally thought. Does it mean something else?

"Well, they don't know. Besides, we're in a castle, so it won't seem nuts."

"Gentlemen, if we could just see a few moments of when Julia is supposed to barge in?"

"Tower it is. Let's go" I say, relieved by this new plan.

This time things feel easier. Even though we get back to that same high point of intensity even faster, we manage to avoid pushing things further. Knowing I can stop it with a single word lets me really put everything I have into it. My hands slide down his smooth and sweaty chest as he thrusts his hips against mine. As his pace increases, Kevin breaks away from kissing me and buries his head into my collarbone, letting out something like a growl. The vibration of his voice travels through me, and I gasp in ecstasy. I feel his hands slip under my ass, and for a minute it feels nice to have him support me. However, the second I feel his fingertips grasping the band of my underwear, I realize he is going to strip me naked if I don't say something.

"Tower," I whisper in his ear. The word works like magic. Kevin begins to dial the intensity back, and I feel safe once more. We fall back into a steady rhythm, till finally he pulls his body off of mine, gives me a quick wink, and then calls out to the audience.

"I'm not sure how much longer we can hold this position."

"He's right, I am going to hurt like hell tomorrow if we do this much longer," I add.

"Sorry, you can stop. We just need to adjust some more for Julia."

Kevin remains seated while I decide to stand up again and stretch. I roll my shoulders and bend back and forth, moaning in delight as the lactic acid releases from my stiff joints

"I'm that good?" Kevin smirks.

"Don't flatter yourself."

"That sound means I don't have to."

"That sound means sex with you is a pain in the neck."

"More like a pain in the balls." I know what he means; all that grinding with no release is incredibly frustrating.

"Well, I know several people in the ensemble who're more than willing to help you out."

"And you?" he asks, though I'm not sure if he is asking if I'd be willing or how I plan to get my own release.

"Eric's going to have a good night," I say, hoping he will make it home before the urge to take care of it myself wins over.

"Lucky guy," Kevin says with a quick smile before standing up and walking down stage.

NINETEEN

THE TECHNICAL REHEARSAL TAKES FIVE days to complete, but eventually it is behind us. We continue to adjust tiny things like lighting and sound, but mainly all we do is run the show over and over. With each passing day I can see how everything is falling into place, and the finished production begins to really take shape. Merchant is pretty good at not stopping us while we run things, but when we finally get to the end his notes are exhaustive. He misses nothing, and gives us countless notes. Then we tinker with those bits before running the show again. Finally, we only have one day left to rehearse without an audience. Tomorrow is our first preview performance, which means we will test how the play works with a crowd. Usually this is something I'm excited about, but over the past few days, with the sets, costumes, and lights, the show has changed a lot. It's all there, but now I'm just not sure I'm ready.

I had hoped the borderline marathon sex sessions I've had with Eric for the past few nights would have helped me to get some sleep, but I am routinely tormented by the nightmares I always have right before a show opens. It's very cliché. I arrive at the theatre, ready to perform, only to be told that we will be performing some other show instead of the one we've been rehearsing for weeks. Everyone is completely prepared for this, except me. To make matters worse, I'm always playing the lead. I scramble around, constantly looking at the script backstage, begging people to explain the choreography and blocking to me, and just barely getting through each scene. Then, right after the last line is said, and the audience is about to either boo or clap, I wake up.

"Mason, wake up," Eric says. When I open my eyes, I find him staring down at me with concern.

"Is it morning already?"

"No, but you were yelling in your sleep."

"Oh..."

"What show was it this time?" he asks, flopping back down onto his back.

"Oklahoma."

"At least it wasn't Sondheim or Shakespeare."

"True, but I don't do a very good Southern accent." As a boy from Houston, this has always been something I am equally proud and ashamed of. I love that no one believes me when I tell them I'm from Texas, but I've lost a few jobs for my inability to play Southern.

"Don't worry about stuff like that. You don't need it for the show you're in."

"Thank God," I say, wondering what Merchant would've done if I had.

"I can't wait to see it."

"Me either." Kevin was right. After the photoshoot fiasco, Eric needs to see the show. He wanted to keep the lights on while we had sex last night, which was fine, but I worry that his real reason wasn't that he liked my new body, but that he thought I'd be picturing Kevin in the dark.

"So what will you do on your final day?"

"Run the show till Merchant is satisfied," I say, leaning over the bed to rummage on the floor for a t-shirt. After all the weight loss, I've basically been forced to wear Eric's clothes. I look forward to finally going shopping for my own stuff, once the show is up and rehearsals are over. I don't even know what the characters on most of Eric's t-shirts are, but since I plan to wear a hoodie over them, I guess it doesn't really matter.

"I guess I shouldn't expect you home early, then."

"I don't know. Merchant has been pretty lax with notes the past few days. I think he just needs to make sure all the technical elements run smoothly with everything else."

"I hope so. When you get a chance, let me know when you'll be home. After last night I think I'll need advance notice," he says, pulling me to him.

"I thought you liked surprises."

"I didn't say I didn't like it." He kisses me, but it's just a peck. We both know that neither of us has daisy-fresh morning breath.

"Well, then you better let me go, so I can come back."

"I'll be waiting," he says, caressing my ass before pushing me off the bed.

WHILE I THOUGHT I HAD seen Merchant's genius at work from Day One, this morning reveals we've only been given a taste of what he can do. With the sets and script finally completed, the stack of papers I am so used to seeing him constantly reviewing have disappeared. His focus is now entirely on the actors. While we are on stage he refuses to take his eyes away from us to write something down, so he has Jenna follow him around. He needs to see everything.

Jenna, too, reveals the depth of her talent, jotting down notes at an alarming pace as Merchant whispers rapidly. This would be impressive enough on its own, but she also manages to do it while dodging as he moves from seat to seat like a pollenating bee. She is like some sort of ninja secretary, constantly shadowing his movements, without ever blocking his view or his path. They almost put the synchronicity Kevin and I have to shame, especially as something seems a bit off with us today. Everything seems dulled, but I try not to worry about it. We've done this too many times; actors need an audience to keep things fresh.

After we finish the first act Merchant can't hold his tongue any longer and demands we all sit for notes. When he joins us onstage, the scowl on his face causes my stomach to clench, and I curse myself for ever thinking he would be easy to please. I should have known better.

"Marshall, what were you doing with your hands in the first scene? Does Dyne have arthritis? I saw nothing of the sort throughout the remainder of the act. You need to be consistent throughout. Don't show me something in the first scene that is later abandoned with no explanation." The tone of his chastising is so serious I worry Marshall might break into tears. Thankfully, he seems to be able to keep it together, though the pen in his hand looks ready to burst as he grips it tightly to jot the note down.

I manage to get through the first scene without trouble, but Kevin isn't nearly as lucky. Merchant picks apart everything, most notably his pronunciation of the word "the," insisting that the correct pronunciation of the vowel is like "bee" not "duh." When Merchant starts talking about when Caleb and Ezio first embrace, the veins around the temples of his forehead begin to visibly throb.

"Kevin, what were you doing? You couldn't have put yourself further from him. You literally pushed your butt out like a flying buttress arch. You looked like you were presenting to Marshall. Let's fix this now, both of you, stand up," Merchant demands, motioning for me to join Kevin. We embrace again, and it feels normal to me, but Merchant lets out an exasperated sigh. He presses Kevin maybe half an inch closer to me, and it makes a difference. My face begins to flush, and I feel deep within myself that this tiny half an inch means a lot to Caleb. It's the light the sparks the fire of attraction between us. When we let go of one another, we exhale together, and only then do I realize we were both holding our breath. Kevin looks at me, and I can tell by the look in his eyes that the half inch also means a lot to Ezio.

The notes take longer than the performance, and to my surprise Kevin seems to get most of them. Every issue Merchant had seemed to trace itself back to Kevin having done something slightly different. With every correction, Merchant puts the pieces of our passion back into place and I become more and more curious as to why we'd assembled them so loosely this time. It's never been like that before. Once Merchant is done, lunch is called, and we are released for a much needed hour to recover ourselves. None of us wants to be alone, so we decide to go down the block and lose ourselves in pizza.

While I had lamented not bonding with the cast yet, I was hoping we would become friends over better circumstances than a scathing round of notes from Merchant. Julia charms the guys behind the counter to allow us to reassemble every table in the joint into one long banquet table. With the strength of all the guys in Kevin's Club, it takes only a matter of minutes, but I'm a little surprised and touched that they leave a seat across from Kevin for me. When I take my seat, Kevin adjusts his chair. After over an hour of adjustments from Merchant, I notice that he is now slightly further away from me.

"So who is ready for Act Two?" Julia asks, pretending to slash her wrists and die at the thought.

"I'm ready for the act, the notes however...." I reply, joining her mime game by pretending to hang myself.

"Want me to replace the dagger with a real one?" Marshall asks, singing the shrill violin section from the stabbing scene in *Psycho*.

"Not yet, but if he starts correcting the rate that I blink, please kill me."

"Will do."

As we wait for the food, each one of us comes up with a preferred method of death during notes. Tiny volunteers to go up to the catwalk and drop a sandbag on Julia. She immediately vetoes letting him be her executioner, joking that he will find a way to convince Merchant that Julia should be played by him in drag. Tiny is on book if we need a prompt, so whenever one us needs assistance, he does his best imitation of us saying the line. His impression of Julia is uncanny. To lighten the mood he pushes his head under her long chestnut hair and rattles off a few of her lines.

"How about it, Mason? You think you could fall in love with me?" Tiny asks, batting his eyes at me.

"Well...maybe...it'd have to be quite a transformation. It takes a lot to compete with Ezio."

"Does it?" Kevin asks, sullenly, sucking the laughter out of the room. I look at him, but he refuses to return the favor. The restaurant goes creepily quiet, with only the sounds of the kitchen to fill the void.

"Ummm...of course it does," I say, with so much sympathy I worry it sounds like pity.

"It better! I lose, and honestly, it takes a lot for someone to turn down this," Julia says gesticulating to her curvy figure.

"Especially those!" Tiny says, widening his eyes and leaning his head close to Julia's epic cleavage.

"Exactly! I mean they even attract gay men!" she says, shimmying back and forth, causing Kevin's club to whistle and howl. We chatter on, except Kevin, until the pizza arrives, and the silence feels easier because everyone's mouth is full. Kevin only takes a few bites before pushing his plate away.

As a slow eater, especially now that Lycan's diet has made my stomach shrink to one third of the size it was two months ago, I get to finally hear from a few of the ensemble members. Whenever I can, I try to compliment something I saw them do in rehearsal, which quickly makes the cast warm up to me. Even Kevin's Club seems to take a liking to me, after I tell them their subtext as former conquests of Ezio is really palpable.

"I'm glad you noticed."

"Of course! I don't think Caleb would really believe men could even be together without you guys looking so hungry for him during the scenes at court."

"At least someone is," Kevin says, once again attempting to kill the mood.

"Well, it doesn't appear you're hungry at all," I counter, eyeing his half-eaten slice.

"I'm not really, but you're welcome to keep pigging out. The next time Caleb's shirtless, do you think Merchant won't notice those two slices you just inhaled?" The insult would have shattered me a few weeks ago, but I've become stronger on the inside as well as out. Still, I can't believe Kevin is doing this.

"Maybe you should apply the focus you have toward counting my slices to working on stage."

"Oh, are we giving out acting advice now? How about you stop thinking about your precious boyfriend when you're on stage with me!" The entire cast looks at me, and I know my face must look just like that sad muscle boy's Kevin left in the street. I want to die. Just when I thought I'd found my place among them, Kevin has ruined it. All the time we've spent in each other's heads has given him a full arsenal of words to hurt me, and – I can see in his eyes – more is on the way.

"Kevin, this isn't the time or the place," I say, trying to implant the suggestion in his mind and spare us both from making a scene.

"Fuck that! I just got ripped apart by Merchant because of you! I'm not about to let the cast think I'm the weak link here."

"Kevin, please. We all got yelled at. We don't think anyone's a weak link," Julia says, trying to minimize the scene Kevin is intent on creating.

"Not everyone. Mason seemed to have no problem letting me take the heat for what is clearly his problem!"

"I wasn't the one who decided to change things up. What was I supposed to do?"

"Oh, I don't know. Maybe…anything?" Kevin says, throwing his arms up in disgust. "If you can't even adjust to a change in blocking, what's going to happen if someone drops a line? Are you just going to pretend they gave you your cue?"

"Of course not, I'll figure something out."

"How do you expect anyone to believe that? You couldn't even adjust to stuff that barely matters. I know you need help up there, but god, I'm only fucking human!"

I'm not sure which hurts more: Kevin's insult, or the sound of gasps from the cast.

"I…I…" I stutter, trying to find something to say.

"What? You what?"

"I don't need your help." I stand up, not about to just lie down and let Kevin use me as a whipping boy. I remind myself that Kevin isn't the only one with ammunition.

"Is that a joke?" he stands up as well, leaning his long frame across the table, until we are staring at one another face-to-face. "You wouldn't even have this part if I hadn't helped you. How many times have you told me that? I should have realized after a while, your ass wasn't worth saving."

"If you'd stop focusing on my ass, we wouldn't be having this fight."

"If you gave me something else to work with, maybe I'd have a reason to."

"I've given you plenty. I'm not stupid, Kevin. I wasn't hired because I was pretty, I'm not like you." Kevin's face darkens, his expression of anger and fury beyond anything I've ever seen before. His hands turn white as he firmly grips the side of the table, and time itself seems to freeze. I can see it in his eyes, hear it inside of his head: I've gone too far.

"Meaning what?" he asks, his voice low and guttural.

"Nothing," I reply, trying to think of something, anything, to help me back pedal out of this.

"No, not 'nothing.' We all heard you. Explain it to me. To us." The entire cast and crew are like statues. Even the kitchen staff seems to have frozen in place.

"Kevin, stop. Please...I didn't mean it."

"Didn't mean what?"

"Nothing. Just stop. Please, stop."

"Stop what? Stop asking you to explain what you meant? I can't help it. I'm apparently just a dumb pretty boy, right?"

"You know that's not true."

"The truth doesn't matter. Perception matters. On stage or off, all we ever are is what people perceive us to be. You might have fooled some of us into thinking you've become this great actor, but you're still just playing pretend. It's maddening to watch you. I see you walk right up to the edge, but never leap. And then you have the nerve to accuse me of being a piece of meat? Because what? Because I didn't need someone to tell me that being in shape was important in this business? Or was it because I walked in and auditioned and got the part, instead of having someone sneak me in, to convince the director that I was worthy of a chance? You know, a real actor doesn't blame the system for being unfair, a real actor transforms himself into something the system can't ignore."

I know better, and yet like a fool I played with the devil anyway. Did I really think I'd actually become as good an actor as Kevin? Someone with whom he wouldn't be able to take the stage, but rather, share it? I might have pierced Kevin's armor with my words, but his reply was far more deadly. The demons I thought Lycan and Merchant had exorcised from my mind return with even greater strength, having merely been playing dead. Now the perfect catalyst causes them to strike. I hear them repeat Kevin's words, louder and louder, telling me that, not only am I bad actor, I'm a bad person. I was the one who told Kevin to keep his distance, and yet when he was being filleted by Merchant, I said nothing. I owe him more than that. Why didn't I say anything? Kevin's right. I'm a fraud.

Without a word, I stand and make my way out the door. It takes every ounce of strength I have left not to burst into tears before I make it around the corner. I want to scream, but the only noise that escapes my lips is this sort of creaky cry, and I can feel that my entire throat is practically closed. I try to breathe deeper, to find a way to use my voice, and eventually it works. I weep like my mother did when I came out to her. I weep for the death of the person I thought I would be.

"Mason?" It's Alex, the last person in the world I want to see me like this.

"Go away!"

"No, I need to tell you something." His voice isn't affected in that stupid nasal tone he normally uses, but is pure and sincere. For the first time, I feel like I'm hearing the real Alex.

"Just go, do my part. Isn't this what you've been waiting for?"

"I'll go, if you promise to just listen to me for one minute."

"Fine."

"Kevin's said all of that before."

"What?"

"Yeah, that same monologue. Almost verbatim. Two years ago we were in a show together, and when the director criticized him, Kevin blamed this girl, and said almost the exact same thing to her."

"But why?"

"Uh, hello? To blame someone else, obviously. Kevin's not exactly used to people telling him he's wrong."

"But he's right."

"If you really believe that, even knowing he's said it before, then maybe I should take your part. You know, just because you fear it being true, doesn't make him right. Only giving up does."

"So what should I do?"

"Prove him wrong," he says, reaching out his hand to help me up. It's odd to hear Alex be so perceptive, or so real. If he'd been like this the whole time, I wonder if we'd have been friends. Or would I have really worried about being replaced?

We arrive back at the theater to find everyone scrambling to get ready. As I pass the members of the cast each of them smiles, giving me a nod of encouragement or approval, I can't really tell which. I brace myself for a confrontation when I open the dressing room I share with Kevin, but thankfully he's not there. After changing back into my costume, I can feel some of my confidence restored. In the mirror I see the actor I've always wanted to be, and know that I have changed. I have. I can feel Caleb – the character I created, that I breathed life into – touch my mind with his. He is part of me, and is every bit as real as Kevin's Ezio. If Kevin thinks I'm running away, then he's in for a big surprise. I'll unleash the soldier within us both. I will fight.

"Mason?" I hear Merchant ask from behind the door

"Yes?" I answer, feeling Caleb's annoyance that I am answering to that name.

"Can I come in?"

"Are we ready for Act Two?"

"What? I think we need to—" Merchant begins.

"Everything is fine," I say, opening the door wide. "See? I'm ready for action."

"You're sure?"

"I've never been more ready to give you the performance of a lifetime." I walk out toward the stage, passing everyone, until I come face-to-face with Kevin.

"Mason, I wasn't expect—"

"You're not even dressed yet?" I ask, cutting him off.

"What?"

"The ball is about to begin. You should prepare yourself. I have a feeling it is going to be the event of the century," I say, not sure if I mean it as Mason or Caleb.

"Five minutes to places for Act Two," Jenna announces over the speakers, and without another word I go over to the one of the backstage mirrors and adjust my glorious coat. Kevin might have shattered me, but I know how to rebuild things that were once broken. This time, I will be even stronger than before.

TWENTY

NLIKE THE FIRST ACT, WHEN we get on stage I am not about to put up with any distance between Kevin and myself. Yet this time, Kevin seems even more determined to avoid me. So whenever he deviates, I correct it, and force him to maintain what we worked so hard to create. He doesn't seem to know what to do with me now that I'm not holding back. I push him, demanding he give me more. Whenever he withholds, I understand why Kevin found it so frustrating. As the second act progresses, things with Kevin just fall apart. It's maddening to watch, but Merchant never calls for us to stop. By the time I die, I can see in Julia's worried eyes that Merchant is about to unleash a tsunami of fury that will make what happened this morning look like a child's play.

"What was that hesitation at the top of the act?" Merchant says, the frustration in his voice barely in check. "What was with both of you the entire act? Mason, since when is Caleb so aggressive? Kevin, why were you running around the stage? You went out of your light over and over. Mason practically had to force you to get close to him, and in the final seduction scene he literally did. He put your hands on him, because you just stood there."

"I'm sorry...I just..."

"Just what? If you want to portray Ezio this way, I'll find that revision where Dyne is the mastermind. Is that what you want?"

"No," Kevin insists.

"Then fucking act! What happened tonight cannot happen again!"

Merchant yells, stomping his feet down as he paces.

"It's not just him," I say, not wanting to let Kevin take the heat again, especially since I know I am equally at fault this time.

"Believe me, I know. Just looking at you two makes me sick. We have an audience tomorrow, and this is what you show me?" He swings his arms wide, and then throws them up in disgust.

"It was just...after this morning...," I start, but not entirely sure how to explain.

"This morning! At least this morning, we had a show. It wasn't a great show, but it wasn't this mess."

"Stop," says Kevin, standing up. "It's my fault. Mason and I had a fight. I told him to stop holding back."

"Only because I have been. He was right. I'm the reason the first act was so bad."

"That is enough!" Merchant fumes. "Kevin, you're an actor, not the director. I don't ever want to hear about you giving anyone notes. Do you see what it's done? What am I supposed to do? Cancel our first preview? We barely have any preview performances as it is! I want whatever is between you two fixed. Tonight! If you give me a repeat of this tomorrow morning, I will replace you both. I'd rather have amateurs up here trying than whatever the hell you were doing. Get out of my sight." Just as Kevin knew how much he wounded me at lunch, I know Merchant's dismissal is breaking Kevin in half. Alex was right, Kevin's always been fortunate enough to be spared the harsh reality of this business. I've been yelled at by directors before, but Kevin has always been a golden boy. Until now.

An actor to the end, he quietly walks offstage with me, his face completely devoid of emotion. A knot of guilt wells up in my throat for causing this, for having reveled in making him look bad on stage. I quietly follow him off, but once we are backstage, he runs.

I follow him, but lose him as I run down into the bowels of the theater to our dressing room door, but there I pause. Unsure if I'm ready to see Kevin so broken, I cup my hand to try and listen through the door. I'm not sure why people do this in movies and TV; it doesn't work very well. Next I try the handle, and am surprised to find it unlocked. To my horror, the room is empty. My chest constricts and I stop breathing. When I feel a hand on my shoulder, my lungs restart and I choke on a quick inhalation of air.

"He's not here?" Merchant asks, retracting his hand.

"What are you doing here? Where is he!" I yell, furious at him for pushing Kevin over the edge.

"I was hoping to talk him down."

"Do you think he'd even listen to you after being humiliated like that? What were you thinking?"

"He was slipping!"

"So you pushed him over the edge?"

"Me? Who was the one chasing him around the stage?" Merchant asks, his words tightening the knot of guilt to a point where I feel like I'm choking.

"Isn't that what you told me to do?"

"You knew what you were doing!"

"I..."

"We don't have much time. I need you to find him."

"What? How?"

"Just like we practiced."

"You expect me to find him how? He could be anywhere in the city." The idea of trying to find him, when there were millions of places he could be, seems truly impossible.

"What was all that training for if not for moments like this? Now, where is Ezio?"

Though it seems ridiculous, I do it. I close my eyes, take a deep breath, and try to focus on the question. To find him, I need to concentrate. I start by throwing up every barrier in my mind to block out the hundreds of thoughts and emotions that attempts to distract me. I slowly lower myself onto the ground to recreate the sessions I had with Kevin and Merchant. Only this time, everything is on a much grander scale, so I imagine that the room extends to the size of Manhattan. I feel tiny, but putting it all under one roof seems to help. Once I've got it assembled in my head, I start tapping into Kevin.

"Where is Ezio?" Merchant asks again.

I dig deeper into my mind, trying to remember every tiny detail about Kevin I have ever known. The amount of data is surprisingly large when I try to organize it into a mental map, but no sooner do I notice this, than I realize I'm going about this the wrong way. I am not going to find the answer by cross referencing some cerebral spreadsheet. Kevin doesn't operate like that. He runs on instinct, feeling his way through life. I wipe my mind of thoughts, forgetting even my goal, and just try and tap into some part of Kevin's essence.

"Where is Ezio?"

The sound of Merchant's voice makes the hair on my forearms stand on end. The pulse of my fluttering heart throbs in my ears as I begin to panic. The voice is horrible; Kevin would hate it. It hits me that my body is reacting to Merchant just like Kevin, and I can sense a shadow of Kevin in the city-sized room. He's running, fleeing as far away from any authority as he can, looking for a place where he feels safe, superior, and wanted. My mind jumps at a supernatural pace, from location to location on my conjured map of Manhattan until the answer finally hits me. I know where he is.

"Tower!"

"What?" Merchant asks.

"I know where he is," I say, jumping to my feet, my breathing already settling into a rhythm that will let me almost spring the fifteen city blocks that separate us.

"Stop!" Merchant grabs my shoulder. "I'm not done with you."

"But there's no time."

"I know, but Mason, it's time I called in my favor."

"Fine, what is it?" I ask impatiently, annoyed at this delay.

"Have you even thought about what you'll do when you find him?"

"Well, no. Apologize, I guess."

"I'm afraid he will need you to do more than that, and so will I."

"What are you talking about?"

"Kevin has lost his way, and I need you remind him of his ability. I need you to save him from himself." The request feels like a direction, one that I don't understand.

"And how do I do that?"

"That's something you'd know better than I. You've spent hours in his mind. You know what he needs. I simply want you to agree to provide it."

"But...what if I can't?" I ask, feeling like Merchant is trying to trap me into another awful agreement.

"Then there's nothing we can do. The show won't work without Kevin any more than it would work without you. The future of your career hinges on bringing Kevin back."

"But how?"

"Mason, use your talent. Remind Kevin of his greatness. Be exactly what he needs in this moment of weakness. Kevin isn't used to being vulnerable. Find a way to give him back his armor."

"I...I'll try."

"That's all I can ask of you. Now hurry, before it truly is too late," he says, letting me go.

When I exit the theater, I'm assaulted by a terrible combination of freezing rain and wet snow. I flip up the hood of my hoodie to shield myself as much I can, but after just a few blocks the cold soaks in. However, I am determined not to care, and push myself to sprint faster and faster. My increased speed causes me to slide on the wet pavement a few times, but just before I am about to topple over I manage to just barely regain my balance in what probably looks like a rather impressive stunt. People turn and stare, forcing me to abandon all traces of politeness and yell for them to get out of my way. Once I arrive in front of the Chinese restaurant, I take a minute to collect myself before walking in.

"Can I help you?" the hostess asks.

"My friend's in the back," I explain as I pass by, making my way to the alley. I knock on the door, and after a few minutes the same thin-faced man as before opens the door ever so slightly.

"May I help you?"

"I'm here to meet someone."

"Name?"

"Tower," I reply, and the man shuts the door in my face. I knock again, and the whole scene repeats, only this time I wedge my foot in the door.

"Sir, please remove your foot."

"No, I know he's in there," I say, trying to squeeze past him.

"That doesn't mean he wants to see you," the man replies, and while that sinks in he manages to knock me back and shut the door behind him.

I knock again, but this time there is no answer. Part of me is happy, knowing that I am in the right place, but it's only a small victory if I can't get in. I wait, hoping someone else will come by, but no one does. The alley is mainly shielded from the ice and snow, but my breath is visible as I exhale. As I'm no longer running, I can really start to feel the slushy snow that has begun to seep into my clothes. I know I can't wait forever. As a kid, I remember watching the movie *Iron Will*, and learning about frostbite. I never really got over it. So I try to think of what else I can do. I tell myself there has to be another way in. Then I remember that when we left, we took a different passage. I quickly jog around the building, calling Kevin's cell phone repeatedly, but he doesn't answer. I take a moment to send Eric a text message saying it's going to be a long night, but when he calls my phone I press ignore and shift my ringer to silent. I can't lose focus. I've got to find that door.

I make several passes, but nothing seems familiar. I curse myself for not paying better attention back then, but how was I to know I'd be doing something like this? I decide I've got to expand my search, which requires me to climb over a short wall that blocks the alley from the patio of the neighboring building. Security lights flick on as I drop down, but no one comes to check it out. Once they click off again, I slink along the wall, until I find a fire escape.

The steps are peculiar in that they reach the ground, which makes me think I might be in the right place, but I'm not sure. The metal steps creep under my weight, so I try to move as stealthily as possible up to the first floor. I find what I hope is the right door, and slowly open it to reveal a black curtain. I'm happy I've found it, but worried about barging in on Kevin. I listen for signs of what to expect, but all I hear is him muttering his lines to himself. His speech is slurred, and he seems to be stumbling around. When I hear a crash, I rush through the curtain to find him hanging off of the overturned loveseat clutching a nearly empty bottle. Based on the random French word on the label, and smell that permeates the air, I'm guessing that Kevin's been chugging cognac.

"Kevin!" I run to him.

"Unh..." he groans in response.

"Kevin, what are you doing? Get up."

"Not again, oh god not again," he cries out.

"Kevin, come on, get up." Even with all my training, I can't lift him. His frame is all muscle, and in his condition he's basically dead weight. "Kevin, I can't lift you. Help me out a little."

"I thought you didn't need my help."

"I was wrong, okay? I need you. Now come on, let's get you off the floor."

I strain, trying to move him, but it's no use. "No, the floor is where I belong."

"Come on Kevin, just stand up. We need to get you home."

"No. No, home. Here. You're supposed to do what I say," he slurs, looking at me, clearly perplexed.

"I'm trying to help you."

"Don't talk back...just be quiet. Just let me pretend," he says, yanking me down on top of him. "Mason, Mason, Mason," he coos, petting my head.

"Kevin."

"You sound just like him."

"Like who?" I ask, in my most patient voice.

"Like Mason. My Mason."

"I am Mason."

"No. No. Not my Mason."

"Yes, your Mason. Look at me." For a long while he stares at me, his eyes blinking rapidly, unable to focus for very long at first. Eventually though, he seems able to see me.

"Wait. Mason?"

"Yes?"

"Oh my god, it's you!" he says, bolting up, and hugging me to him. "It's really you, right?"

"For the last time, yes! It's really me." I say, holding his face in my hands, looking him dead in the eye.

"But why?"

"Why what?"

"Why are you here? You shouldn't be here."

"I came to get you. You ran off, we—" I don't want to say we. I know I can't mention Merchant if I want him to listen. "I was worried"

"How did you find me?"

"Kevin, c'mon. Who knows you better than me? I knew you'd run here."

"I like it here."

"I know."

"I like you."

"I know."

"Do you like me too?" I never expected Kevin Caldwell to sound like a note you pass in middle school. I want to laugh, but don't.

"Yes, Kevin, I like you very much, but I'd like you even more, if you'd come with me."

"Where?"

"Home."

"Will you come too?"

"Yes, but only if we leave now."

"You promise?"

"Yes, I promise, now come on," I say, putting his arm over me and helping him out and down the staircase. Once we're down, I realize scaling the wall wasn't exactly necessary. There's a gate on the opposite wall that is unlocked. We stumble a few blocks until finally I manage to lean Kevin against a streetlight and flag down a cab. It takes some convincing to get the cabby to take us, seeing that Kevin is so drunk, but I offer to pay extra if he vomits. Fortunately, Kevin manages to make it all the way home before violently throwing up in the street outside his apartment. I rub his back between convulsions, making sure to avert my eyes so I won't be sick myself. His legs begin to shake, and I try my best to support him, but it's hard to do given how strong his contractions are.

"I'm so sorry," he repeats, in the brief moments he has between waves. I tell him it's fine, praising him for not getting sick in the cab, until eventually he's done.

"You think you can make it up the stairs now?"

"Yeah, I feel a lot better now." He says, standing up on his own.

"We need to be quiet. If the landlady wakes up, she'll call the cops," he tells me, his face as serious as he was when he defended his chop stick theory. The memory causes me to snicker. "Shhh."

"Sorry."

"And don't judge me on my place. I don't bring people home often," he says, opening the door to his apartment. It appears he wasn't kidding about being quiet, as he motions for us to skip a few stairs on our way up. He points to his ear, to tell me they squeak. I wonder if the landlady isn't already awake, given how loud Kevin's digestive pyrotechnics on the street were, but if she is, she doesn't come out to yell at us. Kevin's hands are shaking so badly that it takes him a while to get the key in the door, but he finally manages to open it.

As I close the door behind us, the place practically swallows me in darkness. I step forward into the unknown, knocking something with my foot and causing a domino effect of tiny tinkles, as the sound of bottles touching bottles fills the apartment. The room is pungent with the smell of sweat and booze, and I have to breathe through my mouth to avoid gagging.

"Can you turn on a light?" I ask, afraid to take another step.

"Fine," Kevin says, followed by the sound of lamp chain being pulled.

The dim bulb isn't strong, but now that I can see, I wish I couldn't. Kevin's apartment is a complete wreck. Liquor bottles, most of which are empty, are strewn all over the place, with a few take-out boxes thrown in here and there. I could almost overlook this, since I always assumed Kevin was a bit of a slob, but as my eyes adjust I see the faint shimmer of gold, silver, and copper reflecting off the discarded condom wrappers that litter the floor like coins at the bottom of a fountain.

"Kevin…"

"I told you, no judgments."

"But…look at this place. What on earth have you been doing here?" I ask, and for the first time in days I feel completely out of sync with him. Seeing him in this place makes it clear that, as much as I thought I knew everything about him, there were plenty of secrets he was hiding from me.

"Nothing, I've just been having a bit of fun."

"I thought you didn't bring people here."

"Sorry. I don't bring people I *know* here."

"Oh…," I say, realizing that I am standing at ground zero, surrounded by the wreckage of an anonymous orgy. I try to make my way toward Kevin, but no matter how careful I am, the sensation of cold noodles squishing under foot, combined with the stench of sex and booze, makes me want to wretch. However, I know I have to be strong. I've got to help Kevin.

"Be careful," he hisses, but no matter what I do every step I take creates even more noise. Kevin, on the other hand, is like a spider, able to navigate his web with ease. While I attempt to reach him, he continues moving around the apartment, stripping off his clothes and tossing them to the floor until he's just wearing a tank top and designer briefs. He makes it to the bathroom, and after a few seconds I hear the faucet on the sink turn on full blast. The sound of running water helps drown out some of the noise I make.

Kevin's apartment is swelteringly hot, which I'm certain has helped increase the decomposition of the food on the floor. My clothes have gone from cold and wet to warm and damp in just a few minutes. After a bit more searching, I eventually find a slightly non-disgusting place on the floor to drop my pack, coat, and hoodie.

"Kevin?" I ask, after the water stops. I think about opening the door, but thankfully Kevin reappears.

"This way," he says, taking my hand.

"Errr, okay…" I start, as he guides me through another doorway. "But, can we talk a bit?"

"I don't want to talk."

"But we have to. We have our first audience tomorrow, or, rather, we have our first audience today."

"If that's the only reason you're here, just leave. Can't we talk about anything other than the show?" he asks, circling me to close the door. This room is even darker than the last; fearing I might trip, I tighten my grip on his forearm.

"Yes, but…"

"Mason, just be quiet," he says, pulling me toward the floor and causing me to bang my knee against the wooden frame of his bed. Before

I can yell, he covers my mouth with his hand, muffling my cry into a wheezing moan. Once I've stopped, he retracts his hand. I sit on the edge of the bed, rubbing the pain out of my throbbing knee.

He leaves my side, and after a bit of rummaging around I hear the unmistakable sound of a match being struck. Next, there's an eruption of light. Shielding the fragile flame, Kevin's hands glow red in the darkness. Using a single match, he gracefully illuminates the wicks of few tea lights that rest in an arched iron vessel on his dresser, as well as a pillar candle on his nightstand. Their combined power bathes the room in a soft but full light. Unlike the rest of his apartment, his bedroom is immaculately clean. I forget that I am no longer hidden by darkness, and my facial expression must reveal my surprise. Without my even asking, he explains. "I entertain out there. You're the first person I've ever brought in here."

"Oh." I swallow hard. "Okay."

"Yeah." He pats the mattress in front of him, inviting me to come closer and share his bed, like I'm a pet. I follow his suggestion, curling up beside him, trying hard to think of what I should do next.

We don't speak.

While I think, Kevin pulls my shirt up slightly and begins tracing his fingers along the knotted muscles of my spine, lulling me with the gentle heat radiating off of his hands. After running around outside in the cold, the warmth is hard to resist, and I close my eyes, just wanting to relax for a few minutes. I visualize the patterns his fingers create as they lightly skate across my body: figure eights, circles, triangles, and stars. With each sweep he nuzzles closer to me, pulling my shirt up higher and higher to increase the canvas he's drawing on. Eventually I'm shirtless, and, as Kevin continues, I almost want to purr with delight.

However, when I feel his hand grasp the front of my jeans, the hazy feeling vanishes, and I knock his hand away. He's too close for me easily roll onto my back, so I roll forward onto my stomach and then onto my side to face him. I can't forget why I'm here: I need to get him to come back, but not like he is now. No, I need him to come back as he was, strong and confident. Without that part of him restored, I'll never see the real Ezio again.

"I want to talk about tonight," I say, grasping his hand and holding it in mine. "I know you don't want to, but we need to. I'm worried."

"There's nothing to be worried about. I'll be fine."

"Merchant thinks you aren't coming back." Kevin winces at the mere mention of his name, and I worry I've screwed up. I squeeze his hand a bit, and he squeezes back.

"I'll come back," he whispers, leaning into me, resting his head on my shoulder. We hold each other for a few minutes, until Kevin starts pressing on my collarbone, trying to get me to lie back down.

"Stop. I'm not done talking."

"Shhhhh…we can talk in the morning. Just stay with me tonight. I don't want to be alone."

"No. Not if you won't even tell me what's going on with you," I say, sitting up and throwing my legs over the side of the bed.

"Okay, okay, don't go. What do you want from me? I said I'd come back."

"Showing up isn't enough. I need you to come back all the way, not like this. I know you can do it, but you have to talk to me. Let me help you."

"I don't need help."

"Kevin, look around this place. You need help."

"Look, I'm sorry about tonight. It won't happen again," he promises, scooting closer to me so I can see the sincerity in his eyes.

"But what happened today? What made you so scared? You've never pulled away before."

"I was scared because of you! You freaked me the fuck out. After everything I said at lunch…it should have…it should have destroyed you, but instead you…you just walked on and came at me with everything you had. It was terrifying. You treated me like a prop."

"I had to. You weren't giving me any other choice. I thought that's what you wanted. I was adapting. I'm sorry you feel like you've been holding everything together all by yourself. I wanted to show you, I wasn't going to rely on you. You don't have to be perfect, we're in this together."

"Oh, now we're together?" Kevin says, the look of annoyance strangely made more menacing by the candle light.

"Of course we are. Kevin, I tell you that all the time. I'll admit, we haven't always been equal partners, but I hope we're closer to being that nowadays. I mean, I'll never be able to forget all the help you gave me. I'll owe you for that for the rest of my life."

"You keep saying that, but whenever I try and cash in, you say no."

"What?"

"It's true. Whenever I ask, you always say no." Kevin brings his face so close that his lips brush mine, and I quickly shut my eyes.

"Kevin, I..."

"I've tried to make it so easy for you. At your party, the bar, Julia's soiree, even the fucking photoshoot," he says, as he plants kisses on my neck and chest.

"Kevin, stop."

"Relax, just listen. Let me do the talking." Kevin pivots until he's behind me and begins to massage my shoulders. Slowly his hands travel lower, but seeing as I'm sitting up his attempts to grab my ass are not particularly successful. While I know what he wants me to do, I resist, but it doesn't work very well. He wraps his arms around me and pulls me backward onto the bed. Kevin's body isn't exactly a great pillow, and thanks to the weight loss I'm not exactly padded that well either. My shoulder blades begin to hurt from resting on his ribs, so I turn onto my side, but Kevin uses this moment to lightly push me over so that I am on my stomach. Before I can roll back onto my side, he deftly swings his leg over me, straddling me like a horse. He strips off his tank top, throwing it off the side of the bed, and lowers his bare chest against my back. The position seems dangerous. He slides the full length of his body over mine, his trapped erection sliding along the denim of my jeans. His dick is so hard that it doesn't bend, and I hear him suck in air through his teeth to power through the discomfort. I think about using this as an excuse to move, but, before I can protest, he lowers his lips to my ear and whispers: "Ask me anything."

"I want you to...to tell..." I say, having difficulty finishing the thought. My brain short-circuits when he finds a cluster of knots in the small of my back; instead of telling him to stop, all I do is let out a low moan.

"Oh my, I think I know where Ezio's hands will go tomorrow night." My muscles pulse with pleasure at the attention, but Kevin's mentioning of Ezio causes me to think about the show, and again I am reminded why I am here.

"Tower!" I yell, and instantly I feel the weight of Kevin's body disappear, as he returns to the empty space beside me.

"Ugh! I hate the word! See! Even now, you resist me."

"Wait...I'm sorry...Are you still talking about the show?" I ask, opening my eyes and looking him in the face.

"God, the show, it was even worse tonight. Most of the time you can at least pretend to be into me."

"Well, most of the time you actually try to get me."

"I know, but I just can't do it anymore. It's bad enough when you act all pure and good, that you're suffering my desire for the sake of art, but this afternoon, I could feel you loathing every second of it. Knowing what I wanted, and giving it to me, but with such hate. Do you have any idea how hard it is to deal with that?"

"Yes! Kevin, I do. What do you think it was like for me when we were in that acting class together? Why do you think we lost touch?"

"We didn't lose touch. You disappeared. We were friends, and then one day you just disappeared."

"I had no choice. I had to cut you out of my life because it was the only way I could stop loving you!" My words come out louder than I anticipate, fueled by a rush of emotions. Everything I thought was dead and buried, the loneliness of countless night spent pining for him, comes back at once.

"I didn't know..."

"Yes, you did. Everyone knew how I felt. You just didn't want to acknowledge it. I couldn't take it anymore. Loving someone who doesn't love you back is hard, but eventually you can see it'll just never happen. You can stop. Loving someone who refuses to even acknowledge it is so much worse. Every time you'd call, or text, or suggest we hang out, I'd feel this tremendous hope, and that made it impossible to move on. It took me more than a year to stop wanting you."

"I'm sorry."

"You should be. You know, I was happy when I saw you again, figuring now that I had Eric, we could be friends. But friendship wasn't enough for you this time. You wanted your old idolizing fan back, and you knew just what to do to push me there. Do you know what it's like to know that my love for Eric isn't perfect? That there's still some part of me that wants you? Why do you think I needed a safe word?"

"I didn't come up with that for you. I did it to stop me," Kevin says, emphatically slapping his palm against his chest. "When you're in that scene with me it seems so real. Every time we do it, I think I've finally managed to get you to give in, but the second they tell us to stop, I realize I'm wrong. You return to yourself, and act like it was nothing, or worse, that it was painful. I come home and replay it over and over in my mind. Seeing just how many times you tried to get me to stop. To tell me nothing I do will ever be enough."

"Kevin, I don't find you lacking. I wish I did. Maybe then it'd be easier for both of us. But it doesn't matter. You have to give me up."

"I've tried! Why do you think my living room looks like that? I've fucked tons of guys in the past two months, just because they vaguely resembled you. All they needed was something that reminded me of you, your hair, your lips, your big stupid grin, anything. I mean, Alex is almost your twin, if he shuts the fuck up." Is that why he kept telling me to be quiet? Did he think I was Alex? Did Alex know he was being used like…an understudy? This is too much. As flattering as it is, it's even more horrifying.

"Kevin…why?"

"I thought if I could have some piece of you, I could move on. The problem was, I knew I was getting closer to you. On the night of the photo shoot, I actually thought you were going to not only let me fuck you, but have Lee take pictures! I was seconds away from just going for it, but then Eric showed up. I couldn't believe you stood there, naked, and blamed yourself. I'd worked you up so hard that you weren't in control at all, and yet you told Eric it was your fault. Worse than that, you believed it." How had I missed these signs? I'd been in his head for hours each day, but I thought all that passion and hunger for me was Ezio, that it was acting. Kevin's entire body is trembling, shivering, even though I know he's not cold. I struggle to find the right words to rebuild him, but it's hard to process everything.

"Kevin, you're taking too much of the blame."

"Bullshit," he retorts, and so I try again, and this time the words come out smoother.

"I'm not saying you're innocent, I'm just saying you can't take all the blame. You know there is still some part of me that wants you. I just never dreamed you could actually be feeling those things for me too. I assumed it was like old times, and that everything felt so real because you were an incredible actor. I mean, you're Kevin Caldwell."

"That doesn't mean what you think it does. I'm just a face who can sort of act." There it is again. Kevin's fear, his insecurity. This I know I can fix.

"Kevin, would you say I've become a better actor since we began working together?"

"Yes."

"And I've told you it's because I learned so much from you?"

"Yes."

"Then trust me when I say your name means something. You're more than just a pretty face. I see hot men every day in this city, but none of them has ever made me question the love I have for Eric. You and your talent have, which shows how powerful it is. Whenever I'm with you, I see a life I might have had, and it's a life I am lucky enough to live when we share the stage. That's the reason everything is so muddled when we perform together. There's something between us, and that just makes it easy for us both to wish our lives as Caleb and Ezio were real."

"Then let's grant that wish," Kevin says, suddenly breaking out the grin he wears when he's plotting a scheme. "The scene is going to get out of control sometime, but maybe we can choose when. Let's do the scene right now. We can do it however we want, it'll be our little secret."

"I'm through with secrets. Besides, you fucked a bunch of guys who looked like me. Did that help? No, it made it worse."

"Because they weren't you! Mason, this will work, it has to. Otherwise I'm going to do something drastic one night."

"The scene won't ever get completely out of control. We can't have sex on stage."

"The only thing that stopped me during the photo shoot was the fact that Merchant called stop and even then I was ready to defy him, but then Eric showed up. Do you even notice the audience when we're doing that scene? We perform eight times a week, twice in one day on matinees, what are the odds one of us will always have the strength to stop the other?"

"That's why we have the safe word."

"Then we'll use it tonight. Just try it. If you want me to stop, I'll stop."

"Ideas like this never work. It's completely stupid," I say, more to myself than to Kevin, still trying – but failing – to think of some other way.

"No, pretending to ignore this is stupid. Look what's happened as a result. If we'd hooked up years ago, the mystery would be gone."

"There's got to be another way."

"Why won't you try this?" he asks, pushing me back down onto the bed.

"Because it makes no sense. Why would us having sex help things?"

"It won't be us, it'll be Caleb and Ezio. Let them have tonight, and whenever things are getting too intense, this memory will help keep us in check. We won't need to go all the way, we can just remember tonight. Trust me, I've never been wrong about acting before. The memory of tonight will be enough for the rest of the run." Before I can reply, Kevin kisses me, and Merchant's words keep rolling around in my head. Is this what he needs? Am I able to do this? I relax and start to give in. Sensing this, Kevin quickly goes to work unbuttoning my jeans, as I begin to kiss him back.

"Ezio!" I gasp, as he breaks off the kiss to throw my jeans to the floor.

"Mason."

"What did you call me?"

"I mean Caleb," he says, as he slips his fingers in the elastic around my boxer briefs.

"Stop!" I say, pushing him away, my body frustrated with the sudden stop of pleasure. "This isn't working. Neither of us are even thinking about the show."

"You're right. I'm sorry, I was just...excited. Let's really do the scene, hold on," he says, disappearing into the other room, and returning with a bottle of wine and single glass.

"Come Caleb, share in my delight, and suck the milk of Venus with me," he says, pouring the wine into the glass.

"This isn't working, it's not the same."

"I've got an idea. Hold on." Kevin leaps off the bed, and starts rummaging through a closet. His lithe torso glows in the soft candle light.

"What are you looking for?"

"These," he says, holding up two masks that look remarkably similar to the ones we wear in the show.

"You just have these?"

"I go to a lot of parties. These are from Mardi Gras." The moment I put it on, I can feel a little bit of Caleb's presence in the back of my head. I close my eyes, and when I open them, I can see Kevin as Ezio. Only instead of dressed as he usually is in the scene, he lays there, nearly naked, and my heart begins to beat rapidly.

"Share in my delight, and suck the milk of Venus with me," he says, his voice making every cell in my body feel alive.

"If you insist then," I say, skipping ahead in the scene a little.

"Very good, drink up, my little angel. But as you do, tell me, what do you know of love?"

"I know that it causes men to do mad things." This sentence has never been truer.

"Indeed, it does. For love emboldens us to risk all, a risk I am finally willing to take. Caleb my sweet angel, all I ask is that you stay with me tonight. Love me as I love you for this one evening, and, once the morning comes, if you still love another, I will resign that you are a war I cannot win," he says, changing the line to fit tonight. The slight modification in the words seems to completely undo me, and for a brief moment I abandon myself to Caleb's pulsing desire, careful though to never once retreat from the experience completely. The four of us share our two bodies, Caleb urges me to let go, but I fight back.

"Wait," I plead.

"What's wrong?"

"This isn't right. It isn't safe."

"Don't worry, I'm always safe," he says, grabbing a condom and lube from his bedside table. His kiss banishes away everything but the pure joy of this moment. As he slowly slides my underwear down my legs I know my last defense is gone. I grab at his boxer briefs, and as I lower them down I giggle when his erection slaps against his abdomen. As I expected every part of Kevin's body is truly perfect. We explore every inch of one another, and I commit each sensation to memory. Caleb and I become one, not shared, but one. With nothing to anchor us to the world, Caleb and I finally submit to Kevin and Ezio, consumed in being the sole desire of the man who has once more become a god.

TWENTY ONE

WHEN I WAKE, IT TAKES me a minute to realize where I am. So many things feel familiar, but are not quite the same. The smell of smoldering ash wafts about the room, and I notice that last night's votives have just expired. As the smoke tendrils snake up into the ceiling, everything comes back to me. Visions of last night flash forth in my head, like a movie that is being viewed in extreme fast forward, but on occasion switches to slow motion. I see Kevin and I sitting in bed and talking, followed by his wild gesticulations as he convinces me to sleep with him. I want to turn it off, but the harder I try, the more in focus it becomes. I slither out from underneath his arm and stumble to the bathroom, turning the faucet on full. I gulp down water, hoping to wash away the remnants of his saliva, which I swear I can feel on my teeth.

After rinsing my mouth out a few dozen times, I return to the bedroom to find my clothes so I can sneak out, but my shirt seems to have disappeared. I decide to borrow one of Kevin's, or at least so I hope, which is draped over a chair. Knowing Kevin will wonder where I am, I rummage through my backpack and rip a page out of my script to write a note. Unsure of what to say, I leave it cryptic yet positive.

Kevin,

*I didn't have the heart to wake you, as I know
you'll need your strength for tonight. I couldn't find
my shirt and borrowed one of yours. I look forward to
tonight.*

Mason

The words feel strange, but nothing better comes to mind, so I fold
the paper and leave it by the bedside table, just inches away from Kevin's
sleeping body. I take one last look at him, sprawled out across the entire
bed. The single bed sheet draped stylishly about his god-like form just
barely covers him. If I hadn't slept here, I would swear a designer came in
during the night to style him this way, as the coverage is artfully placed
to preserve his modesty. I dig my fingernails into my hand, hoping I can
reprogram myself to associate pain with his visage, instead of lust and
longing. Eventually I have the power to turn away and return home.

The early morning sky is gray and overcast, making the entire world
seem as muddled as my own life. The lines and boundaries I've spent
years living within have all been smudged. I no longer remotely resemble
myself on the outside, and after last night, I wonder if there is any part of
my former self left. Walking the abandoned streets, I pull my coat tighter,
as I notice there are small flecks of white swirling in the air. It's December,
and it's snowing like I'm in a Christmas special. I thrust my hands in my
pockets to keep my hands warm, and feel my phone resting there.

My battery is almost dead, but I can see I've missed about twenty
calls. I listen to my voice mail, and when I hear Eric's voice, my heart
breaks.

"Hey, thanks for texting, I know you can't answer. The reviews for
our game are out...and they're really good. My boss's boss asked me to
stop by next week, so that's pretty great huh? Anyway, I'll try to wait up,
I love you so much."

The support and enthusiasm in his voice cuts me like a knife. What
have I done? What am I going to do? How could I forget Eric last night?
What was I thinking? With what's left of my battery, I listen to each call,

and even though they came at three or four in the morning, they all just end the same. "I love you so much." He repeats, and when I think of saying it back, the words feel different. They feel like a lie.

I wander home, on mostly empty streets. The few people that pass by me do so quickly, understandably freaked out by the boy who keeps bursting into tears every few feet. The cold makes me want to wipe away my tears, but I don't have the heart. I deserve to have them freeze to my face, to remind me how stupid I am. I can't even think of what I'll do once I get home. How can I find the words to tell him this? I've done the one thing, the only thing that could truly hurt him. I hope that by telling him, by being honest and showing him my regret, we can get through it, but I fear the look on his face. The anger and pain in his eyes, the knowledge that he, too, will never be able to say "I love you" to me in the same way again, if he can say it again at all, makes me hate myself more than I ever have. Everything I do, the steps I take, breathing, crying, feeling, all of it feels unfair to Eric. When I get to our street, I do what I can to pull myself together. I can't blubber my way through this. I owe him at least that.

"Eric?" I call, as I walk through the door. He's not here. I plug in my phone, and after a few more minutes it comes back to life. I dial him.

"How's my little star?" he asks when he answers.

"Not good, last night was a disaster."

"Yeah, I figured that out when you didn't come home. What happened?"

"Your favorite person had a meltdown, and I had to stay and put him back together," I say, not wanting to even say Kevin's name aloud at this point.

"Kevin?"

"Yes."

"Oh. Well…how bad was it?"

"It was…He…We…" I choke on my guilt, unable to even say it. I can't do this over the phone.

"Mason?"

"Where are you?" I ask, trying to buy myself time.

"Oh, I'm at work. The game needs a patch, so of course they called me in. My boss is still drunk, so I'm leading the team. Don't worry though,

I told them I had special plans tonight. I'll see you after, and you can tell me all about it. Okay?" The show. God, for a full hour, I'd forgotten what last night was even for. The memories flash in my mind, and I can hear Kevin and Merchant, convincing me it was all for the show.

"Yeah, let's talk then."

"I love you," he says, and for a minute I think I might actually be sick. I try to remember how the words used to sound.

"I love you too," I say, just like before, but even though it's pitch perfect, it's still wrong. Hoping this is all just a horrible dream, I crawl into bed, where I pass out, until I'm awakened by the ringing of my phone.

"Hello?"

"Mason! Finally, you're two hours late for rehearsal. Where are you?" Jenna asks, her voice panicked and angry.

"I'm home, I had to sleep."

"Get down here right now. There's a car waiting for you downstairs. Hurry."

"But—"

"I said hurry!" She hangs up the phone, and I try to go back to sleep, but now that I've slept some I can't stop thinking about last night.

When I get downstairs, I find a town car waiting just as she said.

I always found it glamorous, when leads arrived at the theater via town car, but can't enjoy this, now. I'm disgusted with myself, and I must look pretty rough, because when I smile at Tiny while I sign in, he looks way. I quickly scan the sheet for Kevin's name, and am nauseous at the sight of his signature there. Fortunately, it passes, most likely because it's been so long since I've eaten, or had anything to drink. There's nothing for me to throw up at this point.

"Mason, a word?" Merchant asks, pulling me into my dressing room.

"What do you want?"

"To thank you. Kevin seems back to his old self." That Merchant seems chipper makes me want to punch him.

"Yeah, well, he got what he wanted."

"And now so will you."

"No, I can never get that now."

"Mason, the show must go on. Don't dishonor the sacrifices you've made. No one will benefit from that."

"You'd say anything to get me on stage."

"I would, but fortunately, I have the advantage of also being right. Do I need to start prepping Alex?"

"No. You're right, the show must go on," I say, knowing there's no turning back now. Not performing won't make it easier for Eric to forgive me. The best I can do is show him that I thought I had no choice.

I sit in front of the mirror and try to remember what my face usually looks like. My flesh is raw and blotchy from my abrasive cleaning, and although I managed to sleep most of the day away, my eyes are puffy and dark circles ring my eyes. Thankfully, stage makeup can do wonders, and out of habit I began to paint Caleb's face onto my own.

"Hello?" I hear Julia call from behind the door as I finish up. "Everyone decent?"

"All clear."

"Damn, I was hoping to get a peek."

"Afraid it's just me attempting to fix my face."

"Well, alert me when you and Kevin decide to strip down will you?" she asks, making my mind flash images of Kevin's naked body lit by candlelight.

"Have you seen him?"

"Yeah, he's warming up."

"How does he look?"

"Perfect as always." That he is so fully restored feels unfair.

"Well, how about me?" I ask, turning my head for her to get a good look.

"Gorgeous and young. Why?"

"I had a long night."

"Doesn't show a bit. Do you need anything? Sudafed maybe?"

"No, I'm fine, thanks." I smile. "I'm going to go warm up."

As I exit the dressing room I see Kevin lounging in the green room, and his face lights up as our eyes meet. I turn and head for the stage to avoid him, but he manages to grab my hand just before I step onto the boards.

"Hey," he says, happier than I've ever seen him before.

"I missed you this morning."

"Kevin..."

"I know. I remember, it's our secret okay? I just wanted to say...I think it really worked...I can't wait to be on stage with you." These words I've longed to hear him say for so long that I can't stop the flush of joy that washes over me. The moment it does, I feel like I am the worst person in the world. How can I enjoy anything that comes from me cheating on the one person in this world I truly loved? Kevin stares at me, and I can see he's worried. He knows that while he's fully returned to his old self, I'm far from it. Still, after last night, it's almost too easy to read him. I know what he needs to hear, and give it.

"That means a lot coming from Kevin Caldwell."

"Well, yesterday I didn't believe that, but someone convinced me that my name matters. Break a leg tonight," he says, kissing me quickly on the cheek for luck, and flashing me his trademark smile once more before vanishing into the dressing room. I go to wipe his kiss away, but Caleb stops me. I remember I can't hate Kevin or Ezio. If I do, then last night was for nothing. I need to get into character. I need to forget.

I begin to warm up, going through the series of exercises Lycan taught me, and then running through the various tongue twisters I've been doing all my life. I replay the moment I just had with Kevin, and part of me thinks maybe this is all going to work out. As much as I hate to admit it, Kevin was kind of right. I can read him perfectly now, and I know he can read me, too. Throughout the rehearsal process, or really our entire friendship, Kevin's smiles are not just some little kindness he bestows on people, they're clues. His smile is more than a reflection of his own happiness, but rather a reminder that I should be acting happy as well.

I allow myself to put away thoughts of last night. Taking a deep breath, I feel my whole body reviving itself. I settle into my old routine, focusing on preparing for the show. Other actors slowly join me on stage to do their own private warming up rituals. All of us seem to work on movement, voice, and diction, but each in our own way. I've done the same ones for so long that doing them now helps me remember who I was, who I've always been, making last night seem like nothing but a dream.

Kevin arrives just as I finish, which is a relief, as it means I'll get some privacy in the dressing room. Back to my old self, I smile as I head back to get into costume, but he holds out his hand for me to stop.

"Leaving already?"

"I was going to get changed. I assume Merchant's going to want to talk to us right before curtain, so I want to be ready."

"Oh, right."

"All actors please report to the stage," Jenna announces over the speaker system.

"Or maybe he's just going to do that now," Kevin says, slinging his arm across my shoulders like old times.

Merchant takes the stage, and his eyes quickly zero in on us. Kevin pulls me closer, absolutely beaming, and I smile with him. Maybe that's what I have to do now, pretend to be fine until time fully heals this wound. I did that when Merchant marked me on the first day of rehearsal. Maybe that was the point? Merchant nods his head ever so slightly at me, seemingly confirming the thoughts in my head. In a few moments the entire cast is on stage, facing out like we're about to sing "Seasons of Love" from *Rent*.

"I would like to just take a moment of your time," he begins, pacing up and down, staring at each of us in turn with his penetrating gaze. "Tonight is important, but I'm saving my good stuff for our real opening. As your director this is my privilege, not yours. I want you to perform tonight, and every night, as if it is both your first and final performance.

"I am the harshest audience you will ever have, so don't expect the people outside who are anxiously holding on to their tickets to be like me. They are with you in a way that I can never be. They are here to escape into the world we've built. Of course, not everyone is a great guest. So I can tell you now, things are going to feel different tonight. Someone will certainly think the request for silencing a phone doesn't apply to them. There will be gasps of excitement, laughter, and, if we are lucky, thunderous applause. You must take all of these things inside of yourselves, and adapt.

"Which brings me to the last thing I need to say before any of you walks onto this stage. Yesterday, I forgot that adapting is one of the most basic, most important, most vital truths of live theatre. I publicly chided the two individuals who were adapting to the outside changes that had come into our world, and it is one of the worst mistakes I've made as a director. While I will make amends with them privately, I wanted to make certain I did so in front of everyone, so the rest of you will know that adapting is far from a sin. Rather, it is a necessity. I hope you will join me in applauding these two fine actors, for they knew what they were doing was certain to enrage me, but they also knew what they were doing was right." Merchant grabs Kevin and me by our hands, pulls us out of line, and begins to clap. The entire ensemble joins in, and even though it's a small group, the applause feels loud and strong, as if it was coming from a packed house.

I look at Kevin, who simply smiles back, and unsure of what we are supposed to do, we take a small bow. This seems to strike a chord with Merchant, who immediately quiets everyone down.

"That reminds me, you left before I put you into the bows. I would like you both to come in last. Once the lights go down, exit stage left, and come on once Julia has taken her bow. Kevin you will first present Mason, and then Mason, you will present Kevin. Once you two have bowed independently, take one together, and then the rest of the cast will come forward for the group bow."

"Got it," Kevin and I say in unison. Once again we are in perfect sync.

"Jenna! Can we run the curtain call, so Kevin and Mason can practice it once?"

"On it!"

While I had felt aware that tonight was going to be different, rehearsing my bow with Kevin makes me remember that tonight is the first time I'll perform on Broadway. As if that isn't enough of a thrill, I'm the second to last to bow. It has been years since I have been given such an honor, and I can't believe that this time it is on a Broadway stage. As I rehearse bowing my head, I feel determined to earn the right to do so before our audience tonight.

"Would you like to run that again?" Merchant asks, after glancing at his watch.

"No, if you don't mind, I would rather get into costume. I want to check my props, and double check that everything is where I need it to be for my costume changes," I say, knowing that in less than an hour the curtain will rise. Despite never being better prepared, for the first time in years, I am nervous to perform in front of an audience. Especially since Eric will be in the house. For him, I need to prove that everything I sacrificed was worth it—a task that, after last night, won't be easy.

I run to the dressing room and quickly strip off my clothes, so I'm standing completely naked when Kevin walks in.

"Ah!" I yell, covering myself as fast as possible.

"Chill, it's just me."

"Still, you could knock."

"It's my dressing room, too. Besides, I don't think you have anything to hide," he says, dragging his index finger down my bare chest.

"Stop that," I say, slapping his hand away.

"Are you okay?"

"I'm fine, just...well...the show starts soon, and I have a lot to check. I mean I need to move my costumes into the wings for my costume changes, and..."

"Relax, Mason. You're just nervous. The show is going to be fine. Also, c'mon man, you're on Broadway, you don't move the costumes. The wardrober does that," he says, lacing his hands around my neck and leaning in for a kiss.

"Save it for the show," I reply, ducking under him.

"Sorry, right."

Once I'm dressed, I start double-checking, and then triple-checking, that everything is in its proper place. I try to review my lines, but they are so hardcoded it takes me longer to say them than to think them, so it feels like a waste of time. Thinking of coding threatens to summon up thoughts of Eric, and again I have to fight myself to keep from dwelling on last night. I imagine him out there in the audience, dressed up in his only suit, sitting in the fancy box seat I reserved for him. I had such high hopes for what tonight would mean for us. How did I get so close only to ruin it at the eleventh hour? Why couldn't I have figured out another way to help Kevin?

Before I can spiral further into despair, Jenna's voice comes over the wall-mounted speaker. "Places for Act One. Curtain will rise in two minutes."

In the dim blue lighting behind the main curtain, I see everyone arrange themselves on stage. Kevin looks unbelievably dashing, and upon seeing him in costume, I can feel Caleb awaken within me, elated to see his first glimpse of Ezio for the night. Feeling his presence, my nerves slowly begin to melt away, and as the curtain rises to reveal the stage to the audience, I see the fully rendered world of the play through Caleb eyes. A world truly beautiful, for in it, is Ezio.

I walk forward, kneel before him, and deliver the first line. "My liege, I have been sent from the fronts of battle, to deliver unto you this message."

"Such a service is usually performed by a young steward. Why have my generals sent back a man?" Ezio asks, and hearing his voice, my heart begins to flutter fast.

"As I am wounded, the young boys you speak of are of more use to you than I am," I reply, and from there, the show begins.

With an audience, everything seems a little slower as we hold for laughs and gasps. However, when I am backstage, time seems to be drastically accelerated. If I didn't have help changing my clothes, I'd be naked on stage long before the end of the show.

The conversations Ezio and I have repeated almost every day for the past two months feel spontaneous and new. Laughter erupts out of me, filling the theater with the pure and honest sounds of enjoyment, as Ezio dazzles me and the audience with his charm and wit. Of course, when Mina arrives at court, through Caleb's eyes, I see her as more beautiful than I think Julia could even see herself. Still, as drawn to her as I am, I cannot deny my attraction to Ezio. The conflict and confusion in my heart is more palpable than ever before, and I've never been happier for the break that intermission affords me.

"Did you hear that?" Kevin asks, as he bursts through the dressing room door.

"What?"

"The applause. They're loving it!"

"Well, we are giving them quite a show," I say, as I touch up my makeup a little.

"You're brilliant! I didn't think we could get any better, but man, everything seems unreal out there."

"I know! I almost couldn't keep going after you made that lewd gesture behind Lady Farragut! I had to bite my tongue!"

"I just wanted to hear you laugh again. Every time you laughed, I wanted to kiss you," he says, grabbing my head and planting a big wet kiss on me.

"Hey!"

"Sorry, but god, I've been dying to do that all night."

"Well, you'll get more than that soon enough," I say, pulling out my costume for the masquerade.

"Care for a preview?" he says, slowly gyrating his hips side to side as he begins to get changed.

"Kevin, stop." I never thought I'd hate being backstage like this, but I do. It's so much easier to be Caleb.

"I'm sorry, but, it's so hard to control myself with you tonight. You've never looked better."

"That's a joke right? You should see what I look like without all this makeup. It's scary," I say, pulling my shirt over my head.

"It's not a joke. From the second I saw you today, all I've wanted was a repeat of last night."

"That was a one-time thing." And it shouldn't have happened.

"It doesn't have to be," he says, pressing his body against me, tilting my chin and kissing me.

"Hey, boys!" Julia says, as the door to our dressing room opens. I can see her eyes widen as I push Kevin away.

"What's up?" Kevin asks, busying himself with resuming getting dressed.

"Oh, nothing. I just wanted to let you know the call is—"

"Five minutes to curtain," Jenna says over the speaker.

"Five minutes," Julia finishes. With her excuse utterly ruined she just closes the door. Normally, I would be furious, but five minutes is not enough time to deal with Kevin and finish getting dressed, so I focus on getting back into costume and character, as best I can.

Kevin's remarks repeat over and over in my head as I stand in the wings, waiting to go on stage, and I curse myself for having severed the link between Caleb and myself so completely during the intermission. My entrance seems to come before I am ready, but when I hear my cue and step onto the stage, I feel Caleb spring to life within me. And even though I want to kill Kevin for what he just did, Caleb pays no attention to my loathing. Nothing can penetrate the love he feels for Ezio.

The scenes go by faster than they did in the first act, and before I know it I am sitting on Ezio's throne, observing the lavish dance number. With my face obscured by the mask, I observe – as Caleb – everything that is going on. I wish I could see through my own eyes how Eric is enjoying the show, yet, try as I might, I continue to see the world as Caleb, a world where there is no audience, a world that seems to have nothing else in it but Ezio.

Soon we are alone. Though I know what will happen, the scene feels unfamiliar and new tonight. Instead of sticking to the blocking, we constantly bring ourselves close together, and the second before passion would overtake us, we separate again to let the scene continue.

"And how do you plan to do war with a specter?"

"By bringing you here and asking you, not as your ruler, but as your lover, to stay with me for one night. Try to love me as I love you, and when the morning comes, if Mina is still in your heart, I will resign that you are a war I cannot win," Ezio says, his tone a pitch-perfect replica of Kevin's when he finally convinced me to submit to him.

In the moment when I put the wine goblet to my lips, I am inundated with flashes from last night, when we were both ourselves as well as our characters. I am barely able to tell if I am remembering or repeating the event, until I feel my lips meet his. The music swells all around me, and I let out a gasp of pleasure as his hands once again massage the knotted muscles at the base of my spine. His hands go lower, lifting me up off of the ground by my ass, supporting my full weight as I wrap my legs about his waist. I can feel every part of Caleb's body responding in celebration, as if he has never been touched by another person before in his entire life. This goes beyond the courtly love he has felt for Mina. This is passion in its rawest form, and no sooner do I realize this, than I hear a howl of pain fill the room, followed by the sound of fabric ripping as Julia tears down the curtain she was hiding behind.

Upon seeing her, I know I should separate from him, but as much as it pains me to see how my proximity to Ezio hurts her, it feels even more painful to let go. Ezio releases me without hesitation, and I stagger toward Mina, staring at the look of betrayal and disgust in her eyes. I know I should feel guilty or ashamed, but unlike all the other times, I am not confused about what I want. Ezio is the one for me, and instead of wanting to make an excuse, I just want to rush back into his arms. I turn to look back at him, just as he steps behind me, and drapes his arms around my shoulders. I resist the urge to revel in the sweetness of his embrace and stare straight ahead prepared for the rest of the scene.

"Mina, what are you doing here?"

"You dare to ask what I am doing, after I find you like this?"

"It is not as it seems. I would return to you if I thought you would have me." For the first time I'm uncertain if Caleb is telling the truth about this.

"You would dare to think of returning to my side? I will have none of you that his venomous lips have touched, which leaves you…" She looks me up and down. "Nothing to offer." Ashamed, I look away for a moment, until she cries out. I turn in time to see her charge at Ezio, and I manage, just barely, to block her blade with my body. The impact of the prop knife feels horribly real, and I let out a scream that is not meant for the stage. My vocal chords threaten to burst as the noise within me escapes, and I drop to the ground.

"No. Why? Caleb…my love…why?" Mina cries out, giving me my cue for the final speech.

"Because, my sweet Mina, I have played a foolish game. My heart wanted to love two people at one time, and thus flung itself upon your knife, not only to protect, but to rip itself in twain. I fear no one can live with half a heart, and it would take two full ones to truly love each of you as I do. With you, all the pain and horror that I had known in my life vanished into air. With you, I learned what happiness was. I don't want to live in a world where what you've seen tonight would diminish the pure love and affection I felt for you. What we had was something few people have ever known. That I dared to reach for something more must have angered the gods above, but it was only through this cruel trick of fate that I was able to understand there is even more to what I thought I knew of love. Ezio, over the past few days, a great clarity has come to me, showing me that with you there is no choice in love. Loving you is beyond my control. It is as much a part of me as breathing, as living. Your hand has reached in and touched my very soul, revealing who I really am. To most I would be a monster, but in your eyes, I am beautiful. You find joy in every part of me, and there is nothing in this world I would trade for that. Worlds change from knowing that kind of love, and now you can change ours. If I must die, I die happy knowing it allowed you to live."

Ezio's voice shakes and rattles as he sobs like a child. With all that is left of me I pull him down, and when I close my eyes to kiss him, I know I shall never open them again.

"Jesus, did he pass out? Did you actually stab him? I mean that scream..." Kevin whispers to Julia, as they start to drag me off stage.

"I know, I don't know what happened." Julia whispers back before pinching my cheek. "Mason?"

"Ow! I'm fine," I say, getting to my feet.

"Oh, thank goodness! What was going on tonight? I mean before I entered you were..."

"That's your cue!" Kevin says, and Julia runs out, the applause rising to greet her as she does.

"Ready?" Kevin asks.

"Ready," I confirm, and hand in hand we walk out to deafening applause, the loudest I've ever heard in my life. I toss my head up to see Eric screaming in excitement, tears streaming down his face. I can't stop looking at him, and finally he points down to the rest of the crowd to remind me to thank them for their applause as well. I gesture toward Kevin so he can take his bow, and the rest of the cast joins us at center stage. We bow twice more, before finally walking off stage. The second I'm in the wings, the wardrober snaps her fingers at me, demanding I take my shirt off before the stage blood can fully seep into the fibers. The entire cast is abuzz, hugging and congratulating each other. The audience's reaction to us, really has made everything seem worth it. A ton of guys in the cast, whose names I've still yet to learn, pull me into hugs and compliment me. The scene is so chaotic, none of us even notices that Merhcant himself has joined up backstage.

"Listen to that! They are going wild! Get back out there," Merchant says, grabbing Kevin and me by the arms and dragging us away from the cast and back toward the stage.

"One second!" I say, attempting to grab my shirt back from the wardrober, but it's no use. With one strong push, Kevin and I are back in the light. A roar swells from the crowd, and although I know they saw much more of me in the show, I feel far more naked now. I'm no longer shielded by the mask of Caleb; what they see is me.

Kevin hands me his glorious coat so I can cover myself, and then drags me to the very lip of the stage. Once there, he extends both his hands, presenting me once again, and I take a short bow. The crowd manages to scream even louder, and above me I can hear the entire balcony has taken to stomping their feet to make their elation heard. Eric is going wild, and I can feel my pure love for him return.

"I love you," I mouth, and again the words feel real, making me wonder if maybe Kevin and Merchant were right about last night, and it wasn't really me, but just another role, just theatre. After I return the favor and present Kevin to the audience as well, he grabs my hand and leads me back in line with the rest of the ensemble, who have rejoined us. As we back up, Julia enters, dragging a rather reluctant Merchant on with her. She takes a short bow, and then holds up her hands to the audience to silence them.

"Ladies and Gentlemen, we are truly humbled by your response. It has been an honor to perform for you tonight, but we would be lost without the man you see before you. Please join us in applauding the mastermind of the work you saw, our director, Mr. James Merchant." The audience resumes clapping, now joined by the entire cast. Merchant shakes his head in disbelief and humility, which seems utterly out of character for him, but eventually takes a bow of his own. He then retreats back, as the full cast joins hands once more, and gives a final bow. We again walk off stage, waving farewell as we go.

By the time I reach the dressing room, the applause has stopped, but the murmuring of the patrons is wild and exited. I take special care to hang up Kevin's coat, and then rummage around in my pack hoping that I managed to bring some halfway decent clothes since I pretty much ran out of the apartment this afternoon wearing the clothes I wore yesterday. Fortunately, I had the common sense to pack a clean pair of jeans and a hoodie which, thankfully, matches the t-shirt I borrowed from Kevin this morning.

"Can you believe that?" he asks, beaming.

"I know! It was incredible," I start for the door.

"Leaving already?"

"Eric's waiting."

"Oh, of course. But what about the party?"

"Party?"

"Yeah, they just told me about it. We're all meeting at Merchant's apartment for drinks..." Just when I feel myself starting to get excited, he adds, "and notes."

"His apartment? Where is it?" And I guess the better question would be: how does he plan to fit all of us in it?

"The Upper West Side, 88th and Riverside Drive. He's right on the Hudson."

"Oh! Well, great, I'll see you there then."

"Bring Eric!" Kevin calls after me.

The mere mention of Eric's name sends me running out the stage door. There, I'm blinded by the flash from dozens of cameras. Having never stopped smiling since the curtain call, it is easy to pose as I turn to face in the direction of whoever shouts my name. Eventually, the lights cease flashing, and, once my eyes quit seeing their trace images, I'm able to fully take in the crowd that has gathered around. The wall of people is so large that it spills out from the small alley onto the street.

"Mason!" A boy with a lot of acne waves me over and hands me his program. "Can I get an autograph?"

"Oh, sure. But I don't have a pen."

"Here you go," Julia says through gritted teeth, her face locked in a permanent smile as she hands me a pen.

"What's your name?" I ask the kid, who ducks his head and blushes when we lock eyes.

"Justin."

"All right then, Justin, here you go."

"Thanks so much! You were fabulous!" he says, running off. The second he disappears another person asks me to sign their program. And another after him. It isn't hard to be nice, but I am distracted, wanting just a quick second so I can look around and find Eric. After twenty minutes or so I finally see him leaning against the wall, waiting patiently as ever, but it's almost an hour before I'm able to make my way over to him.

"Sorry," I say, wishing we'd made plans for him to meet me backstage.

"Don't be sorry! You were spellbinding tonight; I almost lined up for an autograph myself."

"I'll give you one whenever you want," I say, taking his arm and leading him onto the street.

"Good to know. Where do you want to celebrate?"

"Merchant invited us to a party at his apartment on the Upper West Side."

"Sounds like a plan. Let's get a cab," Eric says, but the second we reach the curb a black town car rolls up to us.

"Mr. Burroughs?" asks a man wearing a chauffer cap, as he rolls down the window.

"Yes?"

"Mr. Merchant sent me to collect you."

"Oh, thanks," I say. As I approach the door, the man pops out of the car and opens the it for me.

"Do actors always get this kind of treatment?" Eric asks.

"Movie stars do, but I've never heard of a stage actor being treated like this."

"Well, after tonight, you deserve it," Eric says, giving me a quick kiss.

"So...you really liked it?"

"Mason, you can't possibly be asking me that. The curtain call, the autographs, this car service. It was unlike anything I've ever seen before. I think you can assume everyone was blown away."

"I don't care about everyone else. I want to know what you thought about everything, every moment of the show."

"Like what?"

For the entire car trip, I slowly interrogate him about every moment of the show. He surprises me by just how much he actually noticed. Microscopic details that Merchant placed in the show, or that Kevin and I discovered, all seem to have made a big impact on the audience. What's even better is that Eric can't stop telling me what he heard the other audience members saying during intermission. Apparently people were calling their friends and telling them to buy tickets as soon as possible.

"The seduction scene was so different than what I saw in the photoshoot."

"That scene was different tonight, in general," I say, unsure if I should really tell him why. This morning, I was certain I had to come clean about last night, but now, I'm not so sure.

"I thought it was going to be hard to watch."

"It wasn't?"

"Not really. I mean, honestly, by that point, I'd stopped thinking of you as you."

"I can't imagine a better compliment," I say, hoping this is a sign that I shouldn't say anything. At least, not now.

The car slows in front of a stone monolithic building that looks like the New York City equivalent of Downton Abbey. The colonnade leading to the door is comprised of Corinthian columns, and the windows all have stained glass. "Mr. Merchant lives in the top floor," the chauffer says, before hopping out and opening the door for Eric and me.

"Thanks," I reply, taking Eric's hand in mine as we approach the building. A handsome doorman dressed in a tailcoat and white gloves opens the door for us and smiles as we pass into the 1920's Gatsby-era lobby. The smell of vanilla-laced pipe tobacco permeates the entire place, and I inhale the sweet scent deep into my nose as we approach young woman with an hourglass figure that rivals Julia's, who is seated behind a heavy wooden desk.

"Hello. Are you here for the party?" she asks, opening a large, leather-bound guest ledger and handing me a Montblanc fountain pen.

"Yes," I reply, signing my name for what must be the hundredth time in the past hour.

"Excellent, Mr. Merchant has directed the cast to join him in our library. The remaining guests are asked to make their way to the drawing room." I'm kind of sad we won't get to see Merchant's actual apartment, but I guess it makes sense. I don't think anyone in the city has enough space to host the entire cast. Still, surrounded by this incredible amount of beauty makes me feel like a true Broadway star.

TWENTY TWO

THE LIBRARY LOOKS LIKE IT would be a pretty great place to sit and read, if it wasn't full of actors projecting their voices over one another in conversation. Green leather couches flank a marble fireplace, while the walls are lined with glass-paned book cabinets. Behind the glass is an impressive collection of books, many of which appear to be ancient, which explains why they are locked up tight. I say hello to a few people in the ensemble, but unfortunately I can't remember any of their names, so Eric has to introduce himself. I try to make a mental note of each name as I hear it, and for the first time I actually manage to commit a few of them to memory. Everyone we meet practically gushes while they congratulate me on a job well done, and I'm happy that I can tell them about little bits of their performances I noticed.

As Eric and I chat with the ensemble, waiters dart around carrying trays of snacks, champagne, wine, and colorful martinis. They are so quick and efficient that they remind me of the waiters from *Hello Dolly!* I wonder, since they are all incredibly attractive, if they aren't actors who view this as a chance to audition for Merchant in some way.

"Mason!" Julia crows, taking two glasses of champagne off a waiter's tray and walking over to us.

"Julia!" Eric and I call back.

"Can you believe that crowd? How many autographs did you have to sign?"

"I honestly don't know, but it was a lot. Thanks for the pen by the way."

"My pleasure. I could probably sell it for a nice sum. Everyone asked about you. And you too!" Julia says, giving Eric a kiss on the cheek.

"Me?"

"Yes, they wanted to know if you and Mason were really a couple."

"But how did they even know I exist?"

"The program. I wasn't even thinking, the first time someone asked. I pointed you out to them, so I am glad to see no one hurt you."

"Why would they hurt Eric?" I ask, equally appalled and confused at the idea.

"You'd be surprised what fans will do. I think some really wanted you to be single," Julia explains.

"Well, there's always Kevin," Eric replies.

"I'm not sure that's an appropriate substitute," Kevin says, holding a tumbler glass with what I assume is yet another Caldwell Clan. This one is closer in color to the amber one he had at the speak easy bar.

"Kevin!" Julia and I yell out in harmony, before each giving him a big hug as if we haven't seen him in ages.

"You were great tonight," Eric says, surprising me by shaking Kevin's hand. Seeing them touch makes me shudder.

"Thank you. You were a particularly good audience member."

I huff in feigned objection. "I'm not sure if I should be jealous you got to see him during the show, or mad that you broke character long enough to steal a glance."

"I don't think you can be mad at Kevin for anything," Julia says, pausing to suck down half a flute of champagne. "Whether he broke character or not, you two were on fire tonight. Besides, there's that bit of drama that went on backstage."

"What?" Eric asks, and I panic, thinking of what she walked in on during intermission.

"Mason took a while to remember he wasn't dead, and Kevin did most of the heavy lifting as we carried him backstage," Julia explains, making me relax once more.

"You did?" Eric asks, his brow furrowing with obvious concern.

"Yeah, I don't know what happened. I think it was just overwhelming.

Plus, you stabbed me pretty hard."

"I did?"

"Yeah, well, it felt that way."

"Is that why you screamed like that? It made me almost jump out of my seat," Eric says, placing his hand on my stomach where I was stabbed.

"It's fine, see," I say, knocking on my relatively solid abs. "I think it's because I was so in the moment that I forgot that it was going to happen."

"Which is exactly as it should be," Merchant interrupts. "Eric, how lovely it is to see you again. I hope you don't mind, but I was hoping you might join the rest of the guests across the hall in the drawing room. The cast will join you there, once I've had an opportunity to give them some brief notes about tonight's performance."

"Oh, sure. Of course. But don't change too much. Tonight was absolutely incredible."

"It certainly was, but my job is to make it perfect," Merchant says, ushering Eric toward the door.

Once Eric and a few other guests have left, Merchant stands in front of the fireplace and makes a sweeping motion with his arms to suggest that we should all make ourselves comfortable.

"Now, this is not going to take long, as I think we can all agree tonight was a great success. However, there is always room for improvement. I will start with the large ensemble notes..." He gives them a few minor adjustments, after which they are released to re-join the party across the hall. Little by little, the cast dwindles, until finally it is just Julia, Kevin, and me.

"Julia, while your performance was excellent in your one-on-one scenes with Caleb and Dyne, your group work was in trouble. Whenever Ezio was in the room, Caleb barely noticed you."

"I agree, but there wasn't a lot I could do about it," Julia responds, eyeing me with an accusatory glare.

"Don't blame Mason, if anything Kevin was the issue. Still, what I found most concerning was that when you saw you were losing, you gave up. If Caleb's eyes wander it is your job to refocus them. It should be a challenge, by which I mean I want to see some of the effort. Obviously, I don't want to see all of it, but giving a glimpse will endear you to the audience. We want them to be rooting for you, too, not just Ezio, and that only sort of half happened tonight."

"I'm sorry, I was caught by surprise. Moments I was used to stealing were interrupted by some new distractions."

"Indeed they were. Kevin, what have you to say for yourself? You made rather bold choices tonight, chief among them that rather lewd gesture in the court scene."

"I'm sorry, I was just really in the moment. Mason's laugh was priceless...I just wanted to keep hearing it."

"Well, you certainly got him laughing, along with most of the audience. I'm tempted to let you keep it, but we will see how tomorrow goes. Mason, while Caleb's laugh was positively infectious, you might want to rein it in a little bit. I think you added a good five minutes onto the running time just by laughing."

"Really? Oh god, sorry. It was just...well...Kevin...er...Ezio was really funny. The audience seemed to remind me I hadn't heard those jokes every day, and so I couldn't stop. I'll do better tomorrow." I make a mental note to compliment Colin on the humor in the script that I seemed to have only realized existed tonight.

"Well, don't overcorrect. Your laugh really imbued the show with some lightness. It made some scenes seem more innocent, which I liked. This is why we have previews, to fine tune little things like this. So keep it up, but don't let it distract you from giving Mina your attention. In fact, seeing Ezio try and fail will help restore the balance in the love triangle to some degree."

"I'll do my best to be a worthy distraction," Julia says, with a slight shimmy that draws Merchant's eye to her jiggling bosom.

"Er...right. Now Julia, you're free to join the party. I look forward to seeing what you come up with, now that you know how stiff the competition is."

"Oh James, I think you know how good I am when things are stiff." I'll give her one thing: Julia sure knows how to make an exit.

"Now I don't have much more to say to you two, but this. Your seduction scene would have been great, had anyone been able to see you. This isn't rehearsal, you can't wander out of the light. So I need to know, which was more comfortable for you? What you did tonight, or what you've done all along?"

"Tonight," we both answer.

"Really? Now, Mason, it was my understanding you wanted to be interrupted before any nudity was involved."

"That's right."

"I see. And are you aware you were partially naked on stage tonight?"

"What? No! When?" I shoot Kevin a look of betrayal.

"It was only a brief moment, but right before Julia entered, the entire audience got a nice view of your backside. Kevin's hands obscured the view, since that was what he was lifting you up by, but when he let you go, well, you didn't seem to notice. Kevin pulled them up, when he came up behind you." Despite Merchant's explanation, I still can't remember it, or even believe that it happened. Why hadn't Eric mentioned this? Or anyone else?

"I didn't know."

"I can probably lift him up so that doesn't happen, with some practice."

"Then let's try it again tomorrow. I'll need you to come in early anyway, to reset the lighting to accommodate the new blocking."

"Anything else?" I ask, wanting to question Eric about this alleged nudity.

"No, you are free to go. Excellent work from both of you. After last night I was worried, but now...well I almost wish the critics had been here. Just remember, this is the minimum I will accept from here on out," he says, dismissing us with a wave of his hand.

"Sorry about the nudity thing. It won't happen again," Kevin whispers to me as we make our way across the hall into the drawing room.

"It's fine. I'm just freaked out I didn't even notice."

"It's understandable, there was a lot going on."

"Well, thanks for covering me back up at least," I smile.

"Any time man, happy to help."

When the doors to the drawing room open, the party seems to have tripled in size. The cast and crew are now highly outnumbered by Merchant's friends, to the point that I'm unable to locate them for quite some time. Every step we take, people engage us in conversation. I do my best to be gracious, but pale in comparison to Kevin. With a simple wink, nod, or handshake, he manages to make each person feel truly special. One by one, he moves forward through the crowd, leaving a trail of enchanted patrons who seem unable to stop talking to the other guests about how wonderful he is. The ease with which he wields his charm on such a grand scale is somewhat comforting to watch. If he can do this to an entire room, did I even have a chance last night?

"Mason!" Alex says, grabbing me in a big hug, allowing me to excuse myself from an elderly woman who is now the seventy-fifth person to tell me how brave I was to show my ass on stage.

"Alex, great job tonight!"

"You, too. Honestly, I'm hoping you just do the whole run, because once reviews come out, people are going to be mad if I'm called in." There is something particularly nice about hearing Alex say this, especially since he is using his non-nasal voice again.

"Thanks, but I bet you'd bring something to this, too. After all, we've both got history with Kevin."

"I'm just glad you fought back. What happened last night anyway?"

"That's a long story," I say, not really interested in ever telling it.

"I bet. Well, whatever you did, you must be pleased with the results. You and Kevin were better tonight than you've ever been."

"Thanks," I say, wishing he'd stop talking about it.

"You okay?"

"Yeah, I'm just far too sober at this point."

"Oh, god, of course. You probably haven't had a second to yourself. Want me to grab you something?"

"Would you?"

"What's your poison?"

"Anything wet and alcoholic," I reply, waving at Eric but failing to get his attention. Unfortunately, I only succeed in attracting more guests who seek to congratulate me.

"I'll get him and your drink," Alex says.

It had never occurred to me how draining it is to mingle with fans, and I can feel my energy start to decline. Kevin, on the other hand, seems to feed off their energy like some sort of compliment vampire. I try to mimic him, but it doesn't work. He's spent his entire life having the world love him.

After what feels like forever, but is likely only a few moments, Alex walks by and very casually places a wine glass in my hand. Eric takes my other one and simply bulldozes through the crowd, dragging me to one of the couches where Julia is sitting.

"Jesus, slow down," Eric says, his eyes widening as I practically chug the entire glass of wine.

"Sorry, I'm dying of thirst and hunger. I've been glad-handing with people since Merchant released us." The wine hits me hard, making me remember that I forgot to eat today. God, how is that possible?

"Here, I made you a plate. Do you even know who these people are?"

"Not a clue. What about you, Julia?"

"Investors, I assume."

I stop pigging out on mini quiches and cheese cubes and look up. "How do you know?"

"They all seem to know David," she says, pointing out Mr. Stein in the crowd. Having not seen him much over the past few weeks, I barely remember him. As the producer, it makes sense he is here and entertaining investors. I consider myself lucky that, I've been spared having to hear about the financial side of getting this show to Broadway.

"Care for another?" Julia asks, noticing Stein's approach and my empty glass.

"God yes. Make it a double if possible," I say, half-joking. I know that a double of wine would just be a big glass.

"I'll go with you," Alex offers.

"The more the merrier," Julia replies. "Eric? Care to come along?"

He gives me a look, and I nod to let him know he should go.

"Sure thing."

Stein extends a hand to shake as he charges toward me. "Mason!" he says, catching me by surprise by using the handshake to pull me into a hug. Considering we haven't spoken since the audition, his level of familiarity is startling. Then I notice the tiny old woman at his side, and figure she has something to do with it. "Smashing job tonight, the entire room cannot stop talking about you."

"Thanks so much. I guess you're happy you cast me."

"Of course, how could we not be? Now, I'd love for you to meet Mrs. Ladwell." Mr. Stein says, directing my attention to her.

"Oh, Mr. Burroughs, you were incredible," she says, clasping my hand.

"Thank you so much," I reply.

"It was just thrilling to watch you. Tell me, is it hard to memorize all those lines?" This is the question I'm asked most frequently. I get why non-actors ask it, but honestly it annoys me to no end. Memorization is important, but anyone can be taught to parrot words back. Acting is about bringing them to life.

"Oh, not really. You have to keep in mind, we rehearse for weeks. I'm sure if you said the same thing day after day you wouldn't even think about it," I say, using my, ironically, canned response.

"Oh, I don't know. At my age, my memory isn't what it used to be. But you and Mr. Caldwell were absolutely unforgettable."

"Oh yes, I should see if we can get a moment with him," Mr. Stein says, quickly guiding her toward Kevin. Once her attention is turned, he discreetly rubs his thumb against his index and middle finger to indicate Mrs. Ladwell is wealthy, and mouths a big "thank you" to me.

"Who was she?" Eric says, handing me a fresh plate of hors d'oeuvres.

"Some investor. Say, did you notice that I showed my ass on stage?"

"Well…yeah."

"You didn't mention that in the car," I say, annoyed that it must really be true.

"It was really brief."

"Well, everyone keeps mentioning it to me."

"I think they want to know if it was an accident," he says, making me wonder if he also wants to know.

"It was."

"I figured," he says, but he sounds unconvinced.

"It was basically just a wardrobe malfunction." I flop down onto one of the couches, utterly exhausted.

"Then why didn't you pull it up once he put you down?"

"I didn't even know it had happened until Merchant told me," I say, throwing my hand up to point toward Merchant at the exact time Alex passes behind me. Time seems to slow down, the second my hand makes contact with the full glass of wine in his hand. Before my ears can recognize the familiar ping of struck glass, I feel the liquid on my head, running down my face over my shuttered eyes. I inhale quickly, expecting to let loose a scream of outrage, but a few drops of the crimson liquid catch in my throat, causing me to cough and sputter instead.

"Oh no!" Alex cries, as everyone turns to look. "God, I'm so sorry!"

"Are you okay?" Eric asks, wiping at me with a cocktail napkin.

"I'm fine," I say, trying to clear my throat.

"I'm so sorry," Alex repeats. "I didn't mean to, I promise."

"Don't apologize. It was my fault," I say, only just realizing that the t-shirt that is now completely drenched is actually Kevin's. This is what I get for trying to order a double. "Still, this sucks, I can't believe I left my pack at the theater."

"Do you need a change of clothes?" Kevin asks, coming to my rescue. "My pack is in the study."

"Maybe we should just go home," I say.

"Don't say that, it's just a little spilled wine. This is your night," Kevin says, disappearing.

"He's right. Let's just go get you changed. Come on," Eric says.

"But where?" I ask.

"Mr. Burroughs! If you wanted to see my place that badly, you should have just asked!" Merchant says, descending upon the scene.

"Oh, no, I'm sure I can just go to the restroom and change."

"Nonsense, we need you to look your best." Merchant replies, gingerly placing a silver key in my hand. "You need this to call the elevator. Now get cleaned up, I have a feeling Shapiro needs you to charm some more of his investors."

"Here you go," Kevin says, passing me his backpack with an expression I can't really understand.

"Thanks," I say, as I walk past him to the elevator. The woman who asked us to sign in takes one look at me and quickly inhales in shock. She ushers us into the elevator and then takes the silver key from me and inserts it into a slot, causing the top button to glow. I notice that instead of a floor number it just says "Merchant." She hits the button before returning to her post. Once the polished bronze doors close, I can see my reflection, and just how pathetic I appear. I look like a watered-down version of Carrie. "I should probably take a quick shower."

"Agreed. Just rinse off while I find you something to wear."

The elevator opens right into Merchant's apartment. Though, to be honest, the word "apartment" seems a silly word to describe it. Merchant's place is massive, he could easily have had the entire cast up here, but considering how immaculately decorated it is I assume he probably didn't trust us to not wreck the place.

"Uh...wow. I didn't know directors made this kind of money," Eric says, equally impressed.

"I'm not sure they do."

"Well, anyway, hurry up, and try not to break anything. I don't think we can afford to replace as much as a lightbulb in this place."

As I search for a bathroom, I notice the walls are adorned with framed photos of Merchant's productions and glowing New York Times reviews. Below his enormous, wall-mounted television there is an ornate curio cabinet with his numerous Tony awards prominently displayed.

I eventually find a bathroom off the living room. Like everything else, it is bigger than most guest bathrooms would be in a New York City apartment. It has a full shower with multiple shower heads, so that when I finally manage to figure out all the dials, streams of water hit my body from numerous angles. It only takes a few seconds before all traces of wine, as well as the remainder of my stage makeup, have been cleared away. Although I know I should be in a rush to get back downstairs, I take a few minutes to let the warm water roll over me, allowing the tension from the past twenty four hours to swirl down the drain at my feet. After I'm done, I use a towel to dry off, wrapping it around my waist before heading back to find Eric.

"There you are. Did you find any clothes I could fit in?" I say, seeing him standing near a couch strewn with clothes along with Kevin's bag.

"I assume you'll fit in this," Eric says, tossing me the shirt I accidentally left in Kevin's apartment.

After I unwad it, my heart drops into my stomach when I realize what I've done. The shirt is one of the ones I borrowed from Eric. I do my best to pretend I don't notice. "Thanks."

"Why was that shirt in his bag?"

"What do you mean? I always keep spare clothes in mine."

"I'm not asking about that. I mean this shirt specifically. It's mine, isn't it?"

"I don't think so," I say, looking at it again with a feigned perplexed expression.

"Really? You think Kevin just happens to have the same t-shirt with Kain Highwind from Final Fantasy on it?"

"Who?"

"Kain Highwind!"

"Oh…well…I guess he must have picked up my shirt instead of his. I'm sure he was in a big hurry, and our dressing room is kind of a mess."

"God, you really are a good actor aren't you?" Eric asks, dropping his gaze to the floor.

"What?" I reply, acting as if I've been accused of something far worse, terrified that Eric has figured it all out.

"I found this in his bag too," he says, hurling a wadded-up piece of paper at me. It hits me in the chest and falls to the floor.

I bend down to pick it up, but the second I see my handwriting on it, I know exactly what it is. "Eric, I can explain, we—"

"Oh, yes, please, let's have another explanation! Please, do tell, what perfectly reasonable thing caused you to go to Kevin's apartment and take off your clothes."

"I was there to calm him down."

"Shirtless?" Eric yells, taking a step toward me.

"My clothes were soaked," I protest. "I'd been out in the city searching for him. I was freezing."

"And I bet Kevin knew just how to warm you up."

"It wasn't like that," I say, trying to remember how it made sense at the time, but failing to find any logic in it now.

"Then what was it like, huh?" Eric takes another step toward me. "If it was something innocent, you'd have told me. No one is forcing you to keep secrets from me anymore, so tell me."

"I didn't tell you because it didn't mean anything."

"What didn't mean anything? What happened?" Eric yells, advancing on me again. I can feel the heat radiating off of him. In the entire time I've known him, I've never seen him this angry at anyone.

"Kevin had a breakdown, we weren't even sure he'd come back, I... we couldn't lose him. Not now, not with the show so close to opening. I mean, we had our first audience tonight. There was no time."

"So you gave him what he's been after?"

"It wasn't like that."

"Did you sleep with him or not?" Eric demands, as tears begin flooding down his face.

"Yes," I admit, wanting desperately to look away, but knowing I shouldn't. "He said he needed me to, he said the show depended on it."

"And you think that wasn't worth mentioning to me?"

"I didn't tell you because it didn't mean anything, because I still love you!" I say, grasping him by the shoulders.

"Not as much as you love this show!" he replies, throwing me back. "God, I can't believe how much of my life I wasted on you before finding out how limited your love for anyone else is."

"That's not true."

"Yes, it is! Whenever you've been in a show before, you've become obsessed, but this show has completely transformed you. I thought there was still some part of you left in there"—Eric looks me up and down, his eyes no longer wet with tears—"underneath your fancy new body, but there's nothing. The Mason I knew would never have slept with anyone for a role."

"It wasn't about that. We were in character."

"How stupid do you think I am?" Eric fumes, his pale skin flushing red. "I might have fallen for that once, but not again."

"But it's the truth. I didn't have a choice. After everything I've worked for I couldn't just throw it all away. This is what I've been dreaming of doing my whole life."

"Really? This is your dream? I thought you wanted to be an actor, not a whore."

"You don't mean that!"

"You're right. I don't, but I wish I did!" he says, looking at me with disdain. I search his eyes, hoping to find something that will help me believe we can get through this, but there is nothing there but anger and disappointment. "You say you didn't have a choice, but you did. You could have come home. You could have let this show fail. You could have chosen me! I would have understood. Hell, I would've been happy to see you. Because at least then I'd know that some part of the man I love was still inside you."

"But he is still in here." I clutch my hand to my chest. "I know it. Listen, I'm so sorry. I know that it's idiotic to try and apologize, because nothing I can do will undo the pain I've caused you, but, please, give me a second chance. I'll spend the rest of my life making it up to you. We can start over."

"I don't want to start over, Mason! I don't want you to love me out of guilt," Eric cries, and as he struggles to breathe all the fight in him seems to drain. "My heart hurts too much to endure trying again. If we weren't strong enough by now, we never will be."

"We were strong. I was the one who was weak."

"That's just not true. A chain is only as strong as the weakest link. If we were strong, none of this would have happened. But it did. I love you, more I've loved anyone in my entire life, and you did the one thing that would hurt me the most. And now you expect me to just forgive you? I can't. I won't. That's not how this works. We're done." Eric turns toward the elevator.

"No, please. Don't go!"

"Why should I stay?" he asks, turning back to face me. "What good could possibly come of it?"

"I want you to understand—"

"It's because I understand, that I am leaving. I'm sorry Mason, but real life isn't like your little play. You broke my heart! There's no way to talk your way around it. So quit trying. Just let me go."

"But I love you," I reply.

"Goodbye Mason," he says, and as he walks into the elevator and looks at me, I can see that I've lost him for good.

The second the elevator doors close, I crumple to floor and let out a scream that makes the one on stage seem like a baby cooing in comparison. I howl over and over, until finally I am too exhausted or too pained to scream any more. Not able to even consider going back downstairs, I crawl up on Merchant's couch to wait, but for what, I have no idea.

TWENTY THREE

WHEN I AWAKE THE NEXT morning, it takes me a little while to figure out where I am, a feeling that is becoming all too familiar. The memory of last night comes back to me, and I try to cry out, but my voice is so ragged and raw that I barely emit any sound. I can feel my tear ducts attempt to push out fresh tears, but there are none left.

"Mason?" Merchant calls from behind the door.

"Here," I croak, but I am not sure it's even audible.

"I'm coming in." He enters, carrying a tray of food and water.

"What time is it?" Every attempt at speaking hurts, and I clutch my hand to my throat.

"Try not to talk, you've been screaming in your sleep ever since I got you into bed. I came to check on you after I saw Eric downstairs yelling at Kevin, before storming off. When I found you, you were catatonic, until Kevin came in. Do you remember anything?"

I shake my head.

"Not even punching him in the face?"

"No!" I flex both hands and pain shoots up my left arm causing me to gasp.

"Yes, that's the one. You've got a mean left hook. He picked you up, put you on the bed, and then you started screaming and slugged him. By the time he knew what hit him, you'd passed out. After that, Kevin spent most of the night filling me in on everything that happened between you two." The images from the night I spent with Kevin flash again in my mind, but this time it feels dirty and seedy. I attempt to cry again, but still have no tears or voice to express my pain.

"Stop. Stop! You need to recover. Have something to eat and drink, and then we'll figure out what to do from here."

"I'm not hungry," I say, meaning it for the first time since Lycan put me on my diet.

"I know you're not, but you need food, even if your body doesn't think so. Just get down as much as you can."

I take the fork, poke at what I hope are scrambled eggs, and quickly shovel them into my mouth. They go down easily enough, but there is no taste, and after a few bites my gag reflex kicks in. I have to fight it to stop myself from vomiting all over the bed.

"Don't you dare," Merchant says, seeing me straining to keep it down.

"I'm fine," I say, swallowing the bile that had crept halfway up my throat.

"Keep eating. I'll be back in a few minutes."

After the first few bites, my body admits how hungry it is. When Merchant returns, I've already cleaned my plate. A small part of me feels a little bit better, but the idea that I could feel good at all makes me start to cry again. This time I manage to produce a few tears, and Merchant doesn't try to stop me, he just sits next to me until I'm spent.

"I don't want to appear insensitive, but I'm afraid I've got ask this before it gets any later."

"Will I be performing tonight?"

"I'll understand if you can't, but if that's true, I need to work with Alex."

"But we're in previews. Can't we cancel?"

"After the scene Kevin and Eric made last night, a canceled performance will most certainly make headlines, and it won't be hard to connect the dots. It'd be good press, but I assume you'd rather not make this scandal more public."

"No. So I guess I've got no choice."

"Alex will be more than—"

"No. I'll make it," I say, trying hard to project my voice to prove it.

I won't lose this role now. Performing is all I have left. "I just need to see Kevin first."

"Are you sure?"

"Yes, I need to know if I can ever pretend to love him again." Though I'm not certain if I fear more that I can or that I can't. Either way, I seem to lose.

"I understand. I'll get him."

"He's here?"

"Yes, he watched over you most of the night, albeit with only one eye. He kept a steak on the one you punched," Merchant says, unable to keep from smiling as he leaves.

In the few moments I have to gather my thoughts I think about what I need to know from Kevin, and it all boils down to one thing: Did he mean for this happen? He couldn't have planned for me to get doused with the wine, but he did offer me a change of clothes. Why didn't he warn me to keep Eric away from the bag? I have to know.

"You asked to see me?" If I didn't recognize his voice, I might not have believed it was him. The beautiful symmetry of his face is now horribly marred by a fist-sized purple blotch extending from his left cheek to the bridge of his nose.

"Oh god," I gasp, horrified by what I've done.

"Don't worry. I've covered up worse with stage makeup. Are you... how are you?"

"Imagine that, only bigger and on the inside."

"Right," he says, taking a seat on the bed, but avoiding direct eye contact.

"Merchant wants Alex to go on tonight."

"Oh..." Kevin says, and I can feel him wanting to say more, but he doesn't.

"I told him I could do it."

"Can you?"

"I don't know."

"I'm not sure if I can do it without you," he says, looking at me for a second before again averting his gaze.

"Look at me," I say.

"I can't."

"Why?"

"Because I'm afraid of what I'll see. Last night, when you punched me, you screamed 'I hate you.'"

"I did?" I ask, wishing I could remember that moment.

"Yes, but the thing is, you didn't need to say it at all. The hate seemed to swirl around you. I could practically taste it in the air. It was like all that passion had turned cold, and sharp. Honestly, it hurt more than the punch."

"Did you mean to hurt me?"

"No. I mean...I hoped you'd leave him. I wanted...I want to be with you, but I...I didn't want it like this. I wanted you to choose me."

"Then why didn't you warn me? Why did you even offer to help, if you knew what was in that bag?" When he doesn't respond I grab his shoulders and force him to look at me. "Tell me why!"

"I didn't expect him to go upstairs with you, okay?" Kevin tries to pull free but I refuse to budge. "I sure didn't think he'd go through my bag. I didn't mean for him to find the note, but part of me was hoping you would. That's why I told you where it was!"

"But why did you keep it at all?" In my frustration I tighten my grip on his shoulders, and the veins in his neck pulse rapidly, revealing how much effort it is for him to even speak.

"Because when I woke up and you were gone, I thought I'd dreamt everything," he says, his voice catching. "I was about to quit, but then I saw your note. It proved it was real. It was evidence that, for at least one night, we were together as I wanted us to be."

Seeing him so broken, again feels even worse, as if last night really was for nothing, and I fight the urge to comfort him. I can't believe there is any part of me that has any compassion for him. "Kevin, stop. Merchant has more than enough work today if he is going to get me on stage tonight."

"So, you'll do it?" he asks, his voice suddenly infused with hope.

"If you can look me in the eye and tell me you never planned to break Eric and I up, then yes."

"I never planned to ruin your relationship with Eric, but I can't lie and say I never hoped for it, or thought about it," he says, looking me in the eye without even blinking.

With his face no longer distractingly perfect, I am able to look into his eyes and not get lost for the first time. Knowing that I might never again be able to look this deep ever again, I stare for as long as I want. I try to search inside of myself to see if Caleb can assure me we can still love this face, even though it has caused us more pain than either of us had ever dreamt. I envy that Caleb is spared this kind of heartache through death, but even as I share my thoughts and memories with him, nothing seems to extinguish the flame in his heart. I can feel him begin to override my own senses, and little by little, I start to see Ezio instead of Kevin. For a brief moment, I have to restrain myself from kissing him, which tells me I can perform tonight. Throughout all of this Kevin barely blinks, and never shifts his gaze, until finally I look away.

"I believe you."

"Thank God!" he grasps me in a hug and runs his hands down the base of my spine.

"Stop!"

"What?"

"Kevin, I'm not ready for anything between us, not personally anyway."

"Oh. I just thought." He shifts his gaze away in embarrassment.

"I'm barely keeping it together. I need time."

"Then I'll wait. I don't ever want to cause you pain again," he says, letting go and standing up.

"Then let's keep the romance strictly on the stage. Now, get Merchant. We don't have any time to waste."

"I'll be there every step of the way to help."

"No, this is something I need to do alone," I say, knowing I won't be able to handle an entire day with Kevin at this point.

"But..."

"I'm sorry Kevin, but for the time being, I only want to see Ezio. So, if you really want to help, stay away. I'm going to switch dressing rooms with Julia for a few days."

"If that's what you need," he says, nodding his head to me as he leaves the room.

With Kevin gone, I explain to Merchant I will do the show, and within the hour my professional medicine man is knocking on the door. Over the next few hours, Lycan hands me a variety of strange drinks. The only one I recognize is the horrible honey and vinegar one he gave me once before.

"Won't this knock me out?" I ask, as I tip the small cup up so that I can down the rest of it as fast as possible.

"That's what this is for," he says, handing me yet another cup. This one contains a bubbling brown sludge that looks entirely undrinkable.

"I can't."

"Smell it first," he says, with an encouraging smile.

"Oh my!" I say, as the unmistakable aroma of espresso fills my nostrils. Excited to finally drink something normal, I take a big gulp, a move I instantly regret when the taste of grass and imitation grape flavoring hits my tongue.

"At least you got half of it down quickly."

"What is this?" I ask, and then proceed to chug water to rinse out my mouth.

"Finish it, and I'll tell you."

"Fine," I say, shooting the rest of it like a shot.

"Espresso, wheat grass, prune juice, and a cough drop."

"A cough drop?"

"Well, basically. It's a recipe I got from an Innuit healer when I traveled through Canada," Lycan says, acting like it was as easy as tuning in to a show on Food Network.

"Any other poisons?"

"Hopefully not. Try saying your lines."

"Your Lordship has been most kind in inviting me to dine here, but surely it is a waste to bestow such finery on someone of my station." I am amazed to hear Caleb's voice come out of me as loud and clear as it did yesterday.

"I think that'll do. Just keep drinking water, and I'll bring some tea for you about an hour before the show. There's a car waiting for you downstairs. Here, eat this on your way." He hands me a foil-wrapped square. "Go on. You don't want to keep Merchant waiting."

In the car, I inspect my lunch. I'm pretty sure it's just a ham and cheese on regular white bread, but I eat it quickly to avoid tasting it, just in case. If anything, I've learned nothing is as it appears to be with Lycan. Once I arrive at the theater, Jenna shows me to my new dressing room, which I will be sharing with Marshall.

"Merchant's inside," she says, throwing me a scowl before stalking off.

"Oh, Mason, you've got excellent timing. I was just explaining to Marshall that I wanted to separate you and Kevin backstage to avoid the temptation of breaking character. I'm not certain it'll work, but Marshall has assured me he'll do his best to not distract you."

"That's right. Although, I have to admit, I didn't notice you being off at the top of the second act last night."

"Oh…yeah, well, nothing gets past Merchant," I improvise poorly.

"Indeed," Merchant confirms. "I assume Lycan is done with you?"

"For now."

"Excellent, I need you on stage to fix a few lighting cues," he says, leading me out of the room.

"Do you think he believed that?" I ask, as we walk down the hall.

"No, but he knows better than to ask questions. If Eric and Kevin hadn't gotten into it at the party, it would've been easier."

"I keep meaning to ask you, what exactly happened during the fight?"

"Oh, just a lot of yelling. Luckily, most people were too drunk to comprehend what was happening, but, for those that were sober, it was clear that something was up."

"I see."

"Don't think about it. Now, I want to go over every scene you have with Kevin."

"All of them?"

"Yes," Merchant says, picking up a copy of the script. "Let's begin."

Going through the show without Kevin feels strange, but Merchant is a pretty decent scene partner. I try to summon forth Caleb's consciousness, but it doesn't do any good. Without Kevin, there is no Ezio, and without him, no Caleb, so it seems I'm left to fend for myself on stage. I am certain none of this escapes Merchant's notice, but he doesn't seem to mind, he just soldiers on until we get to the end of the first act.

"Let's stop here," he says, tossing the script aside and taking a seat on the floor.

"Are you sure?"

"Mason, I am pleased to see you can say your lines. I was worried the similarity in subject matter might make even that difficult. I don't want to exhaust you any more than I have to."

"Okay," I say, fighting back a fresh wave of sadness.

"Tonight isn't going to be easy, so just remember this. When you feel like it's all spinning out of control, remember your training. No matter what has happened to you, out here, on this stage, you are Caleb. I've seen you vanish when you walk on stage, don't get in the way of letting that happen. Channel everything you are feeling into your work on stage. If you can do that, I will try to find a way to help you."

"You've helped me more than enough."

"I shouldn't have sent you after Kevin. I used you to clean up my mess, and no director should ever use an actor for that. I owe you, so just let me be your brain for a few hours," he says, tapping the side of his head.

"I don't think there is a way to fix the situation with Eric, but maybe you can think of a place for me to stay. Or at least a way for me to get my stuff."

"Oh, for the next two weeks you'll be staying with Lycan. He wants to keep an eye on you from now until opening night. Give me a list of your belongings, and I'll have someone retrieve them while Eric is at work."

"Wow, maybe you can help with Eric after all."

"Maybe, but I can only think about that if I'm not worried about you."

"Then don't worry about me. You won't see anyone but Caleb when I'm on that stage."

TWENTY FOUR

TRUE TO MY WORD, I let Caleb run the show that evening, and it seems to work. Keeping Merchant's few notes in mind, Kevin is more restrained, and Julia works harder to make herself a viable option. However, when Mina discovers Ezio seducing Caleb, I feel my heart break. It's like reliving the moment when Eric found the letter I wrote to Kevin. It makes death seem so much easier, but at the end I am still alive. In fact, the curtain call is the hardest part of the entire performance. Even though it's only a few minutes, with Caleb dead, I hate being myself on stage. I cry that night, and every night after, but everyone assumes my tears are of happiness and gratitude for the applause we receive.

Although each day gets a little easier, now, more than ever, I wish I could just forget I exist and live as Caleb every second of my day. I think Kevin would like that, too. I can see it in his face when we hold hands at the end of the show, this look of hope, just before he realizes how badly I want to pull away. Yet, he never seems mad about it; he just tries harder to make things easier for me. He leaves the theater before I do, giving me the chance to avoid a lot of fans. Having been a fanboy so often in my life, I never completely duck out, but when I sign autographs I avoid my bio so I won't have to see my dedication to Eric.

What little free time I have, I spend playing the game Eric helped design. The game is one of the massive multiplayer role-playing ones, where you meet up with people online and go on quests. I learned that there is a thing in the game called a leader board, where the people who do the best on a specific quest get their name emblazoned on a stone tablet in the center of the world. I keep thinking that if I could somehow get onto there, Eric might see it. Unfortunately, I'm not very good at the game at all. A few players have tkaen pity on me and helped teach me some basics, but I'm still nowhere near good enough to get on the board.

Lycan helps keep my mind off of Eric as best he can. During the day he keeps me distracted with additional workouts, long guided meditations, and disgusting beverages that he claims will help me recover my voice. This is a necessity nowadays, as I apparently spend half of every night screaming in my sleep. Waking up hoarse is starting to feel routine, which I could handle, but seeing that I've kept Lycan awake as I sit down to breakfast makes a knot of guilt form in my throat.

"Was it any better last night?" I ask, mortified by my involuntary actions.

"Actually, yes. I haven't heard anything since midnight."

"Really? Did you get some sleep then?" I ask, the knot loosening up a bit in relief.

"Some, yes, but an idea woke me up a few hours ago."

"An idea?"

"Yes, though not my own. Merchant called, he has finally come up with something for you."

"About Eric?" I ask, my whole body feeling alive with hope.

"Yes, though I'm afraid it's a bit risky."

"I'll try anything."

"I figured that was the case. Has he still not returned any of your phone calls?"

"Not one," I say, checking my phone again. I haven't allowed it to be on silent since I woke up in Merchant's apartment, but whenever it rings, it's never him. It feels unfair to miss him, but I do.

"Then I think we need to communicate with him in a way he can't ignore."

"Like how?"

"I am going to insist he meet with me to discuss the apartment."

"What about it?" I say, curious what it has to do with anything.

"Well, you see, I will tell him that you have found a place live, but the landlord is insisting that, in order to give you an affordable rate, you must be released from the lease you signed with him."

"I don't want to lie to him. That's what got me into trouble in the first place," I say, having already promised myself never to lie to him again, if I ever get the chance to speak to him.

"You won't be lying. I'm a very picky landlord."

"You?"

"Yes. Honestly, aside from the late night noise, I've kind of enjoyed having you here. Plus, Merchant has offered to subsidize your rent by pulling some strings with a travel company. Thanks to him, I will finally have a chance to visit Turkmenistan. I've always dreamed of seeing the ancient city of Merv, so really, you'd be doing me favor," he says, looking at an urn that I assume is from there.

"Okay, but even if he's willing to listen to me, what should I say?"

"I assumed you'd given that some thought."

"I've barely thought of anything else, but it's all jumbled in my head," I say, having played the conversation out in my head at least a hundred different ways.

"Of course. Well, I'm afraid words aren't my strong suit, but I would urge you to focus more on being strong enough to listen to him."

"Well, of course."

"It's not so simple. Are you able to hear that it's truly over? I hope it isn't, but you need to be prepared to hear that."

"Can anyone ever be ready to hear that?" I ask, unsure whether I could ever truly give up hope that Eric and I could get back at least part of what we once had.

"I believe so, yes. If you love him, then you won't continue to ask him to reject you. You have to be willing to let go."

"But how?"

"It won't be easy Mason, but that's why you must give this everything you have. One final gesture. If it's not enough, then nothing ever will be," he says, handing me a stack of papers and a pen.

"What's this?"

"A copy of the terms of your potential lease, a ticket to tonight's performance, and some stationary. I thought you might want to write a letter explaining why he should attend."

"But…he'd never want to see Kevin and me on stage…not after what happened."

"It is precisely because of what happened that he should want to see the show. You honor Eric every night with your performance. He should see that, if nothing else, to see that you know what you lost. Besides, if you keep performing like this, I'm afraid that you'll never do another show again."

"Why?"

"You're slowly becoming numb, Mason. I can see it when we meditate. You're beginning to resent performing, and I'm afraid that once this show is over, you won't have the desire to ever build another character again, or worse, you'll retreat into your character. I worry you'll try that to stay close to Kevin, but eventually he won't want to pretend anymore. I fear what might become of you if that happens."

"Why shouldn't I resent it?" I say, raising my voice. "I've sacrificed years to be an actor, only to realize, now, that acting brings out the worst in me."

"No, it doesn't. It merely reveals all of you," Lycan says, using his calming voice to settle me back down. "We all blind ourselves from the harsh reality of our true identities. Like Adam and Eve, you have been tossed out of your own personal Eden and made aware that there are parts of you that are not as virtuous as you would like to have believed. But it is that knowledge, that realization, which makes your performance so much more powerful. The problem is, instead of accepting it, you hate it. You keep trying to get back into Eden, and that is impossible."

"I thought you weren't good with words," I say.

"I know a lot about self-reflection, Mason, but very little about love."

"Love depends on two people. What will I do if he doesn't come tonight?"

"Perform for him anyway," Lycan replies, standing up from the table. "This is the night that will live on people's memories, the one that reviewers will write about. Your grand gesture will live for as long as those things exist. Let tonight be your magnum opus, so that no matter where he is, for the rest of your life, you will always be able to look back on tonight and know there was nothing more you could have done to get him back."

"I wish I'd written that down," I say, already paralyzed by the blank sheet of paper in my hand. I don't even know how to start.

"If you will give me your word that you will stop blaming performing, and once again embrace it, then I will be happy to guide us through a morning meditation. I think a clear mind will help you find the words you seek," he says, extending his hand to me after standing up.

"If you say performing will truly help me, then I'll stop resenting it."

"Then I guess I don't have to go easy on you."

Over the next hour or so, Lycan guides me through a series of incredibly complex poses. I listen to his instructions, focusing on breathing and clearing my mind, and am able to push my body further than ever before. In some poses, I actually manage to extend myself even farther than Lycan, which seems to please him. However, when he demonstrates the Kākāsana pose, which essentially involves lifting my entire body up by my fingers, I only manage to do it by using my palms, allowing me to access the muscles in my entire arm.

"Are you able to give any more?" he asks, as I strain just to hold myself, my muscles trembling from the effort.

"No," I say, trying to breathe through it.

"Then relax. You must accept that even when you give everything you've got, it may not be enough."

"I understand," I say, after slowly lowering myself to the ground. I just hope that tonight I manage to give a performance that is enough.

"Then go grab a bite in the kitchen. Merchant's arranged for someone to help you compose your letter. You don't have much time if we are going to get it to Eric before tonight, so don't think on it too long, otherwise you'll never finish."

When I walk into the kitchen I find Colin Shapiro seated at a table, eating a grilled cheese sandwich. There's something particularly strange about it, not only because I've never seen normal food in Lycan's kitchen, but because Colin's skeletal figure makes it hard to believe he ever eats anything.

"Mr. Burroughs, just who I was waiting for."

"Oh, Mr. Shapiro, shouldn't you be at the theater?"

"Probably, but after talking to Merchant I felt I should pay you a visit. Here." His bony hands shake as he offers me a large envelope.

"What's this?"

"The original ending of *Masque*. I thought it might be of interest to you, given your…situation."

"Why?"

"Because, I have spent a lifetime trying to properly atone for choosing art over love, and while I will never be able to share these words with the one I lost, you still have a chance."

The words on the page feel like Colin has heard every fractured thought I've had, every possible way to express my regret and sorrow, and bound them all together. After the first sentence my body begins to quake, and I have to sit down. I read over it several times, each time catching some new level of meaning, some parallel to my own remorse. I can feel the years of careful consideration in the placement of each word, and wonder how Merchant ever convinced him to rewrite the ending without it. It's so clear that this was not only the true ending of the play, but the reason it existed at all.

"It's perfect, but Eric would never believe I could write something like this. I can't plagiarize an apology."

"No, you can't, but I understand your plan is for Eric to attend tonight. Correct?" Colin asks, sliding a pen and some paper over to me.

"Well, yes."

"And he saw the play before?"

"Yes."

"Then he would notice if you said these words tonight. He would know that while everyone else would believe the show had always ended like this, that you were responsible for changing it. That these words might have been be heard by hundreds, but were only meant for him."

"Yes, but can we really change the play so drastically now? Previews are over—"

"Previews are previews. The show isn't set until opening night. Merchant has left the choice with you. It will no doubt be that much harder for you to perform the original ending night after night if Eric rejects you, but there is a chance it could help you get him back." Colin's eyes are glassy, and I know that as much as I want Eric back, Colin wants this ending, too.

"Then I'll do it." I don't care about suffering more, if it means there is even the slightest chance of getting Eric back. I've learned that every opportunity you take comes at a price, and I would gladly suffer anything if it meant Eric might one day hold me in his arms again.

"I figured you would, so let's work on finding the words to get him to come."

"That won't be easy."

"Nothing about tonight will be easy, true atonement never is."

Over the next hour, I attempt to write something that will convince Eric to come, but Colin crosses out every sentence except for three words: "honesty," "change," and "regret."

"It's not finished," I protest, as Lycan comes in to collect the letter.

"So I see," Lycan replies looking over my shoulder. "Colin, I thought you were here to help."

"I am helping," he says, crossing his arms.

"I'm not so certain. You can't climb a mountain if you try to make each step perfect."

"He's almost there, I can feel it," Colin huffs, circling the words again and again.

"I need more than three words."

"You've got the words that count, all you have to do now is fill in the rest. Each word gets one sentence," Colin says, handing me a fresh sheet of paper.

"But there is so much more to say."

"I know, but you will say the rest of it with your performance. That's how you can truly speak to Eric," Lycan says, hoisting Colin out of his chair, and dragging him into the parlor. "You've got five minutes. Alone."

"You can do it!" Colin yells, scrambling to break free. "Just use the words!"

Without Colin slashing my sentences as soon as they're done, it's easier to write, but nothing really says what I need it to say. I try to think back to what Eric ever liked about me, to find the parts of me he thought were gone forever. Before I know it, the time is up, and Lycan snatches the page away, handing it to Colin, who simply nods with approval. I sign my name, and Lycan seals the envelope before I can try to edit it any more. I've done my best; all I can do now is hope that what I wrote was enough.

Dear Eric,

Enclosed is a ticket for tonight. The show has changed since you last saw it, and so have I, but tonight's performance will be special. It will no longer glorify what divided us, but show you, and only you, that I know and regret the foolish idea that anything was ever worth more than your love. Honesty is rare to find in our lives, especially from actors on a stage, but it will be there tonight. It is my hope you will be there too, but even if you burn this ticket, know that my performance will always be for no one but you.

With all my love,
Mason

TWENTY FIVE

LYCAN HAS YET TO RETURN from his meeting with Eric when the car arrives to take me to the theater. I ask the driver to wait, but he says he has strict instructions to not allow me to delay. Knowing that Merchant probably devised this as part of his plan, I obey, and throw my pack into the car along with a bouquet of roses. Sinking back into the comfy leather seats, I remind myself how far I've come. I think of who I was at my audition and can't help but laugh to remember that my biggest concern at that time was that I had a thirty-two-inch waist. I used to think I'd never want that problem again, but I'd trade back my old body if it meant I could have another day with Eric.

When I arrive at the stage door, journalists are already lined up, but when one of them asks who I am, I tell them I'm just in the ensemble, and so I'm able to get into the theater without much hassle. When I sign in, I'm surprised to find that Tiny is dressed in a tuxedo.

"You look fabulous."

"Thanks, it's for the after party."

"Not for me?"

"I'll wear whatever you want me to," he says, with a wink.

I see Kevin in the hallway. He sees me too, and quickly disappears into our old dressing room. I am tempted to just let him keep on thinking he should avoid me, but given what tonight is supposed to mean, I decide he deserves to know as well.

"Mason!" Julia calls out, in her usual sing-song fashion, as I step into the dressing room.

Kevin is seated at his station, shirtless, absent-mindedly flipping through the script as he reviews his makeup in the mirror. "Hey," he says, the muscles in his jaw flexing to control his enthusiasm.

"I wanted to wish you well, and also make good on a promise."

"What promise?" Kevin asks.

"These are for you, Julia," I say, handing her a large bouquet of roses.

"Mason! How sweet! Oh, I better get these in some water," she says, practically dancing out of the room.

"Kevin, about tonight…"

"Nervous?"

"Did Merchant tell you about the ending?"

"What? No."

"Oh. Well nothing is different for you, but the speech I give at the end will be from Colin's original ending."

Kevin's eyes widen. "The one he wrote for…"

"Yes."

"Okay, but why?"

"Because I asked Eric to be here tonight," I say. Kevin looks away.

"How was he?" I can tell his concern is genuine because, when he looks back, his eyes appear to be a deeper shade of blue, the way they do whenever he's worried about something.

"I don't know. I didn't actually see him. I sent a letter."

"What if he doesn't show up?"

"Then I'll perform for him anyway. Listen, I appreciate how good you've been these past two weeks about respecting my needs for space. I know it hasn't been easy on you. But, whatever happens tonight, well…I thought you should know what it's for."

"And tomorrow? What happens then?"

"Tomorrow I'll start performing for myself again."

"Then I'm happy to help you through tonight." He gives me a one-armed hug.

"I'll need you tonight more than ever," I say, wrapping both of my arms around him.

Kevin pulls me close. "Then I'm happy to help you through tonight."

The door opens, and Julia enters, carrying one of the prop vases, now filled with the roses I gave her. She raises an eyebrow. "Do you want your old dressing room back?"

"Et tu, Brute?" Kevin says, miming being stabbed in the back.

"Just asking! I'm happy to enjoy the space for as long as I can."

"Keep it, at least until tomorrow," I say. "Umm, Julia, won't someone need that during the show?" I point to the vase.

"I'll put it back at intermission. Now your little boudoir will have some fresh flowers."

"Oh, I do love surprises on opening night," Kevin says, inhaling their scent.

"Break a leg tonight, both of you," I say as I exit.

Time seems to absolutely crawl by, and I constantly check my phone, hoping for some word from Merchant or Lycan or...Eric. I warm up, and for the first time in weeks, Kevin and I play the finding game with one another. The synchronicity between us has never been more exact, and when I open my eyes after finding him for the third time, his smile is so warm that it feels like old times. Ever since we had our night together, connecting with him has been easier. I think it was more than just the sex; it was the confessions. Baring the ugly truths we did that night made us something more than just friends. Because of that, I can feel his hesitation with me, his fear that he will do something to push me too far, and lose me all together. It's still hard to believe I have such an effect on him, but I don't deny it anymore. I'm glad I told him what tonight was about.

"Hey Mason," Alex says, in his usual nasal and annoying tone. If he hadn't grown on me so much, it'd drive me nuts knowing that he doesn't actually have to talk like that.

"Break a leg tonight Alex."

"You, too. I hear it's going to be a bit different tonight," he says, his voice dropping to a normal pitch.

"Yes, that's the plan."

"I'm rooting for you. In fact, everyone in the cast is, and, well...I just wanted you to know that I'm really sorry for making your life hard. I want to thank you for reminding me what theatre is about. Over the years I'd forgotten that art really does have power, provided the person telling the story is doing it for something more than just applause." He hugs me, and then, upon seeing a half-dressed member of Kevin's club walk by, lets go of me to follow him.

Shortly before the house is supposed to open, Jenna calls all of us onto the stage, so Merchant can to speak to us. Not all directors give big speeches before a show, but in my experience, the best ones do. I'm also thankful for a distraction to make the time go by faster. The moments just before the curtain rises are always the longest.

"Tonight is the night we've been waiting for. I have purposefully been quiet about which reviewers have already come see the show, but tonight there is no denying they are out there. So I will tell you this, the reviewer from the *Times* has already seen the show, but he is here again tonight. You've managed to capture the hearts of everyone who has walked through those doors, but tonight, I challenge you to take their souls as well. If you feel yourself slipping, remember that in this theater, princes have died, friendships have been forged, and love has caused people to burst into song. All of that energy lies in these walls, in the very floorboards on which you stand. Use it, if ever you find your own strength failing. Let the ghosts of all the shows that have ever been played upon this stage fuel you, so that each and every moment is honest and true. This is more than your opening. This is your entire life in three hours, so make every second count. Now, let's give this audience full of critics a show that will have them laughing and crying so hard they won't be able to scribble their notes, for their eyes will be full of tears!" He lets out a wolfish howl, and we quickly join him.

My voice soars through the room, and I can feel the energy he is talking about envelope me. I look at Kevin, and can sense he feels it, too. The gloom and doom that has surrounded me these past few weeks is gone because tonight I am not performing just because I've finally made it to Broadway; no, tonight is about more than that dream. Tonight I perform to leave my own mark on the floorboards and the walls of this theater, not merely to say that I was here, but that I was here for the one I love.

"Mason, a word," Merchant says, stepping into the wings and gesturing for me to follow.

"Did Lycan meet with him? Is he coming?"

"Lycan met with him, and he accepted the ticket. However, I need you to promise me that you aren't going to sacrifice your performance by checking to see if he's there."

"Is he?" I ask in an unsteady voice, unsure if knowing is a good idea.

"Promise me you won't look for him."

"I promise I won't look for him."

"Good, I don't know if he's here, but Lycan said he read the letter, and then asked for the ticket. So, that's something," he says, clasping me on the shoulder. "And Mason?"

"Yes?"

"I don't think I've ever told you this, but, I'm proud of you." The words immediately cause me to tear up. It's nice to cry out of happiness again. "Now, don't get all blotchy. There isn't enough time to redo your makeup. But you should know this: I've never worked with anyone who exceeded my expectations before, but what you've done these past few weeks is nothing short of a miracle. I look forward to watching you tonight. You'll know I'm with you, when you hear me whistling," he says, with a gleam in his eye.

"Tonight is for Eric, but I couldn't do him justice without you," I say, embracing him, which feels, oddly, both perfect and unnatural.

After a few moments I let go, and without another word, he leaves me to find his seat in the house. In order to busy myself, I check my props and costumes, kiss Julia for good luck, and give Kevin another hug. Before I know it the curtain rises, and the show begins.

Tonight, Caleb and I share a mind in a different way. He no longer feels distinct and separate, but rather just another part of me. As our minds fuse together, I can see the world through his eyes, but for the first time I am not blinded from also seeing things as they really are. Throughout the show, I hear the audience clap, gasp, and cry. Each auditory sign of what they feel helps me fine-tune my performance to make a line funnier or more gut-wrenching. I can see this is something Kevin's done all along, and with me finally doing it too, the audience seems utterly spellbound by us. Julia helps balance us out, emphasizing a joke when we get too serious or grounding us if we start to make our quips cartoonish. She is truly magnificent, and as the curtain falls on Act One, I understand better than ever why Caleb loves her.

"Intermission is going to be a little longer," Jenna says, as I pass her in the hall.

"Why?"

"It's opening night. People want time to have a drink and use the restroom."

"Got it," I say, as I make my way to my dressing room.

I don't speak to anyone, afraid that saying anything might cause me to lose focus. Marshall doesn't seem to mind. He spends the entire time playing Candy Crush on his phone, not even bothering to begin changing his costume until I'm almost out the door. After touching up my makeup, I take my place backstage and prepare for another long wait.

"Hey, Mason," I hear Kevin say, behind me.

Not wanting to cut myself off from Caleb, I don't reply.

"Oh…right. I just wanted a hug before the curtain."

"All right," I say, turning to face him. I know it's the least I can do, considering all I've asked of him tonight.

"I can't wait for you to be mine again," he whispers into my ear.

"What?"

"He's not here, Mason." The words stab into me one at a time, and for a moment I can't comprehend their meaning. Once I do, though, I feel myself slipping.

"I don't care. Tonight is for him," I reply, fighting to keep it together.

"The box is empty."

"It's not over."

"Yes it is! He threw his ticket away, just like he threw you away. Don't you see that you and I are supposed to be together?" His voice is loud enough to pass through the curtains, and the audience has just started to quiet down from the excitement of intermission.

"Lower your voice!"

"No! Tonight should be about us. Tonight you're giving the best performance of your life. You shouldn't squander it on him," he says, grabbing me to him and pressing my head into his chest.

"I love him, Kevin."

"No, you love me! I thought once we were together, you'd see that."

"That's not how it works." I break free of his grasp.

"What we have, what we did, doesn't it mean anything to you?" he says, his voice frantic and wild.

"Yes, it does, but what we did wasn't right. It only happened because of extreme circumstances."

"But you enjoyed it. I know you did."

"I'm not saying I didn't, but there's more to it than that."

"I've given you space, I've given you everything. What can I do to make you love me like you love him?" he asks, grabbing my arm.

"Kevin, stop, you've got to let me go."

"Fine, I'll let you go, but not until I've given it my all. If you're not holding back tonight, neither am I!" he says, releasing me and storming off.

It takes me a while to breathe again, and while normally I hate long intermissions, I am thankful for the delay tonight. When places are called, I am still pretty shaken up by what Kevin said as he ran off. What did he mean by it? I continue ponder it as the curtain rises, but then remember what tonight is supposed to be about. Before the blinding lights once again prevent me from seeing the audience, I decide to break my promise to Merchant and look at the spot I know Eric should be.

He's not there.

The scene begins without my notice and I almost miss my first line, but the Caleb part of me pounces on my moment of weakness and takes over. My vision flickers as Caleb strives hard to make me forget my own world, but I quickly regain the balance I had during the first act.

As the dancers perform their elaborate choreography for the masquerade ball, I let Caleb fully take over, and focus my attention to trying to tap into Kevin's mind like I did when I was searching for him. I know he has something planned, but I can't figure out how he could change the scene to be anything else. Even if we did the old blocking, Julia would still stop us. Before I can think on it any longer, the moment has arrived, and although Kevin's face is hidden behind his mask, I can tell he is smiling as he takes my hand and leads me into our final scene.

He paces around the stage like a caged animal, skipping almost a full page of dialogue, which throws me off. Using this to his advantage, he kisses me way ahead of schedule.

"My lord, you do forget yourself," I improvise, hoping Colin will forgive me.

"No, it is you who should forget, for I see you still pine for that strumpet Mina," Kevin replies, leaving me with no clue how to get the scene back on track.

"I love her."

"Have you no passion for me then?"

"I do feel for you my lord, but passion is but one component of love," I say, remembering a line that was lost in one of Colin's countless rewrites.

"What do you know of love?" Kevin says, finally feeding me a line which will permit us to get back on script.

"I know it causes men to do mad things," I say, staring the truth of it in the face.

"Indeed, it does. For love emboldens us to risk all, a risk I am finally willing to take. Caleb my sweet angel, all I ask is that you stay with me tonight. Love me as I love you for this one evening, and, once the morning comes, if you still love another, I will resign than you are a war I cannot win." It is the same modified line he used the night we were together.

As his lips meet mine, I am surprised how gentle he is being, since he was so crazed just moments ago. Slowly, he traces his fingers over my skin, more sweet than sensual, but when at last I feel his thumbs dig into the small of my back, a strong sense of déjà vu comes over me. In a flash, it all comes back to me. I've done this before. I realize what Kevin is doing – he's recreating the night we shared in his apartment on stage.

"Tower," I whisper, but Kevin looks me in the eye, and I can see he has no intention of stopping.

I try to escape his grasp, but he's too strong, and I can only resist so much without ruining the performance. Keeping his grip on me, he lowers himself onto the chaise, pulling me on top of him. That this, of all things, will be a part of people's memories shatters what is left of my resolve. Tears run down my face, splashing onto his chiseled chest, and at last Kevin's smug smile of satisfaction dissolves.

"I love you," he says in a stage whisper.

"And I love you too," I reply, placing his hand on my heart, as he kisses the tears from my face.

"No!" Julia screams, entering with a look of concern instead of betrayal.

"Mina! What are you doing here?" I say, once again remembering the play is still going on.

"You dare to ask what I am doing, after I find you like this?"

"It is not all it seems," I say, practically taking a nose dive onto the floor as I scramble off and away from Kevin. "I…I would return to you if I thought you would have me."

"You would dare think of returning to my side? I will have none of you that his venomous lips have touched, which leaves you nothing to offer." The look of betrayal and pain she wears is so close to Eric's that I look away in shame, locking eyes with Kevin instead. There is something in his eyes, a sense of defeat, of nothingness, and I know something is off. Confused about what to do, I run into his arms, though Julia has yet to even begin her attack.

"You should choose me. I can make you happier," he says, shifting his gaze slightly above my head.

"We cannot chose with whom we fall in love," I reply.

"No one knows that more than I," he says, kissing me again. "I lied to you," he whispers in my ear, so quietly that I'm not quite certain I hear it.

"He's here then?"

"Yes," he says, and as I turn away from him to look, I see Julia lunge, and I make it just in time. The prop knife stabs into my heart instead of my abdomen, and I grunt, instead of letting out a scream of pain. With what little strength I have left I crawl out of the elaborate light cue into the darkness at the lip of the stage.

Eric.

Although the lights prevent me from seeing much more than his silhouette, I would recognize him anywhere. I forget to breathe, to act, to do anything, for what feels like forever, unable to stop looking at his shadow. I begin to sob, clutching at the spot I was supposed to be stabbed, unable to remember what to say next.

"No. Why? Caleb…my love…why?" Julia cries out, giving me my cue for the final speech.

A full minute passes on stage in silence. I look at them both, but the words seem lost, all traces of Caleb seem to have dissipated since I was stabbed, and I am unsure of how it even begins. I close my eyes, racking my brain for some clue, but nothing comes. Utterly drained, I don't have the energy to even panic, and slowly I feel myself beginning to faint.

A whisper of a whistle blows in from the wings, and it reminds me of Merchant's advice. Placing my hands on the floor boards, I think of the unforgettable performances that have occurred pm this very spot, performances of legend. I feel the energy flow from the wood through my arms, and the words I wanted to say to Eric, the words that inspired this show to exist, tumble out of me with more passion than ever before.

"Because, my love, I have played a foolish game, and lost. During my time within these walls, I sought to become a different man, one worthy of your love. For, although you found no fault within me, I found my own reflection lacking. My time here allowed me to transform myself as I had sought, but at a price I should never assented to pay.

"You would be wrong to blame this man for my deeds, for he was under the impression we were as much in love as you and I. Having become an excellent shapeshifter, I changed myself to be what he desired, knowing that I could twist this to my advantage. But, like a drunkard who drinks too deep, I changed my form so completely that I forgot who I was, and lost myself in his embrace.

"In seeing you tonight, your face reminded me of all that I was. A man torn between two worlds, who attempted to live two lives with one heart. I felt I had become something beyond human, and that I could manage to love each of you as perfectly with half a heart as your whole hearts love me. For such folly, it is only right that my heart split itself in twain upon your blade. I am happy that, in doing so, it has saved one of the hearts I dared love. Please permit it to save the other, by placing the dagger in my own hand and blaming me for all that has transpired here tonight. I know I have no right to make such a request, but it is the last I shall ever make. I am not saddened that each of you knows the truth, but rather relieved that all secrets have now been aired. The only regret I have is that you will remember me not as one who loved you, but as one who wore a mask."

With nothing left to say, I close my eyes and let my body go limp. Julia and Kevin sob over me as the lights slowly fade to black and the applause starts. It crescendos in darkness.

Julia and Kevin reach out their hands and help me up and into the wings, where the entire cast is waiting. They all try to hug and congratulate me before dashing out to take their bows, but Tiny pushes them to get out there and not keep the audience waiting. The applause roars so loudly that I fear the walls might buckle, and, when Kevin and I step onto the stage, they somehow manage to swell even louder. Yet, above it all, I can distinctly hear Eric calling my name, right before a huge bouquet of moonlight lilies falls at my feet. Picking them up, I hear a strange jangling noise as something drops out of them and onto the stage in front of me. Eric's keys. Recognizing them at once I scramble to pick them up, clasping them so tightly that the jagged edges press hard into my palm, but I don't feel the pain. I look up at him, never happier to see his face in all my life. He keeps pointing to me, and screaming something, but all I can hear him say is my name. The rest of it is drowned in the elation of the crowd.

After several additional bows, Julia once again grabs Merchant and drags him onto the stage, but after taking his bow, he holds his palms up to the audience to ask them to stop and be silent once more.

"Ladies and gentlemen, thank you once again. I hope you enjoyed tonight's performance. I despise long speeches. Our playwright will tell you how many of them were cut from the show, but please permit me to say a few words. For those of you who have attended before, I have no doubt you will have noticed some key differences in tonight's performance. Please note that they are not the result of any fault of the actors, and were entirely intentional. Though our audiences have always been enthusiastic, tonight's record eight curtain calls permit me the great vanity of saying they were excellent modifications. However, I am unable to claim all of the credit. Please join me in one final round of applause for our playwright Mr. Colin Shapiro." The audience, as well as the cast, applauds as Colin enters from the wings, escorted by Alex.

"Thank you one and all," Colin says, his voice surprisingly loud considering how frail he appears. "I have waited many years to see what

I saw tonight. I knew it would happen soon after I met Mr. Caldwell, or Ezio, as we have seen him tonight. I was so taken with the talent of this young man that I felt inclined to return to writing. Over the past two years he has been a truly inspiring Muse. Mr. Burroughs, or Caleb, and I have only known each other a short time, but we are connected by shared experiences that date back to the day that love was first expressed between two people. His passion and work made every word he spoke tonight as true in his heart as it is in my own," Col says, before leading the audience in another round of applause.

"We thank you all for coming, and hope you will return soon," Merchant says in closing, raising his hands to indicate the house lights should rise. Bowing once more, we are finally free to leave the stage.

Still clutching Eric's keys in one hand and his flowers in the other, I rush to my dressing room. It takes a lot of effort to set either of them down, but, knowing they'll only slow me down, I manage it. I start pulling my clothes off with such abandon that several buttons pop off; I am fortunate nothing actually rips in the process. My heart jumps when I hear a knock at the door.

"Eric!" I cry out, flinging the door open wide, despite my state of undress.

"Afraid not," Kevin says. He's leering at me, and making no effort to disguise this fact.

"Quite a show," I say, uncertain whether to be angry at him for practically raping me on stage, or happy that by doing so he pushed me over the edge, allowing me to deliver the final monologue better than I would have ever thought possible.

"Yeah, well, I told you. I like surprises on opening night."

"You know how I feel about surprises," I say, angrily thrusting my legs through my jeans.

"After tonight, I think you're right about them. But that's not why I'm here. You dropped this on stage," he says handing me a card.

"I did?"

"It fell out of that bouquet."

"That's what he was pointing at!" I say, ripping it open.

"What's it say?"

"It says he'll see me at home!" I squeal, grabbing the keys and heading for the door.

"You're leaving now?"

"Of course!" I say, zipping up my hoodie and heading for the door.

"But the press, the parties."

"Tell them I had something much more important to tend to."

"Don't you dare!" Merchant says, barging into the room.

"I've got go," I say, trying to slip by.

"I'm afraid that's impossible."

"You're joking!" I balk, unable to believe he would ask anything of me now.

"Believe me, it'll be worth it."

"But..."

"Mason, I told him not to expect you until late. Now trust me," he says, tapping his head for a second, and then personally escorting Kevin and me all the way to the stage door.

"I trust you to think for me about all sorts of things, but when it comes to love, well...I think that's something I know better than even you," I say, glancing at Kevin who can read me so well.

"Mr. Burroughs, be reasonable," Merchant says, stretching out his hand to me. "You can't leave now."

"That's exactly what I can do," I say, flipping up my hood and dashing into the blinding lights of a thousand cameras.

"Anything you want me to say?" Kevin calls out.

"You know what we have to say, Kevin! You have to tell them we couldn't have done it without Julia!" I flash a smile before turning and making my way through the crowd. I'm stopped by a few fans, and quickly sign a handful of autographs, but I keep walking as I do. Nothing is going to stop me this time.

★

THE SOUND OF MY KEY turning in the lock is sweeter than all of the applause I have received tonight. As I step inside, the scent of our life in the apartment fills my nostrils, and for the first time in weeks, I feel like I'm finally home.

"Mason?" Eric calls from the bedroom.

"Were you expecting someone else?" I ask, walking into our bedroom just in time to catch Eric turning off the Playstation. I guess while I was gone, he finally put it in the bedroom.

"No, I just figured you'd be much later than this. What about the party and interviews?"

"They can wait," I say, drinking in the sight of him. Based on the fact that he's still wearing the black socks from his suit with his pajama bottoms, it's clear he barely beat me home. Still, even dressed as he is, I've never wanted him more in my entire life.

"But tonight is your big night!"

"Didn't you get my note?" I ask, taking a seat next to him. "Tonight is for you, and only you."

"How did it go?" he asks, as if he didn't know.

"Oh, you know...performance of a lifetime."

"Really? Such a shame," he says, looking away.

"What? Why?"

"'Cause I missed some of it. You'd be amazed how far you have to go to find moonlight lilies this time of year. Besides, if I'm going to see it as many times as I expect, I don't want to tell our friends 'he was better on opening night.'"

"Then I guess I'll have to find a way to recreate tonight," I say, inching closer to him on the bed.

"Please don't."

"Why," I ask, scooting back.

"By the time I go again, I expect you to be much better," he replies, pulling me to him.

"Well, I'm open to suggestions."

"Stop talking," he says, and kisses me.

No violins play in that moment, no candles are lit, and yet, even though there is nothing but my lips touching his, it is the single most romantic kiss of my life, one to which no opera, play, speech or song could ever do justice. In Eric's kiss I realize I am living the role of a lifetime.

THE END

ACKNOWLEDGEMENTS

First and foremost, I would like to thank my loving husband, Brian, and darling daughter, Natalie. Without them in my life, I would never have found the courage, time, and confidence to bring this story into the world. Thank you Brian, for taking care of our little one almost every weekend so I could finish this manuscript.

I must think this incredible Steve Berman. Thank you for agreeing to meet with me for lunch when I was just beginning to write this novel, thank you for ignoring my yammering at said lunch, and for ultimately believing in me as an author and the importance of this novel.

Thank you to my incredible editor Nancy Beranek; without your patience, guidance, and theatre knowledge, this novel would have more unintentional plot-holes, typos, and actions defying time and space than any reader could forgive. Thank you for loving these characters as much as me, and helping me do them justice on the page. As a debut author, I could not have been in better hands.

Thank you to my various theatre families I've worked with over the years. I couldn't have written these characters without treading the boards with you all. Theatre has impacted my life in so wonderful many ways, both as an actor, and an audience member. I am thrilled that, as an author, I can spread that love beyond the stage and into the entire world.

Special thanks to my Critique Partner, Vicki Weavil. Your encouragement and belief in me and this novel saved me from giving up more times than I count. Thank you for being a wonderful friend, a brilliant cohort, and an inspiration.

Thank you to Sara Davis, who I asked about more bizarre line edits than anyone. Thank you for helping me see that there are always a thousand ways to say something, and for helping me sift through them all to find the perfect one.

To Melissa Laney, who read every version of my novel at least twice, thank you for being the one I could turn to in the middle of the night and ask whether some new idea was worth pursuing.

Finally, this novel was read, loved, and commented on by an incredible group of Beta Readers: Thank you for caring so much about me and my characters.